SILENT MARKER

DI FRANK MILLER TITLES

Crash Point

Silent Marker

Rain Town

Watch Me Bleed

Broken Wheels

Sudden Death

Under the Knife

Old School – short story

SILENT MARKER

John Carson

Cover design by Jimmy Gibbs

This book is dedicated to
Julie Ann Stott and Wendy Haines,
for their enthusiasm, support and hard work.
Thank you, ladies!

CHAPTER 1

'Do you think he's going to turn up?' Kim Smith said. She was standing next to Frank Miller, drinking a cup of coffee, trying to look like another office worker standing having a chat with a colleague.

'He said he's coming, and he said he has a gun. There was no reason to doubt him.' Miller was holding a cup of coffee from the vendor, but it had long gone cold. He felt the Glock 17 underneath his suit jacket. It wasn't often they had to visit the armoury to be issued with a firearm but sometimes it was a necessity. Edinburgh wasn't always kilts and bagpipes.

Despite the early June sun being out, a nippy breeze shot through Princes Street Gardens. They were standing in the shadow of the Scott Monument, which stood like a stone rocket, pointing skywards, waiting for a countdown that was never going to happen. They slowly walked over to the statue of David Livingstone, looming over them on his pedestal, allowing them slightly more cover.

As it was Edinburgh's rush hour they blended in with the workers going about their business. It was too early for the shops to be open, but nice enough for people to be walking about.

'I wish I still carried my gun,' Kim said, looking at Miller's face.

'You don't work for the government anymore so you'll just have to be content.'

'I know, but I still miss it. Unlike you coppers, carrying my gun was all part of being in the Witness Protection department. Working for the Procurator Fiscal's office is a whole new ball game.'

'Talking of the Procurator Fiscal, how is Norma?' Kim had been working in her office as an investigator for the past few months, transferring from her old job just a few weeks after meeting Miller.

'Still over-protective.'

'And nobody in your office knows you're her daughter?'

'I haven't told anybody.'

A voice crackled in the earpiece Miller was wearing. *'Trojan Horse approaching through the west gate.'* Trojan Horse. The woman they were here to protect, Rosie Davidson. Miller's sister-in-law, technically ex, since her husband was dead. Gary Davidson had been a detective serving with Miller's team, but died a few months previously in prison. Miller knew she had been wired before they let her loose to meet the man they were going to take down, and he had told her they'd be listening to her. She wouldn't be alone.

Miller pressed the cuff button on his microphone. 'Rosie, this is Frank. Can you hear me? Just answer yes, if you can, but don't turn round and look at me. I'm over at the Scott Monument.'

'Yes, I can hear you.'

'She looked round at me, didn't she?' Miller asked Kim. His back was to the bench Rosie sat on.

'Yes.'

'It's okay, if he's watching, he'll be expecting her to look around.' He looked at Kim, at the blonde hair falling from her head down to her shoulders, to cover the curly wire coming out of her shirt to the earpiece. Usually she tied it up in a ponytail, just like the first time they met. She had her black jeans on, and black trainers.

'You're not going to go running anywhere, I hope,' Miller said to her.

'I wouldn't dream of it,' she said, smiling at him. They looked like two commuters who had bumped into each other, should anybody be watching.

'I mean it. She's the wife of a dead cop, and your mother sent you here to liaise, but you have to leave the takedown to us.'

'Of course I will.'

Miller shook his head. 'I mean it, Kim. He says he's armed and Rosie's had death threats, so I want you staying well out of the way.'

'Yes, boss.'

'Why do I get the feeling you're not taking me seriously?'

'You worry too much, Miller.'

'That's what your father said to me a few months ago. Like father like daughter, I see.'

'That reminds me, Neil was asking for you the other night.'

'You didn't tell him I stayed over, did you?'

'As if. He might not be as tall as you, Miller, but he's a little stick of dynamite.'

'Hardly little.' He took a sip of his coffee, wishing there was something stronger in it.

'I hope the rest of your team are on the ball.'

'Relax, we're not Boy Scouts. We've done this sort of thing before.' He took another sip of coffee, feeling the tasteless liquid roll down his throat. 'Jesus, this coffee's cold.'

'I'm sorry. I know she's your family, and whoever this guy is, he's really shaken her up,' Kim said.

'Just keep it cool. We've dealt with scum like him before.'

'Possible target located. Main gate near art gallery.' DS Hazel Carter's voice buzzed in Miller's ear and he automatically tensed, like a soldier about to go into battle. Everybody was in position, with patrol cars nearby.

This was the fourth possible target since the handover time fifteen minutes ago and Miller was feeling tense. Somebody was extorting money from Rosie Davidson, but she didn't know his identity. The last email sent to her said he wanted her to meet him with a bag of money in Princes Street Gardens he would hunt her down and kill her.

'Roger, Sierra One,' Miller said, into his concealed microphone. 'Confirm Alpha Victor One on stand-by.' The Armed Response Vehicle sitting on Waverley Bridge, the officers ready to go into combat. The email had been specific about the target having a gun and his willingness to use it.

'Alpha Victor One, Roger.'

'All units stand-by.' Miller watched the man walking into the gardens, looking around. Miller felt the gun nestling in its holster against his hip, hoping it wouldn't be needed. He smiled and bent over, kissing Kim lightly on the cheek. He laughed, reaching out for her hand. She caught on and squeezed back. 'Late twenties, blue blazer, light blue shirt, jeans. Everybody copy.'

'You be careful, Frank Miller,' she whispered.

He smiled and looked into her eyes.

'I mean it.' She tugged on his hand to enforce her point.

'I know you do,' he said. 'Right, let's start walking, but remember one thing; you're here only to observe. I don't want you physically involved in any of this, okay?'

'If you say so.'

'I do.'

Already he regretted allowing her to come along, and had protested to Norma Banks, but the PF had insisted, reminding him she wanted everything to go smoothly so when an arrest was made, it couldn't be construed that the police went in heavy-handed. Making it sound as if she was doing Miller a favour.

It was three hundred yards to the bench where Rosie Davidson sat with the holdall, probably frozen to the wooden seat with fear by now.

The man in the blazer approached and sat down on the bench.

'This looks like the target,' Miller said, into his microphone. 'Stand-by.'

Rosie was wired for sound and they needed to hear the man on tape asking for the money and telling Rosie why he wanted it. They had rehearsed this moment and Miller hoped she wouldn't blow it.

'Alpha Victor One, roll now, code twelve.' *Silent approach, high priority.*

They watched as the man slid closer. Listening as the voices came through their earpieces.

'I'm glad you could make it, Rosie,' Shaun Foxall said, sitting down beside her.

Miller watched Rosie turn to look at the man who had been threatening her with emails, culminating in him asking her for the money or he would kill her. *I have a gun,* he wrote, *and if I don't get the money, I'll blow your head off.*

His hand was in his pocket now, maybe holding a gun. Maybe holding a banana for all Miller knew.

'Shaun Foxall? Why?' Rosie asked, her voice quivering through Miller's earpiece.

'I have to take the bag.'

Rosie held the holdall tighter. *'No. I have to know why. Why me?'*

Foxall sighed. *'I was told to take the bag.'*

'You threatened me. My husband only died three months ago.' Her voice was starting to break up now.

Foxall was looking confused and nervous. *'I just need the bag. I need it to complete the game.'*

'Game? What the fuck are you talking about? You said you would hurt me. Like that would happen.' Rosie managed to make her voice sound incredulous. *'You're just a boy. I'm twenty-eight. My husband was a cop. You're what, sixteen?'*

'I'm twenty-five.'

'You look like you're ten. You can't even grow a proper moustache, you little bastard.'

He looked at his watch. *'Give me the bag.'*

'You wish,' Rosie said, standing up. *'Fuck you!'*

Shaun Foxall jumped up, pulled out his gun and pointed it at Rosie's head.

'Gun! All units go!' Miller shouted, watching as the ARU pulled into the side of the road. The two armed officers jumped out of the car and ran to the entrance as Miller threw his coffee cup down and started running towards Rosie. Kim was running too.

Miller pulled the gun from its holster.

Foxall turned when he saw the tall man and the blonde woman running towards him. He turned the gun in their direction and fired it, smiling.

Miller watched the movement, bringing his own gun up. The three safety catches built into the Glock's trigger disengaged one by one, as he pulled the trigger farther back. Five and a half pounds of pressure was all it would take to squeeze off a round from the deadly accurate gun, yet despite all its features, it was rendered useless.

The man was standing behind Rosie and Miller couldn't get a clear shot. He diverted his attention for a split-second, just before Foxall's gun went off again. He collided with Kim, landing on top of her as they rolled onto the grass. As Miller lay on his back, Kim was up and away.

'Kim, no!' Then he was up and after her. Foxall was running. He heard the shout, 'Armed police!' but with so many people about, they didn't have a clear shot.

Sirens cracked the air as Miller gathered speed, heading for the exit on The Mound. Tam Scott, another member of Miller's team, stood in his way, but the young man had too much momentum and knocked Scott onto his back, winding him. He saw Kim going through the gate, chasing the target.

'He's in Princes Street, heading west, south side opposite Hanover Street,' Miller managed, between breaths.

A patrol car rushing down Hanover Street as the ARU car drove at the red lights, its siren trying to split the traffic, stuck behind a tram. The armed officers were on foot, running along the pavement, cradling their Heckler and Koch MP 5's.

Miller was ahead of the other team members, pumping his arms, his jacket flapping like a pair of black bat wings. He tried not to think about Kim being shot. What did she think she was doing? *Just what Carol would have done.* His wife had been a fine detective and took her job seriously. She too would have been after Foxall.

He was outside the gardens, past the mobile food vendor. Miller could see Kim rounding the corner on the opposite end of the art gallery. Foxall was nowhere in sight.

A patrol car headed down The Mound, each of its headlights flashing in turn, the blues on top enforcing the message.

Where was Kim?

Then he saw her opposite, the black jacket running down the stairs of the Gents toilets. *Oh fuck, no,* he thought, knowing if the target was down there, Kim would be like a rat trapped in a corner.

The patrol car screeched into the side of the road as Miller stopped at the top of the stairs leading to the subterranean toilets. The Mitsubishi ARU arrived ahead of the two officers running round the corner.

'Get this area cleared,' Miller ordered, pointing to the bus shelter opposite and the people waiting inside it. 'Get teams into the gardens down there.'

An unmarked car pulled up behind the patrol car that had come down The Mound. DCI Paddy Gibb, Miller's immediate boss.

'I was just leaving the station when I heard this going down,' he said to Miller. 'What's going on?'

'Kim Smith chased the gunman down there,' he said, nodding to the toilets. 'Turns out Rosie knows him. I'm not sure from where, yet. He really was armed. We thought we had him covered, but he opened fire. Luckily he didn't kill anybody.'

'I think I might just kill one of you lot if this hits the fan.' Gibb spoke into his radio, and then turned back to Miller. 'The negotiator's on his way, but if all else fails, we'll storm the place.'

'No we won't; Kim's down there with him.'

Gibb shook his head. 'How did she end up down there?'

'She can run faster than me, that's how!' Miller snapped. 'Never mind that now. We have to make sure she's safe.'

'Miller! Miller, can you hear me?' Kim's tinny voice sailed up from the toilets and all the attention turned in that direction. An ambulance flashed down The Mound.

Miller stepped closer to the entrance, flanked by an armed officer pointing his Heckler and Koch MP5 down the stairwell.

'I can hear you.'

'Shaun wants you to come down.'

'Just stay calm, Shaun. We can talk about this. I'm coming down now.'

'You can't go down there, boss,' Scott said beside him, his breathing heavy from the quick sprint, still feeling winded.

'I can't risk him shooting Kim. I'll be alright.' He handed the gun over to Gibb.

He took his jacket off before slowly making his way downstairs. 'I'm coming down Shaun,' he called out. Rounding the corner at the foot of the stairs, he saw Foxall holding the gun by his side. It was an old-fashioned pistol. An island of washbasins stood between them. The smell of disinfectant and piss was almost overpowering.

'Why don't you put the gun down, Shaun, and we can talk?' Miller was holding his hands out to show he wasn't carrying a weapon. It was cold down here, but Miller didn't feel it. He didn't have time to feel it.

'I'm not sure how it ends. They didn't tell me.'

Miller looked puzzled. 'Let her go and you can keep me. Surely a detective is worth far more to you?'

'I don't know what to do anymore.'

'Look, Shaun, I'm not armed. You're the one with the handgun.' Miller was still connected to his microphone so the team would be listening upstairs. 'Just let the girl go and we can talk about this.'

''I don't know what to do. They didn't tell me how the game ends.'

Miller wondered if the younger man was high on something, which would make him even more dangerous. 'Just take it easy and nobody will get hurt.'

'I want to go home now. I don't want to play anymore. This place smells.'

'Just give me the gun, Shaun, and then we can take you home,' Kim said.

Foxall gave her the gun and Miller, pumped full of adrenaline, ran round the sinks and body-slammed him against a cubicle door, twisting him round and cuffing his hands behind his back.

'Get down here!' he shouted at the top of his voice. Seconds later, boots thudded down the stairs. Scott came in after the ARU officers. Miller handed over the gun.

'You okay, boss?'

'Oh yes, I'm okay. I just need to have a word with a little lady.'

Kim looked at him. 'Right, I admit it, things got a little out of hand.'

'Kim, we really need to talk,' he said, as she made her way up the stairs.

'Is Rosie alright?' she asked.

'She'll be fine. Now, what the hell do you think you were doing? I can't believe you just did that. You could have been shot.'

One of the armed officers came back upstairs, looking for the paramedics. 'The gun's a starting pistol, boss,' he told Miller.

'See?' Kim said. 'I wasn't in any danger after all.' She smiled at Miller.

'That's not the point.'

'I'm going to tell your bloody mother,' Gibb said to her, only realising how it sounded after the words had left his mouth. 'Make sure you both write up a bloody report about this.'

Miller found Kim greatly irritating and absolutely sweet all at once. 'Learn a lesson from this, Kim.'

'I will, I promise.'

Scott came up the stairs, twisting the cuffs a little harder than he needed to. 'Push me down in front of my team, you little bastard?' he whispered. 'I'll put the word round in Saughton, see how you like pushing those boys around.' He gave Foxall to the uniform team who had come round with the van. Foxall was still moaning and bent over as they put him in the back.

'That was a close call, Tam,' Miller said, but was interrupted by Gibb who had just hung his phone up.

'We're wanted down in Warriston cemetery, Miller.'

'Warriston? What's up?'

'There's something there you should see. It has to do with the Terry White kidnapping.'

And with those words, Miller's past came back to haunt him.

CHAPTER 2

The long grass swayed in the chill wind as if the dead were waving.

A yellow JCB backhoe sat with its bucket on the ground next to the partly demolished house, as if it was sulking and refusing to go back to work. Workmen dressed in dirty overalls stood around it, smoking, huddled together like union conspirators.

Police vehicles were parked on the gravel driveway, which had long ago given up trying to keep its gravel. Grass had started reclaiming the land between the wheel ruts, creating a sharper camber than there had once been. The canopy of trees shadowed the driveway, making the place look dreary and foreboding.

Gibb stopped the Mondeo behind the last of the patrol cars. A member of Miller's team, DS Jimmy Gilmour, walked over to their car. 'Morning, sir,' he said to Miller. 'Sir,' to Gibb.

'What's the rundown on this, Jimmy?' Gibb asked him.

'That pile of rubble over there is what's left of the old caretaker's house. It's been standing empty for the past couple of years after it burnt down. Only the thick stone walls were left, and the council are shitting themselves in case some glue-sniffer pulls a wall down on top of himself, so they finally got around to demolishing it. One side of the house fell into the basement. The crew started knocking down what was left of the house yesterday, and this morning, they were clearing more of the rubble away when one of them noticed a bone sticking out of the ground. So they had a look and called us. A uniform had a look and he saw a backpack strap sticking out of the ground nearby. It was open and he pulled out a notebook. It has Terry White's name on it.'

Miller turned round and looked at what was now a building site. Farther north in the cemetery was the new, extended burial ground where his wife, Carol, was buried, near her father.

Miller hadn't been back to her grave in a while and had no intention of coming back until it was time to lay flowers on the anniversary of his wife's death, which was months away. The light wind blew at him, making him shiver.

Miller saw the mortuary van parked up ahead behind a patrol car. A BMW 5 series parked behind it, a car he hadn't seen before. 'Whose car is that?' he asked.

'You haven't met her yet. She's the new pathologist. She just started on Monday,' Gibb said.

'You met her?' Miller asked.

'Of course I have. We'll be having a lot of interaction with her, so I went down to the mortuary and was introduced to her.'

'What's she like?' he asked.

They started walking up the path, towards the blue tape strung across the road.

'Early thirties. Bit of a snooty cow.' They all put on overshoes.

'It's through this way, sir,' Gilmour said, and led them past the fallen stones that had once been somebody's house. The wall at the back was still standing, charred in places, with remnants of the old wallpaper stuck on others. A wall joined onto the side of the house, with an opening where a gate had once stood sentry.

The long, unkempt grass crept up gravestones hugging the wall. At the back of the house was a pitiful vegetable garden. Miller imagined it had once been quite a pleasant plot of land. A high wall separated them from the cemetery on two sides, the third wall keeping them from what was once a railway line, now a walkway leading down to The Shore in Leith, if they chose to walk it.

Miller saw a ladder coming up out of the ground and looked down. Several people in white suits crouched round what looked like a fresh grave. Two faces turned to look up at them; Jake Dagger, pathologist and Charlie Warner, head mortuary assistant. The third suited person kept their back to them. The two men stood up and only then did the third person stand.

The owner of the BMW.

Miller felt a tightness in his chest for one moment. This woman had replaced Julie Davidson, the former pathologist who was now dead, the woman who had been his sister-in-law.

This woman smiled at them. 'DCI Gibb. We meet again. And you brought some friends round this time. Couldn't you wait until the wine and cheese party?'

Gibb ignored her. 'Dr. Kate Murphy, this is DI Frank Miller and DS Tam Scott. Two members of my team.'

She put a hand up to shade her eyes. 'I'll have to ask you to stay there while we dig around the body.'

'That's fine,' Miller said. Looked her in the eyes. Seeing Julie's face there for a moment.

'Are you alright, DI Miller?' Kate asked.

'I'm fine. Why?'

Kate's smile stayed in place but was devoid of any humour. 'You look pale, that's all. If you're going to puke, I don't want it shooting down here.'

'Frank's fine. This case means a lot to us,' Gibb said, feeling his hackles rise.

'My wife died because of this case,' Miller said. 'She was the DC chosen to do the ransom drop that night, and she was run down by a hit-and-run driver and later died in hospital.'

'Oh, I didn't know.'

'Is that Terry in there?' Gibb said, nodding to what was now essentially a shallow grave.

'Yes. They sent me a copy of his dental records to my iPad. It's him alright, but we'll double-check it with the DNA sample given by his mother when he went missing.'

'When will he be taken out of there?' Miller asked.

'Probably mid to late afternoon. SOCOs are coming to give us a hand to get him out and process the scene.'

Miller looked at the grave, and the bony hand sticking up through the dirt. 'How come he was unearthed?'

'They were clearing some of the rubble and the backhoe pulled up one of the prefab concrete walls that had fallen down here. That's when they saw his hand.'

'So the crime scene is pretty messed up now.'

Kate drew in a deep breath and let it out slowly. 'I'm afraid so, but we wouldn't have known it was here if it hadn't been dug up.'

'We were hunting his kidnapper on Guy Fawkes Night, three years ago this coming November. Can you tell from his body if you think he died close to that time, or a bit later?'

'As I said, he's badly decomposed,' Kate said, patiently, 'so I would say more likely he was killed around that time, rather than say, kept alive and killed a few months ago.'

Miller turned to Gibb. 'It could be that the kidnapper killed him after he didn't get the money, but Carol said she thought he was already dead. When the kidnaper played his voice over the phone, it didn't sound like they were in the same room.'

'That's possible.'

Miller had stood and watched his wife die in the Accident and Emergency room as the doctors battled to keep her alive, but a traumatic head injury had been fatal. She died because somebody had been greedy. Had taken a little boy and wanted money in exchange for his safe return, knowing full well young Terry had been given a death sentence. Miller wanted to find the bastard more than anything.

'They're through there, ma'am,' Miller heard a uniform say. He turned and saw Norma Banks come in with Kim Smith behind her. Mother and daughter. Procurator Fiscal and lead investigator.

'Hello, Miller,' she said. The overshoes clashed with the immaculate suit she wore.

'Mrs. Banks.'

'And who would this be?' she said, nodding down towards the pathologist.

'I would be the new pathologist, Kate Murphy. And you would be, dear?' Kate said.

Gibb made a slight face as if he had just bitten into a lemon whilst chewing a wasp, wishing he wasn't in the vicinity of the two women. This would be a battle to the death, and Norma banks *never* lost a battle.

'I am the Procurator Fiscal. *Dear.'* Norma said, in her best *You don't want to start a war with me* voice, a war she was more than capable of winning. 'This is my lead investigator Kim Smith.'

'Hi, Kate. Pleased to meet you. Call me Kim.'

'It's Dr Murphy, actually, Miss Smith.'

'It's Dr Smith, actually.' Kim kept her smile in place, as a Great White does even after it's been reeled in. She had obviously learnt a lot from her mother.

'Okay, ladies, let's not have a pissing contest, here. Let's leave that to the blokes, shall we?' Norma looked at her daughter. 'You will liaise with Dr Murphy and report back to me. I remember this case well. Because of it, we lost one of our own detectives. So we will all pull together on this. Do I make myself clear on that, Dr Smith?'

'Yes.'

'Dr Murphy?'

Kate just looked at her without answering, as if she was about to say, *You're not my boss.* Instead he cleared her throat. 'Yes.'

Norma stepped back and looked at the grave. The garden area was sheltered from the wind and the sun was out in full force, and Miller could see the woman sweating. 'Who needs to go on a South Beach Diet when you can just come and look at an open grave?' she said. 'I hope the restaurant we're going to at lunchtime does a nice salad.'

More graveyard humour. Miller knew it was a safety valve and nobody was being flippant when they came out with something like that at a crime scene, but he'd known men who had taken early retirement because they couldn't take seeing the aftermath of what one human being could do to another.

Norma Banks nodded, as if she had just finished a small prayer for the young boy, and walked quietly away. Kim stayed, looking at the pathologist.

'I'm sorry, we got off on the wrong foot.'

Kate stared into her eyes. 'Or the right one, depending which side of the fence you're on.'

Gibb was also sweating, not because of the sun, but because he needed a cigarette. He took his lighter out and held it tightly in his hand, as if it was his child. *Daddy, I insist you use me to light up one of those bad boys you have in your pocket. Go on, light one up. GO ON!* He took a deep breath and put the little errant child back in his pocket.

'Still trying to give up the smoking, boss?' Miller said, seeing the lighter being put away.

'Not any longer. It's making me strung out.'

'Well, don't be smoking here,' he said.

Gibb walked up to her just like Norma had moments earlier. 'Nobody's that stupid. And I don't know what you've been told about our last pathologist, but we all have a distrust for you lot now.' Gibb's Irish brogue became more pronounced when he was angry. He walked away from Kate.

'Miller, take Kim and go and see Terry's mum. Tell her the news.'

'Okay, I'll go and see if she still works up in Morningside.'

He walked out of the gardens with Kim, depositing their overshoes in a small receptacle outside.

'We can take my car,' Kim said. 'I brought my own because my mother's driving sucks. She swears more than a truck driver when she's behind the wheel.'

'Okay.' His thoughts were far away. He was thinking of a dank, cold night when fireworks lit up the sky. Of a little boy who may or may not have been dead, and a woman who he loved very much, running around from pub to pub, taking calls from some evil, slimy bastard who had full control over her actions, some filth who needed hanging, who-

'You okay, Frank?' Kim put her hand on his arm. They were standing at her car, an old Mondeo belonging to the PF's office, and Miller didn't remember getting to it, such were his thoughts about his wife's death. He was sweating.

'Yeah, I'm fine. I'm sorry about what happened in there. It just brought back memories of our last pathologist. I couldn't help it.'

'Nobody's blaming you, least of all me.'

She smiled. 'Hey, the good news is, now you're going out with me, you can see my mother more often after hours.'

'I really don't have an answer for that.'

Kim unlocked the car and they climbed in. Miller switched the air conditioning on. Nearly three years ago, Miller let Terry White down. He wasn't going to make that mistake again.

CHAPTER 3

Miller sat down in his office chair as Kim closed the door behind her.

'I really am sorry about earlier, but Kate just rubbed me the wrong way.'

'Don't worry about it. Things happen.' He looked at her. 'You know how we went bowling on Emma's birthday, and had a good time?'

'Yes, of course.'

'I'd like you to be around for her seventh birthday. You running after that clown this morning might have taken that chance away. Don't ever do that again to me. I lost one person who meant more to me than anything. I don't want to lose another.'

She sat down opposite him. 'I never thought about that. I'm so used to being armed, I just chased after him.'

'Just don't get all gung-ho. That could just as easily have been a real gun he had.'

'I didn't know you cared about me like that.'

'Of course I do. You're my one and only girlfriend.'

Maybe one day you'll be my wife, he thought, *and I don't want to lose two wives.*

'I love you, Miller.'

'I love you too.'

The words still sounded strange to Miller. He'd known Kim for four months, had been dating her for three, and felt a buzz of shock when she had told him she loved him one night after they'd been out for a drink.

His wife had been dead for over two years, but something primeval deep inside him felt as if he was still cheating on her. He knew Kim had fallen for him, and told him she was in love with him, but there was something holding him back. He said they would move in together when the time was right. Her little girl had just turned six, and he wanted her to get used to him being around before they lived together. *Keep telling yourself that, Frankie boy,* a voice in his head said. *Keep telling her it has to be right for little Emma. That sounds better than it has to be right for you.*

'Down in that toilet, I wonder what Shaun meant when he said he didn't know how it ended? That they didn't tell him?' Kim said.

'I don't know. I think he was maybe on something.'

He brought his computer to life and took a sip of the coffee he'd bought them as the screen appeared before him. He started looking through the database on his computer, digging through the folders until he came to the one he wanted. The addresses. The mouse slid around the mouse mat as his finger deftly clicked the button.

Somebody had made a good job of updating all the old case files to computer. Some unknown PC who had been typing in the names, dates, and figures without having a clue what story lay behind them, or who had been affected changing their life forever. He often wondered if the officers detailed to do this sort of mundane work ever bothered to consider the human misery enmeshed in the pages of information. Yet, how could they? Sometimes there were thousands of details to enter into the database.

He waited for his terminal to connect with the server, extracting the information he wanted like an unseen robot, delivering the outcome without fuss or altercation.

The page opened on the screen and Miller watched as the name appeared before him as he took a sip of the now tepid coffee.

'I just want to refresh my memory before we go and see the mother,' he told Kim.

'What about the father?'

'They divorced shortly afterwards, so I heard. She called me to let me know, and to ask me to call her first if there was ever any news. Apparently, he was sleeping around.' He looked over the desk at her. 'Don't worry, we'll pay him a visit as well.'

Kim sat opposite Miller, holding onto her own coffee. There was the bustle of activity coming from the main investigation room, as they brought out everything they had on the original investigation.

'I'm assuming the case was never closed,' Kim said.

'It's always been active, but it's human nature I'm afraid. It wound down as other crimes took precedence. We never forgot about the wee boy, but there's only so many of us to go around. Now we'll bring it up to the front again. I for one want more than anything to catch the bastard.' He looked back at his screen.

Carl White. Last known address, 34 Whitehouse Mews; an old established development in Barnton. He saw a note saying Jill White had updated her address to Barberton Mains, after her divorce. A real comedown for her, but that's the way of a divorce. He wondered why the husband hadn't moved out. He remembered what Tam Scott had said once; marriage was like watching a tornado in the distance: it made you feel excited and nervous at first then you ended up losing your house and your car.

He jotted down the telephone numbers for the couple, in case he couldn't find them in person. Then he looked at the panel describing their occupation.

Carl owned a sports car dealership, dealing in high-end cars.

Jill was a psychologist. More chance of catching her if she still worked.

He called the hospital where she worked and after identifying himself, was told she was working.

'The mother's at her work. We'll tell her first, then go and visit the father.'

They walked down to the back car park behind the High Street station, and it was cold in the shadows. Strangely, Miller didn't feel cold on the outside.

Just on the inside.

CHAPTER 4

Terry White stood on the toilet seat, trying to look out the small window set high up in the wall again. He thought he saw daylight peeking through whatever covered the outside of the glass, but it wasn't. He thought if he could open it and get past whatever was out there, then he could escape.

He jumped down at the sound of the door closing upstairs.

He flushed the toilet and went back into the basement again. He couldn't tell what time of day it was other than by the DVD player. They had left him some cartoons to watch and a pile of books and comics, but he was bored. He didn't know how long he'd been down here, or what day it was. They told him nothing, and didn't answer any of his questions.

He watched the same cartoons over and over. It stopped him from screaming out for his mum.

He didn't know why he was here, but he was scared. The man who came in the car said he had been sent by his dad to pick him up from school, but then they had driven away from the city and the man said there was something wrong, and his dad was going to meet them here because there was some trouble. Nothing to worry about but they had to hide.

He had driven through a gate onto a grass-covered driveway. Up to an old house.

'When's my dad coming?' he had asked the man. He didn't recognise him. He knew all the salesmen in his dad's showroom, and this man wasn't one of them.

'He's coming right now,' the man answered. Terry turned round and saw the old van bouncing up the long driveway behind them.

'In that old van?' he said, and before he could turn round, a cloth was clamped over his mouth. He kicked and screamed, and pulled at the man's arm, but he was strong. He heard the van pull up behind them, but he wasn't struggling anymore. He felt tired, like the time he'd been to the dentist and he'd been given gas and had felt the room spin round. Now he heard the van door shut and

somebody walk up to the driver's side.

His eyes were very heavy and he tried to stay awake but couldn't.

'He not in the boot yet?' the other man said.

'Doesn't look like it, does it?' the driver said.

Terry looked over at the driver's window just as the van driver bent down to look in, but then he slipped into darkness.

Now he was in this underground room in somebody's house. They didn't tell him when he could go home, or why they were keeping him here. They brought him food, which he wolfed down, and one time they brought his favourite, jelly and ice cream. Which was nice, but it didn't make him feel any less scared.

Nights were the worst. He knew it was night because the lights were switched out and it was dark outside the little bathroom window. That's when he really missed his mum. He would cry himself to sleep and hug the teddy they gave him. His friends would laugh at him if they knew he was sleeping with a teddy, but he didn't care. At least teddy was somebody he could talk to.

He wondered if his mum was missing him. Was she crying herself to sleep at night like he was? Did she have her own teddy bear now?

His dad would be furious when he found the men who had taken him. The man had said he was being driven to see his dad, but that was a lie. So his dad would be furious that a man had taken his little boy by lying to him.

Now he heard the footsteps above him. He didn't know what it was like up there because after the man had put the cloth over his face, he went to sleep and woke up on the bed down here.

They gave him pyjamas to wear and clean clothes every day, so he wasn't too bothered about that. They didn't hit him or touch him in any way. They even gave him a nice toothbrush. The bathroom had a shower in it so he was able to wash. The man with the mask told him if he shut his eyes, he could pretend he was in a swanky hotel in New York, or Hong Kong.

Terry liked the idea of going to New York, to see the Statue of Liberty, and walk through Times Square and go to the Toys 'R' Us there. He'd seen pictures of it. They had a huge Ferris wheel, and each of the cars was a different design. Terry's favourite was the Cozy Coupe. He'd had one when he was little and it would be brilliant to ride in the one in Times Square.

Maybe tonight, when it was time for sleep, he would lie awake in the dark and pretend to be riding it. That way he'd be in New York and not in this horrible basement with these horrible men.

He heard footsteps coming down the wooden stairs. He sat on the bed and picked up a book, pretending to read. Then somebody turned a key in the lock and opened it.

The Mask.

Not like Jim Carrey in the movie The Mask, but one you could buy in the joke shop down Victoria Street. It was pure white with black hair painted on top, and the mouth was grimacing, as if it would be in pain if it were real. It wasn't though, it was a Halloween mask. He knew Halloween was close. Had it been yesterday? Was it today? Or was it going to be tomorrow? There was no point in asking, as he wouldn't be told.

The Mask had frightened him at first, but he saw the real eyes looking out of the holes in the rubber face. The voice inside told him not to be scared, that he would be back with his mum and dad soon.

He was carrying a tray of food. It smelled good. Fish fingers and chips. His belly rumbled and he wanted the food so bad, but didn't want to anger the man either. He had to know though. Had to ask the question, even though the man had said he'd take the food away from him if he kept on asking.

'When can I go home?'

The Mask put the tray down and then stood up straight, taking in a deep breath. Terry thought he was going to get a slap, maybe worse. After all, the threats had been implicit and he thought his captor probably meant it.

'I've already told you I'll have to wait and hear from your mother and father. These things take time, and the more you worry about it, the longer it will take to resolve. Jilly's not a silly woman, she'll come up with the money.'

Terry shook his head. 'My dad will pay you anything you ask for just to get me back.'

'I know he will. He's a good man. He loves you.'

This voice was different from the man who picked him up in the car.

Terry had been scared at first, his mind running wild with thoughts of his own death and what the man would do to him but the more he listened to the man's voice, the more he was convinced of one thing: he knew his kidnapper.

CHAPTER 5

'I can't believe we've got another pathologist with attitude.' Kim smiled at Miller. 'I don't want you to think I'm a lunatic.'

'I already think you're a lunatic,' he replied. 'Don't worry; it seems our new pathologist is a bit combative. I'm sure Jake Dagger will put her in her place. If not, Leo Chester certainly will. I'm sure your mother will fill him in when he has lunch with her today.'

'My mother's having lunch with Leo? I didn't know that.'

'When she said she hoped the restaurant had a salad on the menu that was what she was referring to. Apparently her and your dad are working a case and Leo is involved with it.'

'She didn't tell me. How did you find out?'

'Dagger sent me a text. He thought it was funny. Kate Murphy is a bit of a bossy boots apparently, and you know Jake; he's a sweetie wife when it comes to gossip.'

'Like you, right now.'

'Just keep your eyes on the road,' he said, pointing through the windscreen.

'I'm a better driver than you, Miller.'

'You won't get any arguments from me there, sister.' He yawned. Looked at his watch. Mid-morning and he felt as if he'd been on a full shift already.

'You look like you could do with another coffee.'

'After this, we'll get one.'

'You coming round for dinner tonight? Emma's dad picked her up this morning and they're taking the train down to London. We have the place to ourselves.'

'Sure, I'd love to. You're going to miss Emm though, aren't you?'

'She's my daughter, of course I am. It's only for three weeks. His wife is nice, and they get along well, so I'm sure she'll have a good time.'

'I'll miss her too. I'm used to seeing her.'

'Pack a bag, don't pack a bag, the choice is yours if you want to stay over.'

'On a weekday? You must be getting to like me, Miss Smith.'

'It's Dr. Smith, actually.'

'I knew you were going to say that as soon as the words left my mouth.'

'It's not all beauty with me, Mr. Detective.'

He sat back as they cut into Whitehouse Loan and followed it into Morningside where Kim connected with Canaan Lane.

The Astley Ainslie hospital situated in the heart of Morningside was in an almost park-like setting, although this park had high walls and an ambulance sitting at the entrance. He knew where he was going, instructing Kim as to which turning to take, following the sign for Clinical Psychology.

They parked in a handicapped space opposite the main entrance to the single-storey building. It looked like some sort of throwback from World War Two, taken over by the hospital and painted but never updated. A man stood leaning on a stick in the bike shelter with its tin roof and grit box. He smoked a cigarette, defying the sign telling patients not to.

Miller and Kim left the cool of the car and went inside, turning right to the reception area. Miller asked the receptionist if Jill White was on duty while Kim put change into the coffee machine.

'She is.'

'Could you tell me where to find her?' he asked, as the machine whirred and dropped a cheap plastic cup for Kim's brew.

'She's in the room at the far end of the corridor, round to your right.'

'Thanks.' He turned round as Kim took her coffee, wincing as she took a sip of the burning liquid.

'This is awful. I'll bet the staff don't drink this stuff.' She made a face.

The sun shone through the windows. Posters lined the walls. Messages about healthy eating, giving false hope to the afflicted. *Fruit is better than a chocolate bar* one read. Miller could easily see how somebody could be hooked on chocolate but not on a Granny Smith.

They could hear a voice talking from behind the door. A woman's voice.

'Ready when you are,' Miller said, standing near a rack holding rubber floor mats. His nerves on edge now, something that didn't normally bother him.

'Sure you're okay?' Kim said.

'I'm never going to be okay for this.'

****

'What is chronic pain?'

Jill White looked around at the blank faces of the people sitting in the chairs facing the white board. Nobody ventured an answer. An overgrown bush lurked outside one of the windows at the back of the room, the branches scratching at the glass like bony fingers as the light wind pushed them around. A lawnmower sounded in the distance.

Jill looked at the words she had written on the white board before moving on to her answer.

'There are two different kinds of pain: acute and chronic. Does anybody know the difference?'

Blank faces. Ignorance of the subject or not wanting to answer wrongly in fear of making a fool of themselves in front of the others.

'Okay then; acute pain is like having a broken leg. You will be in acute pain, the body's way of telling you there is something wrong and you have to get it sorted. If you get the right treatment, in this case having your leg put in plaster, the pain will go.

'Chronic pain is different; this is pain that has been going on for six months or more. The pain may have started out as being acute because of the injury, but then the pain stayed long after the injury healed. Around eleven percent of people living in this country suffer from chronic pain.'

Jill looked at the faces to see if what she was telling them held their attention, but apart from a few people changing position in their chairs, they could almost have been dead.

'Unfortunately, there is not much training given to doctors when they are learning their craft, so doctors seem to treat chronic pain as acute pain and administer painkillers. They advise the patient to rest. Both are inadequate when dealing with chronic pain. If your pain has become worse over time, we aim to tell you some of the reasons why. One thing we don't do is offer a cure. We are here to help you understand your pain and show you ways that might help you live with your pain better, through exercise and deep relaxation techniques.'

Jill cleared her throat, feeling tired today. The morning session had gone quite well but the afternoon lot looked as if they were here on a school trip. One old woman had already moaned at her because she was sitting in the wrong chair, and one of the men had kindly let her have his, a high-backed one. She had grumbled as she sat back down. Another man looked as if he was about to drop off at any moment.

'Now,' Jill continued, 'a broken leg will show up on an x-ray, but an injury to tendon, muscle or nerve, will not. Sometimes when the pain is in the body, it won't show up on any scans or x-rays. No one knows for sure why the pain doesn't settle down after an injury, but some reasons are starting to emerge. I'd like to look at some of them now.'

She turned to the board once more and started writing on it. One man who had back problems, and had been suffering for years, stood up and went behind the high-backed chair to stretch his back.

'If some of the soft tissue in your body becomes damaged, this can be the cause of your pain.' She underlined the words *Soft Tissue* on the board.

'Body tissues are made up of either bone or soft tissue. The bones make up our skeleton and the soft tissues connect to the bones. Now we'll look at some of the soft tissues in the body.

'First of all, muscle.' She wrote this on the board and was about to face the group again when there was a knock on the door. Helen, the assistant psychologist who had been writing notes, got up and answered the door.

'Sorry to bother you, but I'm looking for Jill White. I'm DI Miller.'

Helen turned to look into the room. It was as if somebody had pulled the plug on Jill's blood supply and it was rapidly draining out of her body, starting with her face.

'I'm here,' she said to Miller, walking over to the two detectives standing in the open doorway looking ominous and she knew what this was about.

Her boy was dead.

****

Miller's words sounded hollow as he asked for Jill, but then he saw her standing in front of the board, looking much the same as the last time he had seen her, but thinner, as if not knowing the fate of her boy had quelled her appetite.

'Can we talk in private?' Miller asked.

'Can you take over, Helen?' Jill asked, handing the red marker pen to her assistant before leading them to a room down the corridor.

Inside, a bank of fluorescents came on, lighting the room with artificial daylight. Outside, dark clouds scudded over, taking the light with it, promising a downpour.

'This is investigator Kim Smith with the PF's office. She's assisting us.'

'It's about Terry, isn't it?' Jill said, sitting behind a desk, waiting for them to sit.

'It is, I'm afraid, Mrs. White. Earlier today, we found a skeleton, which we believe to be your son. The pathologist confirmed it on site from dental records and we'll run a DNA test, but I wanted to let you know we have found a body.'

Jill put a hand over her mouth as if she was about to vomit. 'Oh my God. Terry. My poor little boy.' She sniffed, trying to control herself. With a shaking hand, she reached into a drawer and took out a packet of cigarettes, lighting one up, not caring that hospital policy forbade anybody smoking in the grounds, never mind inside the buildings.

Miller looked at her face, at the lines that had crept round her eyes since the last time they spoke. The eyes themselves like candle holders, dark places that hadn't seen light since the candles had been snuffed out.

'Where...where was he found?' Her voice barely holding together, hand shaking as the cigarette made its way to and from her mouth.

'In the old caretaker's house in Warriston cemetery.'

Tears made the journey south, running over wrinkled skin, gathering at the corners of her mouth where they fell off.

'How did he die?' The voice quivering, lips curled at the corners.

'We don't know yet. The pathologists will have a look and see if they can determine the cause of death, but it won't be easy unless there are any broken bones to indicate how he died.'

Broken bones. Acute pain for Terry, chronic pain for her.

'I see you got divorced, Mrs. White. Does your ex-husband still have the dealership at Newbridge?'

She looked at Miller as if she would rather forget that part of her life. 'As far as I know. We divorced not long after that night.' The night when the police lost the money and she lost her son.

'Do you keep in contact with him?'

She shook her head, the nicotine having a slight calming effect on her. 'No, I don't want anything to do with him. I haven't seen him since the day he left. The lawyers did all the dirty work.' There was an awkward pause for a moment as Jill's eyes travelled to another place in the past.

'We'll have to talk to you again, Mrs. White. We'll let you know when the Procurator Fiscal releases Terry's body.'

'Can I see him?' she asked.

Miller hesitated for a moment. 'I don't think that's a good idea. Best to remember his smiling face.'

She nodded at them, almost absently. She had prepared herself for this moment for a very long time, rehearsing in her own mind how she would go about arranging the funeral, how she would tell other members of her family, how she would react when she saw the coffin holding her little boy, but nothing could prepare her for the reality.

'Your husband will have to be told. I would expect a phone call from him, if I were you. I know it might be tempting for you to call him, but I would ask you not to. If he reacts in an aggressive manner, which can happen, better to let us deal with it.'

She looked at Miller as he stood. Carl White was the last person on Earth she wanted to see. If she ever came across him again, she'd kill the bastard.

CHAPTER 6

'I'm interested in the Ferrari,' the young man said.

I'm sure you are. 'It's a very nice car,' Martin Crawley said, beaming his best *Stop wasting my time you little wanker* smile.

'Maybe I could take it out for a test drive.' The man looked to be in his early twenties, and probably had several convictions for drunk driving, or at the very least, speeding convictions. The last thing Crawley was going to do was let the little tosser sit in the car, never mind drive it.

'The thing is we can't just let a potential customer out in the car. You would have to make an appointment and we have to run background checks.'

'Background checks? You think I'm some kind of scally that doesn't have money?'

Crawley looked at the scuffed leather jacket and the faded jeans, which really meant nothing. Some of his customers were millionaires and dressed worse. However, there were two differences setting them apart from this reprobate, their shoes and their watch. Two dead giveaways. This guy had trainers on and wore a plastic Casio. Crawley knew the lottery had created a lot of millionaires now, but even if this piece of pond life had come up with six numbers, he still wasn't going to get to drive the car.

'Nobody is suggesting anything of the sort, sir. I'm merely stating company policy.'

'Maybe I'll take my business elsewhere then,' he said, shuffling towards the exit, drawing his greasy fingers over the bodywork as he left.

There's a Toyota dealer across the road, Crawley was about to say, but thought better of it. It cost the company a fortune in security at night as it was, without encouraging the filth to come back after dark with some friends and a can of petrol.

A woman approached Crawley from behind. 'Little bastard. Did he think you were going to hand him the keys and just let him give it a belting on the A9?' Cindy Shields said.

'That's exactly what he thought I was going to do. Oh here, pal, take the keys to one of the most expensive cars in here and shag it up the motorway. Remember to take it up to the red line before you change each gear. And bring it back whenever you want. With no petrol left in the tank.'

Cindy laughed out loud and put her hand on Martin's arm. 'I just sold a Five Series this morning to a guy who has more money than that little spurt.' At the side of the showroom outside was what they called the bread-and-butter machines, the second-hand Beemers and Jags, easier sells, the cars that made up ninety percent of their sales.

They walked back over to their desks at the back of the showroom, stopping at the coffee station first. Cindy put a little cup in the Keurig machine, and waited a couple of minutes for it to brew.

'Have you seen Louise today?' she said to Crawley, in a whisper.

'No. I didn't know she was coming in to see us today?'

'Neither did I,' Cindy said, taking the little K cup away from under the spout and replacing it with a new one.

'Remember when she first started here?' Crawley said. 'All flashing teeth and batting her eyes. Being nice to everybody. Sometimes her skirts were so short, you would think she was wearing a belt and had forgotten to wear a skirt at all. She was a good laugh, and she certainly knew how to get the sales. I wish I had legs like hers. Maybe get a few more sales that way.'

'You're a pig.' Cindy smiled at him as she took his mug out and added milk to them both.

'I'm not sexist. I respect all women.'

'Then why did you stand there and let me make the coffee?'

'Because if I didn't, you would claim inequality.' He grinned at her.

They both heard the sound of high-heels clicking towards them and turned round. 'Still gossiping round the coffee machine, I see,' Louise White said, flashing an expensive smile at them.

'Everybody needs a coffee break, Louise dear,' Cindy said. 'You of all people should know that. After all, this was your favourite spot when you worked here. This and the boss's office.'

'A big coffee break with a little bit of work thrown in,' she said, laughing. 'Hi Marty. Good to see you again, sweetheart.'

'You too.' He kissed her on the cheek. 'How's life over at your new dealership?'

'Being my own boss is the best move I ever made. And my offer still stands; if you ever get fed up with that arse up there, you can come to me.'

'Things that bad, eh?'

'I'm glad I got rid of him, Marty. He's a monster behind closed doors.'

'I wouldn't know. I don't socialise with him and don't intend to. Taking a pay cheque from him is what it's all about.'

'You keep it that way.'

'So what brings you here?' Crawley said.

'Just some unfinished business.'

Crawley looked up to see Carl White standing, watching them from the landing overlooking the showroom, before turning and heading back into his office.

'I'd better go upstairs.' She walked over to the stairs leading to the upper offices.

They walked over to their desks, sitting opposite each other. The air conditioning felt good in the showroom, especially as the walls were mostly glass.

'He had a good thing going with Louise,' Cindy said, 'but he spoilt it for himself.'

'Poor bastard.'

'Poor bastard nothing. That'll teach him to think with his small brain.'

He looked up and saw a car pulling into the customer car park at the back. 'You can have that one,' he said to Cindy. Then he saw the marked patrol car pulling in behind it.

Cindy turned round and laughed. 'And you can have that one. See if they want to upgrade their Vauxhall Astra to that Bentley GT.'

Crawley laughed. 'Snow to Eskimos, Cindy.'

CHAPTER 7

'I've never seen the attraction myself,' DS Tam Scott said, from the back seat.

Kim had stopped the car at the traffic lights in Newbridge. In recent years, car dealers had moved their dealerships out here to the western outskirts of Edinburgh, into brand new premises. Lexus, Mercedes Benz, Land Rover, BMW and Toyota had all moved here.

'Attraction to what, Tam?' Miller asked, from the front passenger seat.

'All these fancy cars. It's a tin box on wheels whatever way you look at it. Whether you have a pure bred racehorse or a donkey pulling a cart, it's still a cart at the end of the day.'

Miller shook his head. 'You're in the minority on that one, mate. Kim has a brand new Audi TT after her first one got torched, Jack has his A6 and to be honest, if I won the lottery, I'd have a big house and a Ferrari.'

'Because you already have the supermodel.'

Kim smiled and looked at Scott in the rear view mirror. 'I love you, Tam Scott, can I just tell you that?'

'I got your back.'

Miller made a noise. 'Clearly I meant that as well.' He turned, and gave Scott an *I'm going to boot your bollocks* look.

'Keep telling yourself that, boss.' Scott smirked as Kim moved on green, turning in between the Lexus and BMW dealers.

Carl White Exotic Cars was on their right.

'This is a purpose-built dealership built on land left over from when they sold and demolished the chicken factory a few years back,' Miller said, filling Kim in. 'Carl White had gone after a combined Ferrari/Maserati franchise but was beaten to it by a dealer on the east side of Edinburgh.'

'He'd only just finished it when his son went missing,' Tam said, all business now.

'What sort of bloke is he? I've known a lot of guys like him who are arrogant,' Kim said, pulling into the customer car park, the patrol car coming in behind them.

Miller opened the door as the car stopped. 'He was a decent sort of guy,' he said, stepping out. 'Quite down to earth.' He closed the door.

'So was the Yorkshire Ripper,' Scott said, getting out of the back.

Miller felt the sun beating down on him, feeling good after the long, hard winter. He could see the expensive cars through the big windows. Truth be told, he'd have a reasonable house and a nice, cheap car if he won the lottery. He'd only worry about a Ferrari being stolen if he had one. They looked nice and he supposed it would be good to have a collection in a huge, secret warehouse somewhere, just for him to look at.

Miller waited for the two uniforms to get out of their car and the five of them walked into the showroom, and changed Carl White's life forever.

Miller was first in the showroom, ignoring the expensive metal trying to entice them. He stood and looked around, his eyes falling on Martin Crawley as the salesman walked across to them.

Miller had his warrant card out. 'Police Scotland. I'm DI Miller. I'd like to speak to Carl White.'

'I'll see if he's available,' Crawley said, but then they all heard the voice from above. White standing on the balcony again.

'Send them up, Marty.'

Miller walked up with Kim and left Scott and the others with the sales people. They climbed the stairs and Miller got a better view of the gleaming metal below. They stepped into White's office, and Miller looked at Louise.

'Mr. White, could we talk in private, please?'

White looked at Louise. 'You can leave.'

'Gladly. I've said what I came here to say.'

White took a deep breath through his nose and let it out slowly. 'Now.'

Louise got up from the chair 'Remember what I said. I'm not going to keep coming here.' She walked out without looking back at White.

'This is Investigator Smith from the PF's office,' Miller said, making the introductions.

'He's dead, right? My son!' Carl White's eyes bored into Miller's, a technique he'd used on car buyers, and now something he was unconsciously doing with a murder squad detective. Miller met his stare, unfazed.

'I'm here to tell you that the body of a young boy was uncovered today, and we believe it to be your son, Terry. There's going to be further tests of course, but you need to prepare yourself in case it is him.'

'How sure?'

'The pathologist at the site compared dental records, so we're putting it at a ninety-nine percent probability.' Miller cursed himself for sounding so clinical, but the words had to be said in a certain way so they couldn't come back to bite them later on.

'I'm so sorry we came here without better news,' Kim said. 'Although I wasn't on the original investigation, I've fully read up on it.'

'Why are you involved?' White said, seeming to slump in his chair.

'The fact that a police officer died while the ransom drop was being made means the PF wants her office to have a hands-on approach in this case. That's why I'm working with DI Miller.'

'You know it was his wife who died?'

'Yes, I'm aware of that.'

'Where did they find him?' he asked Miller.

'In the old, burnt-out caretaker's house in Warriston cemetery. He was under a wall that had collapsed.'

White stood and walked over to the window of his office. He could see partway down into the showroom. 'This is all meaningless shite now.' He swept a hand in front of the window and turned back to face Miller. 'I envisioned Terry growing up and joining me in the business before finally taking over one day. He loved cars. Talked about nothing else.'

'He was a good kid, from what you told me. My wife wanted to grab the bastard who did this, more than anything. I was in contact with her the whole time the night she died, except for the last few minutes,' Miller said.

'I remember you telling me all about it. He gave her the run around, didn't he?'

'Yes he did.'

'I remember sitting talking with Carol. She was a bloody good police officer. Her old man was a cop too, wasn't he?' White sat back down at his desk, the colour leaving his face.

'Yes he was. Harry Davidson.'

'He was murdered too, if I remember correctly.'

'Yes, a few months back.'

'Anyway, I remember Carol sitting with me, and she looked me in the eye, and told me she would do absolutely everything in her power to get the guy who took my son. And she made the ultimate sacrifice. Then some thieving bastard stole the money. I read about that in the papers too.'

'I'm sorry we didn't recover that.'

White waved away the apology. Miller was starting to feel hot, despite the air conditioning. 'The money was nothing compared to you losing your wife. My mother's loaded. It was a drop in the ocean to her. I would gladly have given a million to get him back. Hell, I would swap places with Terry if it meant he could still be alive.'

'We told your ex-wife.'

'How did she take it?'

Her son is dead, how the fuck do you think she took it? 'Pretty badly.'

'She's a cold-hearted bitch. Did she tell you I was shagging around?'

'Not in so many words. She said you were divorced now,' Kim said.

'She didn't go into the nitty gritty then? If you asked her, she would tell you I was sleeping with my customers, that I would shag anything that gave me a smile, yet she was the one who was cheating.'

Miller wasn't interested in anybody's gossip, unless it could be construed as motive. 'Did you two have marital difficulties during the time of Terry's kidnapping?'

White nodded. 'It started a while before Terry went missing. She was shagging one of Terry's teachers. As if the money I was lavishing on her wasn't enough, she wanted excitement. All the sneaking around got her pulse racing, she said.'

'She called me at my office a while back to let me know you were divorced. She told me you were the one sleeping around.'

'Our marriage was over by the time Terry was taken. We were in the same house but living separate lives. She likes to tell everybody I was a player, but that isn't true. We didn't even sleep in the same room. Sure, I went with some women, but for all intents and purposes, we were separated.'

'Why didn't you tell Inspector Miller that at the time?' Kim asked. 'It might have been relevant.'

'I didn't think. I couldn't prove it, and she denied it, saying it was in my imagination. We just wanted to concentrate on Terry, so we put our problems on the sideline. We thought if we got him back that would be the new start we needed. She promised me she wouldn't go with another man again. I believed her, I really did. But when the money went missing and your wife died, we could see the chance of getting our little boy back fading to zero. That's when the arguing started again. Then she started staying late after work, and coming home drunk, and then staying out overnight. Who knows who she was sleeping with.'

'What about you, Mr. White?' Kim asked. 'How long have you known Louise?'

'Has this got any relevance to Terry's kidnapping?'

'No. I'm just filling out some background detail here.'

'She was a sales executive here when we met. I fancied her, but I rarely mix business with pleasure, but she has a fantastic personality. We hit it off, started going out after my divorce, and eventually we were engaged. Now we've split up.'

'Does Jill know anything about your private life now?' Miller asked.

'We have no contact. Anything she says to me is through a lawyer. Nothing gets misunderstood that way.'

'How many of the original staff still work here from the time Terry went missing?'

'All of them. They're very loyal, and they get a decent basic salary and a healthy bonus. I need people I can trust, especially since I have all that precious metal out there.'

'We'll need to re-interview them, just to keep ourselves up to date. The case has never been closed, but you know how tight budgets are. Cases with higher priorities come up.'

'I understand,' White said. He sighed, as if he'd been avoiding the next question, but knew it was inevitable, and he had just been dancing round the campfire. 'Where will Terry be taken to?'

'The City Mortuary. The pathologist there will be working closely with our head of forensics, Inspector Maggie Parks.'

'Will I be able to see him?'

'I legally can't stop you from seeing him, but you wouldn't want to see him. Remember him the way he was.'

'Thank you for being honest with me, Miller.' He stood up from behind his desk again. 'You'll let me know when I can go ahead with the funeral? Assuming it really is him.'

'I'll let you know. He won't be released until the PF says so, and it might be a while. We will be in touch again, with a confirmation. We have both you and your ex-wife's DNA. I'll call you.'

They stepped out onto the landing and looked down into the showroom.

Louise Walker was looking back up at him. And she wasn't smiling. The last time a woman looked at him like that, was just before she tried to kill him.

Miller's phone rang. It was DCI Paddy Gibb.

'I need you back at the station, Miller. All hell's broken loose. Kim's mother is here about to take somebody's head off. We were about to charge Shaun Foxall when his lawyer turned up. You're not going to like this one little bit.'

CHAPTER 8

'If he's playing games with me, I'll have his head on a spit. You do know that, right?' Norma Banks was pacing up and down the corridor, outside the interview rooms in the High Street station, when Miller opened the door and stepped into Hell.

'Norma, you and I both know there's nothing we can do.' Detective Chief Superintendent Dennis Friendly stood with a grim look on his face.

'He took a shot at your officers. How the bloody hell were they to know it was a starting pistol?' She walked up to Miller. 'I heard you threw my daughter to the ground. Once again I have to thank you.'

'Just doing my job, ma'am.' He looked at Friendly. 'What's going on, sir?'

'Let's go into the observation room and you can see for yourself.' Friendly turned and opened the interview room door, nodded and closed it again. Then the three of them went into the observation room, and sat down. They looked through the one-way mirror into the interview room.

Shaun Foxall sat in a sweatshirt and tracksuit bottoms that had been supplied to him. Next to him sat his lawyer. 'That's Richard Sullivan,' Miller said.

'Yes it is,' Norma said.

'How did he get involved?' Meaning, *How can Foxall afford him?* Sullivan came at a high price and was usually hired by celebrities who had gotten themselves into a spot of bother. At one time, Miller had thought Sullivan had been responsible for his wife's death, as it was *his* stolen car that had run her over.

'One of Foxall's family member's paid for him,' Friendly said.

They listened to the men on the other side of the mirror. Detective Superintendent David Elliot, head of Serious Crimes, sat with one of Miller's team, DS Hazel Carter, both of them looking across the table at Foxall and Sullivan.

Sullivan looked at Elliot. 'Under Section 85 (A), subsection 27 (C), of the Mental Health Act Scotland, 2010, Mr. Shaun Foxall is not responsible for his actions earlier this morning, or at any time leading up to today's actions. All charges are to be dismissed. Under Section 114, subsection 17 (B), after such an occurrence, Mr. Foxall will be re-admitted to the Royal Scottish Psychiatric

Hospital for a period of seven days for re-familiarisation. After which, he will be released into the care of his family once again. He will then attend a day clinic every day for a further seven days, after which he will resume his life as a citizen in the *Care in the Community* programme.

'Are there any questions?'

'No, all answers to any questions have been duly satisfied, and the detainee may now be released into the care of his lawyer until he leaves the custody of Police Scotland and relegates his position to a non-governmental area,' Elliot said, reciting verbatim from the instruction manual he'd just brushed up on after Sullivan arrived in the station.

'Until his arse is booted out of your station into the High Street,' Norma Banks said.

'How did this happen?' Miller asked.

'I'm as pissed off about it as you are, Frank, but as the PF, my hands are tied. I can't proceed with any charges.'

'You know how it is, Miller,' Friendly said. 'Foxall has mental health issues and after they closed down Gogarburn years ago, all the nutters who were in there are suddenly roaming the streets as if they were cured.'

'Although we don't call them "nutters" these days,' Norma said.

'Yes, of course,' Friendly said, his face going red. 'However, even though the *Care in the Community* programme has had many success stories, there are some who have slipped through the cracks.'

'I know most of them are okay, but it's the ones who think they're okay, but go off their nut. Like the guy who stabbed one of our uniforms in George Street after that stand-off.'

'It's the Russian Roulette effect, I'm afraid.' Friendly stood up as he watched the four people in the other room stand up. 'They're leaving now.'

They all went out into the corridor. Foxall didn't look at Miller.

'My client would like to change back into his clothes,' Sullivan said. He looked at Miller but said nothing.

'We'll be paying Mr. Foxall a visit while he's in the Royal Scottish,' Miller said.

'Really?' Sullivan said.

'Section 121, subsection 19 (D), *the police have the right to make sure that the conditions of the release back to the hospital are being strictly adhered to.*'

Sullivan nodded. 'Yes, of course. Anytime.'

'You'll also be aware that we don't need to make an appointment and neither do we have to advise you in advance of our intentions.'

'Yes, I'm aware of that. That won't be a problem.' Sullivan turned to Foxall. 'Come downstairs, and we'll get you your clothes back.'

'One more thing, Mr. Sullivan,' Miller said. Norma Banks looked at him, a slight smirk on her face.

Sullivan stopped and turned back to Miller. 'Yes?'

'He doesn't get the gun back. Scottish Firearms Law, Section –'

'Yes, I know,' Sullivan said, interrupting Miller.

Norma, Friendly and Miller watched Foxall until they turned left at the end of the corridor as David Elliot and Hazel Carter led him away.

'I didn't know you knew all about the Mental Health Act, Miller,' Norma said.

'Unfortunately, this is not the first time I'll be visiting the Royal Scottish.' He looked at Friendly. 'Unless you want another officer to do the follow-up, sir?'

'No, I would rather you do it,' Norma said before Friendly could reply. 'Then report back to me. Take Kim with you.' She looked at the senior officer. 'That is okay with you, isn't it, Dennis?'

The two red spots seemed to glow more fiercely on Friendly's cheeks. 'Yes, yes, of course. Miller is the man for this job.'

'Good. I need a cup of coffee. And not that cheap stuff you keep for visitors. I want a real cup.'

'Of course.'

Miller's phone rang. 'Excuse me, I need to take this,' he said, looking at the screen. 'It's the mortuary.'

Both Friendly and Norma stayed where they were as Miller answered. 'Yes, I'll tell them.' He hung up, put his phone away and looked at the two faces staring at him. 'That was the new pathologist, Kate Murphy. Forensics are still going over Terry White's grave site, so it will be a while until they can move the body.'

'Okay, keep us in the loop,' Norma said, walking away with Friendly.

Miller looked at his watch. It was way past lunchtime and he was starting to get hungry. He went back downstairs to the main investigation room. He walked over to Gibb, who was organising the crew and putting the old Terry White case on the front burner, indicating for his boss to join him in his office.

'I suppose you heard about Shaun Foxall being released without charge?'

'I don't know where to start me ramblings, old son.'

'Apparently the *Care in the Community* programme gives them a free pass.'

'It's this shitty world we live in, Frank. Some of them are fine; some go on to be axe murderers.'

'Ah well, at least the big wigs who sold the psychiatric hospital don't have to deal with them again while they sit in their Ivory Towers.'

'Oh, I can feel me blood pressure rising as we speak, Frankie, me old son.' Gibb's Irish brogue starting to get thicker again.

'I know, we have to go with the flow. Besides, Friendly and Norma Banks want Kim and I to liaise with the hospital.'

'Yeah, make sure the wee bastard is getting his hot cocoa at night, and all that stuff.'

Miller laughed, despite himself. 'It's not the first time I've been shot at, and I'm sure it won't be the last. Oh, and Kate Murphy called and said forensics are still processing the scene.'

'Right. She was supposed to call me, but I think I pissed her off this morning.'

'She's not making many friends, that's for sure.'

'She's not here to make friends, Frank. I don't care, as long as she can do her job.'

'We'll have to deal with her on a regular basis, so let's hope she gets off the defensive.'

'Just keep young Kim there in check.' He nodded through the door window to where Kim sat at a desk, a phone clamped to her ear.

'Hey, I'm not her keeper.'

'You're her bloody boyfriend.'

'She could beat the crap out of the both of us without breaking sweat.'

'You're a big softie, Miller.' Gibb pulled out his packet of cigarettes and lit one, opening the window wide to waft out the smoke.

'So you couldn't handle the pressure to quit smoking, I see,' Miller said.

'The wee fellas were in the packet, shouting out to me, *Smoke us you big bastard, before we go out of date.*'

'Do cigarettes go out of date?'

'How would I know? I don't keep them long enough to find out. Anyway, that's what they were shouting to me, and who am I to upset them?'

'You never cease to amaze me, Paddy.'

'That's what my wife used to say.' Gibb flicked the remainder of the cigarette out the window as Kim knocked on the door.

'Come in,' Miller said.

'I'm not interrupting, am I?'

'No, Chief Inspector Gibb was just giving me a lesson in willpower.'

Kim held up a piece of paper. 'I was doing some research on Shaun Foxall. He said his mother was Annie Foxall, deceased, and his father was Patrick Foxall, also deceased, both of which is true. What he didn't tell us, and what I found out by making a phone call is, his grandfather remarried, to a woman called Margaret, who now goes by her previous name, White. Margaret White. Carl White's mother. Shaun Foxall and Terry White have the same grandmother.'

CHAPTER 9

Miller felt the office cloying and needed to get back out into the sunshine. Paddy Gibb said they were setting up the stuff from the kidnapping and he could have an hour.

The mid-afternoon sun was high above the city centre, creating little pockets of cold shadows in the Closes off the High Street. The tourists had arrived and it was only a few short weeks until the Edinburgh Festival got into full swing. The street in front of the station would be closed off and only used by police vehicles in an emergency.

Miller loved the High Street, not just working there but living there as well. He looked towards the North Bridge and at the old building that was once a multi-level furniture store now converted into apartments. He looked up at his own apartment, imagining his wife standing there, waving down at him, as she should have been, but she was in the cold ground. She would never stand in front of the windows looking out again.

He took his mobile phone out and made a call. Spoke to the man on the other end and hung up, putting his phone back in his pocket and started walking down towards Hangman's Close. Walking into it, his thoughts went back nearly three years, and the worst day of his life.

'I'm not going to ask if you're alright, because I know you aren't,' Jack Miller said to his son. 'Even Charlie knows there's something wrong. He's not been himself all morning.'

The cat looked up at Miller as if he knew Jack was talking about him. He walked up to Miller and rubbed himself against the dark material of Miller's suit trousers, shedding fur on them. Miller petted him, running a hand along his back, and rubbing the spot on his back at the base of his tail. Carol said cats liked that spot to be rubbed, and she was right. Charlie would always come up to her wanting attention, especially when she was in the kitchen. That signalled it was treat time, and she always spoiled him.

Now she would never spoil him again.

Miller stood, and saw his wife standing in the kitchen doorway. This couldn't be the day of her funeral after all. There had been a mistake, because she was standing right there. He could see her.

'Dad, it's okay, she's not dead after all. She's here, I can see her.' He wanted to scream the words, but nothing came out. Tears streamed down his face, and when he blinked, she was gone. He walked from the living room across to the kitchen, Charlie following him, but she wasn't there.

He stood in the middle of the kitchen and cried hard, just standing there, holding onto the back of a chair, his head bent, his shoulders heaving with each heavy sob, until he felt his father's hand on his shoulder.

'I'm going to leave you alone, Frank, but I'll be in my room if you need me.' The hand was taken away and he suddenly felt lighter.

He sat on one of the chairs, his head down on his arms when he heard her voice.

'It's going to be hard, Frank, I'm not saying otherwise, but you have to be strong.'

Miller stopped crying and looked up. Carol was sitting at the table opposite him, a glow around her, as if he couldn't focus properly for the tears.

Now he found his voice. 'It's so hard being here without you, my darling. I miss you so much. I thought we were going to grow old together, that we would plan our retirement and go live in the sun somewhere. Have our kids come over for a visit. It was a little boy you were carrying, did you know that?'

Carol smiled at him and nodded.

'The pathologist confirmed what the consultant said in the hospital, that it was you falling and banging your head that caused you to...leave me. He also said you were three months pregnant with a little boy, but he didn't make it either. Nobody knows that. I couldn't tell anybody that, and the pathologist said he wouldn't reveal that detail.'

'I don't want to go and leave you worrying like this, Frank.'

'You don't have to go. You can stay with me. I want to be with you again.' He picked up the packet of painkillers that lay on the kitchen table. He had popped two at breakfast time. 'I can get more. I can take them all. We can be together again.'

'Frank, you're hurting, and you'll hurt for a long time, and you and I both know time is not the healer everybody says it is; time just dulls the pain, makes it easier to laugh again, to go about your everyday business. This is not your time though, sweetheart. You were my first love, and I can say I married my first love. But this is not your time, honey.'

He cried again and felt her hand on his, her gentle skin caressing his, her slender yet strong fingers rubbing gently over his knuckles. He looked at her beautiful blonde hair and her blue eyes, and knew he would never meet anybody like her again.

'I know you say that, but there's nobody else I want to be with other than you.'

'We'll be together again one day, my sweet Frank, but not just now. It's not what I want.'

'You don't want me to be with you?' The words stung him.

'More than anything, but only when the time is right.'

'I want you now. I don't want to be on my own.'

'You have to be strong for Charlie. He needs you right now.'

'He's a cat. He has my dad.'

'Listen to me; it's always hard on the ones left behind. You're consumed by grief right now, but it will pass. You have to trust me. If you love me, you'll stay behind. Charlie is not just a cat, it's what he represents. He's ours, and I need you to look after him, because I can't. I have our baby here, Frank, but where you are, you have Charlie, and he needs you. When you pick him up and hold him, you'll feel the same little animal I picked up and held. I didn't choose to leave you and Charlie, and you can't choose to leave either. One day you'll be beside me again, but until that time, you have to live your life. Promise me you will.'

'I don't know if I can.'

'Promise me. I have to go, Frank, but I have to hear you promise.'

He looked at his wife's face, at her smile, and knew he had to do what she wanted. 'I promise.'

'I have to go now, Frank, but you have to know I loved you more than anything. Till we meet again, my darling...'

She stood up, still holding his hand and then Frank saw him for the first time; Carol was holding the hand of a little boy, around two years old. Not three months, but two years. How?

'Bye, Daddy,' his son said, holding up a little hand and moving his fingers up and down in a little wave. Under his arm was a soft toy. A cat.

'Bye, Son,' he said, and then he felt his whole body rack with his crying.

He closed his eyes for just one second, just one lousy second and they were gone. He couldn't feel the touch of her hand anymore. Couldn't see his little boy.

'They're coming, Frank,' his father said, from the doorway.

Miller jumped, startled. Got up from the table and walked through to the living room, trying to stop the tears and failing. One corner of the room was part of a turret, and had windows looking down on to the High Street.

Police outriders had stopped the traffic on the North Bridge. A police car with its blue lights flashing drove slowly past the station, leading the hearse, a funeral car behind. Officers in uniform and plain clothes stood outside the station and saluted as the car went by.

The hearse stopped briefly, and the funeral director got out and walked in front of the car. Miller knew this was called 'paging' and it allowed time for the officers to get in their cars and fall in line.

The other members of Carol's family, her father, sister and brother were in the funeral car, having left with the hearse from the funeral parlour, but Miller stayed at home because he had wanted her to come home one last time.

The hearse rolled slowly down the setts towards their apartment. It was a dry day, in the first week of December, but cold outside. A weak, watery sun shone down on the High Street.

Charlie jumped onto the back of the couch that was against the wall with the big windows in it, and looked out, as if he knew.

The hearse turned round into the North Bridge and stopped outside the entrance to the building.

Miller grabbed his jacket and overcoat and put them on before grabbing a lint roller to get the cat hair off the bottom of his trousers. Then he stopped. There wasn't much there, not so anybody would notice. In a strange way, it would almost be as if Charlie would be there at the funeral. Carol would have liked that.

The funeral director knocked on the door and walked into the living room.

'Mr. Miller. Your wife is here.' It was said quietly and not without feeling, and Miller nodded, unable to speak. Jack already had his overcoat on, and they followed the director out of the room. Miller turned to look at Charlie, still sitting on the back of the couch, still looking out the window.

As if he was saying goodbye to his mummy.

****

Miller rubbed at his eyes as he crossed over The Cowgate and walked up into High School Wynd. The dour grey building of the City Mortuary on his left as he climbed the steep street. He turned into the courtyard of Edinburgh University's Psychology and Criminology campus. The main building had been a church, built around the start of the nineteenth century, and other wings had been added on over the years.

He walked past the parked cars on the right and straight over to the double doors facing him. Inside, a servitor sat at his station, and Miller showed him his warrant card telling him he was expected. He also knew where he was going.

The hall was large and magnificent, wood panelling adorning the walls as if they were works of art, and there was a sense to the place, not of decay, but of sights unseen and sounds unheard. He could only imagine the sort of people who had walked through these corridors hundreds of years before him.

He took the wide, marble stairs up to the first floor. His footsteps echoed in the quiet as he went along to the third door on his right and was about to knock when a loud voice boomed from within.

'Come in!'

Miller went in and for the first time that day, felt like smiling. Then he started crying.

The man behind the desk stood up. 'I've been expecting you for a long time, Frank.'

CHAPTER 10

Margaret White sat back in the rear seat of the Jaguar XJL, and closed her eyes briefly. She couldn't drive in Edinburgh, not now. Back in the day, when there weren't so many cars or foreigners on the roads, she could. Barnaby, her dead husband, had been fiercely English, and like many of his generation, felt Britain built the best cars in the world and wouldn't dream of setting foot in a Japanese or German car. Dear Barnaby died of a stroke before his time. If he worried less about superior German engineering and all the ills of the world, maybe he would still be here today.

He would have baulked at the idea of her being driven about in a luxury Japanese car. Which is why Margaret still bought Jaguars.

Barnaby Foxall had been Margaret's second husband, and although fate brought them together one sunny afternoon, she would have to wait years before that day arrived.

Duncan White's family had owned several woollen mills in the Borders of Scotland, and had made their fortune there. Who could have predicted a future where cheap, imitation cashmere scarves would sit on the tables of souvenir shops and the woollen mills of the Scottish Borders would be a shadow of their former selves?

Real cashmere was still popular when Margaret and Duncan married, and it wasn't long before they had their first - and only - child. Carl White came into the world in the same year Margaret Thatcher became the first woman leader of the British Conservative Party, Bill Gates co-founded Microsoft and while most Americans celebrated Independence Day, a victim of serial killer Ted Bundy disappeared, from Layton, Ohio. Carl White's only appearance in a newspaper was in the Births column of *The Edinburgh Evening Post.*

Margaret was brought back to the present when the Jaguar stopped suddenly. Her driver looked in the mirror. 'Beg your pardon, ma'am. Cyclist.'

'It's fine, Edward.' At least he hadn't knocked the man over.

She closed her eyes and went back to her thoughts.

Her son was her pride and joy, and her husband was all she had dreamt a husband would be. Duncan had been prudent with his money, and it was almost as if he had looked into a crystal ball and saw the world fall out of the textile market.

Which is why he had invested his money in new technology, and made an absolute fortune. Although he had spent his money wisely, he had instilled in his son a passion for cars.

A passion Carl still had when his father died, when Carl was only sixteen. His father opened one of the first Rolls-Royce dealerships in Edinburgh, and it had flourished. Duncan made sure Carl was used to working hard and getting his hands dirty, and had given his son a job on a Saturday morning, washing the expensive cars until they were gleaming.

Carl loved it and soon started to pick up everything there was to know about cars. He was to start at the bottom and work his way up, but that all changed one Saturday morning when Duncan had been sitting in his office and a massive heart attack had claimed his life.

Carl had suddenly gone from the bottom floor to the top, overnight, and Margaret had thought her son would flounder, but with the help of some experienced salesmen, he had taken the challenge head-on and succeeded.

He was making a small fortune by the time he was in his early twenties and met a young woman called Jill McLean. She had just graduated from Edinburgh University and was starting her work as a psychologist in the Royal Scottish Psychiatric Hospital in Edinburgh.

It was shortly afterwards that Margaret met and fell in love with Barnaby Foxall. He had walked into the Rolls showroom and over to her as she sat behind one of the empty desks. "Can you help me, love?' he had said. 'I need to speak to somebody who can help me with the cars.'

His accent was somewhere around Yorkshire, brash and not at all friendly.

'Well, let me help you find your way back to the door. Love. I don't just work here, I own the place. My son knows everything there is to know about these cars, but even if he didn't, I wouldn't sell you one anyway. We're very particular who we sell our cars to.'

He had laughed then. 'I like you. I like you a lot. Please excuse my ignorant self, but I'm not here to buy a car. I'm here to buy the dealership.'

Barnaby had been Barnaby Foxall, who owned a myriad of car dealerships in London and along the south coast, but his mother had been Scottish and he felt the lure of the 'old country', as dear old ma would have called it. She was a cantankerous old cow, but very wealthy. Margaret White was merely "comfortable" compared to old ma Barnaby's wealth.

So they had talked over dinner, and Carl had thought it would be good for business to be part of a group that had dealerships all over the south coast of England, so they went into partnership.

After some time, Barnaby proposed to Margaret and she accepted. They planned to get married six weeks later. Barnaby said at their age, there was no point letting the grass grow under their feet. Margaret moved to London, while Carl headed up the Scottish end of the business.

She had known what she was getting into of course; Barnaby was a widower, and his mother lived with him. As did his son, Patrick, himself a widower who also had an eight-year-old son. A young, troubled boy, called Shaun. He had autism, and went to a special school where his disability could be cared for. Shaun called Margaret, *Grandma*, and she loved it.

Carl told her he had asked Jill to marry him and she had accepted. They were making their wedding plans, and Barnaby was looking forward to having an extended stay in Scotland, so Patrick could meet his new stepbrother, and introduce his own son to the Scottish side. Barnaby's mother insisted she get a dress in London, in case there was nothing that would fit her in Scotland. She wondered if they even had TV there, despite Patrick assuring her they had, and in fact, a Scotsman had invented television. Patrick loved his grandmother and their regular debates and arguments about all and sundry.

He had offered to drive her from their home in the country into London, where she would be measured for a new dress followed by lunch at the Ritz.

It was only a few hours later that two uniformed police officers – a constable and an inspector, out of deference to the family – had turned up at the house and broken the news to Barnaby that his son and mother had been involved in an accident. A truck had veered over the centre line and hit the car Patrick was driving, and the car in turn had hit a tree at sixty miles an hour. The mother died instantly, while Patrick died shortly after being taken to hospital.

Barnaby was distraught. His mother and his son, gone, leaving them with his grandson, Shaun.

Although they had gone ahead with it, the wedding was a somewhat muted affair.

Margaret knew Barnaby had strong opinions before she married him of course, but the world had taken his little boy, and now he hated the world. He would get drunk and yell obscenities at the TV, and for some reason, his bigotry and racism would come to a head. Then he started talking loud outside, so much so that Margaret would get embarrassed and found herself apologising more and more for her husband's behaviour and outbursts.

Barnaby would get furious with her, telling her not to apologise for him, that it was a free country and he would say what he liked, when he liked to say it. He was permanently angry.

It was while he was having an outburst at a BBC news article that he had his massive stroke. He never regained consciousness and died seven days later in a hospital bed, looked after by people who he had grown to hate before his stroke.

Margaret went back to using her previous married name, White. Barnaby Foxall had been building up quite a reputation, and that was the last thing she needed, to have a name that was linked to a bigot.

Barnaby left her half his money. The other half went into a trust for Shaun. Technically, Margaret could have walked away from Shaun as her step-grandson was twenty now, but she had known him for twelve years, and couldn't let strangers look after the boy. Besides, Carl's wife was a psychologist, and said Shaun could be cared for up in Scotland. His autism had gotten so much worse, and he needed more and more care, and paying for it wasn't a problem. He wasn't too much to handle. He just needed that extra little bit of care.

The only reason he was in the psychiatric hospital was for hitting somebody. It wasn't Shaun's fault.

The boy had been shouting at Shaun, making fun of him. Shaun had temper problems now, and was always asking when his dad was coming back to get him. It was some sort of regression the doctors said.

Shaun would have been fine, but the boy, technically an adult as he was sixteen, had pushed Shaun so hard that Shaun fell down. And Shaun being Shaun, had got back up and punched the boy so hard he'd broken the boy's nose. The boy's father had been a judge. And had it not been for the doctor saying he wasn't fully responsible, Shaun would have gone to prison for a long time, provocation or no provocation.

Instead, he was admitted to the Royal Scottish Hospital under the care of the Mental Health Care Act. It would be a while before he would be allowed out on his own again, and only then would he be admitted into the *Care in the Community* programme. Somebody would have to be legally responsible for him.

'We're here, ma'am,' Edward said, as he stopped at the security gate of the psychiatric hospital.

There was a large, steel gate across the road leading into the hospital, and a guard came out of the guardhouse to speak to Edward. The driver showed the guard some ID and Margaret's name was checked off on a clipboard. They were expected, and Shaun's doctor had cleared it for her to come in and see Shaun.

As the gate glided out of the way and the Jag drove slowly through, Margaret couldn't help wondering one thing: where did Shaun get the gun?

CHAPTER 11

Harvey Levitt was American, born in New York, but transplanted to Scotland after he married a Scottish girl. Now he was a psychologist with Edinburgh University, and was the Psychologist for Police Scotland, Edinburgh Division.

'Coffee, Frank?'

Miller walked over to Levitt's desk and sat down. 'Black, Harvey, thanks.'

Levitt walked over to a sideboard where the coffee pot sat brewing. 'It's not long made, so it won't taste stewed.' He poured two cups and sat back down, passing one over to Miller.

Levitt was around forty, Miller guessed, but he had never come out and asked the man. He looked young anyway, not what he had always thought a psychologist might look like. He sipped his coffee and put the cup down on Levitt's desk.

'How did you know I'd be here one day?' Miller asked.

Levitt held out his hands, as if he was a magician who was demonstrating hiding a bird and was letting the audience see it was gone. 'You've opened up to me before, especially after Carol died, but it was always in the office at the station. You haven't come here on a personal basis. So I thought one day, sooner or later, you would come here.' He drank some of his coffee. 'Is it because of your friend and mine, Kim Smith?'

'Am I that transparent?'

'Hey, it's my job to figure these things out.' His hands were back together, as if he'd just caught the invisible bird and was about to reveal it to the audience. 'It's what I'm good at. My wife tells me I'm no good at making Spaghetti Carbonara, but a man has his limits.' He smiled.

'You might know I'm in a relationship with Kim now.'

'I don't listen to office gossip, but having said that, I bumped into I a few weeks ago, and he updated me on all aspects of your life. Tell you the truth; I enjoyed having a few beers with him. So, to answer your question, yes I did know.'

'When I met her under those circumstances a few months ago, I liked her a lot. I don't know what it was, Doc, but I felt something stirring inside me, as if I could feel this connection, but it was alien. I knew I shouldn't have felt that, because I was married.'

Levitt held up one hand. 'Let me stop you there, Frank. You *were* married. Until almost three years ago, and then you became a widower. I know that's such an archaic term, but it is what it is. That's what you became, whether you like it or not.'

'That's as may be, but I still felt in here that I was married.' Miller said, touching his chest. 'I still do. I loved Carol more than anything.'

'Do you still love her?'

'I always will. Is that wrong?'

'No. You will probably have feelings for Carol for the rest of your life, and nobody will blame you for that. To have somebody you loved more than anything just ripped away from you like that, is a terrible wrench.'

Miller drank some of the coffee. 'Earlier today, I started thinking about the day of Carol's funeral. I haven't told anybody this, but I saw her that day, in the house. She spoke to me. I thought it was her ghost.'

'What did she say to you?'

'It's what I said to her that scared me; I told her I wanted to be with her. That I could take a load of painkillers and be with her, but she told me no, it wasn't my time, and I had to stay behind and look after our cat, Charlie. He's just a cat, I told her, but she said he needed me.'

'It wasn't Carol you were talking to, Frank; your own mind had projected you there. Imagine your brain split into two halves; one half is mad with grief. It makes you think you can't go about your life as normal. That you don't know how you're going to cope with the grief of not seeing your loved one every day, wishing you could, but knowing you're not going to. So the solution is to take your own life so you *can* be with her every day.

'The other half of your brain is telling you, no, you can't do this. It's this half that's gone into self-preservation mode. It doesn't want you to make this rash decision. It manifests an image of your wife, so in a way, if you won't listen to yourself talking sensibly, then maybe you'll listen to your wife. It happens more than you think. Something primeval inside our brains is responsible for our survival, and that something told you that you should stay alive. It doesn't work with everybody, as some poor souls take their own life, but in this case, it made you see sense.'

'I haven't told anybody this, but Carol was three months pregnant when she died. The day of her funeral, I saw her with our little boy, but he was about two. I don't understand why I didn't see a baby.'

'That was your son, Frank, your future. You saw the little boy he would have grown into. Maybe some time you'll think of him as a teenager, or a young man. At that moment in time, the half of your brain dealing with the grief was showing you the little toddler he would have been.'

Miller took a deep breath and let it out slowly, and then drank some coffee. A few minutes of silence went by before Miller felt he could speak again. 'I'm having a problem with Kim; with making a commitment to her.'

'You feel guilty that you shouldn't be giving this woman attention when you're, quote, unquote, still married.'

'That's it exactly. Carol would not be happy.'

'I agree, were she still alive, but she's not, and she wouldn't want to see you hurting like this, Frank. Nobody wants to see a loved one being hurt. However, you feel you're cheating on her by going out with Kim.'

'Sort of, especially now Kim is talking about us moving in together.'

'I know that's not the sort of thing that should be rushed, and not for the reasons you're thinking of. It's a big commitment to each other, sometimes bigger than getting married.'

'Kim has a little girl, who just turned six, and she's a little beauty. We always have fun when we're out, and she's as cute as a button, but...'

'But?' Levitt drank some of his own coffee. 'So now you feel guilty about little Emma? Yes, I know her name. Jack told me that too.'

'I do.'

'Don't. You have nothing to feel guilty about. Life is for the living, Frank. I'm sorry to hear about losing your little boy, but just think of all the happiness you can bring to this little girl. Nobody is asking you to forget you would have had a son, but you can have more children and still preserve his memory.'

'So you don't think I should call it a day with Kim?'

'It's not for me to tell you how to live your life, but my advice is, cherish the memories, but learn how to make new ones, and be happy while you're doing it.'

Miller drank more coffee and sat back in the chair for a moment, reflecting. Then they had a bit of idle chit-chat and then Miller got up to leave. 'Thanks, Harvey. You don't know what a relief it's been to unburden myself.'

'You're welcome. Just take things easy. Only make a decision when you're ready to.'

CHAPTER 12

Margaret White walked along the corridor, her shoes squeaking on the polished floor, and came to the doctor's office.

'Come!' came the terse reply.

She walked in and the doctor rose to greet her.

'Mrs. White, please take a seat.'

'I'd like to see, Shaun, Doctor.'

'He's settled in very well.'

'Considering he's used to being in this place, I should hope so.' She looked around the functional if dingy office. The window let in the sunlight, and she could see trees and grass below, as if they were in a park.

'I won't sit. I would rather just cut to the chase and go and see my grandson, if that's all the same with you.'

'Ah, well, there's a slight problem with that.'

'Oh, really? Do tell.' Her face clearly showed her anger at not getting her own way.

'It's just that Shaun is in a vulnerable state just now. He's had a very traumatic day, and is not in a receptive mood. Don't get me wrong, he's comfortable, but he needs some stabilisation at this moment.'

'What do you think I'm going to do, Doctor? Give him some crack? Maybe throw a party and have the nurses take all their clothes off?'

The doctor almost laughed but caught himself. 'No, no, nothing like that. You have to understand though, what he did today was very serious. Anybody else who shot a gun at a police officer would be looking at a very long stretch in prison.'

'I don't need a lecture on the law; I just need to see my grandson.'

The doctor held up his hands. 'I fully understand, believe me, and that won't be a problem. Tomorrow, perhaps, but not today. He was very anxious when he arrived here. He needs some quiet. Sometimes that's all our patients need, just to rest and recharge their batteries.'

Margaret felt as if all the air had rushed out of her, and wished she could take something to relax herself. 'I don't want Shaun to feel scared. He didn't like it when he was here before. He often talks about the bad times he had here.'

'Patients often have a difficult time in the transition between home and here, that's all. When they see they're in no danger, they start to assimilate and become very productive. Then they make new friends and learn new things. People don't understand mental health. They think because patients are in the Royal Scottish they are all serial killers waiting to escape, whereas the exact opposite is true. Each patient has some problems adjusting to the outside world. They need to live in a different structure, as Shaun did. Some of my patients learn new skills and can adapt so they can join society again, albeit under supervision. We all know some patients can't and won't re-join society, as their fear of the world is transposed onto the public, who then see them as a threat.

'Shaun was one of the lucky ones. We treated him and because it is acceptable to release patients like him into care, he is part of a programme where he can live an almost normal life. However, sometimes there is a sideways slide, and those people have to go through a little retraining, that's all. Then he will be back amongst everybody else. You have to take a step back, Mrs. White, and let us treat him so he can go back home with you. The sooner we can get on with that, the sooner Shaun will be back in familiar surroundings, and I'm sure you'll agree that's what we all want?' The doctor smiled at her, his most charming, disarming smile.

Margaret took a deep breath and closed her eyes, feeling a calmness washing over her.

'Of course you're right. I want Shaun home with me as soon as possible.'

'The Procurator Fiscal has put Shaun back into the programme, so we legally have to keep him here for seven days, but that's a *minimum.* The sooner we get him on the mend, the sooner it will be over and before you know it, he'll be home. Then he'll come and visit us every day for another seven days, just staying for an hour or so, to make sure he's comfortable being back and then life will be back to normal.'

Margaret took a moment to think about it. 'I'll be back sometime tomorrow morning.'

'Come anytime. Shaun will be woken up for breakfast at seven am.'

'Thank you, Doctor.' Margaret turned and left the office.

She often wondered how many killers were really in this place. Today, there was only one.

And he was following her.

CHAPTER 13

It was late afternoon by the time they got all the old files and everything from the old Terry White investigation sorted out. Miller sat in his office writing a report when Gibb called them all into the main investigation room.

'Listen up,' DCI Gibb said, from the front of the room. 'As we all know, Shaun Foxall was taken back to the Royal Scottish after being interviewed by senior officers and the PF. Norma Banks is not happy about it, but legally, her hands are tied.' A groan went through the room. Gibb held up his hand. I know, people, I know. Some of us would like to see Foxall strung up.' He looked over at DS Andy Watt, one of the old school, who was nodding his head.

'So he takes a shot at police officers and he's let off with a slap on the wrist. What kind of society do we live in nowadays? The criminals are given more protection than the cops,' Watt said.

'It's a PC biased society we live in, Andy, and I don't mean police constable. Heat. Kitchen. You know what I'm saying.'

'I'd like to have seen what would have happened if he'd pointed his gun at one of the ARV boys. They know how to do it right in America, that's all I'm saying.'

'Think about all the gun crime they have over there though, Sarge,' one of the younger officers said.

'Oh, and we don't have gun crime in the U.K., is that right, son? Nobody's allowed to carry a gun over here unless you're a wee scally, then you can shove a shooter in your tracksuit pocket.'

'Okay, ladies, enough,' Gibb said. 'Apologies to the real ladies in here who are behaving. Andy, my office after we're done.'

'Whatever.'

'Right, Foxall; he's been taken in as a resident for the required seven days. Then he'll be back in there every day for a check-up for a further seven days, then we'll send a posse round to string him up when he gets home, if that's alright with you, Andy?'

A burst of laughter from the room. Miller, standing at the back, couldn't help smiling.

'Oh fuck off,' Watt said, not quite under his breath.

'To serious business now. Terry White. The pathologist called me ten minutes ago. They extracted Terry from his shallow grave, and forensics are going over the ground in what remains of the basement. There's also a fair sized garden to check. The decomposed body was taken to the City Mortuary, and the first thing they did was run dental records again, just in case. Kate Murphy confirmed a few minutes ago that it was indeed young Terry in there.'

A hand shot up. 'When are we going to tell the vultures?'

'Chief Super Friendly is handling that one. He'll give a press conference later this afternoon. An initial conference as we don't know how the boy died yet, and that's going to take a while. Meantime, we are going through all the paperwork from almost three years ago when the kidnapping went down.' Gibb nodded towards Miller. 'Back to when we lost one of our best detectives, DI Miller's wife. For those of you not on the team at that time, DS Carol Miller was bounced from pub to pub, answering the phone in each one so the kidnapper could give her further instructions as to what to do with the ransom money.

'After the last run, she was knocked down by a hit-and-run driver. The money was stolen by an opportunist. I won't give you all the details just now, but I want you all to read up on it.

'And we have now found out Shaun Foxall is related to Terry White,' Miller said. 'I called the PF and she said there is absolutely no legal reason why we can't interview Foxall about where he was the night Terry was taken.'

Gibb pointed to Miller. 'I'd like you on that, Frank. Take Kim with you. As part of the *Care in the Community* pish, he can still be interviewed in the hospital, as he did commit a crime. Legally, he doesn't need a lawyer present as he's under the care of the hospital, and as long as we get permission from his doctor, we can talk to him. And a rep from the PF's office will be there too, so we have all the bases covered. In fact,' Gibb looked at his watch, 'can you go there this afternoon? Now we have a formal ID on Terry it gives us cause to interview him.'

'Will do.' He looked over to Kim who smiled at him.

'You'd better go and have a word with the grandmother as well. Her address is in the notes. She's known in influential circles so we had better give her the courtesy of telling her to her face that her grandson is dead.'

'I know where she lives. I'm assuming she's still there,' DS Hazel Carter said.

'Right. Get onto it. Take Gilmour with you.'

The team got up from their chairs. Miller and Kim left the station by the back door, into the car park. 'There are rumours they're going to close this place,' he said, unlocking the door to his Vauxhall Insignia. The sun had gone over them, heating up the car's interior, and leaving it stuffy.

'It wouldn't surprise me,' Kim said, as she got in the passenger side. 'Now Police Scotland is in full force, they'll be making a lot of changes.'

Miller wound the windows down to let some cooler air in as he backed out of the space. 'Including reducing the hours of the public counters, so I heard.'

'Just wait another hundred years when all the policing will be done by robots.'

'Man is slowly making man extinct.'

They drove past Quartermile, the old Royal Infirmary changing beyond all recognition into apartments.

'There are changes everywhere you look,' Kim said, pointing to the old hospital. 'My Emma was born in Simpson's Memorial. Now it's been torn down to make way for yuppie flats.'

'I thought Emma was born in London?'

Kim gave a brief laugh. 'No. My ex wanted her born down there because he's English, and he had my dad's backing because he's English too, but my mother's from here and so am I.'

'And the women won at the end of the day.'

'I told Eric, when you're carrying the child, then you can decide where you're giving birth.'

Miller wondered if his girlfriend missed her ex like he missed his dead wife, but it was something he hadn't come right out and asked her. Maybe he wouldn't like the answer.

'Are you still coming down for dinner, tonight?' she asked him.

If she'd asked him an hour ago, he would have said, probably not, but he felt so much better after talking to Harvey Levitt. The American had made perfect sense to him. 'I'd like that.'

'I think Jack and Neil went out drinking the other night. Jack was so hungover the following morning that Charlie almost fainted with the booze fumes.'

Kim laughed. 'I haven't seen the cat for a couple of weeks.'

They drove down Morningside Road and Miller turned off for the entrance to the Royal Scottish Psychiatric Hospital. Home to both secure and non-secure patients, hence the gate.

Miller showed his ID to the guard. 'We're here to interview a patient who was brought in today.'

'Are you expected?' the guard asked.

'No.'

'Okay, follow the road to reception. They can deal with you in there.' He stepped back into the guardhouse, and seconds later, the heavy steel gate slid back on its tracks. It had been a while since Miller had visited this hospital, interviewing one of the secure patients before he transferred to the State Hospital down in the Borders.

Inside, the old building was cool. After identifying himself and Kim, they were escorted up to the second level and dropped off at a nurse's station.

'Did you know this was originally called the Edinburgh Lunatic Asylum?' Miller asked Kim.

'Really? I thought that was Fettes HQ.'

'I'm sure we can't tell the difference sometimes.'

'Can I help you?' a stern-faced nurse said. They showed their ID.

'We'd like to interview Shaun Foxall,' Miller said.

'Oh, I don't know if that will be possible.'

A doctor was standing looking at a chart behind the nurse's station. He looked over at Miller before going back to reading the chart.

'Under the *Care in the Community* programme rules, if any patient commits a crime and is re-admitted for evaluation, the police have the right to interview the patient for further details so a report can be drafted for the Procurator Fiscal,' Kim said. 'I work with the PF, and we need to have a talk with him. Since we're at the hospital, his lawyer doesn't need to be present.'

'Or we have the authority to remand him in custody until he is able to talk with us,' Miller said.

The doctor quickly put the chart down and stepped over, smiling at them both. 'There won't be any need to take Shaun away. I'm Dr. Borthwick, Shaun's doctor.' He stuck his hand out and Miller shook it.

'DI Miller. We just have a few questions we need answered.'

'Fine. He hasn't been given his sleep assistant meds, but he's just tired at the moment, so we'll bring him along to a room for you. Nurse, please show the detectives along to the office.'

Borthwick walked away along the corridor, while the nurse showed Miller and Kim into an office round the corner.

It could have been a student's lounge, with a few padded chairs strewn around. A camera sat up in one corner, a little red eye unblinking underneath the plastic casing.

Five minutes later, Borthwick returned and held the door open. 'His grandmother wanted to see him, but I was afraid seeing her so early might upset him.'

'Why would he be upset at seeing his grandmother?' Miller asked.

'Right now, she would have been a receptacle for his desire to go home, and that would have set him back before we even got him started. Although the order is for him to stay for seven days, there is one caveat; he needs to show progression. If he doesn't, then I have the authority to sign an order that can keep him here longer. Nobody wants that. We all want what's in the best interest of Shaun, and that is to get him on track again. So please treat him with respect.'

The same respect he showed when he was shooting at police officers, you mean? Miller thought.

'Of course we will.'

Borthwick turned his head to look out the door and nodded. A nurse brought Shaun Foxall in. A male nurse followed Foxall in and stood to one side.

'Nurse Brannigan will stay here in case you need assistance.' The man was large and looked as if he would have no problem taking care of any unruly patient. Borthwick left with the female nurse and closed the door.

'I'm detective Miller, this is Dr. Smith. We want to have a word with you, Shaun.'

'Do I know you?' Foxall asked, looking at Kim.

You should do, you shot at me this morning. 'No.'

Foxall looked at Miller. 'I know you though. I saw you a long time ago.'

'It was this afternoon, Shaun. Back at the police station. Remember?'

Foxall shook his head. 'Before that. A long time ago.' He took a deep breath, his eyes shifting back and forth, rubbing his hands together. 'Not you. The police. Gary.'

'Gary who?' Miller looked up at the camera. Looked at their "bodyguard".

'Gary the bad man.'

'Is there a café we can go to?' Miller asked Brannigan.

'I don't know if he's allowed to go,' the nurse said.

'I'll tell that to his lawyer, will I? Richard Sullivan would chew you up. You'd drown in the paperwork the lawsuits he would throw at you.'

Brannigan's cheeks brightened a little and Miller could see the muscles tighten in his jaw, as if he really wanted to show Miller some of his restraining skills. 'There's one down on the next level. I should maybe go with you.'

Miller stood up. 'I'm a big boy. I'll deal with Shaun. He's not going anywhere, are you Shaun?'

Shaun shook his head. 'Nope. I'd like a Coke. They won't give me Coke here. They said I have to have a special diet. I just want something fizzy.'

'We'll get you a Coke, Shaun,' Kim said, smiling. They stood and left the room. The nurse at the station looked at them as they walked towards the lift. 'Café,' Miller said to her.

'Fine,' she replied, obviously more aware of the law than Brannigan was. The big man walked out of the room towards them.

'I'm going out the back for a cigarette,' he said. 'I need a break.'

They all rode the lift down one level, Brannigan going one way, Miller and the others following the sign for the café. 'Rules say we can question him away from electronic audio visual equipment,' Miller said. 'I doubt there will be anything like that down here.'

It was quiet late afternoon, and they were serving dinner. It actually smelled quite good. 'You want something to eat, Shaun?' Miller said.

'They give me fancy vegetables and stuff I don't like,' Shaun said, yawning.

'You tired?' Kim said.

'Yes.'

'Did they give you any medicine yet?'

'Yes, Andrew did. Some pills. But I didn't take them.'

'Andrew?'

Shaun looked at him. 'Dr. Borthwick.'

Miller looked at Kim. *The doctor lied to us.*

'What would you like to eat?' Kim asked.

'Fish and chips,' Shaun said, eyeing up the food in front of him. The woman behind the counter dished the food up and they took the tray to pay for it, Kim adding a bottle of Coke. Regular, with sugar in it.

'Is there a reason you wanted to bring him down here?' Kim asked Miller, in a quiet voice.

'I'm sure they were recording the whole thing, including the audio. He mentioned Gary. It could only have been Gary Davidson. Gary the bad man. And besides, Borthwick said Shaun hadn't been given anything to make him tired. Why would he lie?'

'I'll bet they keep him doped up enough in case we turned up, not expecting us to turn up so soon.' They sat at a table. A few other members of staff were starting to filter in, followed by visiting family members.

Shaun started tucking into the food as if he'd been starved.

'Can you tell me about this man Gary?' Miller said.

Shaun swallowed his food washing it down with some Coke. 'He was a policeman, just like you. I didn't like him. He didn't buy me dinner.'

Kim smiled. 'You didn't like him because he didn't buy you dinner?' Kim said.

Foxall shook his head. Ate some more. Miller and Kim waited patiently. 'No, I didn't like him because he said they were going to kill me.'

'Who was going to kill you?' Miller asked.

'Them. The people he hung about with.'

'Do you know these people?'

'No. He was drunk one night when he came in here to pick up Rosie. I like Rosie. I think she was frightened by our game today, but I had fun. They said it would be just like in the movies. I like movies.'

'Do you know Gary's last name?' Miller said, getting a sinking feeling in his stomach.

Shaun laughed. 'Of course. He was Rosie's *Special Man.* That's what she called him. When she wasn't angry with him. I used to listen to them fighting.'

'What's Gary's last name?'

'He's gone now. He died. He was a bad man. He made Rosie feel sad.'

Tell me his last name. Miller knew who he was talking about, he just needed Shaun to say it so he couldn't say he was coerced. 'What was his name, Shaun? Can you remember?'

Shaun put his fork down. 'Davidson. Gary Davidson. He hated me. He said they were all going to kill me.' He put his fork down and started crying. 'I want to go home, Frank. They're going to kill me.'

'Why would Dr. Borthwick want to kill you?'

'Not him. The other men who come to the hospital. They're not doctors. They don't wear white coats like Dr. Borthwick. I like Dr. Borthwick. He's nice to me, but I don't like the others who come here.'

'You're safe in here, Shaun. Nobody can touch you,' Kim said.

Shaun rubbed at his eyes. 'You don't understand: I know who killed Terry. And now I'm in here, they're going to kill me. I heard them talking about it.'

'That was almost three years ago,' Miller said. 'A long time ago. You're safe now.'

'No, no, I don't mean back then. I heard them say it today. They said now I'm back in here, I won't be getting out alive.'

CHAPTER 14

Neil McGovern's department was located in one of the basement levels in the new Scottish Parliament Building in Holyrood. He was sitting at his desk when the call came through. He was envisioning a juicy steak with his wife at her favourite restaurant, washed down by a nice bottle of wine. She had been working so hard recently, juggling too many balls, thinking the office wouldn't run without her, so he was going to surprise her with a nice relaxing evening, even though it was a weekday.

He debated whether to answer his phone or not. Curiosity won him over.

'Hello?'

'You were actually thinking about not answering that, weren't you?' Kim said.

'Well, I'm glad I did, now I know it's you, sweetheart. What's up?'

Kim paused for a second before speaking. 'We have a situation, Dad. You're going to have to trust me on this one.'

'I always trust your judgement. Except when it comes to men. Frank Miller not included.'

'He's here with me.'

'So tell me what the situation is, Kim.' McGovern knew it had to be work related as she'd tried his office first.

'I don't want to go into detail, but you have to trust me. We have a young man with us who has learning difficulties, and needs witness protection.'

'That's my speciality. So where are you now?'

'I'm at the Royal Scottish Hospital in Morningside.'

'You're not trying to break out one of their patients, are you?'

'That's exactly what I'm doing.'

'You're kidding me.'

'I'm not joking about this, Dad. Mum will freak when she finds out, and believe me, the new chief constable is going to be going after her job, but this young man's life is in danger.'

'Okay, first of all, the chief con can go blow. I have friends in Holyrood who could have him removed before he's had his first coffee in the morning.

Your mother and I can handle him. If this is a life-or-death situ we're in, then it won't be a problem. Is he a long-termer in there?'

'No, he was only brought in today. He's a re-evaluation case. Seven days then he's out.'

'Can't you just wait until he's out next week.'

'That's the problem; it's somebody in here who wants him dead.'

McGovern took a deep breath for a moment and let it out slowly. 'That is a problem. Tell me, what was he admitted for?'

A pause before Kim answered. 'For extortion and discharging a weapon at police officers.'

'Oh, nothing serious then?'

'Dad, nothing is what it seems. To be honest, Frank and I brought him down to the café, but the longer we stay here, the longer he's in danger. While we're in here with him, I don't feel safe either. Accidents happen.'

'Right, get out of there. I'll issue an immediate protection order. My secretary will have it filed in thirty seconds. That way, it's all legal. Get out of there. If anybody tries to stop you, get Frank to arrest them. As of right now, that boy is under the protection of Her Majesty the Queen. And nobody argues with the Queen.'

Kim looked at Miller as she hung up, and then at her watch. 'As of right now, Shaun's with us.'

Miller had no doubt they would be watched as they left the hospital with Shaun, and maybe Dr. Borthwick would have the wherewithal to call Miller's superiors or not, but Miller guessed the good doctor would have to put up a verbal fight, or people would want to know why.

The message was already being broadcast on his Airwave by the time they got to the car. 'You drive,' he said to Kim, giving her the keys. 'I need to call a friend of mine.'

'Call for Detective Inspector Miller,' Control said, but Miller ignored it.

Kim made sure Foxall was secure in the back before driving towards the gate. The security guard wouldn't open the gate. 'I've had a call that a patient is trying to leave the premises without consent,' he said, looking a little flushed. Miller got out of the car.

'I don't want to sound like a bully, pal, but get the gate open. You're messing with an investigation. I'll arrest you and I will personally see to it that every aspect of your life is looked into. Every little detail. I will make sure you're remanded in Saughton while the investigation is taking place.'

'You can't do that,' the guard replied, but didn't look too sure.

Kim looked at him. 'I'm with the Procurator Fiscal's office. He damn well can, and he damn well will, if you don't get that fucking gate open right now.'

The guard sniffed and gave her a last defiant look, as if to say he was doing this under duress. 'You remember that you forced me to do this when the shit hits the fan.'

The gate slid open and the car passed through. Miller looked behind him and saw two orderlies running along the road towards the gate. Borthwick was standing at the entrance door.

'I think we just saved your life,' Miller said to Foxall.

'I knew a nice lady once. I wish I had saved her life, but I didn't. She died.'

'Oh really? What was her name?' Miller asked.

'Carol. She had the same name as you.' He looked at him. 'Carol Miller. They killed her too.'

CHAPTER 15

Cameras tracked their movements as they walked along the brightly coloured corridor. McGovern had been pleased when offered this part of the building. One thing the Scottish Parliament Building wasn't short of, was high-tech security.

'This building is so fascinating. We were lucky to get a suite of offices here, as well as space downstairs. We have rooms down there for some of our guests that are better than the Four Seasons.'

'Fascinating, Dad,' Kim said, 'but we're not after a private tour.'

'Spare the rod and spoil the child, isn't that right, Frank?' McGovern smiled. His accent couldn't quite betray his East London upbringing.

'I wouldn't know, Neil.'

McGovern laughed. 'Young Shaun will be alright here. I have some people looking after him in one of our restaurants downstairs.' He motioned for them to sit on one of the settees at the far side of the room. He sat on a chair opposite them and poured coffee from the pot that had been brought in.

The door opened, and Norma Banks, Procurator Fiscal and Neil McGovern's wife, walked in.

'This is getting fucked up,' she said. 'You still have that little something in your drawer, husband dear?'

'It's medicinal,' he said, looking at their daughter.

'So, now we're all here, let's talk about why you absconded with a patient from a psychiatric hospital,' he said.

'This had better be bloody good,' Norma said, opening one of Neil's drawers and taking out the small bottle of whisky that lived there. She poured herself a coffee and poured a stiff measure into it. 'Not only have I had the chief constable on the phone, but the hospital and the justice secretary. They want to know why a boy was kidnapped from the Royal Scottish. I told them to hang fire as there's an operation going down.' She looked at Miller. 'Tell me I still have a career, Frank.'

'We're going to hear why things went down,' McGovern said.

'The lord advocate himself was on the phone to me, just so you know.'

'Just have a seat and sip your drink. Relax and we'll get to the bottom of this.'

Norma sat down and slipped her shoes off.

Miller looked at Kim, who nodded, and then addressed the two older people in the room, hoping he wasn't going to sound like a clown. 'Do you know what happened with Foxall this morning?' he asked McGovern.

'I do.'

'So, he was apparently writing to my former sister-in-law, Rosie Davidson, extorting money from her. Not at first, mind, but he led up to that. So today, we executed a plan we'd put together, to lure him out. Rosie didn't know who was emailing her, but he knew a lot about her. I asked a friend of mine to do some background checks on the quiet.'

McGovern looked at his wife. 'Ian Powers, a computer guy. He works for me now, but he's been a friend of Frank's for a long time.'

Norma looked at Miller. 'I know him; his brother murdered his wife and tried to blame Ian for it. That's the same man, isn't it?'

'Yes, that's him. Carol and I believed him when he said he was innocent. Anyway, he did some checking, and found the IP address for the emails that were being sent: Lothian Buses.'

'So he worked for the bus company?' Norma asked.

'No, a lot of the new buses have free Wi-Fi now. He could just go on a bus, make up an email address and only use it when he rides a bus.'

'And we know he rode the buses,' Kim said. 'We asked him and he said he did. We also came out and asked him if he had a smartphone or an iPad he could use on a bus, and he confirmed he had both.'

Norma drank some of her coffee. 'We would need a warrant to look through those devices.'

'No we wouldn't,' McGovern said. 'Now he is officially under the wing of the Witness Protection programme, we can have those gadgets in here in under an hour.'

'Except he's already given us permission to look at them, but considering he's also under the health care system, we have to tread carefully,' Kim said.

'His lawyer could argue that because he has mental health issues he could give you permission to burn the Scottish Parliament down but it doesn't mean to say you can.'

'Witness Protection trumps everything, my dear,' McGovern said. 'Richard Sullivan and I spoke on the phone a little while ago. As you know, we go way back. When I found out he was representing Foxall, and Frank here had taken his client for a ride, I gave him the courtesy of a phone call.'

'I'm sure Dickie got his pants in a knot over that,' Norma said.

'Nah, he understood. He'll get a call from Margaret White but he can blind her with legal mumbo jumbo, but she's still not getting her grandson back until I know what's going on.'

'I don't suppose you called Dennis Friendly?' Miller said.

'*I* did,' Norma said. 'I told him what was going on and if he wants, he can come down here and sit in, but considering he craps himself every time Neil walks into his office, I doubt we'll be getting any flak from him. In fact, I told him I expect full co-operation from him, and you and Kim were working on an operation known only to me and my associates.'

'I appreciate that,' Miller said.

'That's what they'll carve on my tombstone.' Norma looked at her watch. 'What are we going to do about Emma?'

'She's away down to London with Eric, remember love?'

'Oh, yes, I forgot. I hope his wife can put up with her, being pregnant and all.'

'Right, to Shaun,' McGovern said. 'He's having a Coke and watching TV, and Ian Powers is going through his phone. We told him the truth; if he thinks somebody is out to kill him, we need to look at his stuff so we can try and catch them.'

'Does he know who's after him? And do we know for a fact this isn't a deluded mind at play here?' Norma said.

'I know what you're thinking,' Miller said, 'somebody with mental health problems is thinking people are out to kill him because he's been playing too many video games or watching too many of the wrong movies, or whatever. And to be honest, I thought the same thing, except I thought he had a bad streak in him, something he could control, something that would make him threaten Rosie, but now I think there's something else going on.'

'What convinced you?' she looked him in the eye.

'This morning, when I arrested him, he said he didn't know what to do, now they didn't tell him how the game ends. He knows who Gary Davidson was. He says Gary threatened to kill him, as did the others. I wouldn't have believed him if I hadn't seen Gary under duress for myself, and knowing Gary was involved in my wife's death, then I want to hear more of Shaun's story, even if it's so we can dismiss it as the ramblings of a mind that is not quite as there as ours are. However, he said in the car that "they" killed my wife. Whoever "they" are. Again, if my wife had just died or had been run over and Gary hadn't been involved the way he was, then I would have dismissed it. But there's something there that strikes a chord. And if there's more to Gary Davidson than we know about, I want to fully investigate it.'

'Good,' Norma said. 'You know his grandmother will be on the phone to all the powerful people she knows, trying to overturn this?'

'I'll get Richard to talk to her. Make her see reason. He'll baffle her, but make her see that her grandson is safe. Maybe let her think some proper paperwork wasn't signed or some BS like that.' McGovern seemed unflappable.

Norma tapped her fingers on the arm of her chair for a moment. 'Right, let's have a talk with Shaun. Then I'll make a phone call to the lord advocate. And then we'll see if we're all going to prison or not.'

CHAPTER 16

Jack Miller hit the bottle of wine and it smashed against the lift doors.

The woman who had been stepping out of the lift jumped a little as the bottle flew out of her hand.

'Oh, jeez, I'm so sorry,' he said to her 'I am so clumsy. And you've got red wine on your trousers.' Jack put one hand up to his forehead. 'I am such a clot.'

The woman smiled at him. 'I can't disagree with you there, my friend.'

Jack couldn't miss the American accent. 'Please, let me get you a wet towel or something. I live in there.' He pointed to his front door.

'Don't worry about it. I was heading home. I live just round the corner.' She pointed to the opposite end of the hallway that went round to the apartments overlooking Cockburn Street.

'I've seen you a couple of times. I thought you were visiting somebody.'

'No, I moved in last week.'

'And I just smashed your house-warming bottle. And ruined your clothes.'

'I'll get them dry cleaned.'

'And I'll foot the bill. And if they can't clean them, I *will* pay for new ones.'

'I'll go and get something to clean that up with,' she said.

'No, I'll clean it. And my name's Jack Miller, by the way.' He smiled and held out his hand.

'Pleased to meet you, Jack Miller-by-the-way.'

He laughed.

'My name's Samantha Willis. Sam for short.' She shook his hand.

'Pleased to meet you, Sam-for-short.' He held onto her hand for a few seconds longer than necessary. Then something clicked in his head. He let her hand go. 'Samantha Willis, the crime writer?'

Sam smiled even wider. 'Yes. And this is the part where you say, *Oh, I've heard of you but I've never read any of your stuff.*'

'I have read your stuff, actually.'

'Smartass.' She smiled.

'I'll go and get the brush and clean this glass up before somebody cuts themselves. Which will probably be me.'

'Seeing how clumsy you are.'

'Guilty as charged. Hang on a minute, I'll be right back.' He went into the apartment and found a brush and pan. Samantha was still waiting by the lift.

'Is that how you introduced yourself to all the new neighbours?' she asked him, still smiling. 'By smashing their bottle of wine?'

'No, you're the first. And hopefully the last.' He swept up the big chunks of glass and then went back for his vacuum cleaner, giving the carpet a quick once over.

'You would make a good house cleaner. I'm looking for one, if you're interested.'

'Sorry, I can't fit into my maid's outfit anymore.' He laughed. 'Well, this conversation went downhill fast.'

'Yeah, that's an image I'll never get out of my head.'

Jack held up one finger. 'I'll just mop whatever's left of your wine off the walls and the lift,' he said. Five minutes later, he was back, slopping water about until the walls were reasonably clean.

'I take it back, about wanting to hire you as a cleaner. You just failed the manual dexterity test.'

'Well, I was a cop for over thirty years, so my cleaning skills are a bit rusty. Luckily I'm not looking for part-time work.'

'A cop? Really?'

'Yes, a murder squad detective. My son's a detective now. Carrying the family torch.'

'Interesting.'

Jack picked up the mop and bucket. 'I'll nip out and get you a bottle of wine. What was the make?'

'Forget it, Jack. I was only going to sit in, watch TV and have a couple of glasses.'

'Now I feel bad. I have beer in the fridge. You could have some of those instead.'

'Sure. I like beer, although it's best not to mix the grape with the grain, isn't that what they say?'

'Exactly. I'm surprised an American would know that saying.'

'My ex-husband is Scottish.'

'Ah. That makes sense.'

'Do you have time to have a beer with me? Unless you have something on? I know you were on your way out,' Sam said.

'I'd love to have a beer with you. I was just on my way to have a few beers with my mates, but they see me all the time.'

'Give me half an hour to get showered and changed. I'm at number fifty-five.'

'Great. I'll be there.'

'I must warn you, I might want to pick your brains regarding police procedure.'

'Pick away.'

Sam walked away and turned back to look at Jack Miller as he opened his door, then she rounded the corner.

Jack went into his flat feeling happier than he had in a long time. It had been a long winter, what with all that had gone on with Frank, and finding out who really killed his wife. Jack's own wife had died a few years earlier, and though there were some women who hung around their local, it was nice to talk to some different female company now and again.

'Mickey, it's Jack,' he said, calling his friend on his mobile phone. 'Something's come up. I'll have to catch you guys later.'

'What's her name?'

'What? Can you not keep your mind out of the gutter for ten minutes?'

'Again: name.'

'As if I would tell you.'

'I'm your best mate. You tell me everything.'

'There's nothing to tell. I just have to go out somewhere.'

'I was a copper just like you, big man. I can tell when somebody's lying to me. Spill.'

'Don't make me hunt you down and smack you around.'

'As if, Miller. You couldn't smack your way through a piece of wet toilet paper.'

'Anyway, I have this important date I can't get out of.'

'So it *is* a date? Come on, man, just tell me.'

'And have it all over the Rebel?' The Rebellion pub, named after the Jacobite Rising of 1745.

'Seriously, Miller, anybody would think you're sixteen.'

'I feel like I'm sixteen at times, hanging around with you. Anyway, I'm going now. Stay alive.' He hung up and took the six-pack of beer from the fridge, still in their cardboard carrier. He looked at the cat. 'I know, Charlie, I said I was only going out for a few beers, but I'm only going to be along the corridor. Don't judge.'

He left, locked up, and walked along to number fifty-five. He tried to remember who had lived here until recently. An old guy. He'd taken ill and had gone to live with his son. *Just like you're doing,* he reminded himself.

He knocked, and Samantha answered the door a few minutes later. Her hair still damp after her shower, and she had changed into a casual shirt and shorts.

'I'm not sure what vintage these are, but they're cold,' Jack said.

She laughed and stepped aside. 'That'll do for me.'

The Royal Mile Apartments used to be a furniture store, so each apartment was unique. This was a two-bedroom compared to Frank's three, if Jack's memory served him correctly.

'Did you know the previous owner?' Samantha asked, as she led Jack down the hallway into the living room.

'I met him a few times, but I believe he went to live with his son after he took ill. Nice guy though.'

'Take a seat,' she said, after Jack gave her the beers. 'I'll put some of these in the fridge.' She took two out of the carrier and gave him one.

'Great stuff, thanks, but I feel a bit of a fraud, bringing you the beers and then drinking one.'

'I hope you'll have more than one,' she said, smiling. 'Besides, I have more in the fridge.'

'Sounds good.' He twisted the top off, taking a pull from the long neck, before putting it on a side table next to the couch. Samantha came back in and sat on the opposite couch. A large screen TV was on the wall above the fireplace.

'You've done this place up nicely,' Jack said.

'Thanks. It was a labour of love. I don't mind painting. Although, most of my time is taken up with writing.'

'I take it you work from home?' It sounded stupid when he put his thought into words. Of course, she was going to work from home. Where else would she work?

'Yes, the spare room is my office. It overlooks Cockburn Street. It took me a little while to find something suitable, but it was worth the wait.'

'I have to admit, since I was a copper, I enjoy reading Scottish crime fiction. There are a lot of writers writing crime set in Edinburgh, and in Scotland.'

'I know. I'm one of them. At a signing, someone once said to me, "Don't you think the public will get fed up with reading about Edinburgh detectives?" I said, no I don't think so. Once you've read the annual outing of the favourite fictional detectives, are you going to wait another year, or look for something similar, if that's what you enjoy reading? I think authors like myself fill a void.'

'Authors like you? You're famous. There are a lot of writers who self-publish and don't get the proper recognition.'

'I started self-publishing a few years back. It took me a while before an agent noticed me, and I took off. Some of the writers don't need an agent; they do well on their own, because their writing is so good.'

'You sound passionate about it.' The living room window was open and a gentle breeze filtered into the room, blowing the nets a little. It felt good to Jack.

'I am passionate about it, Jack. Just like I'm sure you were passionate about your job.'

'I was. I got as far as DI, and then there was too much paperwork after that. I enjoyed going out with the boys, and luckily for me, my wife was happy about that. Frank's more ambitious.'

'You married?' She asked the question casually enough, but her smile had dropped slightly.

'I was. She died a few years back. My son, Frank, owns the flat I live in. I moved in with him and his wife after my wife died, but then Frank's wife died, and I've stayed on. It suits us both.'

'I'm sorry to hear that. How old is your son?'

'He'll be thirty in a couple of months. His wife has been dead for almost three years, and he's only just started dating again. Carol was a detective as well. Long story.'

'I don't mean to pry.' She took a pull of her own beer.

'No, no, I didn't think you were prying. Just being nosey. I mean, neighbourly.' He smiled to show he was joking.

'I can see I'll have to watch what I'm saying around you, Jack Miller. First you throw wine all over me, and then you suggest I'm a nosey cow.'

'Hey, if the shoe fits, that's all I'm saying.'

She laughed and they made more small talk. 'I don't know about you, but I'm famished. How do you fancy grabbing some pizza from downstairs?'

'Sounds good. Let me get it. Or we could just walk downstairs and let somebody else do the washing up when we're finished.'

'That sounds even better. Then we can grab a beer in a pub, if I'm not holding you back?'

'Pizza then beer, what's not to love?'

They took the lift down into the cooler evening air. Pizza Hut was right next door and they waited for a table, making more small talk. Jack was beginning to feel even more relaxed. They sat at a table next to a young couple, tourists who were talking with what sounded like a German accent.

'So, how long have you been retired, Jack?' Sam asked, as the waiter took their order.

'Two years. I just turned fifty-six. I had enough years in, so I took early retirement. They're wanting young guys like my son now, and some of us old dinosaurs wanted out. There are still a lot in the force, but it's all politics now.'

'Especially since the unified police force kicked in, so I heard.'

'Oh yes. That pissed off a lot of people, both in and out of the force. It was nothing more than a cost-cutting measure. Same with the fire brigade. I mean, what other country has one police force and one fire brigade? Ridiculous.'

'I can see you're still passionate about being a police officer.'

'I was, Sam. I'm passionate about the job I had, not about the one I would have been doing now.'

'So what do you do with your time now?'

'My friends and I do some work for a government department. Boring stuff.'

Sam smiled. 'Which means it's something you can't talk about.'

Jack laughed. 'Something like that.'

'That's okay, I understand.'

Their drinks arrived followed shortly by their entrée.

'You said you moved in there after you were divorced?' Jack said.

'I did. His name is Ralph, and I thought I'd found the perfect man until I discovered he was going on the internet and hooking up with other women when I was away on book tours, and meeting my publisher.'

'I wasn't prying. I was just...well, yes, I was prying.'

She laughed. 'You were gently asking me if there was a man in my life after my divorce, Mr. Detective.'

'Was I really interrogating you? Jeez, sometimes it's hard to switch off.'

'It's okay. There's nobody in my life right now.' She took some pizza, washing it down with Coke. 'How about you? You met anybody else?'

'I have some female friends, but they're just friends we hang about with in the pub. Ex-colleagues. I don't have anybody special in my life.'

They ate in silence for a moment, and Jack was eager to change the subject now he had the answer to his question. 'Tell me about your latest work,' he said.

'What? So you can go away and write it for yourself? Steal my idea?' She looked seriously at him.

'No, I'm interested in your work, that's all.'

She burst out laughing. 'I'm kidding, Jack.' She leaned in closer. 'Callahan takes down a government contract killer. That's the gist of it just now.'

'Sounds good. I've read them all. I don't want to sound like a fanboy, but I look forward to the new ones coming out.'

'I'm glad, Fanboy.'

'Tell me how you got started.'

'I self-published the first four then was picked up. My new one will be number nine.'

'And here I am having dinner with DI Jimmy Callahan's creator. I am honoured.'

'You're making me blush. It's not as if I'm Patricia Cornwell or anything.'

'I like your stuff better.'

'Oh, stop, please. You're embarrassing me.'

'Oh okay.'

'On second thoughts, heap all the praise on me that you want to.'

Jack Miller felt more and more relaxed, and if he knew what was coming, then maybe he would have been more alert, had he been able to foresee the danger that night. At that moment though, he was swept up in having a good time.

'Before we finish our meal, I want to take a selfie with you.'

Jack leaned in, and Samantha snapped a photo of them with her phone. 'I promise this won't go onto my Facebook page.'

They chatted some more whilst they waited for the bill.

Outside, it was still light and would remain so for the next few hours. There were still plenty of people going about, walking up and down the North Bridge, so the man standing watching Samantha Willis and the stranger she was with blended in perfectly.

It wouldn't be the last time he saw them.

CHAPTER 17

This part of the Scottish Parliament Building was air conditioned. *And to the Lord we thank it,* Miller thought as they walked along the corridor. He knew McGovern's new Witness Protection programme was given this basement level as the previous occupants had moved to Victoria Quay, into the new government building there. This level also had direct access into the underground car park.

'Do you have a place where Shaun can be taken?' he asked McGovern.

'We have a few places here now. Since I was only put in charge of getting the Scottish branch up and running a few months ago, we're still building our network. We have a few safe houses and are working on getting more. We're getting there but it's not finished yet.' He stopped at a door and opened it. The guard sitting behind a counter with a bulletproof glass wall buzzed McGovern in.

'You don't think anybody would...' Miller said, indicating towards the glass with his head.

'This is closing the barn door *before* the horse decides to go walkabout,' Norma said, behind him. 'We'll be dealing with a lot of pond life and some of them were brought up on a diet of watching movies like *Die Hard*, so you never know.'

'And we have a veritable arsenal here,' McGovern said, as he held the door for his wife. Miller and Kim followed. They walked down another corridor that opened up into a large café area. Shaun was sitting at a table with his handler, a young woman called Sarah. Nobody was at the other tables. This was a café for witness protection staff only.

'Thanks, Sarah, we'll take over for now. You can get off now.'

'Right, sir.' The young woman left and the four of them sat at the table with Shaun, who was watching the TV that hung on one wall.

'How you doing, fella?' McGovern said.

'Great. I'm going to a house where I'll be safe,' he said. 'And they have an Xbox there.'

'Yes we do. And there are so many games, you won't know how to get through them all.'

'I like Call of Duty.'

'We have that.' McGovern looked at Foxall. 'I need to talk to you about some stuff, Shaun, and you know you can trust us. Okay?'

Foxall looked at Miller, who nodded at him, and then he looked back at McGovern. 'Okay.'

'We're going to talk about some of the things you were telling detective Miller here. You okay with that?' McGovern knew some people opened up more when they knew they were in a safe environment and in a casual situation.

'Yes. I think my grandmother is going to be angry with me.'

'No she's not,' McGovern said, not knowing or caring whether the old woman was or not.

'That's good.'

'Why don't you start by telling me about the things Gary said? What was his last name again?' McGovern made a show of looking for something in his pocket, as if he'd mislaid a piece of paper.

'Davidson. His name was Gary Davidson, and he was Carol's brother. He was a bad man. I didn't like him and he didn't like me. He said he was going to kill me.'

Miller looked over at Norma Banks. The PF was looking intently at Foxall.

'Tell Neil what you said in the car, Shaun. About Carol,' Miller said.

Foxall looked uncertain for a moment, as if he'd been caught stealing cookies from the jar.

'It's okay, you can tell me,' McGovern said. 'You can tell me anything you like. You're safe here, and you're going to stay somewhere safe until we can get all this sorted out.'

'Gary said they killed Carol.'

'Do you know who "they" are, Shaun?' McGovern asked, careful not to look toward the corner and alert Foxall to the covert camera they used to record witness statements.

'Some men who know the doctor. He thought I took my tablets but I didn't. They make me feel sick. They used to hit me if I refused, so I started pretending to take them. I wouldn't swallow them and then I'd pretend to fall asleep. My door wasn't locked. I could open it. I wasn't like the bad men they had in other parts of the hospital.'

'Of course you're not a bad man,' Kim said. 'We know that. Can you tell us how Gary knew your doctor?'

Foxall stared into space for a moment before answering. 'He would come into the hospital and I would see him talking to Dr. Borthwick. I heard him say he had killed Carol, the nice lady I met a few times.'

'Why did Gary say he had killed Carol, do you think?' McGovern said.

Foxall shrugged. 'He was upset.'

'Did Dr. Borthwick hear Gary say this?'

'I don't think so. I just saw Gary in a room with some men. They looked like they were bad men. One of them looked at me before he got up out of his chair and slammed the door.'

'What do you think Gary was doing at the hospital?' Kim asked.

'I don't know.'

'Are you thirsty?' Neil asked him.

Shaun nodded. 'They gave me a slice of pizza but I had already had dinner. I'd like some Coke, please. They don't let me have it at the hospital.'

McGovern looked over to the counter at a woman who was listening to him. She came round with a cold can. '

Anybody else like anything?' he asked. Nobody did. He thanked the woman and she left.

Foxall popped the tab and took a drink, burping the gas out. 'Excuse me. My grandma said it's important to have manners.'

'Your grandma's right,' Norma said.

'How did I do in the game this morning?' Foxall asked. 'Did I win?'

'Yes, you did,' Miller said. 'You got the most points. Who made the game up?'

'A man. He was nice. He came to me when I was getting a check-up in the hospital, and said we were going to play a game, and he would get me the new Xbox when it came out. He even gave me the gun for it. It's new and looks like the ones they have on the TV. He said some men were going to play the game with me, and all I had to do was pretend you were all the bad guys. Even Rosie was a bad guy, he said. He made it sound like fun. I could shoot at the bad men and they wouldn't get hurt because it was a game.'

'Do you know how to use the internet?' Miller asked. 'Like using emails?'

Foxall made a face. 'No. I only play games.'

'Shaun, I want to talk more about the hospital,' McGovern said.

'Okay.'

'You said somebody was going to kill you in the hospital; was this Dr. Borthwick?'

'Oh no, not the doctor. It was one of the bad men.'

'You know Gary's dead, so do you know who wants to kill you?'

'The same bad man who shut the door on me that time. He was there again today. I saw him. I think he was talking to another man in the room he was in.'

'Where were you, Shaun? Standing outside?'

'No, I was walking past. I left the room with an orderly. I needed to go to the toilet. I wasn't in my own room yet, as they said somebody had been sick and I had to wait. There's a toilet in there but I had to wait.' He looked at Kim and repeated himself. 'Somebody was sick and I had to wait.'

'Did you see the man?' she asked him.

'I didn't see the man, but the door was open a little.' He held his hands, about six inches apart. 'His back was to me. I heard him tell the others they knew I was there. They were waiting for me. They said they would do it tonight. I had to be taken care of.'

'Were those their exact words?' Norma asked. 'That you had to "be taken care of"?'

'Yes.'

'Do you think you may have misunderstood? That what they really meant was they were going to take care of you, like look after you.'

'No.' Foxall shook his head. 'I was scared.'

'Are you sure it was the same man as before?'

'Oh yes. He said he would take care of me later. He had something to do first, then he would come back when the hospital was quiet and then he'd kill me.'

'Maybe you didn't hear him right,' Norma said.

'No, I did. He said he would make it look like an accident. Just like Gary had with that copper's wife.'

CHAPTER 18

'Thanks for picking up the bill,' Samantha said to Jack, as they waited to cross the High Street.

'Last of the big spenders, that's me. Next time I'll ramp it up and take you to McDonald's.'

'You really do know how to treat a lady. And who says there's going to be a next time, Mr. Charmer?'

'Well, I'm guessing as you didn't get a friend to call you on a pretend emergency to get you out of the pizza place, this is not quite torture for you.'

She laughed as the green man came on for them to walk. 'Not quite torture, no.'

'And now you're going to let me buy you a glass of wine or two to make up for smashing your bottle.'

'That I can let you do. Where are we going, by the way?'

'To a nice quiet place I know. Logie Baird's, straight ahead. In the Bank hotel. I would take you to my local, but my friends would be round you like a pack of hyenas.'

'Maybe I like hyenas.'

'Not these ones, most of them are former detectives. Nice guys, but a bit rowdy at times.'

'I've been in my share of dive bars in New York City.'

'You'll fit right in here, then.'

They went inside and up to the bar. Caroline, the regular barmaid was on.

'Hey, Cas, I'd like you to meet a new neighbour of mine: Samantha Willis, this is Caroline, or Cas as we call her.'

'Pleased to meet you,' Caroline said. She was in her late forties, with brown hair and too much red lipstick. *It gets more tips,* she had told Jack one night. 'What can I get you?'

Jack ordered a pint and a glass of red wine for Sam. Then they sat at a corner table in the back. Quite a few people were in, including some with backpacks. The High Street was in shadow now, and although there were summer tourists, it was nothing like the rush that was August.

'There's a sitting area upstairs called Logie Baird's Gallery. It's nice and quiet when you just want a wee chat.'

'I like this place. I don't often go out on my own, and I have one or two friends here who I call real friends, but I don't go out drinking on my own.'

'Neither do I. It's always with my mates.'

'Or some young neighbour you almost knocked out with a bottle.' She smiled and took a sip of the wine.

'Thankfully that doesn't happen too often.' He smiled back at her. 'I'm sure you have a lot of young suitors beating a path to your door, now you're divorced.'

'I wish. I'm turning forty-nine soon, and my time for finding a "young suitor" went out the window a long time ago.

'Forty-nine? Away. You don't look a day older than thirty-nine.'

'This blonde hair comes out of a bottle, Jack, but thank you anyway.'

Jack's mobile phone rang. 'Excuse me, Sam, I have to take this,' he said, when he saw the number. He stood and walked to a quiet spot at the back of the bar. 'Hello?'

'Jack, it's me. How's things?'

'Not so bad, Neil.'

'Listen, I have your boy here with me and the missus. My little girl as well.'

'And you wanted to invite me to the party?'

'I wish it was a beer we were having, me old son. Turns out, our offspring have gotten themselves into a bit of a tizzy. Gone and absconded with a lad from the asylum in Morningside.' Jack heard another voice say something to him. 'My wife informs me that's not politically correct, and I have to use the term psychiatric hospital. Bit late for being correct, if you ask me.'

'Kidnapped? What the hell is going on, Neil?'

'Nothing as dramatic as kidnapping, so get your heart rate down. It's all above board, and the long and the short of it is I need a babysitter at short notice. A team of two. I have Richard Sullivan on board, and it's going to be at his flat. Just for one night. We have a full-timer moving out of a place tomorrow and this guy will be taken there, but for now, we need him kept somewhere.'

'You still at your office?'

'I am indeed. We've been questioning the subject, but he's tired and needs some rest before helping us again tomorrow.'

Jack looked at Samantha and she looked back over at him. He turned away again. 'I'll be there. I'm with a friend, but I'll tell her I have to go. I'm at the pub on the High Street.'

'You've not had too many to impair yourself, have you?'

'I would have told you, Neil. I'm fine. See you in around fifteen.'

'Come down to the underground car park. The guy will be waiting in the back of a car for you. One of the drivers will take you to the flat.'

'Right, I'll see you shortly.' He hung up and walked back over to the table. 'I'm really sorry, but I have to go. I've been called to do a little job.'

Samantha looked uncertain for a moment. 'That's okay.'

Jack sat down beside her. 'It's not another woman, I can promise you that.'

'Hey, Jack, we're just neighbours having a bite to eat and a drink. You can do whatever you like, honey.'

'I know that, but I was brought up the old-fashioned way; I wouldn't invite you over here and ditch you for another woman. Believe it or not, I don't have a group of women beating a path to my door either.'

'You go do what you have to, and you can give me a call sometime. She took a pen and a piece of paper from her handbag, wrote her number on it and handed it to him.

'I can see you home.'

'Don't be silly, Jack. It's a shame to waste this wine and besides, it's just across the road.'

'Okay. I'll call you when I can.' He left the bar and Samantha watched the TV playing above the bar. The man who had been watching her and Jack across the road from Pizza Hut sat down beside her.

'Well, well, look what the cat dragged in,' he said.

CHAPTER 19

Jack walked down Niddrie Street, thinking about Samantha Willis and how at ease he felt with her. He'd been with a couple of women since his wife died, but nothing serious. Nobody had rung his bell the way Samantha had.

She's a neighbour he scolded himself. *She was being nice to you. Letting you buy her dinner and a glass of wine because you were acting like a fucking mugger, skulking about in the hallway.*

He walked past the City Mortuary, where he'd spent many an hour attending the post-mortem of victims of crime, and poor souls who had decided to end their life, and others who had been in the wrong place at the wrong time.

The Cowgate was like a canyon; old buildings on either side, and Jack felt a sudden melancholy. *Too much thinking about death, Jack, you old twat,* he scolded himself.

This part of the town was hundreds of years old, yet it too was seeing its share of change. In hundreds of years' time, it would look totally different, he thought, crossing over St. Mary's Street.

Five minutes later, he was walking into the car park of the Scottish Parliament Building. The security guard checked his ID, and Jack walked down into the underground car park.

He was expecting to see a Range Rover, but a nondescript Mondeo sat with its engine running, and the driver flashed the car's headlights. Jack walked over and saw a huddled form in the back, hiding under a tartan blanket.

'You know the address, son?' he said to the driver.

'Yes, sir,' the young agent answered, and drove out into the early evening sunlight.

****

'Ralph, what the fuck are you doing?' Samantha said, slamming her glass down a little too hard onto the tabletop.

The man grinned at her, his teeth a perfect row of little white tombstones. Samantha remembered just how much those teeth had cost her, and shuddered to think where they had been since she had left him.

'Little Miss Perfect doesn't go out with other men.'

'Not while I was married to you, I didn't.'

'Who's the old bloke?'

'None of your goddamn business. We're divorced, remember?'

'*Almost* divorced.'

'Oh, yes, I forgot, you've still to sign the papers. I take it you've brought them with you?' She gritted her teeth.

The man reached into the inside pocket of his lightweight jacket. 'Here they are.' He made a show of looking for them, but his hand came out empty. 'Oops, I seem to have forgotten them.'

'You son of a bitch. I want those papers.'

'For somebody who's desperate to get rid of me, you're not being very nice.'

'We've already agreed on what you'll get. You're getting a lump sum, half the house and half the apartment in New York. What else do you want?'

'Half the royalties from your next five books.'

'What? Oh give me a break. You're not getting that, and you know it. You'll only get what's coming to you when you sign the papers. You're only ruining it for yourself, Ralph.'

'I am not ruining it, Princess, I'm messing you about, plain and simple.'

'I was good to you. I looked after you when you lost your job, we always had a good vacation, and you had a new car every couple of years. What else did you want?'

'I wanted you to be a whore in bed.'

Samantha grimaced. 'You are such a filthy pig. Is that what those little tramps were? Whores in bed for you?'

Ralph smiled. 'I guess they were. More than you were, anyway.'

Samantha stood up. 'You ever come near me again-'

'And you'll what?' he said, no trace of humour on his face now.

'You'll find out the hard way.'

She walked away and Ralph stood up quickly. Another man came from his side and knocked into the table, spilling the glass of wine over his trousers.

'Look what you've done, you-' He stopped himself when he looked at the man. He was wearing a black suit, white shirt and black tie. His hair was jet black, but it was the eyes that got Ralph; they were so dark brown they were almost black, as if they were two, round holes in his eyeballs. They bored into Ralph. 'Never mind,' Ralph said, walked away, and when he got to the door, he turned round.

The man was gone.

****

Jack looked into the back where a figure was lying down with a blanket covering him.

They made their way down Easter Road and into Duncan Place, following the road until they finally connected with Constitution Street in Leith.

Jack knew where they were going, though the address wasn't to be spoken aloud in front of the witness.

Five minutes later, they stopped at Tower Place in Leith docks. The car pulled down into the underground car park and parked in a visitor's space.

'Keep your hoodie pulled up right over your head,' the driver said to the witness. 'Keep the scarf covering your face and the sunglasses stay on.'

They all stepped out of the car and rode the lift up to one of the penthouse suites. A woman opened the door to the apartment as they stepped out of the lift.

'Please, come in,' she said.

Jack smiled at her. He'd known Tai Lopez for a few months now.

Through in the living room, Richard Sullivan stood with a whisky glass in his hand. He swallowed some of the liquid before putting the glass on a table. 'Don't worry, that's all I'm having. God knows I should be getting blootered now. You know, this blows all kinds of professional ethics.'

'Relax, Richard, this is just a babysitting job,' Jack said. The living room had a window with a sea view and a door that led out on to a balcony with the same view. The sun was starting its slow death for the day. Jack loved the view from here. The lights would be coming on in Dalgety Bay across the water in a little while.

'It's alright for you to say, but this is just a part-time, casual job for you. This is my whole life. I could still get disbarred for this.'

'Jack's right, relax, Dick, your job is safe,' Tai said. 'Neil wouldn't drop you in it. He knows what he's doing.'

'Can I play some games?' Foxall said.

'Sorry, I don't have any. There are plenty at the house you're going to tomorrow. Why don't you watch some TV?'

Foxall shrugged, and sat down in front of the large screen playing around with the cable TV remote.

'I'll be leaving now, sir, but I'm going to give you a card with some numbers on it. Any problems, call any of them and help is only a few minutes away.' The driver handed over the card and left.

'I don't know what I'm going to tell Margaret White.'

'Tell her Shaun's been taken into custody. Make up some bullshit. You're good at that.'

CHAPTER 20

'Your mum's going to miss Emma,' McGovern said, taking a sip of whisky.

'You are too, you big softie,' Kim said, looking out the pub window at the High Street. It was a lot cooler now, and plenty of people were still milling about.

Miller thanked Casey and brought his pint and Kim's Coke upstairs with him. The pub was busier now than when Jack had been in. They were up in the gallery, having the place to themselves. The bar below them was busy, but nobody could hear them up here. 'Nobody knows about you-know-who's place?' he said, meaning Richard Sullivan's flat.

'No,' McGovern said, 'his place is not on the list of safe houses. Nobody would think to look there, but it's only until tomorrow morning. We have another name moving out from one of the real houses, and the subject will move in there.' *No names, McGovern,* he reminded himself.

'We have to go through his story, see if he's not imagining this, but as I said in your office, I don't think he is. He knows about Gary, he knows about Carol,' Miller said.

'I want to know what he meant by, this being a game he was playing this morning, when he was shooting at us,' Kim said.

'We'll talk to him more tomorrow, but he wasn't working alone. He as good as said that, and knowing what we know about Shaun, he isn't capable of acting like that alone, so somebody was pulling the strings.' Miller took a pull of his pint, feeling the cold liquid slide down his gullet. He was starting to feel more relaxed. Kim excused herself and made her way to the ladies.

'Why would they have him be the patsy in an extortion scam?' McGovern said. 'I mean, Gary had that money three years ago, and there's been no sight of it since then.'

'He told me he'd paid off debts with it.'

'So if he did, then why would somebody want Rosie's pension money? I'm sure she got a pay-out when Gary died, but not a fortune.'

'There's one thing that wasn't spread about.'

'What's that?'

'It was reported that the ransom was a hundred grand. It wasn't; it was half a million. Gary didn't steal a hundred grand, but five times that.'

'So now somebody realises it was him, and maybe four hundred K is lying about somewhere. And where better to start looking than Rosie, his widow?'

'That's what I'm thinking.'

'We need to find out who those blokes are, Frank.'

'I know. I thought about going to have a word with Rosie tonight.'

'Good. Take Kim with you so she can keep her mother up to speed.'

They heard somebody coming up the stairs, and Miller thought it was Kim at first, but then he heard another familiar voice.

'Hey, Detective Miller. I thought I heard your dulcet tones up here.'

Miller turned to the woman who was walking over to them. Tall, brunette, good-looking, she smiled and flashed her expensive teeth at the two men.

'Lena. Long time, no see,' Miller said. He looked at McGovern. 'This is a friend of mine: Neil. Neil, meet Lena Finn, reporter extraordinaire.'

McGovern stood up and shook her hand. 'Pleased to meet you,' he said.

'Likewise. Are you two gentlemen requiring a top up? Oh, I can see you have company,' she said, eyeing up the third glass.

'We're fine, thanks anyway,' Miller said.

'I heard what happened this morning, Frank. I didn't cover it, but it must have been scary.'

'Turns out, he only had a banana in his pocket.'

Lena laughed and playfully slapped Miller on the shoulder. 'Cute.' She looked at McGovern. 'So, what did you say you did again?'

'I didn't.'

'That's right. That was a pathetic attempt to try and get you to tell me what job you have. If you're a copper, or if you're a friend of Frank's. Just the reporter in me, love, no offence.'

'None taken.'

'So, let me be blunt; what went down today, Frank? Anything you can give me the skinny on?'

'I don't think I'm at liberty to talk to the press, Lena. Besides, that would be classed as a scoop, and we don't want to piss off any more sharks than we need to.'

'Tut tut, Frank Miller, just you wash your mouth out with soap. Sharks indeed. You'll give young Neil here a bad impression of me.'

'I think Neil's old enough to make up his own mind.'

'So, any more news on the bank robberies?'

'Investigations are ongoing at the moment,' Miller replied.

Lena smiled. 'So I'm getting the stock answer now? You and I go back a long way, Frank.'

'You've been bugging me for years now, isn't that what you mean?'

'Seriously, any news on the robbers? Things have been quiet for a couple of months now.'

'Maybe they've gone away. There's still a team after them. Just because they haven't struck again, doesn't mean to say we've let them off.'

'Can't blame me for trying.' Linda flashed a smile at McGovern. She was only twenty-nine but had fought her way to her position as head crime writer for *The Edinburgh Evening Post*. 'I'm just an honest girl, trying to make an honest living.'

'I know you are, but if you bought me a drink, Standards would be all over me like a rash.'

'Don't you worry about them; I'm building up files on every one of them, just like MI5 do to all the politicians. Everybody's dirty at some point in their life. Present company excepted of course.' She raised her glass to McGovern. 'Nice to meet you, Neil. Maybe we'll meet again.'

'I'm sure we will.'

Linda went back downstairs.

'She's a pistol,' McGovern said.

'I'm sure she's been called worse.' Miller took a sip of his beer. 'She leant me a shoulder to cry on when Carol died. She's a good friend, that's all.'

'Some men can have female friends, some men see all women as play things.'

'I like to think I'm intelligent enough to have relationship with a woman that won't go past the friendship stage.'

'I hope you're not meaning me, Miller,' Kim said, walking back over to the table.

'Of course, not, honey.' He smiled and leant over to give her a peck on the cheek. 'I mean, you father there would make sure I was part of the foundations of any new building he chose.'

McGovern put on a grim face. 'There you go, once again putting a slur on my good character. I should have a couple of my boys have a word with you.'

'He says, proving my point.'

'Luckily I'm not the jealous type,' Kim said.

'Is that why you just spoke to Linda Finn?'

'How did you...?'

'Smoke and mirrors. She's standing smoking, next to one of the big brewery mirrors.' He nodded to a point over the gallery.

'I guess that's why you're a detective.'

'Did she know who you were?'

'She does now.'

'I hope you were nice,' McGovern said.

'I'm always nice, Father. How can you even think otherwise?'

'I know my own daughter. Marksman trained, expert in hand-to-hand combat. Need I go on?'

'Well, now I'm an expert at hand-to-hand after I spent the last couple of months brushing up.'

'You're the ex-wife of an SAS soldier; I would hope some of it rubbed off.'

She looked at Miller. 'You guessed he was SAS, didn't you? Although I never came right out and used that term.'

Miller shrugged. 'Special Ops, SAS, same diff, I think.'

'Well, it's a lot more complicated than that, but basically, yes.'

Miller looked at McGovern for a moment; Kim's ex might be a hard man, but Miller knew the more dangerous of the two was sitting right across from him.

CHAPTER 21

Back home, Miller dished out the Chinese food as Kim poured them a couple of soft drinks. Miller didn't mind a pint, but that was it. Even now, it was rumoured the law was going to change in Scotland, so there could be even less alcohol in the blood stream to make a drink driving conviction.

Charlie wolfed into his meat. He ate dry food during the day, but got his can of meat at night. He looked at the cat eating, and thought Carol was right when she said he, Miller, had to stay and look after him. Whether that was his own mind talking to him the day of her funeral or not, it was right that he stayed amongst the living.

Whatever he was feeling that morning, it had been lifted by Harvey Levitt's words.

When the food was on the small table in the kitchen, they sat down to eat. 'This has been a fun-packed day,' he said, feeling the tiredness hit him.

'It's not over yet, honey.' Kim smiled at him. He remembered the first time she'd told him she loved him. The words felt like an icicle had exploded in him, taking his body temperature down until his blood froze. Just for a second. He hadn't heard those words uttered to him for a long time. He had said them back, not knowing if he really believed them or not, but his feelings for her had grown stronger.

Now as they sat eating their dinner, he wanted to hold her hand across the table, to tell her he really *did* love her, but couldn't bring himself to do so. Not round the table where he saw the image of his wife. He didn't know where they were going to go if they moved in with each other. Here? That was a little way off for now, but it was something he was working on. It didn't feel as if Carol had been dead for almost three years; it felt like three months, because that was how long he'd known who really killed her, and it seemed to reset his grief clock.

'What do you think?' Kim said.

'I'm sorry, I was miles away there.'

She smiled, having the patience of a saint at times.

'I said it might be nice if we could have a long weekend away somewhere while Emma is down in London.'

'That would be nice. Where would you fancy? North Berwick? Maybe somewhere closer to home? I hear South Queensferry is nice this time of year.'

'You're funny, Miller, but knowing how tight you are with your money, maybe we should just go to the USA.'

'America?'

'No, *Up Stairs* in the *Attic.* That would suit your wallet.'

'I really don't think you should give up your day job.'

She laughed. 'What do you really think of the idea though?'

Miller ate some of his sweet and sour chicken. *Make new memories* Harvey Levitt had said. 'I think it's a brilliant idea. Some place we can just kick back and let ourselves go. Got any place in mind?'

'Don't laugh, but I've always wanted to go to Blackpool. Gaudy, brash but it sounds like fun. Walking along the promenade, strolling on the pier, doing the rides at the Pleasure Beach. Just you and I.'

'Sure. I'd like to go to Disney World one day, with Emma. Blackpool sounds like fun for just the two of us.'

'Great. I'll look into some hotels. We'll see how this case works out, and we can book something. If we get the chance in the next couple of weeks, that is.'

'If not, then we can go some other time. If it's just for a long weekend, maybe your mum and dad can take Emma.'

'I'm sure they would love to.'

After they finished and Miller put the dishes in the dishwasher, Kim sat with her feet up while Miller fired up his laptop. He opened some of the files. Areas that had misted over with time came bang right up to date as if they had merely been lurking in the passages of his mind waiting for this day.

Terry White and his demise absorbed his mind once again. Terry White, ten-years-old. A pupil at Daniel Edwards. A bright boy by all accounts without a worry in the world. A bit withdrawn his mother said, didn't have many friends, just one or two close ones but he seemed happy enough.

Nothing unusual about the day Terry went missing. He went to school as usual. Carl had been working at the dealership. Jill had been working at the hospital. Everything had been just as it was every day.

Until Terry didn't come home.

Jill didn't worry at first. Terry sometimes went round to hang out with a friend of his. She rang a couple of the mothers to ask if he was at their house, but he wasn't.

As the clock wound round to nearly eight o'clock, she had phoned the police. An officer had come round, asking questions, and then said he would get things going right away, organise a search party, get in touch with people at the school.

Jill had been sitting with the Family Liaison Officer when she got the first call.

Miller now read the transcript of the interview she had with two of the detectives who had been of higher rank than Miller at the time.

Jill White: He sounded as if his voice was rough, or disguised. I couldn't make out the accent. He told me he was going to kill Terry.

DCI Harry Davidson: And you had no reason to doubt him?

Jill White: My son was missing. How would he know Terry was missing?

DCI Harry Davidson: What demands did he make?

Jill White: He didn't, not exactly. He said he wanted me to do exactly as he said or Terry would die. He said he'd call back later.

DCI Harry Davidson: That was all?

Jill White: He hung up after that.

****

The kidnapper had phoned once after that, to let Terry speak to Jill. By all accounts, it was the last time she spoke to her son. The kidnapper had been clever, dealing with the police. It wasn't like on TV where they said, *Don't contact the police, or else.* The phones were set up in the investigation suite, and the kidnapper had called, demanding the money, issuing threats.

They told him the money would take some time to get together, which was a stalling tactic, and he had given them a deadline: two days. After which he would start posting bits of Terry through the mail.

They got the money together, Margaret White financing it. She said she would pay anything to bring her grandson back to her.

Then the kidnapper had one specific request after that: he wanted Carol Miller to do the ransom drop.

'What are you looking at on there?' Kim asked.

'Just some old notes from the original kidnapping case. I copied them to my laptop so I could read through the files at home.'

'Sounds interesting. Why don't you show me them since I wasn't on the case first time round?' Kim muted the TV.

'Okay. First of all though, let me go and get my map of Edinburgh so you can get a better picture of what I'm talking about.' He laid the computer down on the settee and came back from the bedroom a few minutes later with a map. Unfolded it on the kitchen table and then they both went through to the kitchen, and Miller put the laptop on the counter.

'Harry Davidson, Carol's father and our boss at the time, was livid when Carol said she would do the ransom drop. He said it was a man's job, and that infuriated Carol, so he relented. I still wish to this day that I'd gone.'

There were unspoken words between them then: *That way, Carol would still be alive and here with you.*

'It doesn't change the way I feel about you. I'm not living in the past. What's done is done, but hopefully now we can get Terry's kidnapper.'

'I know, honey.' She kissed him then, and gave him a hug. 'What do you think is different now to back then that might let us catch him this time?'

Miller looked at her. 'Shaun Foxall for a start. Knowing Gary Davidson stole the ransom money. That could lead us down a different path.' He ran his hand over the map, flattening out the folds, before tapping his finger on a point.

'I told you about her being at the White House in Niddrie.'

'Yes, you told me that.'

'Panic broke out after that. She came out of there and some bastard had stolen the car.' Miller felt sweat jump onto his forehead. Just thinking about that night made him feel like punching somebody's lights out.

'What happened then?' Kim asked.

'There were so many headless chickens, it wasn't even funny. We thought somebody had seen her go into the pub with the bag and stolen the car so they could rob her. I despatched an ARV to the scene, plus patrol cars from Craigmillar. My first priority was Carol's safety. What a fucking palaver that was. We thought some arsehole had nicked the car without realising it was a polis car. Maybe he was pished and didn't have money for a taxi, so he took the shiny car just sitting by the side of the road. We tracked it with the GPS. It was only down the road on a piece of wasteland, but by the time we got a patrol car to it, a rag had been shoved in the fuel filler and set alight. There was nothing left of it. By then it was too late; Carol was running out of time. We got a car from Liberton station but it didn't have GPS, it was just a bog-standard Astra. The Armed Response Vehicle was there in minutes so Carol was safe, but we didn't know if the wee boy was going to be found alive...'

CHAPTER 22

Fuck me, Frank, the car's gone.' Carol looked all around, trying to think if she'd parked it somewhere else, but she knew it was gone.

'What do you mean, "Gone?"' Miller said into her earpiece.

'Stolen, Frank. Somebody's stolen the car.' She looked at her watch. 'Eight minutes to the Grey Horse or that kid dies. Simple as that.'

'Stand by, Carol. I'll have somebody there in a minute. They're close by. If anybody comes near that bag, light 'em up.'

'Count on it.' She felt pumped up, not nervous, as she should have, standing in a dark street in Craigmillar. She had a can of Mace in her pocket, and a leather sap tucked into her boot. Something that could be easily put in an attacker's hand after she'd kicked the crap out of him.

Then she saw the blue lights of the Mitsubishi ARV rushing towards her. It skidded to a halt beside her. 'Get in!' the front passenger ordered through the open window.

Carol ran towards him and got in the back, slinging the heavy bag in first. Besides the driver, the two armed officers cradled their Heckler and Koch MP5s, ready to do business. They had been briefed and given the green light to lock and load. Somebody would be getting a hell of a headache if they tried to take the bag from her.

'Thanks, boys,' she said, struggling to put her seatbelt on as the car pulled away at high speed, the siren blaring through the dark night.

'Frank, I'm in the ARV. Make sure you get that car to the Grey Horse ASAP.'

'It's already on its way.'

'Make sure the suit is waiting outside with the keys when I come back out. I don't want this one going missing.'

'Roger that, he'll be there.'

For a big car, the Mitsubishi could move. Straight along Craigmillar Road, right into Prestonfield Avenue and up to Old Dalkeith Road. The Grey Horse Inn was practically across from the traffic lights, tucked in between a kebab shop and a bookies. The ARV pulled in and stopped.

Carol was out of the car with the bag and snatched the keys from the DS who was holding them out for her. She saw another DC she knew standing by an old Ford Focus farther up, making sure nobody stole this one.

Fireworks exploded in the distance, some banging, some whistling, others crackling. As if they were in a war zone. You had to love a country where it was legal to let children play with explosives strong enough to blow their face off, Carol thought, as she walked through the doors with the bag.

This pub had a smoky atmosphere too, but not as many mental cases. It was on the periphery of the schemes, and the nutters had to get a bus to get here, but sometimes they made the effort.

There were one or two nutters in here already. Guys who were hard enough to go out on a cold November night wearing only a T-shirt. A TV sat on a dodgy-looking shelf at one end of the bar, high up on the wall so it would give a good view and would be harder to nick. The barman looked at her, looked at the bag she was carrying, and then looked at her chest.

'Where's the payphone?' she asked.

He nodded to a short corridor where the toilets were. Didn't smile, didn't ask if she wanted a drink. She walked down it. Could see a theme; go for a piss, then get on the blower to arrange a kneecapping or a bank job, or a quick fix. No matter what your fancy was, you could order it with a modicum of privacy. A taxi company's sticker was on the side of the phone shelf, partially peeled off, and partially doodled on.

'I'm heading for the phone now,' Carol said, in a low voice. She looked at her watch, trying to keep her breathing slow. Two minutes to spare. At this rate, she'd have a heart attack before the night was out. Deep breaths, deep breaths she said to herself. If somebody tried to get this bag, then she'd break his skull.

Nobody even approached her.

'Watch your back, Carol,' Miller said. 'Give us the word if you need back-up. They're outside ready to move.'

She didn't reply, and almost jumped when the phone rang. She looked around at the punters to see if any of them were on a mobile phone. None of them was. One young guy got off his stool and walked towards her, about to go past.

'Leave it,' she said.

'I'm going for a piss. Officer,' he said.

'Fuck off,' she said to his back, as the Gents door closed behind him.

'Answer the phone, Carol,' another voice said into her ear. David Elliot. Head of Serious Crimes and the big boss in the department.

'Got it,' she said, picking up the receiver. 'It's me,' she said.

'What if it was the local Chinese takeaway calling back to confirm an order,' the disguised voice on the other end said in a light tone.

'Then I'd tell them I'd changed my mind and I want Sweet and Sour Chicken now instead. With egg fried rice. I know brown rice is healthier, but the egg fried is so much better, don't you think?'

She could hear Harvey Levitt's voice in her head now. They'd sat her down earlier and he'd told her how to play it; "Don't be aggressive, but be assertive. Let him think he's in control without you being totally submissive. Then when you ask to speak to the boy, he'll know you're not messing about. He'll want the money at the end of the day, not the boy, but we want Terry back alive".

'I see you got there on time,' he said, ignoring her. 'Just as well. I won't accept you being tardy.'

'Really? You won't accept me being tardy? You would throw this bag of money away because I'm late?'

'Of course not. If you're late, I'll cut off one of Terry's fingers and let you listen to him scream as I'm doing it.'

Bastard! she wanted to scream, but kept her breathing even. 'I want to hear Terry again.'

She heard him sigh on the other end. 'Want, want, want. Never a please or thank you with you, is there?'

'Let me speak to Terry. Please.' She squeezed the handle of the bag, imagining her fingers constricting this guy's throat. She realised she had just handed more power to him.

The boy came on the phone again. 'Please come and get me. He says he'll let me go if you give him some money. That's all he wants, he says. Please come.'

'Are you okay, Terry?' Carol asked.

'I want to go home.'

'You'll be going home soon.' She thought for a moment. 'What day is it, Terry?'

Then suddenly the boy was gone as quickly as he had appeared

'That's enough. Don't keep asking every time I call. It's wearing thin. I want the money, you want the boy. That's why we're doing a swap. It's in your hands not to fuck up.'

'What? You don't trust me? Sorry, what did you say your name was again?'

'Oh fuck off, Carol.' He hung up.

****

Miller sat on a chair for a moment. 'I just wish I had insisted going that night instead of letting Carol go.'

'You had to do what the man wanted, for Terry's sake. You had no way of knowing how it would turn out,' Kim said. She went over to the fridge and came back in with two cans of Coke. 'Caffeine time.'

He took one and they popped the tabs. 'Not the same as a tinny, but we need to stay focussed.'

'What happened next?'

'Right,' Miller said, standing and putting his can down on the counter. 'So Carol was talking to me over the radio...'

****

'Frank, listen to me; I don't have long. He's going to call back shortly. He won't leave it like this.'

'I know. He wants that money so badly.'

'Listen; he's in control of all this. Manipulating everything. He had somebody steal that car. Somebody he's working with. The other guy steals the car while he has Terry. He doesn't want me riding around in a new car that's filled with GPS and all sorts of tracking shit. He wants me to drive around in an old piece of crap. Like the one they have waiting outside. Some old scrapper that's a bog-standard unmarked. No GPS, nothing. Just a set of wheels for me to use.'

'How would he know what we would give you?' Miller asked her, his voice alternating with scepticism and acceptance.

'It's Bonfire Night, Frank. Are the fire brigade at our burning car yet?'

'No, they're on a shout. Some bonfire out of control.'

'There you go; he didn't just close his eyes and shove a pin at a calendar. He picked November the fifth for a reason; the police and the fire brigade are running about mental. He'd know we're all going to be busy, so he might have figured that most of our cars would be out. Who knows? But he's right, isn't he? Fires everywhere. The only spare car you could find at short notice is some old piece of shit out of Liberton. So they have an old scrapper lying about, and we had ten minutes to get me to this place and make sure we have a car for me. He's clever, Frank. We've been underestimating him all along. Or "them", I should say.'

'We know he's clever. That's why you have to watch what you're saying to him.'

'When I was talking to him, he let me speak to Terry. I heard his voice, then I heard nothing. No background noise, when I expected to hear crying maybe, or some kind of rustling noise as the boy moved about, but it was silent after that. I mean, completely silent. As if his voice had been recorded and he was just playing it back over the phone to keep us happy.

'Maybe he had Terry taken out of the room.'

'No, neither of them left the room. I don't think Terry was even in the same room; the kidnapper's voice echoed. Terry's didn't. As if Terry's had been recorded somewhere else. As if he had been told what to say beforehand. When I asked him what day it was, the kidnapper stopped. He knew I wouldn't get an answer. Play the conversation back.' She knew they were recording everything through her mic.

'I can't explain it, Frank. It's just a feeling and I'm shooting in the dark here, but I think Terry's dead.'

****

Miller felt his heart rushing. Just thinking about somebody talking to his wife like that made him want to smack the shit out of him.

'You okay?' Kim asked him.

'Yeah, I'm fine. I want to catch this bastard more than anything.'

'I know. I do too, now I'm part of the team.' She rubbed his shoulders. 'Maybe we should just relax for a little while. Watch some mindless TV.'

Miller folded the map up, feeling the skeletal hands of a cluster headache creeping over his skull, threatening to crush the fragile bone with its own. Then the Reaper would whisper a cold breath in his ear and tell him he should try to close his eyes now, because his heart had stopped beating and the headache in his brain was really an aneurysm, rupturing, the tiny blood flow as deadly as molten lava...

'Frank?' Kim said, standing in front of him now.

'Sorry, I was miles away.'

'I asked if you wanted coffee.'

'Yes, thanks.'

She turned to put the kettle on. Some people stayed away from caffeine, especially when they felt a headache coming on, but Miller found the taste soothing. Besides, taking three painkillers would help. He put the map away, back in its place in the spare room where he kept files in an old filing cabinet.

The TV was showing a cop show with David Tennant. He liked the actor but felt the need for something a little lighter; surfing through the channels when his phone rang.

'Hello?'

'DI Miller?'

'Yes.'

'It's Sergeant Murray up at the station, sir. Somebody called here asking for you.'

'Who is it?'

'A young woman. Louise Walker. She said you would know her.' The name stuck for a second, but then it clicked; Carl White's girlfriend. 'Okay, put her through.'

A few seconds went by as the call was routed through the station to Miller's phone.

'Detective Miller? Sorry to disturb you at home, but I needed to talk to somebody, somebody I can trust.'

'Okay. What's wrong?'

She took a deep breath and let it out, as if she was deciding whether she should tell him or not. 'I think I found out something about Terry's kidnapping.'

'Go on.'

'You know Carl and I split up? Well, he moved in with me at my farmhouse but I've kicked him out. My friend has moved in. She works for Carl at the car dealership you were at today. Cindy Shields is her name.'

Miller waited patiently for her to get to the point.

'I was up in the attic, gathering some of the stuff Carl had stored up there, and I picked up a box and the bottom fell out of it. I saw a bundle of cash with the band still wrapped round it. It says on the label it's a thousand pounds. And there's something else; I found the owner's document for a car. It was for a red nineteen-eighty-four Vauxhall Nova.' She paused for a moment.

'I think it's the car your wife was told to use by the kidnapper.'

CHAPTER 23

She turned the car into the driveway of the farmhouse and drove round the side of the old building, not wanting her car to be seen from the main road. Just in case.

She loved the summer and even this late, there was a slight tint to the sky, as if the sun hadn't really gone down, but had just slipped behind a curtain.

Locking the car, she walked to the back door and let herself into the kitchen, switching on a light.

'It's me. You home?' She hadn't seen a car outside, but there were garages round the back, some filled with old farm machinery, but one or two were kept for cars.

She took her light jacket off and walked through to the living room, switching on some more lights. The old farmhouse was cold, but turning on the gas fire for a little while would work. Just enough to gently heat up the room. Oh, she loved this old place, imagining the characters who had walked through these rooms before her. Had they been extremely rich? No, or they would have been living in a mansion. Well off, certainly. She wondered if the lady of the house had invited her posh friends over for tea, and if they gossiped about their friends.

There was modern furniture in here, but an old pine dining table graced the kitchen, and whoever had bought the house many years ago had kept the old porcelain farmhouse sink.

She walked upstairs, up the old, dark wood staircase to the upper level, switching on the landing light. Pulling a towel out of the airing cupboard, she made her way into the bedroom where she stripped and stepped into the shower. It was hot and steaming. That was one thing she didn't think she'd like about living back in the old days; filling a steel tub with hot water.

It was funny how people took things for granted. How the simplest things we use every day were a luxury for some people. After rinsing off, she stepped out of the shower and took her towel from the heated rail and began towelling off. She took clothes from the wardrobe something old and casual; a pair of sweatpants, an old T-shirt and a pair of old, comfy slippers. As she walked out into the hall, she noticed the little door that led into the attic was ajar. There was the faintest sound of music playing.

She pushed the door open farther, feeling a shiver run down her spine. It wasn't fear. *Keep telling yourself that.* She flicked the switch at the bottom of the narrow staircase. This wasn't a horror movie; the light came on. She stood and listened for a moment. The music was still faint but a little louder. Then she walked up the narrow staircase. The stairs didn't creak in here either, testament to the quality of the craftsmanship. She wouldn't be announcing her arrival to any serial killer waiting for her. *Shut up you stupid cow!*

At the top, a little banister ran round three sides of the open staircase as it entered the attic. The music, although still not loud, was louder. It was coming from somewhere in here. She stepped up into the well-lit room and looked around at the boxes and old toys stored there. A rocking horse sat in one corner, and for a second she imagined it was moving back and forth, but it was only her imagination.

A train set had been put back in its box many years ago, and now sat atop a bunch of cardboard boxes, waiting for a new owner to come along and give it a new lease of life. Many more boxes sat, some of them collecting dust. They had writing on them, identifying which rooms the contents were to be taken to, and presumably, they were empty.

The music was very low, coming from farther in the attic.

She had never been up here before, not really. Not right into the attic itself. She had come into it of course, but that had been to put some of her own stuff here. The room itself ran the length of the house, but an extension had been added to the farmhouse, and the attic continued round a corner. She presumed more boxes and toys were there, but curiosity made her feet move seemingly of their own volition, and she walked along the central aisle, seeing old stuffed toys, their glass eyes inquisitive, and more trucks, yellow Tonka's, plastic, not tin like they were years ago, each of them with a light coating of dust as if they'd just come from a hard day's work in a quarry. Her heart was beating faster. 'Hello? You up here? If you're trying to scare me, it's not working!'

That's a lie right there. What the hell am I doing up here?

There was a flickering light on round the corner. She walked closer, and that's when she saw the figure watching her. She gasped and saw the figure was a mannequin, wearing a jacket and trousers, as if somebody had started a sewing project years ago and then abandoned it. The flickering was from an old oil lamp, sitting on a desk.

Her heart hammering, she walked forward, and then turned right again, and that's when she saw it.

The wall with Terry's face on it.

Sitting above an old hi-fi unit. Some eighties music was coming from the speakers. She stepped forward and saw a tape playing. Who had turned it on?

Maybe somebody had left it on, it had jammed and then somehow started playing again.

Then who lit the lamp?

She switched the music off and looked at the many faces, cut from many newspapers, stuck to a large corkboard. Headlines cut from local and national newspapers, detailing Terry's kidnapping. *Local boy still missing!* one headline screamed. She saw a story from *The Edinburgh Evening Post,* Lena Finn.

There was an old table sitting below the corkboard, with a maze of stationery items, tape, scissors, paper, bottle of glue. An old chair sat off to one side. An ancient oil lamp on the end of the desk, a box of matches next to it.

She thought about little Terry. Now they had found his body, seeing his face looking back at her from the newspaper clippings gave her a sudden feeling of deep sadness. How could anybody kill a little boy and bury him? Just for money? It was amazing the things some human beings would get up to just for money.

This was creepy. She had a sudden urge to run and flee.

Then the power went out.

The whole attic went into darkness, except for the alcove with the lamp burning in it. She had a bad feeling about this. She turned to leave and saw the figure again. Her brain took a second or more to process this wasn't the mannequin this time. This figure was dressed in a black jumpsuit, wearing a hood and a breathing respirator.

She didn't have time to scream. He punched her hard in the gut before his other hand went round the back of her head and smashed her face against the brick wall. She fell down to her knees, feeling the blood running out of her nose, trying to scream but feeling the wind had been knocked out of her.

She heard footsteps coming up the stairs. *That's how it only took him seconds to put the power out and get up here; there's more than one.*

She'd read about home invasions happening in America, where a bunch of guys would burst into a home, and either rape the female before killing all the family, or beat them all up before robbing them.

She saw the other man approach. He was dressed just like the first one. They said something to each other, but she couldn't make out what because of the respirators, but it was apparent they both knew what the other one was saying. The first one grabbed the lamp while the other one came towards her.

The second one dragged her to her feet, and she thought for a moment he was going to help her, but before she knew it, her final moments on Earth were playing out, as he dragged her towards the railings covering the attic entrance. Grabbing her hair with one hand, cupping her chin with the other he twisted savagely, hearing the audible snap, and threw her lifeless body over.

The man with the lamp picked up a can of kerosene, carefully knocking it over, as if it had been kicked over when the lights went out. When he was certain he and his partner were at a safe distance, he dropped the glass lamp, watching it smash and then the puddle of kerosene burst into flames.

The fire spread rapidly as the two men walked calmly down the stairs, the first one stopping to make sure the woman was dead. He gave the second man the thumbs up and they made their way out of the house.

They had hidden their van in one of the garages where they waited for the woman to come home. They quickly stripped off their jumpsuits, putting them in the back before calmly driving away.

CHAPTER 24

Miller cut along the A8 Glasgow Road dual carriageway, past the slip road for Edinburgh Airport, the blue flashers beaming behind the grill on the car. The journey would have taken twice as long without the siren cutting a swathe through the traffic heading west out of the city.

With the airport on their right, he looked for the sign he had been told would be on his right, in the middle of the traffic reservation, indicating their destination.

'There it is,' Kim said, as the headlights picked out the brown sign with the little blue Scottish Tourism logo on it, on the right, it's arrow pointing left. Miller slowed the car and turned into what looked like a country road, and sped up the paved lane.

The old house was at the top of the hill, lit up from the inside, looking resplendent. Miller switched the flashers off as he came up the lane. No point in scaring the guests.

'I wonder what this place was before it became a hotel?' Kim asked, eyeing up the new structure on the far side of the old stone building, housing the new spa and rooms they built a few years back.

'It belonged to the Usher brewing family,' Miller said, turning off the engine. 'Then it was turned into a hotel.'

Kim got out and looked up at the illuminated sign: *The Dominion House Hotel and Spa.* Miller got out and locked the car.

'Nice swanky place,' he said. 'I've been here before, one of the lads lived locally and we had a piss up in here when he retired. *Jimmy something*.'

'That's a funny name for a bloke,' Kim said, as they walked into reception. Miller knew where he was going and led them through to the Drayman's Lounge, apparently in keeping with the Usher family heritage.

They walked in and a waiter came over to them, holding a tray with a towel draped over his arm. 'Can I help you tonight?'

Miller flashed his warrant card. 'We're looking for somebody.'

'Very good, sir,' he said, and pounced on another couple who had come in behind them. Then he saw who they had come to meet, sitting in a far corner, staring into a small glass.

'Louise?' Miller said.

'Oh thank God.' Louise Walker looked at both of them. 'I'm so glad you could come. I've been scared to go home. Carl's not answering his phone and my calls have gone to voicemail.'

They sat opposite her.

'You said something about finding the V5 registration document for the red Nova that was used in Terry White's kidnapping?'

Louise looked as if she might burst into tears at any moment. 'You don't think Carl had anything to do with his son's death, do you?'

'He had an alibi for the night the boy went missing, and was accounted for at all times the night the ransom drop took place.'

'That's not what I asked you.'

Miller looked at Kim before answering. 'I have to say I don't think he was involved. That was the general consensus.'

'Why would he have the V5 and that bundle of money in his attic?'

'I don't have the answer to that. Do you have the money or the document on you?'

'No. I was scared to touch it again after I looked at it. I had this feeling he would walk in and catch me holding it and then he would...do something to me.'

'Has he ever hit you?' Kim asked, feeling the hackles on the back of her neck rise.

'No, but he can shout and swear when he gets in the mood. He drinks too much and that's when the abuse starts. Verbal abuse.' She looked at Miller. 'He's never laid a hand on me, but he was scary nonetheless.'

'Do you still live together?'

'No. He moved into my house, and we lived together for eighteen months. It was good at first. He'd split from his wife, and needed a shoulder to lean on. I worked for him so I saw him every day. I wasn't around when Terry went missing. I started at the dealership a few months after that. We got on well, as I said, and then he asked me out one night. I accepted, and we started dating. I don't think his wife was very happy about it, but that was her loss.'

'How long did it take for you to get to know the real Carl?' Kim asked.

Louise finally took a sip of the drink in front of her. Miller noticed her red lipstick was wet after the liquid went into her mouth. She was a very attractive woman, and he wanted to ask her age, but guessed she was around early thirties.

'I noticed it within the first six months. He'd had a little bit too much to drink then he threw the remote at the TV one night when he saw the football scores. I asked him what he was doing, and he turned on me. It was quite a shock, I have to admit, but I ignored him and he fell asleep on the settee, drunk.

I went to bed.'

'So he moved in with you?' Miller said.

'Yes. I own a farmhouse just outside Ratho. Actually, the back road to the hotel leads to the village.

'He asked if he could move in with me. I thought it would be a good idea, and he brought a lot of stuff with him. It wasn't a problem as I have a big attic. It was already loaded with stuff from my childhood. I grew up there and bought the house from my parents when they were elderly. They're both gone now, so the house is all mine.'

'Where's Carl right now?' Kim asked.

'I don't know. He moved out a few weeks ago, so I assumed he would go back to his mother's house.'

'Where does she live?' Miller asked.

'In a big house down in Barnton. Cramond Mews.'

'He didn't sell that house after his divorce?'

'Sell it? He doesn't even own it.'

'What do you mean? He owned it before he got divorced, didn't he?'

'Is that what he told you?'

'I just assumed. We dealt with him and his wife when they lived down there.'

'I can see why you might think that, if he and his wife were both there, Inspector, but Carl White and his wife didn't own that place; his mother does. Carl White owns nothing. Not the dealerships, not his own home. Nothing. His mother owns everything. She just let them stay at that house.' Louise took a sip of her drink and put the glass gently back onto the table.

'Everybody thinks I'm a gold digger,' she said, 'but the reality is, I have more than Carl White does. If anybody needed that ransom money, he did.'

CHAPTER 25

They saw the smoke before they saw the flames lighting up the night sky.

Driving up into Ratho village, they heard the siren coming closer and soon Miller's rear view was filled by a fire engine. He pulled over and let it past, then put on his own blues and followed it.

'That looks close to where the farmhouse is,' Louise said, from the back seat, and a few minutes later, she confirmed it was indeed her home that was ablaze as the fire engine stopped on the main road.

Other fire trucks were already on the property, which had a long driveway leading up to the farmhouse. A patrol car sat on the other side of the road, blocking it, the blue lights flashing through the dark. Another one was behind the fire engine with one further up the road.

'Oh my God, my house is on fire,' Louise said, about to leave the car.

Miller parked the car and told Louise to stay in the back out of sight. He and Kim left the vehicle and walked up to the back of the fire engine. 'I need to speak to whoever's in charge,' he said, showing his warrant card.

'I'll go and get him,' the fire fighter said, as the others strapped on their breathing apparatus.

Ten minutes later, a harassed older man walked round the back of the truck, his face soot stained. 'I'm Station Commander David McKay. Help you?' he said to Miller.

'I just need to know what happened here.' Again, Miller showed his warrant card. 'I have the owner here with me.'

'Man or woman?'

'Woman? Why?'

'I need to speak to her, Detective.'

'Okay. Come over to the car.' They walked over in silence, and Louise's eyes widened as they approached. Miller opened the back door.

'Louise, this is Commander McKay.'

'I need to know how many people were in your house.'

'There was nobody when I left. My friend lives with me, but I sent her a text to meet me.'

'And did she?'

'No. I thought maybe she was working late. She's a car sales executive, and sometimes she has long hours. Why?' There was alarm on Louise's face now.

'We took a body from the house, and early indications are it was a female.'

Louise made to get out of the car. 'Let me see her. I need to see if it's Cindy.'

McKay put a hand up. 'No, I can't let you do that.'

'You need to stay in the car,' Kim said, putting a hand on her arm. 'Let the fire fighters do their job.'

Louise sat back and started crying. Kim got in beside her and put an arm around her as Miller closed the car door.

'I'm assuming the mortuary are on their way?' Miller said.

'They are.'

'Does it look suspicious?'

'It's too early to tell, but it looks like it started upstairs. The metal base of an oil lamp was found near the body, and she was found at the bottom of what was left of an attic staircase.'

'So it could be an accident?'

'I would peg it as one right now, but an investigator will go over the scene later.'

'Okay, thanks. I won't hold you up much longer. I'll have Wester Hailes CID liaise with you in case it comes back as suspicious.'

'Very well.'

'How long ago do you think the fire started?'

'Fifteen, twenty minutes, tops. We can tell how far the spread is, and if it had been longer, the place would have been burnt to the ground.'

'So it couldn't have been half an hour, forty-five minutes ago?'

'No. No way. It was contained on the upper level.'

'Thanks.' Miller walked over to a uniform who was standing by his patrol car. 'I need you to do something for me.'

'Yes, sir.'

Miller walked with the man over to the car and opened the back door. 'Louise, I need to take your picture.' He turned to the uniform. 'You got your phone on you?'

'I have.'

'Take a photo of this lady.'

Louise looked mystified for a moment. 'Bear with me, Louise,' he said to her. The uniform snapped a photo with his iPhone. Then Miller closed the door.

'Drive down to The Old Dominion and show that photo to the barman in the Drayman Lounge. Ask if he remembers what time she came in. Then text me.' He gave the man his number.

'Right, sir.'

'Blues and twos. I need this in a hurry.'

The officer jumped into his patrol car. The older fire fighter walked away back into the farm. Miller got back behind the wheel.

'I know that was Cindy in there,' Louise said. 'It had to be.'

'It seems as if she may have fallen down the attic stairs with an oil lamp. They found evidence to support this.'

'Why the hell would she be up there with an oil lamp?' She asked, tears rolling down her face.

'Who knows? There were electric lights up there, I assume?'

'Yes, of course. It was a large walk-up attic.'

'The investigators will go through there with a fine tooth comb to find out what happened.' Miller had an idea about what happened; somebody went to the house to get the money but who? And did they kill Cindy Shields in the process? The detective in him programmed to think this way until he knew the facts.

A few minutes later, the grey mortuary van pulled up, with mortuary assistant Gus Weaver behind the wheel. Miller got out to speak to him.

'Hi, Frank,' Weaver said, climbing out of the vehicle. 'What brings you here? I thought Divisional CID from Wester Hailes would be here?'

'They will be. I just had to check something out, that's all.'

'When I got the call, they said it was a bad one, but if you ask me, all fire victims are bad ones.'

'I'll be liaising with your new friend, Kate, tomorrow.'

'She's starting to make a name for herself already, so I hear.'

'No comment,' Miller said, and winked at the older man. A few minutes later, his phone played a tone. He read the text message, replied and then got in the car.

'The barman remembers you coming in about an hour ago and you didn't leave the bar. That fire wasn't going at that time, according to the Divisional Commander. He can tell by how much of the house is burnt, apparently. So when Cindy fell down the stairs, and the fire went up, you weren't in the house.'

'You don't think I had anything to do with that?' Louise looked shocked. Miller studied her for a moment. In the years he had been a detective, he had come across many liars, and Louise was either telling him the truth or she was a very accomplished liar, and his gut told him it was the former.

'In our line of work, we have to check.' He started the car and they drove away.

'You need to tell me how Carl White is involved in his son's kidnapping,' he said to her, as they entered the village.

'I don't think he was. That's not what I'm saying. It didn't have Carl's name on the registration.'

'I know it didn't,' Miller said. 'We spoke to the owner of the car back when, well, you know, when Terry was kidnapped.'

'I can't remember the name on the registration document now.'

'Brian Sewell,' Miller said.

'That's it.' Louise looked out the window as they passed by the Bridge Inn. 'Do you know him?'

'Where was the document?' Miller asked, wanting to see if her story changed.

'In a box in the attic of the farmhouse.'

'Did Cindy know about the money?' Kim asked.

The tears were still running down Louise's cheeks. 'I don't know. Maybe she found them when she was in the attic. When she moved in a few weeks ago, she brought her stuff with her. That's why I went to the showroom today, to tell that lazy bastard to move his stuff out.'

'Did White know she had moved in with you?'

'I don't think so. I'm sure he would have given Cindy a hard time if he knew. Do you think the fire was set deliberately?'

'I can't say, but an investigation will take place because a body was extracted from the scene.' He looked at her briefly in his rear view mirror. 'It's protocol.'

She looked at Miller as he drove down Harvest Road to connect with Newbridge and the roundabout to bring them back to Edinburgh.

'Your house is pretty much gutted,' Miller said. 'Is there anywhere you can go?'

'No. I have no family. Friends are girls I occasionally go out with for a drink. Cindy was my only real friend.'

'We'll take you to the station just now and get your statement.'

'That's fine.'

They rode the rest of the way, mostly in silence, and Kim sent a few texts from her phone.

In the interview room, Miller and Kim sat with a recorder going and made sure it was videotaped as well.

Louise gave her story of how she found the box in the attic with the bundle of cash and the V5 registration document in it.

'How come you just found that box now?' Miller asked.

'Carl has been out of the house for weeks now, and Cindy asked if I needed a new housemate. She was looking for a new place, and I said yes, as I've known her for a long time. We were friends socially and I even stayed over at her place when we'd been out on the town. So she moved in with her things, and she had quite a few boxes. I started to move Carl's stuff around to make it easier for him to grab, and that's when I saw this particular box. I'd been in to see Carl today and told him to come round and get his boxes. I was moving them nearer the stairs when the bottom fell out of this particular one and the money fell out.'

'Did you tell him you'd found it?'

'No. I was too scared to call him.'

The rest of the interview was just getting a record of how Louise had called Miller, how they met her at the hotel and when they took her home the house was on fire.

When it was over, Kim sent a text from her phone.

The interview room door opened and Neil McGovern walked in with another man.

'Louise, this is my father. He's in witness protection.'

'Hi, Louise. I've already issued an order of protection so you can come with us now.'

'Where?' Louise looked alarmed. 'Why do I need protection?'

'It's just protocol,' Miller said. 'Considering Terry was found today and now your house was on fire. We don't have young Terry's killer, so we just want to make sure you're safe.'

'Where will we go?'

'Tomorrow, we'll go to a safe house. They're being vacated tomorrow, but for tonight, you'll sleep down in the Scottish Parliament building. I have a level there, and we have what we call a Transition Room, where people can grab forty winks while we're waiting for a safe house to be readied, or what not. It's not the Hilton, and it's not designed for long-term use, but you can sleep there tonight.'

'Okay. I'll feel safer I suppose.' She got up and the man with McGovern led her out.

'*Transition Room?*' Miller said. 'You make it sound like a torture chamber.'

'Now, now, Frank, that place is like a spa, let me tell you.' McGovern said.

'What is it really?' Kim asked.

McGovern turned to his daughter. 'It's a little room where I grab a kip when I know I'm not going to be able to go home for a day or so. Don't worry, I have a spare wardrobe there. Not for the young lady of course, I meant for myself. I don't want you to think I don't bathe when I don't go home.'

'Oh we think a lot worse of you than that, Neil,' Miller said.

'Oh dear, I fear I underestimated your wit once again, Detective.' He slapped Miller gently on the arm. 'You know that will come back to bite you in the arse one day, don't you?'

'I'd be disappointed if it didn't.'

'Right, kiddiewinks, I will be off now. Let me know what the pathology report says. I will be in touch with the Scottish Fire and Rescue Service tomorrow.'

'How's Shaun Foxall doing?'

'Fine and dandy. Watching TV with your dad. Richard Sullivan and your dad get on like a house on fire now, I must say. If you'll pardon the poor choice of words.'

'Good.'

'So you think somebody set this fire to get rid of some evidence and this other woman got in the way?'

'I'm not sure, Neil. It's a bit of a coincidence that Louise tells White to get his stuff, then she calls me and the house goes up?'

'Yeah, I smell a rat. Let's get together tomorrow sometime and compare notes and you can bring me up to speed.'

'Will do.'

They walked out of the station through the back door. Louise was sitting in the back of a black Range Rover, the driver waiting patiently for McGovern.

Miller and Kim watched the car drive away.

'Right, let's go home,' Miller said. 'And maybe we can start making plans of our own.' He took her hand and for the first time since they had started dating, didn't feel guilty.

CHAPTER 26

'This is where the serial killer comes up to the car unnoticed and kills us both,' PC Greg Norman said.

'Don't talk shite,' his partner, PC Alec Wardlaw said. 'Just 'cause we're in a cemetery after dark and nobody would hear us scream, doesn't meant to say we're going to be murdered.'

The patrol car was parked across from the old caretaker's house, or what was left of it, with the police tape going round the JCB sat in the front and tied to a window.

'Poor wee bastard, eh? Were you here when it went down?' Norman asked.

'Nah, I had just started Tulliallan. I read about it in the papers and they were talking about it in the college.' Wardlaw, sitting in the passenger seat, looked through the windscreen at the derelict house. 'Nobody would have guessed he was in here, buried in the basement. I wonder why his killer chose here?'

'It's out of the way,' Norman said. 'I mean, there used to be a caretaker living here at one point, but the place burnt down.'

'I wonder if he did it? The caretaker.'

'I don't know if they even know where the caretaker is. It caught fire a couple of years ago and it's been empty ever since.'

'I wonder why they want to pull it down now?'

'In case some numpty starts climbing about it and pulls a chunk of it on top of himself. That's why they had to pull over all of those gravestones, because some kid got killed in a cemetery when he was playing in it. Poor wee sod pulled a gravestone on top of himself,' Norman said.

'It's not surprising when you see how old some of them are. But it's not a playground.'

'Did you never go into an overrun cemetery with your mates when you were a boy and start whacking down giant hogweeds with sticks?'

'No.'

'Neither did I.'

They both started laughing.

'How about that sergeant, what's her name? Hazel Carter. CID,' Wardlaw said.

'What about her?'

'I think she's a bit of alright, that's all.'

'She's way above your league, Alec. I'd give her a wide berth if I were you.'

'What? She wouldn't be able to resist my charm if I turned it on full.'

'She'd be able to resist your pay grade though.'

'Aye, I suppose. She's probably out to grab the likes of Frank Miller.'

'So, you out for CID yourself, eventually?' Norman asked.

'Isn't everybody?'

'No. Who do you think would patrol the streets in high-speed numbers if we were all in CID?'

'You're never thinking about going into Traffic?' Wardlaw seemed incredulous. 'Tell me you're having a laugh.'

'Piss off. I suppose you would like nothing better than to be taking down gangsters, and having shootouts with hitmen.'

'I dunno, look at that Robert Molloy. He swans about like his shit doesn't stink. I wouldn't mind giving him a good belting.'

'Yeah, well make sure you have a big team behind you when you decide to go knocking on his door.'

'You watch too many movies, Greg.'

'Just sayin', that's all. Let the heroes in CID take on the Robert Molloys of this world.'

They sat and listened to the radio chatter for a while, until one call came in and grabbed their attention. Somebody seen round the back of a house in Inverleith.

'That's just a few minutes from here,' Wardlaw said. 'Call it in and we'll check it out.'

'Our orders are to stay here until the relief comes on at midnight.'

'Fuck 'em. We can sit here twiddling our thumbs or we can go and get a bit of action.'

'MIT would go mad if we left here.' Norman looked worried, seeing his career ending up with British Transport Police if things went tits up.

'MIT. They were called Serious Crimes Unit until a month ago, and now they have a fancy name with fancy initials, then they walk on water. Call it in, Greg, and let's get somewhere we can stretch our legs.'

Norman nodded and called it in, and they were given the address. What harm could it do? They would be back in no time.

He turned the engine and the headlights on and they made their way out of the cemetery.

When they left through the main gate, they passed a car but neither young officer gave it a second glance.

****

Lena Finn watched the patrol car disappear in her rear view mirror. It had come out of the cemetery as she turned into the street. She pulled into the side of the road where she had planned to park, and watched, as it turned into Inverleith Row. That was a bit of luck.

She walked into the cemetery, sticking to the grass at the side of the road. Even though it was after dark, there was nothing to be scared of. *Dead people can't hurt you* her father had always said, but he obviously hadn't watched *The Walking Dead.* It was only a few minutes' walk to the old caretaker's house, and she wanted to have a peek around the site where they'd found Terry. Just to get a feeling for the place. *For when you write that best-selling book about the case,* she reminded herself.

She took a circular route, planning to come in from the left hand side, just in case the car that left only had one uniform in it, and one had stayed behind. They wouldn't be so stupid as to both go, would they?

She knew there was a walled extension to the cemetery, about the size of a football field, maybe built for the elite who couldn't get into the catacombs. She didn't know what it was really for, but what she did know was, it bordered the garden attached to the caretaker's house, and there were two arched entrances, almost covered in ivy bushes it was so overgrown, but easily accessible.

As Lena reached the bottom of the road, she made her way through one of the arched entrances, gently pushing aside the ivy bush. She walked towards the wall, hearing a car go by on the other side of the wall bordering Warriston Road.

She faced the high wall bordering the garden. Normally she wouldn't be able to scale it, but there were ornate gravestones here, planted firmly against the wall, the carvings on them hand grips and places to put your feet if you used your imagination.

Grabbing hold of a jutting piece of granite, Lena hauled herself up as quietly as she could. There was the Water of Leith Walkway between the cemetery and Warriston Road. There was always the chance somebody could be out walking a dog, so it was better to err on the side of caution.

A hand reached up and grabbed hold of another piece of carving, her foot found a foothold and then she was up; all done as if she were rock climbing.

Ivy crept along part of the wall, giving her cover from prying eyes from the main road. She reached up to the top of the gravestone, keeping her head down until she took her iPhone out. *Make sure the ringer is off.* Check. She held her phone tightly in one hand as she carefully raised her head above the top of the wall, as if she was about to go up and over the trench.

She expected to see a crime scene tent, maybe some tools from the crime scene people or crime scene tape. Evidence of digging.

What she didn't expect to see was two men digging. Men dressed in dark blue overalls, and wearing gas respirators. She took a quick photo of the two men, who both had their backs to her and put her phone back in her pocket. It was dark, but in Scotland at the start of summer in June, it was never truly pitch black. They were pulling something out of the ground. Something wrapped in black plastic. When their treasure was free, one of the men walked out of the garden at the far end. She took another photo of the man carrying his find. She took another photo of the remaining man filling the hole back in. She felt fear creep down her spine. Who the hell were they, and why were they here digging something up? This had to be the men who were involved in Terry White's kidnapping. Hadn't the money gone missing? Yes, and a couple of months ago, it was revealed who had taken it.

This couldn't be money.

Her mind tried to compute what she was seeing, but it was having a hard time.

They were digging up a body.

She would just stay here until they were gone and they wouldn't even know she was there.

And it would have stayed that way if she hadn't slipped and let out a groan.

The man filling the hole back in — *not a hole, a fucking grave!* — turned to look up at the wall. Lena kept her head down. Suddenly it was so quiet. She kept her breathing shallow, trying to breathe through her mouth. She wanted to see if the other man had come back and whether she would be able to sneak away, so she just had to have a quick peek. She slowly raised her head above the level of the wall until her eyes could see over and...the mask was looking right back at her.

She screamed and lashed out at the mask. She felt a jolt of shock as both her and the man fell backwards, hearing him land with a thud and groan as if he was in pain..

Oh fuck, no! she almost screamed out loud. What to do? Call for help? She took her phone back out, about to call treble nine. That idea was shot down as she saw the man immediately sit up. She put her phone away.

Luckily, the same ivy bush that had crawled up the wall also bunched up a few feet from the wall and broke her fall as she jumped down.

Fear jolted through her like a bolt of electricity, and she leapt to her feet.

She expected the man to leap over at her, but he wasn't there. Why wasn't he chasing her? *Because he can't shout to his friend while he's wearing the mask. He's away to get him.*

She ran the length of the extension, running parallel with the wall separating this part from the main part. The grass long, unkempt and uncut due to council spending restrictions. More ivy crept along the wall. A worn pathway ran around in a circle in here, where people would walk, looking at graves or more likely walking their dogs so the animals could shit and nobody would have to pick up after them.

Those guys would be expecting her to come out through the archway she had come in by, so she ran as fast as she could towards the other entrance, her heart beating fast enough to explode, feeling a stitch starting in her side. Her breath was coming in rasps as she reached the stone archway, also overgrown, affording her some cover. She stood under the stone, which was only about a foot wide, keeping close to the ivy but not so close to make it move, she crouched low and peeked out. Nobody was there.

Then she heard the unmistakable noise of a diesel engine starting up and headlights came round from the direction of the old house.

She knew then one of them was going to get out and go through the first archway, and the driver would belt down here and come through this one and they would trap her like a rat.

She waited, knowing staying alive would depend solely on her timing. The dark van drove fast along the driveway then stopped. The passenger was getting out, just as she suspected he would. She would have maybe two seconds while he crossed in front of the van. No interior lights came on as the passenger door opened and closed again, and then she saw one headlight being blocked out as the passenger crossed, then she was out and running.

She wore black jeans and a black hoodie, wanting to keep a low profile in the darkness of the cemetery, and was so glad she did.

The van roared along the drive and she ducked behind a huge gravestone as the droning engine noise came to a stop, becoming a loud clatter. The driver got out and raced through the archway.

She knew she would only have a few minutes as they cleared the extension. There weren't a lot of places somebody could hide in there, and it wouldn't take them long to check behind the ivy bushes clinging to the walls. Then they would have to figure out if she scaled the opposite wall and tried to find a tree to climb down, as it was too high to jump. Or would she have managed to get into the cemetery itself without being seen? Those were the questions she'd be asking herself if she were pursuing somebody.

She stood into a crouch and ran, bent doubled-over; hoping the height of the gravestones would give her some cover. On her right was where

Warriston Road continued, and lampposts were above the height of the perimeter wall, throwing this part of the cemetery into relative light. There was a gate in the wall further up, but she didn't know if it was locked at night. If she went for it and it was, it would leave her exposed. She tried to go deeper into the cemetery, under the thick canopy of an old oak tree, its branches like an umbrella, protecting her from the streetlights.

She didn't hear the van doors opening and closing again, but the unmistakable noise of the diesel engine couldn't be disguised. She realised these guys were professionals; amateurs would have just jumped into the van, banging the doors for everybody to hear.

Out the other side of the tree, Lena started running again, the stitch getting worse, but the adrenaline giving her a boost. She made it onto the top driveway, the incline going up to where it would go over the old catacombs.

Just for the briefest second, the headlights swept across her back, and then she heard the engine being gunned.

They'd seen her.

She took a left where it went downhill, farther away from the main gate, but off the roadway. Her feet slipping on the grass, she narrowly missed banging her head on a gravestone. She could hear the van up top, and kept running, not looking. Past the gates to the catacombs, and she remembered it was where Frank Miller had been shot.

Funny how you remember the little things just before you die, she said to herself.

The van's engine slowed to a stop. This time there was no need for stealth, and she could hear the van door being slammed shut and the engine racing again. The passenger was running after her on foot.

She reached the far end of the catacombs, and started up the other end, her feet once again slipping on the grass. This time she saw the little mausoleum, standing out white in the dark, with red Perspex roof panels. She ran up to it. The gate's lock had been broken long ago, and now the inside sported some inventive graffiti. A large sarcophagus sat in the middle of the floor. It was much larger in here than she figured on.

She moved quickly round the huge stone sculpture and sat behind it. Waited. Then the lights from the van partly illuminated the inside of the small building as it was brought to a halt. The diesel clatter settled to an idle. Then she heard the footsteps outside, the feet crunching broken glass. She heard the old steel gate slowly opening. One foot crunched more glass and stone debris just inside the mausoleum.

Lena held her breath and closed her eyes. She didn't want to see it coming. She couldn't fight and she couldn't run, but at least she didn't have to look her killer in the eyes.

'Three, the cops are coming back!'

She clearly heard the voice from outside. She guessed the man had taken his respirator off. The man inside here with her didn't hesitate for a second. The footsteps left quicker than they had entered. The van door slamming shut. The engine not gunning this time, but moving at a pace barely above idle. The lights suddenly being cut.

She heard the van's tyres crunching the gravel on the worn drive outside, as if it were retreating from the police.

She looked round cautiously from her hiding spot. There was nobody there. She inched forward at a crouch keeping to one side of the gate, which afforded her a hiding place. Then she peeked out through the gate.

The van driver had killed the lights, and it was moving up the driveway that ran parallel to the one where the police car was coming back. If she were to hazard a guess, those guys had called in a fake emergency call to get the police car away from the cemetery, enough so they would have time to do what they had to do, and would have been away by the time the officers found out it was a false alarm. They would have already been gone if they hadn't chased her.

The windows in the back of the van were part of the doors; no glass windows. There was little chance of them seeing her coming out of the mausoleum, even if they were both looking in their mirrors, but the van kept on going, slowly but steadily. It reached the far end of the driveway, and the driver turned the van onto the road that led to the gate.

She slipped out and watched as the van rounded the corner for the exit, the headlights coming back on. Then she faintly heard the van accelerating and moved from grave to grave, slowly making her own way to the exit.

The gates were always open, set into the perimeter wall where it became lower, round a corner leading into Inverleith Gardens. She peeked her head up above the wall, expecting to see the mask again, but saw nothing but houses on one side, the rugby ground on the other and parked cars, including her own. There was no sign of the van on the long, straight road that led out to the main road. It had either gone up a side street, or it was long gone.

She sighed with relief as she got into her car and locked it. As she drove away, one thought stayed with her, the sound of the van driver shouting to the man who had been so close to her in the mausoleum: *Three.* He had called his friend *Three.*

What kind of a name was that?

CHAPTER 27

'You want a beer?' Miller asked Kim.

She shook her head. 'No thanks. If you don't mind, I'm going to have a long soak in the tub and then hit the hay.' She smiled and shook her head. 'So much for a night of passion, eh?'

'Don't worry about it. I'm feeling pretty bushed myself. It's been a hell of a long day.'

He got his laptop out again and started skipping through files as Kim left the room and he heard her running a bath in the main bathroom.

Was it just a coincidence that Louise Walker found the money and the V5 document, and her house burnt down? Miller, like every other detective, thought if something looked like a coincidence, then it probably wasn't. Who else had Louise told? Nobody according to her.

Then a thought struck him; *she told Carl White.* Inadvertently, she told White she found the money when she went round to the showroom that morning and told him to clear his stuff out of the attic. What had Louise said she did for a living now? Miller couldn't remember if she had or not. He made a mental note to talk to her in the morning. He'd call Neil McGovern first.

He heard Kim in the bathroom, and for just a moment, felt the guilt hit him again. He knew he shouldn't. Harvey Levitt had put his mind at ease, but Miller knew there were going to be times when he would feel as if he was cheating on Carol, until his mind kicked in and told him she was dead.

He got up from his chair, putting the laptop on the settee, and walked over to the side window that looked down onto the North Bridge. Charlie was on the back of the settee, sleeping but ready to leap five feet into the air if he got a fright. He lazily opened his eyes to see if his dad's movement meant he was getting a reward, but no treats were forthcoming, so he closed them again.

Miller looked down onto the traffic. There were still a lot of people milling about. Unhappy faces looked out the windows from the upper deck of a Lothian Buses double-decker. It was a number three, heading out to...where? He wasn't sure. Dalkeith, or somewhere like that. He had his hands on the windowsill, and somebody across on the opposite pavement looked up at him briefly, as if he knew him, but then he walked on. Probably thought Miller was being a curtain twitcher.

He put his face closer to the glass. He could only see so far down the bridge, but he pictured the cemetery perfectly in his mind. Warriston Cemetery. Not only the scene where a little boy had been buried, but where Carol had been buried. *At least she was in a coffin and had a marker,* he reminded himself. Not like Terry. The old, burnt-out house was his silent marker. There were no names engraved on the stonework, no date of birth, no date of death. That would come later when Jill and Carl laid their son to rest.

He knew Carol would have been upset to know the little boy she so desperately wanted to find alive, was dead and buried in a place beside hundreds of other dead bodies, only nobody knew where he was, and it took a demolition team to discover him.

What if the house had never caught on fire? What if they decided to let the cemetery reclaim it after it had? What if a little boy hadn't pulled a grave on top of himself, and the council didn't bother about securing anything dangerous in the cemetery? There were a lot of "ifs" and "buts", but right now, a little boy *had* pulled a grave on top of himself, the house *had* caught on fire and the council had decided it *was* safer to get rid of the house.

They had to find out who had lived in the house. The council were checking through records. They had moved from their old offices on George IV Bridge to a brand new, purpose-built building down by Waverley station and were having teething problems with their IT system.

His breath fogged the window for a moment. He knew his wife was down in that general direction, lying in her grave. He silently wished her goodnight. Was it wrong to keep talking to her like this in his head? Probably. Did he care? No.

Of course his wife's death had been a shock, but not knowing who had killed her meant that – to him at least – her death wasn't final. Then, when they found out who had killed her a few months ago, more than two years after it happened, it felt as if he was really grieving now. That he had only just laid her to rest. Nobody would understand, so he didn't bother telling anybody.

He came away from the window, and once again the cat looked at him, its sense of self-preservation putting its body into DEFCON 2. 'It's okay, wee man,' he said to the cat, and Charlie accepted this, took a deep, contented breath and went back to sleep.

Miller didn't know why he had done this at the time, but he had wanted to know when Carol's body had been taken from the mortuary to the funeral home. If he looked down onto the High Street, he could judge where the mortuary was, in relation to the flat. So he could mentally look across in her direction and tell her she wasn't alone. Then, when they moved her to the funeral parlour that sat in the shadow of the Castle down in the Grassmarket, he could assure her he was still with her.

He couldn't sleep the night before her funeral, which he expected everybody experienced, but he had sat up most of the night talking to her. Thinking about his unborn son. Gone away with his mum. A little boy he would never get to hold, or play fire trucks with, or teach how to shave or talk to women. His little man. His little buddy.

Miller felt something hit him like a steam train. A feeling of complete and utter dread, as if something had just sucked all the life out of him, and he felt as if he wanted to sob like a child again, but couldn't.

He walked quickly through to the kitchen, opened one of the cabinets and saw the packets of painkillers, reached out for them for a moment, and then grabbed a glass. *Maybe I should just grab a hold of the whisky bottle now and down it in one.*

Instead, he ran the cold-water tap, and filled the glass, taking two of the painkillers to combat the headache he felt coming on.

Get a grip of yourself, he heard a voice in his head say. *Life is for living. You have a life. Live it.*

Charlie came walking into the kitchen and meowed, as if reminding Miller he was still there, Carol's cat, and he needed to be looked after. Miller picked him up and hugged him. The cat wriggled free and jumped down to go eat his food.

If they could only see you now, the boys in the station. Drinking water and hugging a cat. What next? Eating gluten-free food and taking up yoga?

He smiled to himself. Carol would have laughed at that.

He picked up his laptop again and sat back down with it, opening a file. Part of the transcript of his statement for the night Carol died. The kidnapper had said he liked Carol's spunk. Always had done. From afar. That's why he picked her.

At the time, they knew he had picked Carol to do the ransom drop, but in their eyes, he had done so because she was a woman, and thought she was an easy target, not knowing Carol would take on anybody.

Now he was convinced there was something going on at that hospital. And tomorrow he was going to find out.

CHAPTER 28

Miller woke feeling refreshed. He hadn't had an exhausted night's sleep like that for a long time. Sometimes it was better to go to bed when you were dead on your feet; that way you got to sleep like the dead. *Dead.* He vowed to get through the day without thinking of that word in context to his wife.

He blinked and looked over to Kim's side of the bed. *Carol's side.* No, it was going to be Kim's. Besides this was a brand new bed. When he started dating Kim, he couldn't have his matrimonial bed still in the flat, so had paid the council to come and uplift it. So it really was Kim's side of the bed.

She wasn't there.

He always wore shorts and a T-shirt to bed, even in winter, but this morning, the daylight was behind the curtains. Not the sunshine, as his window faced northwest. He pulled on a pair of jogging bottoms that he kept on a chair outside the master en-suite, and looked at the clock; 7.17 am. He used his bathroom before going through to the living room. The TV was playing, showing a news channel.

The sound of cooking came from the kitchen. He walked in and Charlie ran up to him, winding his way between Miller's legs. 'Morning,' he said to Kim, bending over to pet the cat.

'Morning, honey,' Kim said. She had on a light housecoat, and he noticed she had slipped on a pair of shorts. She was cooking bacon in a frying pan, along with a couple of eggs.

'This is a bit different from when I first met you,' he said, walking up behind her and putting his arms around her waist. 'I can see my father living here has rubbed off on you.'

She turned and kissed him. 'I don't mind taking a turn cooking breakfast. Every time I'm round here, you cook for me, so fair's fair.'

'Just so you know, I don't eat a cooked breakfast every morning, but this smells good.'

'I was going to get you up shortly. You were dead to the world.'

Dead. 'I was. I can't remember when I last slept like this.'

'I wonder how Louise got on last night? It can't be easy, seeing your house go up in smoke like that.'

'It must be hard,' Miller said, switching on the coffee pot. 'I'm sure your dad's crew looked after her.'

Kim switched the frying pan off, and dished the food on to a plate. 'Sit down before it gets cold. I'll do the coffee.'

'As long as you understand that we share this. I don't want you to think if we move in with each other, then you'll be running after me.'

'*If*, Frank? I take it you've still not decided yet?'

He smiled at her as her face dropped. 'I'm sorry; I meant *when*.'

'Look, you don't have to. It's a big step, I've got Emma, we're both used to leading our own lives.'

'I want to, honestly. It was just a slip of the tongue.'

Her face brightened. 'You know, I fell in love with my husband, but not nearly as fast as I've fallen in love with you.'

He kissed her and she held onto him for a moment. 'Now sit, and eat your breakfast. I'll make us coffee. Gibb is having us meet at eight-thirty so we can go through the Terry White case. I have a feeling it's going to be a busy day.'

'I think so too.'

They ate breakfast, and talked about mundane things, which Miller enjoyed. It had been a while since mundane was the norm for him.

He showered, even though it had only been about eight hours since he'd last showered, but there was nothing like the tiny hot needles bouncing on his skin to make him forget things.

As the water hit him, he knew he was making the right decision about Kim, and if he didn't commit to her, he would end up pushing her away. If he was honest with himself, he really did love her, and would prove it to her. First, though, he needed to prove it to himself.

After he towelled off and dried, he came back into the bedroom and noticed the dressing gown lying on the bed. Kim was already dressed.

He dressed in his suit, a lightweight cotton one, and headed into the living room where Kim was waiting. With another woman.

'Hi, Frank,' Lena Finn said.

'I know you want a scoop, Lena, but don't you think this is going too far, even for you?'

'Oh, Frank, I've gone and done something stupid,' she said, her face looking as if she was going to burst into tears.

'I said you would have been better off joining the force instead of being a journo.'

'If only things were so simple.' She looked at Kim, who nodded. 'I made a mistake last night, Frank. And if they find me, they're going to kill me.'

Another woman walked out of the kitchen. 'Hi, Frank. You don't know me but I've heard a lot about you.'

CHAPTER 29

There were five men in the room. *One, Two, Three, Four and Five.*

They never used names when it was only them in the room. Not that they had to, but it was a way of getting used to calling each other by their monikers. They had agreed on this simple system a long time ago, basing it on nicknames Vietnam Vets would give each other, like Ghost, and Joker and Ace and whatever else they could think of. So they had adopted a simple number reference for themselves.

After all, they'd all seen a TV show where one crook shouted out, 'Watch your back, Jimmy!" or some such nonsense. Giving witnesses a chance to report to the police that one of the masked men was Jimmy. That sort of thing happened in movies. Maybe it happened for real, too, but not to them. Number Five was adamant they used their numbers. *Put a number to a face. Get used to it. That way nobody slips up.*

Which is why they were in the room together that Thursday morning, early.

'I called this meeting this morning because something unexpected happened last night.' Five looked around at the other faces. Three's especially.

'Nobody's putting any blame about here, but sometimes things go off at a tangent, and we have to regroup and have a debriefing, so we can learn from it. Do we all understand this?'

The other four men nodded.

'Number Three, the floor is all yours.'

Three, who was taller than One by a good two inches and would see that he weighed an extra fifty pounds if they were to each stand on a set of scales, walked up to the front of the room and looked at the others, while Five took a seat. There wasn't a man who walked God's Earth who Three feared, but knowing Five was listening intently to every word, every sentence, every nuance, made him feel just a little bit sweaty.

It was nothing to do with machismo. It was more to do with reputation. In their unit, they all tried to outdo each other, while working as a perfectly oiled machine, but it did no harm to stick out, to keep you ahead of the game.

'As you know, myself and number Two were doing a job last night. It was a retrieval, brought on by the unexpected, how can I put it, abduction of Shaun Foxall. That little plan went sideways, but we have our contingency to fall back on. So it's not a problem. What *was* a problem, was the woman who was watching me last night. I don't know what she was doing there, but she was watching me. We tried to take care of her, but the patrol car that was sent on the fake job we called in, came back. We would have had time to do the job, and get back out again, if this woman hadn't turned up.'

'Do you know who she is?'

'We do now.'

'So what do we do about her?' number Four asked.

'We have something up our sleeves for her, don't worry.'

'Why do you think she was in there after dark? Was she a junkie or something?'

'No. She's a reporter. She was there snooping. Obviously the police were hanging around, but she clearly knew if she climbed up that wall, she could gain access to the private garden without being seen and then get to the back of the old house. Those two coppers were just sitting around, not expecting to have somebody climb over the wall,' Three said. 'If they did see anybody, it would most likely be somebody coming up the driveway, but if it were ghouls coming to have a look, there was nothing to see.'

'I think they would have had a field day when they saw you digging up a corpse,' Four said. 'I can see that photo on the front page of *The Sun*.'

They all had a laugh at that, as if digging up a corpse in a cemetery was an everyday occurrence for them.

'Where is the corpse now?' One asked.

'In the van in the barn. We're going to transport him to his new location.'

Five stood up and looked at his watch. 'Right boys, I will have a word with our esteemed leader and explain the situation. Right now though, rush hour will be starting to kick in, so it's time everybody got a move on.'

They all got up and left the room.

CHAPTER 30

'You're our new neighbour,' Miller said to Samantha Willis.

'I was going to introduce myself to you when I got settled. I spoke to one man downstairs, and told him I was a writer, and he said he didn't read.' Samantha smiled.

Kim laughed. 'Well, I've heard of you. I didn't know you lived in these apartments, but I did know you're American, living in Edinburgh.'

'You said you knew my dad?' Miller said, as they all sat down at the kitchen table. Charlie walked up and introduced himself to the two new women in his dad's life by rubbing himself on their legs.

'I just met him last night.' She rubbed the cat's chin as she told them the tale of how she and Jack met.

'So how do you know Lena here?'

Samantha looked across at her friend and smiled. 'She's the *Evening Post's* crime writer, but she also doubles as their crime novel reviewer. She asked me for an interview one day, and we had coffee and hit it off right away. We've been friends ever since.'

'Small world. What part of America do you come from?'

'Originally from Connecticut, but then I moved to New York State in my twenties. My first husband was from the Hudson Valley. He died. And I felt so lost, but then I came over to Scotland to look up some family history, and I met my second husband. He's from here in Edinburgh, but he's a jerk. We're about to finalise our divorce.'

Miller drank some of his coffee. Lena caught his eye. He smiled at her and gently put his hand over hers. 'Don't worry, we'll keep you safe. Now, why don't you tell me what you've been up to?'

Her tale of watching a man dig something up from the private garden next to the caretaker's cottage seemed far-fetched, and it had crossed his mind that maybe she could be making up some cock-and-bull story to get close to him so she could bleed information out of him regarding the Terry White case. She had lost her phone so she couldn't show him some photo of a man bent over in the dark in the cemetery. She had said she'd cancelled that phone, but whoever had it might still be able to get into it, even if he couldn't make a call. Now he had to hedge his bets, although, if she was making this up, she was a lot better than he ever gave her credit for.

'The forensics team will be back at the cemetery around nine-thirty. By the time they get the team assembled and get down there.' He looked at the clock on the kitchen wall. 'That gives you about forty-five minutes to get there and have a quick scout around. Although I'm not advocating disturbing a crime scene, but if we wait for Maggie Parks and her team, we could be waiting all day for access. She's good at her job and goes by the book, so she won't let us near it before she's cleared it. However, I want somebody to have a look at it now.'

'You're going to the mortuary this morning, aren't you?' Kim said.

'Yes, then the council offices.'

'Why don't I take Lena down and have a look? Meet up with you later?'

'Okay, you do that.'

'I'll get back to my apartment,' Samantha said, getting up from the table.

'Thanks for letting me stay last night, Sam,' Lena said. 'I really was too scared to go home.'

Miller didn't tell her that staying away from her house was probably a good idea, considering what had happened to Louise's house.

He made a mental note for somebody to talk to the uniforms who had been on patrol duty in the cemetery last night, and see what call they had gone on. Then he could see they were put on school crossing patrol. If it was true what Lena said about one of the men telling the other the police car was coming back, then it meant they had left their post. The man hadn't said, *Here's the police coming,* but, *The cops are coming back,* according to Lena's account of things.

Samantha left, saying she was working on the plot of her next novel. Her new one would be out in September but she needed to get busy on this one. 'DI Callahan won't write himself,' she said, bidding goodbye to them.

Miller left the apartment and walked down into the sunshine, walking through the shopping arcade connecting the North Bridge with Cockburn Street. His pool car was parked in front of Kim's TT.

He was still unsure of Lena and whether the man in the jumpsuit was her photographer friend helping her with her ruse, but he would find out.

He drove down Cockburn Street and turned along Market Street, taking a long circuitous route to the mortuary down in the Cowgate.

The sun was baking the inside of his car, making his shirt feel sticky. He parked in the mortuary car park, next to one of the grey vans. He walked up to the back door and rang the bell.

One of the new assistants, a young Polish girl called Natalie Strozewski, opened the door for him. 'Come in, Detective Miller.'

He smiled at her as he crossed the threshold. 'Thanks, Natalie.' He waited until she closed the door. 'When I told my dad you were Polish and you had the nickname "Sticks", he wanted to know if they call you that because your last name is Strozewski.'

She looked at him as if he was daft. 'No, of course not. They call me Sticks because I play drums in a band.' She laughed, and Miller could feel his face going red.

'Deary me, Lothian and Border's finest getting ridiculed by a wee lassie,' Gus Weaver said, coming into the receiving area where they stood.

'Less of the wee,' Sticks said, walking away. She turned back once to look at Miller, smiled and winked at him.

'Never mind, Frank, you can't be right all the time. How you doing anyway?'

'Fuck off, Weaver, and get the kettle on. And it's Police Scotland now.'

Weaver guffawed. 'Oh, look, now I've insulted the wee laddie.'

'You've been drinking too much with my old man. Besides, it wasn't such a leap to think "sticks" came from her name.'

'And yet...nobody else makes that connection.'

'I am going to find something on you one day, Weaver, and when you're in Saughton begging me to bring you in some soap-on-a-rope, I'll be the one who gets the last laugh.'

'Never happen, Frankie boy. I'm squeaky clean. If you'll pardon the pun.' Weaver laughed again, leading Miller to think, not for the first time, that the older man had a drink with his breakfast.

'Where's Kate Murphy?' They were walking towards the offices that were down a little corridor off the receiving area.

'She's having a conference with the PF. Fourth day on the job and she's late. Professor Plum will go off his head.'

'Especially if he hears you calling him that.' Professor Leo Chester was the head pathologist, and ran a tight ship.

'He knows we call him that behind his back.'

'I hate to think what you call me behind my back.'

'As if we'd have a name for you, Frank.' He walked into a small eating area where the kettle lived. 'Come on William Wallace, I'll make you a coffee.'

'What? Away with yourself. I don't even look like Mel Gibson.' He looked at his watch. 'I'll wait a wee while and see if she turns up. I have other places to go, but it can wait a bit longer.'

They chatted idly while the kettle boiled. 'So, where does Sticks play?' Miller asked.

CHAPTER 31

Neil McGovern liked to keep fit, but that didn't include running for ten miles every morning before drinking a glass of juice made from squashed carrots. He and Norma had made a small gym at home in their large, detached house in Merchiston, complete with a treadmill, exercise bike and some weights. Just enough to fend off old age without giving himself a heart attack.

They'd both been enthusiastic about using the equipment when they first got it, but McGovern was the first to admit his bright idea had dwindled to a mere, *I'll get round to it when I have time* attitude. Norma Banks thought the exercise bike made a great hanger for drying wet clothes.

So now, on this bright Thursday morning in June, the most exercise he was getting was hopping into the back of the Range Rover that was waiting for him in his driveway.

'How were things during the night?' he asked his driver.

'Miss Walker was a bit unsettled, sir,' the man said. 'I called one of the female members from the department, thinking the lady might want another female just to talk to, to reassure her she was safe.'

'Did it work?'

'Yes, she relaxed after a little while. The agent is a medical doctor, so she gave Miss Walker something to help her relax.'

'That's good. Take me to the office now, then we can get going with the safe house. Is that all sorted yet?'

The car glided away, the supercharged engine needing little effort to move the heavy SUV. 'Yes, sir. The safe house was cleaned after the previous occupant was moved. It's all set up ready for new visitors.'

Visitors. As if they were all going on a trip to Blackpool.

McGovern unfolded the newspaper he had been holding. *The Edinburgh Evening Post's* sister paper, *The Caledonian*. He personally knew the editor, a man he had come to know very well over the past few months. They'd had dinner one evening in a quiet restaurant, where the ambience was light, the food good, and the threat very clear. McGovern sometimes felt he was part of a large Mafia family, and that meeting could certainly have come straight from an episode of a TV gangster show, but the editor had been making verbal threats against a man who was under the umbrella of McGovern's department. The last thing McGovern needed was the man's cover blown.

Now he and the editor had an understanding.

The paper was full of tripe. Sometimes he disgusted himself by reading it. Some of the news articles were just nonsense, yet here he was, sitting in the back of a luxury four-by-four that had a veritable arsenal in its boot, still reading the damned thing.

The story about the fire on the outskirts of the city caught his attention on page five. Just a little bit about the house being burned out. After McGovern's phone call early that morning, he was glad to see the name they had printed was indeed that of Louise Walker. It wouldn't do to have somebody read it and find another name there. It would buy them some time, if nothing else.

Whoever had torched the house and killed the woman would think they had gotten away with killing Louise.

'Did you acquire the CCTV footage?' he asked his driver, putting his paper down for a moment.

'Yes we did.' The driver stopped at a set of lights at Newington Road, waiting to make the turn for Holyrood Road. He briefly looked in the rear view mirror. 'The inn just down the road was accessed after we paid them a visit, and a dark van passed by shortly before the triple nine calls were received. It was an old thing, dark grey. We traced the plates; they belong to a Massey Ferguson tractor registered in the Highlands.'

'So they switched them. Which means our thoughts that maybe this is a professional job is turning out to be right. I'll need to give Frank Miller a call so he can have a wee chat with Carl White again. I want him brought in this time, and given a proper going over.'

The driver pulled away from the lights and headed through the Queen's Park towards the Parliament offices. The car stopped at the car park barrier and a guard checked the ID before the barrier lowered flush into the ground. He drove forward and into the underground car park.

McGovern walked in to the cool offices, the climate control operating perfectly. He sat in his office and started looking through some paperwork when his secretary came in with a coffee.

'Thank you, just what I need.' He took the cup and had a sip before laying it down on his desk. 'Did you get the ball rolling regarding that background check I asked for last night?'

'I did, sir. Louise Walker is clean. There are no mental issues with her or her family, and she doesn't have a criminal record.'

'What about her friend, Cindy Shields?'

'Nothing on her either. Both of them worked for Carl White Exotic Car Sales, as sales executives. Cindy still does. Or did, if it turns out it was her in that house.'

'What does Louise do for a living now?' McGovern drank more of the perfectly brewed coffee.

'Believe it or not, she's just started her own business. Selling used German cars. High end stuff.'

McGovern's eyebrows rose. 'So she's a rival for Carl's business now. I wonder if he would be pissed off enough to try and get rid of her?'

'It takes all sorts, as we very well know, sir.'

'How many times have I asked you to call me Neil? This is going to be a very informal department.'

His secretary smiled. 'I'm so used to working in London where they all expect to be called sir.'

'I was one of them. Trust me, we weren't all like that.'

She smiled back at him. 'I know that now, Neil.'

'I'm going to go through this paperwork, and then I'll get down the road. I'm sure Jack Miller will have strangled Richard Sullivan by now.'

****

Kate Murphy stood looking at the bottle of wine on her kitchen countertop, and thought she could do one of two things; down the wine and spend the rest of the day in bed, or go to work.

The wine won her over and she was just reaching for the bottle opener when her front doorbell rang. She walked cautiously up the hallway, and thought about looking through the peephole, when an angry fire exploded inside her. She stormed up to the door, unlocked it and swung it wide.

'Right then, you-'

'Good morning, Kate,' Norma Banks said, smiling at the pathologist.

The fire went out as quickly as it had started. 'Oh, Norma, I'm so sorry. I'm just fed up.'

'Well, get the kettle on and we can have a coffee.'

'Of course. Come in.' Kate stepped aside and Norma walked into the cool hallway.

'This is a nice place.'

'It's much better than my old one in London. Property is so expensive down there. Coming up to Edinburgh makes my salary go that bit further.' She led the PF through to the living room. It was open plan, with the kitchen and combined dining room at the far end. A door from the dining room led onto a small, private balcony.

Norma walked over to the window, which overlooked Holyrood Road, and the old *Edinburgh Evening Post* offices. 'How are you settling in?'

Kate switched the kettle on and poured coffee from an instant jar into two mugs. 'I'm settling in fine. There's twenty-four-hour concierge, secure underground parking. It's a really nice place.'

Norma turned from the window and walked into the kitchen. 'No you're not,' she said, picking up the wine bottle.

'Almost fine.'

Norma put the bottle back down. 'I think I may have overdone it a bit yesterday in the cemetery.'

Kate smiled. 'You were fine. Nobody will ever suspect, and I don't plan to socialise with them, so there won't be any awkward questions coming up.'

'It's okay to socialise with them. They don't bite. In fact, you would find them to be good friends if you got to know them better.'

'I'll see.'

The kettle boiled, and Kate made the coffees. They sat down in the living room. 'I'm going to be late. Talk about getting off to a bad start. I couldn't sleep, that's all. I took more painkillers than I needed to, and overslept.'

Norma held up a hand. 'I already made a call and spoke to Gus Weaver. I said you were having a conference with me, and that you'll be late.'

'Was he alright about it?'

Norma smiled. 'Kate, my dear, Weaver knows more than to be alright with it. He may not be happy, but he won't say anything. Leo Chester and I go way back.'

They sat in silence for a moment, the sun streaming in through the window, and Kate watched as dust motes floated through the beam of light like tiny invisible bombers that were vulnerable only when they passed through the sun's rays.

'Do you think we can pull this off?' Kate asked eventually, putting her mug down on the coffee table.

'Of course we can. Don't worry about it.'

'Okay. I'd better go and get dressed. After our coffee.'

CHAPTER 32

'It's along here,' Lena said, as Kim parked her car. Another patrol car was parked at the house, and Kim showed her ID to the young officer in the driving seat. Then they walked along to the extension and through the archway, where Lena had run for her life a few hours before.

'I was in here. I figured I could get a birds-eye view, sort of. Get a photo with my phone.' They turned right, and everything seemed different in the daylight.

'Lena, whatever possessed you to come in here by yourself?' Kim said.

'Hey, I'm always chasing a story, always trying to get an angle. It's a very cut-throat business now, especially since you can read news online without paying for a newspaper. I'll be lucky if I'm not out of a job by the time the editor hears this.'

'It must be hard. I can't say I envy you.'

Lena led her to the huge gravestone sitting against the wall overlooking the caretaker's private garden. 'I'll show you what happened,' she said, and was about to climb the grave when she looked down and saw her phone sitting at the pedestal. 'Look. It's still there,' she said, picking up the device.

'Well, at least you know they didn't take it.'

She picked it up by the edges and had a pained look on her face. 'I know I should hand this over so it can be dusted for prints, but...'

Kim pulled a bag out of her pocket, a little Ziploc she kept there. It was force of habit as she used it to put her keys and change in when she went through the metal detector on her way to the PF's offices, before she worked there.

'Dammit, Kim. Just as well I have a throwaway phone.'

'I won't ask why you have one of those as well,' she said, zipping the bag up. 'To pester former boyfriends, perhaps?'

'I wish I had time for a boyfriend. Then maybe I'd have one to pester.'

Kim put the phone away in her pocket. 'Let's climb up there. I want to see what you saw.'

'It was dark, mind, but light enough to make out the figure digging.' She started climbing up the gravestone anchored firmly against the wall. There was no fear of this one falling down. When she was on top, she scooted herself a long a bit, and waited for Kim to climb up. Both women fit and managing the climb with confidence. Once they were both on top of the ivy-covered wall, they sat and looked around them. Things were always different in the daylight, and Kim could see the tenements across Warriston Road. She was also aware this was where Frank's wife was buried, and for a moment, she wished he were there so she could give him a hug.

On the other side of the wall, they could both clearly see where something had been dug up. 'It certainly seems like something was there,' Kim said. The sun was up high, and they felt the heat burning into them. 'Come on, let's climb down this side and see what he was digging up.'

On the drive over to the cemetery, Kim ran different scenarios through her head, mostly involving Lena and whether she had experienced some kind of breakdown. What if she was just looking for some new angle for a story? Although she hadn't known Lena for as long as Frank had, she had a sense that the reporter was genuine here

It wasn't so much a climb down the other side, but rather a *hang down as far as you can, let go, and hope you don't break your ankle* affair. The wall was high so she grabbed hold of the ivy and was starting to let herself go down when it came away from the wall. She jumped down hoping to God there weren't any old tools in the overgrown weeds at this end of the garden.

There weren't. Lena climbed part of the way down and jumped too. That's when they saw the old, rusty, overturned wheelbarrow somebody could have used to shimmy up the wall. Like a man in a jumpsuit, wearing a respirator.

'This is like being back on school holidays, trying to amuse ourselves,' she said to Kim.

'If this wasn't such a serious business, it would be fun, I have to admit.' She walked to the far corner where a six-foot long strip of earth was freshly dug over, or dug up.

'You saw something that had been wrapped, being lifted out of here?' Kim said.

'Oh yes. I got a photo too. It will be on the phone. You'll see for yourself.'

'It was shaped like a body, you said?'

'Yes, wrapped in heavy-duty polythene.'

Kim took her phone out and snapped off a few photos, and then switched to record mode, making a short video. When she finished, she put the phone away.

'Show me where the guy fell after he'd climbed up there, Lena.'

Lena walked forward and pointed to a spot where the weeds and grass looked as if they had been flattened. 'I think it was about here. It was dark, so I can't be a hundred percent certain.'

'Right. I'll call Frank and let him know what we saw. He can get Maggie Parks and her team to comb this area. The question remains though; if it was a body, what did they do with it?'

CHAPTER 33

Miller felt good around Gus Weaver. He didn't know much about the older guy, but whenever the mortuary staff had a night out, Miller was inevitably asked along. Jack was always going on about how he always had a good relationship with the staff there. Obviously it helped with Julie Davidson, one of the previous pathologists, being related to Miller through marriage.

'So there I was, Frank, dancing on one of the tables. Now, you know me, I like a good drink, but I was well pished this night. They had this old eighties song going, and there I was giving it yahoo when the manager came across and asked us to leave. I couldn't understand why, so I gave him a bit of lip. Of course, your dad was working that night on some case, and heard my name coming over the radio. He told the patrol officers he would deal with it. He came down, settled it with the manager, and got me in a taxi. And to this day, I still don't know who the woman was. It wasn't the wife, that's all I know.'

'I can just see you belting it out on a table top, Gus.'

A woman stopped at the doorway. 'Morning, Gus. And you too, Detective..?'

'Miller.'

'Sorry, I forgot your name.' Kate Murphy smiled at them both before walking along to her office.

Miller followed, and Weaver went off to do his own thing, saying, 'Catch you later, Frank,' as he went.

'Apologies for the tardiness. I had a meeting with the PF. She wanted me to give her a quick update.' Kate slipped off a light blue blazer and hung it on a coat hook on the wall.

Miller felt a shiver run down his spine for a moment. Thinking about when his now-dead sister-in-law was sitting in this very office. As soon as the thought entered, it went out almost as fast.

'Don't worry about it. I'm just here to see how you're getting along with young Terry.'

Kate pulled on a lab coat and walked past him. 'Come on, I'll show you.'

They walked along the corridor into the receiving area and on into the storage area. 'I read up on this case last night.' She stopped and looked at him.

'It must have been hard for you at the time.'

'It was.' An ice ball fell into his stomach as they walked into the refrigerated room where the drawers were. She walked past the drawers holding the long-term bodies, the ones that were in dispute with the families and couldn't be released for a funeral just yet.

'I can't even imagine what you went through.'

'You married, Kate?'

She shook her head. 'I was going to say I'm married to the job, but that would be a bit of a cliché. I do enjoy my work, but I work to live, not live to work. I do have a life outside of here.'

'In our jobs, it's sometimes hard to find a social life.'

'Tell me about it. You end up going drinking with the same people you work with all day. Not that that's a bad thing, but when you've finished the entrée, you have to leave room for the ice cream.'

'True.' Miller found her analogy to be spot on. He himself had a good friend in Ian Powers, a computer guy he investigated a few years back, and had helped prove the man's innocence. Now Powers worked for Neil McGovern. He and Ian sometimes hit a few pubs together and they would talk about different things, and Miller made a point of not talking about how his day went, unless Powers asked him. 'That's not to say you're not welcome in The Rebel with us. Or we sometimes go to Logie Bairds.'

'Thanks, that's very kind, but I'm not much of a drinker.'

'We can soon sort that.' Miller smiled at her, warming to the woman. He put her bad mood the previous day down to nerves.

'Maybe I'll pop in one night if you let me know when you guys are going.'

'I'll give you a call.'

Kate stood before one of the drawers at waist level, the new addition deliberately placed there as people might want to inspect the corpse. She pulled on the handle and the flat drawer slid out easily and Miller stared at the form beneath the white sheet.

'You ready, Frank?' Kate asked him.

'You'd think this was my first one,' he said. He felt the blood drain from his face. *Under here is the reason my wife died. The little boy she was trying to find that night. Running around with a bag of money in the hope the kidnappers would give her Terry's whereabouts.* He looked her in the eyes and nodded.

Miller didn't gasp out loud, but he felt his blood pressure shoot up, as if all the blood in his body had just been pumped into his head. The boy's decomposed body looked as if it had been underground for a hundred years. Most of the internal organs were gone, leaving pieces of ragged skin covering his bones. Same with his skull. After he had been brought here and transported to the lab for examination, all his clothes had been cut off and a cloth covered his groin area.

'Bugs had eaten away most of his flesh, organs and skin. Being a cemetery, there were plenty of them around to eventually find their way into a coffin, but Terry had simply been put into the ground in his school uniform. Had he been taken from his school?'

Miller took a deep breath and thought his head was going to explode. A cluster headache belted through his brain at top speed, making him wish he had some painkillers on him. 'He was supposed to go over to a friend's house, but he didn't make it. This friend didn't go to the same school, but they hung out together.'

'I had a look at him, and because the decomposition is so bad, there isn't a definite ruling on how he died, but we took x-rays, and there are two broken vertebrae in his neck. I'm going to hazard a guess and say he died of a broken neck, but I will have to write *undetermined* on his death certificate because I can't actually prove that's the cause.'

'Can you tell if somebody snapped his neck?'

'Yes. When somebody has their neck broken by another human being, there are a number of characteristics, and I'll have a closer look later. We still have to tidy him up a bit and take more x-rays.'

'A car accident?'

'No. Once again, if I was to hazard a guess – and it's only because I've seen it for myself a few times – I would say Terry fell down a flight of stairs and broke his neck at the bottom. Again, I'll have a closer look along with Professor Chester.'

'So the question for me to find the answer to is, did he fall or was he pushed?'

'That's it exactly.'

'And you still think he died around the same time Carol died?'

'I would say so, Frank. I can't give you an exact date, but around that time, looking at his condition.'

Kate slid the drawer back in place and closed the door. 'I've scheduled the PM on the lady who was burnt in the house fire last night. I wasn't here when she was brought in, but since it wasn't a suspicious death, I've pencilled her in for this afternoon.'

'We've had some new information in on that, and it could be suspicious. We're looking into it today, just to keep you in the loop.'

'Okay. Duly noted.'

Miller's phone rang and he spoke to somebody on the other end before hanging up. 'I have to go. Thanks for letting me see him.'

He walked out of the storage room and the noise from the fridge motors sounded thunderous in his ears. Now he wanted to have a word with Carl White.

And the phone call told him he didn't have to look far.

****

The station was buzzing as Miller walked in through the back door. It was like a giant machine slowly warming itself up to operating temperature. In the same way as a Ferrari will run better, when its engine oil has warmed up.

Instead of going up to the investigation room, Miller headed downstairs to where the holding cells were.

'Right noisy bastard he is, now that he's woken up. Doesn't even know where the hell he is,' the sergeant in charge said.

Miller stepped forward and slammed open the steel viewing flap in the door and peered into the cell.

'About fucking time,' the man said. He was dishevelled, one side of his shirt sticking out of his trousers, his hair sticking up at irregular angles, his face in need of a shave, but apart from that, Carl White looked the same as he did the day before.

'Now, now, Mr. White, we don't want to piss off the staff here, do we?' Miller said.

'Where the bloody hell am I?' He stepped forward. 'Is that you, Miller?'

Miller slammed the flap shut, and turned round to the uniform. 'How long's he been in here?'

'Since seven-thirty last night. According to the bar staff, he was blootered by seven. They gave him a chance to leave; he wouldn't, so they called us. A patrol van with six guys brought him in after he started swinging a chair about. Off his head he was.'

'You got his belt and laces?'

'I have.'

'Is he being charged?'

'We were on the fence with giving him a caution or not, and the bar staff don't want to press any charges. Technically, we could do him for breach of the peace.'

'He just heard yesterday we found his son. You know the Terry White case?'

'Who doesn't?'

'That's Terry's dad. I had to tell him yesterday morning that we found his wee boy.' He looked at the sergeant. 'I think I would have got blootered as well.'

'You want me to release him without charge?'

'I don't think the PF would pursue it. Right now though, I need him sobered up. I need him to answer a few questions upstairs in an interview room.'

'Give me ten minutes and I'll release him to you.'

'Fine. I'll sign his release, and depending on how the questions go, hopefully you won't see him back down here.'

CHAPTER 34

'So, you don't work for Robert Molloy anymore, I hear?' Jack Miller said, sitting down at the dining table with another cup of coffee. The back door leading out onto the balcony, open, letting in a nice cool breeze.

Tai Lopez sat down opposite him. 'That's right. I told him I was opening my own little restaurant, which I did.'

'Was he annoyed?'

'Not at all. I gently reminded him that my uncle was coming over from Columbia with some of his friends to help me get it off the ground. Which they did. And I took them on The Blue Martini where I used to work, and my uncle loved the idea of a floating restaurant. I introduced them to Molloy. I won't get any trouble from him.'

'I know Molloy, and he'll keep his ears open regarding any trouble at your restaurant. He doesn't want a war with your family, that's for sure.'

'I haven't had any trouble.'

Jack took a sip of his coffee. 'How are things with Richard?'

'I moved in permanently, and to be honest, things are far better than I ever imagined. He treats me like a lady, something I've never had before.'

'I'm glad to hear it. I've actually come to like him myself. We've had a few pints together recently.' He looked across at Tai and could see why Sullivan would be attracted to her. She was Scottish through and through, but her father's Columbian heritage was evident. Her slight accent also showed that she lived in Columbia for the longest time when she was a little girl.

'I'm glad you two are able to have a drink with each other without you wanting to rip his head off.'

Jack laughed. 'Water under the bridge now.'

Sullivan walked into the room. 'I just got off the phone with Margaret White. I managed to calm her down and reassure her that Shaun was being well taken care of. I mean, it's not like he's locked in a dungeon somewhere, being water-boarded.'

'Why can't you refer her to another lawyer?'

'Well, Jack, don't you think it would be better if I controlled things from this end? If I hand the reins over to somebody else, it will make life difficult for all of us. This way, I can ease her mind and make sure Shaun is kept safe.'

'Good point.'

The doorbell rang. Sullivan answered it. McGovern walked in with Louise.

'Good morning, everybody.'

'Hey, Neil,' Tai said, getting up and walking over to him. She gave him a peck on the cheek. 'Hi, Louise.'

'Hi.'

'You two need some coffee?'

'Tai, my darling, you read my mind. But Richard can get it for us. Don't want him thinking I'm being sexist.'

Sullivan sighed and waved an arm in the general direction of the dining table. 'Make yourself comfortable, and I'll be mother.'

'How are you feeling?' Tai asked Louise.

'Shattered, to be honest. I need to get to work though. I have my own business to run. The cars won't sell themselves.'

'Don't you worry about that, Louise,' McGovern said. 'I already have one of my men at your showroom just now. He's the temporary manager you put in place to run things while you're taking a break. Anybody asks, you're away to Spain. If they see the news report on the TV about your house burning, then the manager will say he knows nothing about it.'

'What if Carl comes looking for me?'

'He won't. Trust me. I called Frank Miller earlier and he's about to have a chat with Carl.'

'He won't like being disturbed at work again.'

'Two things: first, I don't care what he likes. If Frank has to go there forty times to talk to him, he will do, and second, that's not an issue, because Carl's not at work.'

'Then where is he?'

****

'I need a coffee,' Carl White said, leaning his head down on the table.

'Drink the water,' Miller said.

White looked up, his eyes bloodshot and his face pale, after he'd just thrown up in the toilets. He drank the glass of water. Miller nodded to the uniform standing at the door; *go fetch another glass.*

The officer left, and Miller wanted to feel pity for the man sitting across from him, but if he was indeed involved in his son's kidnapping, there was no pity to be had.

'Tell me where you were last night,' he said.

White took a deep breath as if he was going to be sick again and let his foetid breath out. Miller took a packet of Polo mints from his pocket and gave one to White.

'I think you can gather I was out drinking,' he said, the round mint clanking against his teeth as he spoke round it.

'Where?'

'I started off in the Grassmarket, at the Last Drop. Then I went on to a few others.' He rattled them off and Miller wrote them down. 'Then I can't be sure, because the more I got pished, the less I remember.'

'So you don't remember being in the Tumbler in Home Street?'

'Is that where I was?'

'It's where you were picked up by one of our patrol vans. You were getting stroppy with the barman, so he called us.'

'If you say so.'

The uniform came back with a glass of water and Miller made White drink it. 'Why don't you tell me when you went out to Louise's farmhouse?'

'What? I didn't go there.'

'You just said you can't remember things. We think you went out to Louise's house and set fire to it.'

'What?' He looked shocked. 'What do you mean, set fire to it?'

'You got angry with her. I mean, it's understandable; Louise came into the showroom to tell you to pick up your stuff from her house, then you had bad news about Terry. What then? You got mad, went out there and burnt the place down? Maybe you had a fight and killed her. Decided to try and cover up the crime by setting fire to the place.'

'Louise is dead? Oh God, no. Please don't tell me that.' He looked at Miller and tears started streaming down his face.

'Maybe you love her so much that you don't want anybody else to have her.'

'My relationship with her wasn't like that.'

'What was it like? She like it rough so you just happened to throw her about in the name of sex?'

'I didn't put a hand on her. Ever.'

'That's not what she said. She told us you gave her a bloody good belting at times. That you had a temper and couldn't control it.' The lie came easily to Miller. He'd lied to so many suspects, trying to trip them up.

'That's not true. Why would she say that? I treated her like a Princess.' He started sobbing louder. 'I can't believe she's dead.'

Miller didn't want to put him out of his misery just yet. If the fire *was* set deliberately to cover up a crime, then he wanted to keep Louise safe.

Miller's phone rang. It was Kim. 'Go and get him cleaned up a bit,' Miller told the uniform. He answered his phone.

'I'm at the front desk. They told me you were interviewing somebody.'

Miller waited until White had left the room. 'I'm talking to Carl White. I don't think he torched Louise's house, if it *was* torched. So far, there's nothing to say it was, and I would have been inclined to go on the word of that fire commander, if Louise hadn't told us about that money and the vehicle registration document.'

'Which were conveniently burned in the fire.'

'I know we need to err on the side of caution. That's why I'm glad your dad has her in protective custody right now. That way we can keep an eye on her without her knowing we're checking on her.'

'I've handed in Lena's phone. To be taken to the lab. It was at the cemetery where she dropped it. I've left a note for them to download any photos from it and email me the ones from last night.'

'Good. Is Lena okay?'

'She's in good spirits, but she called her boss and told him she needed to take some sick leave as she's not feeling well.'

'Where is she going to go?'

'She's going to stay at Samantha Willis's flat.'

'Great. That way we can keep an eye on her as well.'

'I'm sure Jack will like an excuse for popping along there.'

'Now they've been introduced, I'm sure there will be no stopping him.'

'She's a nice woman, and a great writer.'

'Listen, I'm going to take Carl White home. You want to come with me?'

'Sure. I'll meet you at the back door.'

When White came back with the uniform, his shirt was tucked in and he had obviously run some water through his hair, dampening it down a bit.

'A colleague and I are going to run you home.'

He nodded and followed Miller out of the room. Miller made him walk downstairs in front of him, just in case he got it in his mind to give Miller a shove. At the back door, Kim was waiting for them.

'Mr. White. We meet again.'

'I look a bit rougher than yesterday, as you can obviously tell.'

'We've all been there.'

'I've got my pool car out here,' Miller said, leading them out to the car park. 'Did you move back to Barnton?' Miller asked, as he started the car. Miller figured White had maybe rented his house out when he moved in with Louise, but Louise's words hit him again; Carl White owns nothing.

White gave a laugh that had no humour in it. 'I haven't stayed there in a while.'

'So where to?'

'Fife. Land of the coal miner.'

'Nothing wrong with Fife. My grandparents lived there.'

'I'm not saying there's anything wrong with it, but you know what a snob I am. I lived in Barnton, now I'm living over there in the great Kingdom.'

The drive up to Kelty took half an hour.

'Tell me what you remember from that night,' Miller said.

'It was nearly three years ago, man.'

'It's been fucking three years for me as well, White. Now, just tell me what you remember before I drop you off in the middle of nowhere.'

White sighed. Thoughts from so long ago fought for space with the thoughts of the here and now. 'I was out the night Terry went missing,' he started to say, as if he was reading it from a script inside his head. He had probably gone through his story a million times before.

'Out where?' Miller knew the answer, mainly because he had read through the files again. But he wanted to see if White came up with the same answer. It would normally be a stretch to think somebody might remember what they were doing three years ago, but he himself knew what he was doing. It sounded unfair, because that was the night his wife died, but it was also the night this man's son was taken by a stranger. *Or was it really a stranger, Carl?* he thought to himself.

'That bitch said she got a call from a guy demanding money.' That bitch. Jill.

'She told you the next day when you got back. After your little drinking session.'

'That's right. And let's not forget the whoring. I was a womaniser back then as well as a drunk.'

'Why didn't she call you?'

'We lived together in those days. Marriage is a term for people married to each other, who still want to be together. Jill and I stayed under the same roof.'

Miller remembered the bitter arguments in front of the officers from the Serious Crimes. He knew White and his wife were on the brink, maybe had been for a long time, and Terry's disappearance seemed to push them into the divorce courts.

'The thing we never got to the root of was why Terry was picked by the kidnapper. So he went to an exclusive school, but from what I gathered, there were a lot of other rich boys there. Why did he single out Terry?'

'I don't know. I've asked myself the same question a million times over.'

'It couldn't have been a random kidnapping,' Kim said from the back seat. 'He knew to phone your wife. He knew your phone number.'

'We knew that and pulled in everybody who had access to the number,'

Miller said, keeping his eyes on the road in front. 'Even though the number was unlisted, there are times when people give it away. It was impossible to know who had it, although we figured it wouldn't be a stranger.'

'He was clever, though,' White said, a line of sweat running across his brow. 'He kept everybody running around and still he didn't get caught. But why did he have to kill my boy?'

Miller didn't have an answer. He watched the Odeon cinema slide by at the Halbeath interchange at Dunfermline. It had been a while since Miller had been to the cinema. He couldn't even remember what movie he had seen. It had to have been with Carol though.

Both Kim and White were silent now. The only sound, the noise of the cold air being blown out of the vents and a DJ on Scot FM playing past hits. *China Crisis. Wishful Thinking.* Released before he was born, but he liked 80's music.

The Kelty turnoff beckoned at the top of a steep incline on the motorway. Turning right, he headed into Kelty itself, slowing down at *Welcome to Kelty* sign, as if it was the hub of the tourist trail round Fife. It didn't have quite the same ring as *Welcome to Vegas.*

'Where to?' Miller asked.

'First on the left,' White said, perking up. 'Up to the roundabout, left again.'

Miller drove as directed. A group of youths looking for trouble hung about outside a corner store, throwing sweets at each other and shouting. A few of them stared after his car, the prospect of a stranger to hassle. One of them stuck his fingers up at the car, asking for a confrontation.

You're picking on the wrong fucking guy, Miller thought to himself, watching the reprobates dancing about in the road.

This wasn't an affluent town. Professional people bought the detached houses in the new estate on the back road to Cowdenbeath. Five minutes' drive to the motorway to escape to work in the morning, returning at night where they would be cordoned off from what they saw as the poverty and depravation of the council houses up the road.

White told him to stop in a driveway with a narrow entrance, waiting to trap an unwary driver. Loch Leven Terrace, a refurbished block of four.

White stumbled up the outside stairs to his flat. Unlocked the door and stepped in followed by Kim. Miller took up the rear.

A few more carpeted stairs led up to the lobby. White turned right and went straight into the bathroom. 'Go right through,' he said, shutting the door on them.

The smell of stale cooking hit their nostrils as they passed the kitchen. The living room was on the right, the door open, and cigarette smoke hanging in the air like the aftermath of a shootout. Miller sensed the presence of

somebody in the room before Kim walked in.
By then it was almost too late.

CHAPTER 35

Years before, a hand-to-hand combat instructor had told Kim, *In the time it takes you to think about striking back, you're already dead.*

The agents in her department had to constantly practice their combat skills, and the same people who taught MI5 agents trained them. Another tactic that stuck in her mind: *Use anything you can grab as a weapon. Pencil, lamp, anything at all. In the right hands, anything can be a deadly weapon. If you don't have one, and he does, take it from him and use it against him. He might be fast, but if you want to stay alive, you have to be faster.*

Now, as she walked into the living room, her senses kicked in and she turned, her body already going into fight mode. Her eyes tracked the trajectory of the bottle in the woman's hand and she grabbed hold of it, using her momentum to throw her round and down, taking the weapon from her. For a second, Kim was about to bring the bottle down on the woman's head, incapacitating her in case she had a knife, or worse, a gun.

The woman's housecoat had ridden up, revealing a short nightdress underneath. Kim kept hold of the woman's wrist, bending the arm at the elbow.

'You fucking bastard!' the woman screamed.

Miller took out his handcuffs and clamped her arms behind her back.

'You've met then,' White said, as he came into the room.

'I'll fucking meet you in a minute. You've got a lot of explaining to do,' Miller said, his eyes boring into the other man.

White shrugged his shoulders, picked up the smouldering cigarette and put it out in an ashtray. 'Let's just call it police protection.'

'You'll need protection, you weasel. You should have warned me about her.'

'Police?' the woman shouted. 'I didn't know you two were coppers.' The fight went out of her like a rapidly deflating balloon. Kim stood up straight and grabbed the woman by the arms, dragging her to her feet.

Her hair was in a mess, spread over her face. Her breathing was rapid and Miller could smell the contents of the empty bottle on her breath.

'I thought it was that bastard coming in.' She looked at White. 'Where the fuck have you been? You said you were going down the road for a pint.

Wanker.'

'I went into Edinburgh.'

'Fucking Edinburgh? Why? To see that slag of a wife of yours?'

'Ex-wife, actually, and no, I didn't see her.'

'Lying bastard.'

'Suit yourself.'

Miller was technically in the middle of a domestic, on a patch where he had no jurisdiction. He felt like throwing White out of a window or something.

'Both of you, shut up. I'm taking the handcuffs off now and I don't want any of your nonsense. Right?'

The woman shrugged as Miller took the cuffs off.

'What's your name?' he asked her.

'Whatever you want it to be, sweetheart.'

'Just answer the man!' Kim said, getting worked up.

'Keep your hair on, tiger.' She looked at Miller. 'Susan Tay.'

'Well, Susan Tay, I suggest you keep your temper in check from now on.'

'He keeps winding me up. Bastard.'

White walked away into another room. Miller followed him.

'Nice girl,' he said.

'Snitch and Snatch. She's a Gemini. One minute she'll be your best friend, the next, she'd take your head off with an axe.'

'How long have you known her?'

'A while now. We hook up now and again. I knew her before Louise kicked me out. I had nowhere else to go.' He took a suitcase out of a wardrobe and hastily began filling it.

'Why didn't you go home?' He could hear the muted voices of the two women in the other room.

'I don't have a home.'

'What about Barnton?' Miller asked the question, wondering if White would back up what Louise had said about him owning nothing.

'And live with my mother? I didn't think that was an option. Now I don't think I have a choice.'

'Can't Jill put you up for a while?'

'She's probably got some fancy man in there with her now.'

'Why don't you stay here and try and patch things up with Susan.'

White looked at him. 'You were in the room, right? You did see how nuts she is? I've known her for years, and she's good for a bit of fun but I don't want to be tethered to her. Besides, I want to go back to Edinburgh to help look for my boy's killer.'

'If that's your reason, then you'd be better staying here. We can't have you interfering with our investigation.'

'Why?'

'The police are dealing with it.'

'Look what a fucking mess you lot made of it three years ago. What makes you think you'd be any better this time round?' White pointed his finger at Miller, his temper flaring. Maybe he and Susan were well suited.

'Remember one thing, White: keep out of my way.' Miller walked out of the room and nodded to Kim in the living room.

'Let's go.'

White was standing in the bedroom doorway. 'Are you not taking me back to Edinburgh with you?'

Miller stopped and looked at him. 'You wish.'

He was at the end of the hallway with Kim in front when White spoke to him again.

'So you don't want to know who I think killed my son?'

Miller stopped in his tracks.

'I thought so,' White said, picking up his suitcase.

CHAPTER 36

'So, I have Callahan tailing this guy, who he suspects has killed his brother over a dispute regarding their business. Only it turns out...well, I'll let you buy a copy of the book to find out what happens.'

'It's too early in the morning to be playing games.' Jack Miller smiled at Samantha Willis as she poured him a cup of coffee. He thanked her and yawned.

'I hope I'm not boring you,' she said, teasing him.

'Not at all.'

'How did your job go last night?' They walked through to the living room and sat down. It was in shadow, keeping the room cool.

'It was okay. Some people needed help, and I was there with some others doing some babysitting.'

'Ah. The life of a government spy must be tiring.'

'Spy? I wish it had been that exciting.'

'So what do you normally do with your days?'

Jack took a sip of his coffee. It tasted good, but he didn't want to impose. He'd only popped in to say he was sorry about leaving her in the lurch the night before. He put the mug down on the coffee table.

'I just hang out with some of my friends. We go to the pub. We just do stuff together. We were all in the force together and retired within two years of each other.'

'Sounds good.'

'Do you have friends who you hang out with?'

'I used to, Jack. Since I was a stranger in town, I had no friends over here, but I became friends with the wives of Ralph's friends. When we split up, his friends sided with him, and I didn't get any return phone calls. He poisoned them against me. Said I was fooling around on him, when it was the other way around.'

'I was married for over thirty years to the same woman. Never cheated on her once. I got the opportunity mind, but it wasn't for me. I loved her, and we had our little boy. Some guys though, they can't help themselves.'

'Ralph was wonderful when we first met, but he wasn't working and I was bringing in money from my writing, then I landed an agent, and got a contract. He didn't work at all after that.'

'What does he do now?'

'Nothing. I have to pay him money.'

'Jeez. What a piece of pond life.'

'It's over now though, Jack. Well, I thought it was over until last night.'

Jack sat forward on the settee. 'What happened?'

'He was in the pub. He must have been watching us, because as soon as you left, he came over to me and said he won't sign the divorce papers until I agree to give him more money, even though he's getting plenty.'

'He didn't cause a fuss in the pub, did he?'

'No, he just tried to piss me off.'

'If he keeps bothering you, I can ask Frank to have a word.'

Samantha waved a hand at him. 'No, no, it's nothing I can't handle.'

Jack looked her in the eyes and saw something he had seen many times over the years as a copper; she didn't believe her own words. 'So what happened with Lena?' he said, changing the subject, but mentally filing it away.

Samantha told him the story of Lena's exploits the night before. 'Kim said she was going to the cemetery with Lena to have a look. Lena dropped her phone there and was worried somebody had found it.'

'So they were digging up something from the garden that's attached to the caretaker's house?'

'They were. She said it looked like a body.'

'And Frank knows all about this?'

'Yes.'

Jack thought for a moment. 'This is just the detective in me playing around here, but what if Lena made this up to get closer to the investigation? Said she saw two guys digging something up, so she would be nearer Frank and the team?'

Samantha smiled. 'I think you need a holiday, Jack.'

'I've just had one. With my mates in Spain. Seriously, what do you think, as a crime writer?'

'I've known Lena for a couple of years, and I honestly can't think of her doing something like that.'

'No, neither can I, but I just wanted to voice my opinion.'

'Hey, nobody blames you for thinking outside the box. I have to think, *What if?* all the time, so I can make up mysteries.'

'I wonder who those blokes are?' he said.

'The crime writer in me finds it intriguing that two men would be in a cemetery after dark digging up a body that wasn't in a proper resting place.' Samantha went through to the kitchen to get the coffee pot. 'What do you think, Jack?'

'I'd like to know who he was.' His phone rang, and he listened to the caller. He stood up when Samantha came back into the room. 'I have to go, Sam.'

'Was it something I said?' she asked, smiling.

'No. I know this is getting to be a habit, but I have to rush.'

'Okay. Call back whenever.'

Jack left in a hurry.

****

'It's obvious to me now' Carl White said from the back seat. 'I didn't see the signs at the time.' He looked at the back of Miller's head and then across to the rust red of the Forth Rail Bridge, watching as a train moved slowly across to Fife.

'What are you talking about?'

'Jill was seeing somebody behind my back.'

'I thought you two were living separate lives?' Kim said.

'We were. I was the one who was seeing other women. Then I started going out with Susan.' A train crossed over the bridge, leaving Dalmeny, heading for North Queensferry. 'I just didn't see that, you know? That Jill would be sleeping with somebody else.'

'Do you know who it was?' Miller said, indicating and pulling round a slow moving truck.

'I didn't even know until yesterday afternoon. That's when I called Jill, you know, just to talk about things, and then she ripped into me. Told me she was sleeping with some bloke who was better endowed than me, better looking, had more stamina where it counted and he knew how to make her happy. She gave me the full works yesterday. Oh, and apparently Terry met him and liked him.' He looked at Miller in the mirror. 'I don't know him that I'm aware of, but she said his name was Brian Sewell. She wouldn't tell me anymore.'

'Do you believe her?' Miller asked.

'I wouldn't have, but I remembered one time Terry had a new toy car and I asked him where he got it, and he said from his mum's friend. I didn't put two and two together then. I don't know what crap she was filling his head with, probably telling him we were separated.'

'Which you were.'

'To all intents and purposes, yes.'

'Is that why you went out and got pissed?' Kim asked.

'That, and thinking about my little boy. He was the one thing I lived for, had any hope for. I loved him so much. I would never have done anything to harm a hair on his head.'

Miller believed him at that moment in time. He didn't know how some of the money got into a box belonging to him, or the vehicle registration document, but he could see it in the man's eyes. 'Where to?'

'Just drop me off at my mother's house.'

When they were at the Barnton junction, Miller turned left and drove down the road until he came to the new development. 'I can't go in with you.'

'I don't expect you to.'

Miller was about to tell White what had gone on with Shaun, but left it alone. He was sure old mother White would tell her son all about it.

Carl White got out of the car and walked up the driveway to the big house, carrying his suitcase.

They drove away, heading back into town. 'I have to go and see Rosie,' Miller said.

'That's fine. I'll come along and see how she's doing. Where does she work again?'

'At the new Council offices at Waverley.

It took Miller fifteen minutes.

****

Reporting in Edinburgh wasn't like reporting from the front lines of Iraq or some other far-flung theatre of war, but it had its moments. Lena Finn had had bricks thrown at her when she followed a fire crew as they were attending suspicious fire scenes. Hooligans in some of the poorer parts of the city would steal a car, set fire to it, and then when the fire brigade turned up, they would steal from the fire engine and then brick the firemen.

She did an exposé on a Romanian gangster, who thought he could waltz into Scotland and start his human trafficking scam here as well as back home. She had been instrumental in his downfall, something he vowed he would seek revenge for. One of his men had approached her in a pub one night and told her she would be raped one day, but she wouldn't know where or when.

She wasn't scared of anything, a trait her father said she got from him. A six-foot-five bruiser, he would regularly come back from the pub with bruised knuckles. He had told her early on in life; *Don't take shit from anybody.* And she didn't. Did it make her popular? Of course not. Did she stand by and let somebody abuse her? No way. She had stood up to fighters, both men and women, and looked them in the eye just before a physical altercation. Nothing scared her.

So why did she feel scared now?'

Because her front door was open.

Just a little, as if somebody had carelessly pulled it behind them and it hadn't clicked shut properly. She was sure she had closed it when she left last night. Her first reaction was to take her phone out and connect to the Wi-Fi cameras inside, but then she remembered she didn't have her phone.

At that moment, she regretted buying her home in Dalmeny, a little village outside Edinburgh, on the way to South Queensferry. It sat in its own grounds, not much, but it was surrounded by fields, bordered by tall trees. Nobody could spy on her from afar. She could see any car approaching, long before the driver would see her. She felt safe here, not isolated as her mother had said she would be. This was her own castle, something she protected with the diligence of a defending Army.

Now she felt scared. There were no cars parked in the only places a car could park. She turned off the engine of her own little Mini Cooper and stepped out. The day was getting warmer, and the heat hit her as the air conditioning stopped. She looked around, back down her driveway, which was over a quarter of a mile. She saw old Mr Lang's car in his own driveway, her nearest neighbour.

Then she felt silly and the only thing she started worrying about was whether any animals had gotten in. Like field mice. *And a mouse won't hurt you, silly cow,* she thought, locking her car and walking into her house.

It was cool in here. It was an old house, belonging to a groundskeeper or somebody like that years ago. Now it was all hers, and she was damned if she was going to be scared in her own home. She'd be as well going back to live with her mum and dad, if that was the case.

Some of the trees put part of her little car park in shadow, and as she walked through this to the front door, a light breeze tugged at her, as if it didn't want her to go in the house.

She thought about all the horror movies she'd seen, where the girl walks into the house, shouts *Hello?* just to alert the killer inside that she was there. Then she's all la-de-da about the house, thinking it was okay, and just at the moment she let her guard down, she would be chopped into a thousand pieces...

For fuck's sake, get a grip she scolded herself, as she walked into her hallway. She kept the door open anyway. If she was being chased, then she wanted a quick exit. The house was silent. Almost too silent. She walked through to the kitchen and grabbed a knife from the kitchen drawer. Would she be able to use it if push came to shove? Yes.

Walking round the house, she found nobody lurking anywhere, even in the linen closet. She went back to the front door and closed it. *Who opened it?* She asked herself again.

You did! You left it open.

She actually laughed at herself then. Laughed out loud. The sound felt good in the empty house. Key word; *empty,* she told herself.

She wanted to run a bath, to soak in the big tub she'd had installed. The house was old and the rooms much larger than a new build would have been, and she had been excited when she'd seen the old tub for sale. A big, freestanding, claw-foot ceramic tub. After having it lovingly restored, she'd picked out fancy fitments for it, and it was the one oasis she had after working a long day.

In the bedroom, she undressed, wrapped herself in her robe, and took her towel. She was about to open the bathroom door and stopped for a moment. This was the one room she hadn't checked. What if he was in here? *If there was somebody hiding, then he would have had plenty of chance to leave when you were getting changed. And if there was somebody waiting to attack you, surely he would have come into your room. I mean, what if you didn't use your bathroom? He would still be there waiting.*

She realised she was being stupid, opened the bathroom door and walked in.

A dead man lay in her bath, dressed, but very badly decomposed.

Lena screamed, turned round to run and ran straight into the figure who was standing in the doorway.

CHAPTER 37

Miller parked in East Market Street and left the Police Scotland sign on the dash. The new building housing Edinburgh Council sat on the corner of New Street. Miller could see graffiti-covered fencing bordering what used to be the old SMT bus garage. It had been pulled down and levelled for a development project that was to include a hotel, shops and apartments, but the developer had gone under.

He and Kim walked across to the small plaza in front, towards the main entrance. The council had called their brand new building Waverley Court, and Miller wondered if this was a nod to Sir Walter Scott's famous novel, or because it sat beside Edinburgh's main station. 'What do you think of that?' Miller asked, nodding towards a statue.

The Everyman looked as if it was made out of paper Maché, and he was standing on what looked like a piece of multi-coloured scaffolding.

'What is it?'

'The Everyman. It's supposed to represent all the people, apparently.'

'It's different.'

They walked into reception and across to the front desk. The building was only a few years old, and it was the first time Miller had been in it.

'I'm here to see Rosie Davidson, Development Officer,' Miller said, holding out his warrant card.

'Is she expecting you?'

'Yes, she is.'

'Hold on one second and I'll call through for you.'

The receptionist picked up a phone and dialled a number.

'Very impressive,' Kim said.

'I wish they would update our station, but knowing our luck, it will be sold off and made into a boutique hotel.'

'She'll see you now, sir,' the girl said, hanging the phone up. 'It's on level two, just up the stairs and round to the right. Third office on your right.'

'Thanks.'

They made their way up the stairs and followed the directions until they reached the office, with Rosie's name on the door. Miller knocked and she beckoned them inside.

Rosie Davidson got up from behind her desk, walked over to Miller and Kim and gave them both a hug. 'Thank you both so much for yesterday. I was so scared. Please, sit down and I'll pour coffee. Or would you like some water?'

'Coffee for me, Rosie, thanks,' Miller said, feeling a caffeine fix coming on.

'Water, thanks, Rosie.'

Rosie poured the drinks while the others sat down.

'This is a nice building,' Miller said. Rosie's window afforded them a view of the arches opposite, which had had doors added to them and leased as small industrial units.

'We've had a lot of flak, Frank, let me tell you.' She put the coffee down and handed Kim a glass of water. 'First of all, the council liquidated assets to help pay for the place. Forty mil sounds like a lot, but the old building was falling apart. This is so much more energy efficient. We even have a grass area with our life-size ornamental cow that sits over the Waverley Station underground car park. It's a really nice place to work.' She sat down behind her desk.' But I don't think you're here to talk about ornamental cows.'

'I want to talk about the former caretakers of Warriston Cemetery.'

'I found the information you wanted. Much of the council information has yet to be updated, but it's being done in order of priority. Since the house is no longer standing, it wasn't a priority, but I managed to prod somebody in building services, who then redirected me back to the old personnel files. I have a list of names, but the one you're interested in is the last one I believe?'

'Yes, the one who was there last.'

'Well, the house caught on fire two days after that night.'

The night my wife died. 'Two days?'

'Yes, it was a chip pan fire. The man we gave the job to was Brian Sewell.'

A look passed between Miller and Kim. *Brian Sewell. Jill's boyfriend.*

'Who would have hired him?'

'Me. I hired him. I worked in HR before I moved over to Development. Now I work with the director of services for communities.' She looked at Kim. 'One of the departments I deal with is refuse collection.'

'Did anything stick out about the man?'

'No, nothing. He was in need of a job, he applied and I considered his application.'

'Can you tell us more about him?' Kim said.

'You don't think he had anything to do with the kidnapping, do you?' Rosie said.

'We don't know anything yet, Rosie. He was the last caretaker, Terry's body was found in the basement of the caretaker's house, so we can't rule anything out yet.'

'I understand.' Rosie opened the file in front of her. 'Brian had been in the Army. He came out after serving his time, and had done two tours of Iraq and one of Afghanistan. He had PTSD.'

'How bad was he?' Miller asked, putting his coffee mug on the desk.

'Brian was very quiet, and said he didn't have many friends in Edinburgh, which I took to mean he didn't have *any* friends in Edinburgh. He had seen a lot in battle, and just needed a break.'

'How well was he vetted?'

'Standard vetting, but Dr. Borthwick vouched for him.'

'Andrew Borthwick up at the Royal Scottish?'

'Yes. I'm a volunteer on the patient council up there. Andrew and I got talking one day, and he said he was treating a man with PTSD, and was ready to sign him off as being ready for work, and did I think it would be worth Brian's time applying to the council? I said yes, of course. We have all sorts of people with disabilities. I knew the position of caretaker was coming up, so I suggested it to Robert. He said that would be perfect, and he would help Brian apply.'

Kim smiled. 'Did you give him a break? Brian, I mean.'

Rosie gave a slight smile. 'I suppose I did. I honestly reviewed all the applicants but Brian had the sort of qualifications we were looking for. He would be good at security, and he would be able to supervise the other gardeners. When he got the job, he was over the moon, and he was good at it.'

'No problems with him adjusting?'

'No. Jill made sure he kept in contact with her.'

'Jill?' Kim asked.

'Jill White. She was his day-to-day caseworker. It was needed for Andrew to sign off on Brian's performance record. It's to make sure he is able to function on a normal level. Jill assessed him after he was in treatment with Andrew, and then she signed him off. He had to meet with her once a week.'

'So he would get to know her pretty well,' Miller said.

'On a professional level, yes.'

'What about on a personal level?'

'Oh, I don't think she would go beyond the basics, which is just giving snippets of her personal life.'

'So, let me get this straight,' Miller said. 'Brian comes out the Army, but he's having problems adjusting, so he goes to his doctor, who then sends him to see Borthwick at the Royal Scottish. He gets treatment, but still needs some after care, and that's when Jill gets involved. She gives him the okay as well, and he gets the all-clear.'

'Not exactly the all-clear, Frank. It just means he's more able to deal with the outside world, but with the support of the hospital.'

'Right. He's on the mend, but still has Jill to fall back on if he feels things are getting on top of him?'

'Correct.'

'How long was Brian in the job before Terry was kidnapped?'

'About three weeks, I think.'

'Do you know where Brian is now?' Kim asked.

'I have no idea.'

'Was he sacked after the fire?' Miller asked. The sun was coming in the window and he was starting to feel hot, wishing he had taken up the offer of a glass of water, and wondered if Kim would mind if he took a sip of hers. He closed his eyes for a second. Of course she would mind, you clown.

'No. He left.'

'Did he give notice?'

'No. I mean, he just left. There was no resignation, no forwarding address, no nothing. He didn't come back to the hospital, didn't keep his appointment with Jill, nothing. Brian Sewell just fell off the face of the Earth.'

CHAPTER 38

The voices upstairs were raised again. Terry tried to drown them out, but it was difficult. He played the games and read the books the man had brought.

'Thought you might be getting fed up reading the same stuff,' he said.

'Thanks.' Terry smiled. Somehow, this man wasn't frightening. He knew him, he was convinced of that, and if only he'd take the woollen mask off, he'd be able to tell for sure. Just now though, he couldn't let on. What if he said something and the man hurt him?

He was hungry now, his stomach rumbling. There wasn't a clock down here, but he could tell what time of day it was by the type of food they brought him. Cornflakes in the morning, soup at lunchtime and then a main meal. They'd brought him pizza a few times now, and it was good. Even a bucket of KFC one time.

He felt hungry, but wasn't sure if this was because he was particularly hungry this afternoon, or whether dinner was late.

Whatever it was, they weren't in a hurry to bring him food when they were too busy arguing upstairs.

The door at the top of the stairs slammed shut, and then he could hear heavy footsteps thumping down the stairs.

This wasn't the nice man who brought him food. This was another one. He didn't know this man.

'Here's what's going to happen, sonny Jim; I'm going to bring one of those little pocket recorders out of my pocket, and you're going to talk into it.'

Terry was glued to every word as the man started speaking. He too had a mask on, a woolly one just with holes for his eyes and mouth.

'You are going to speak the words I tell you to speak, you got that?'

Terry nodded.

'I said, have you fucking got that?' the man said, raising his voice. He quickly stepped towards Terry, grabbed his hair and yanked his head back. 'Answer me!'

'Let him go,' a voice from the doorway said. Another man he didn't know, but at least he seemed to be on Terry's side.

The angry man let Terry's hair go and turned round. 'So you tell me what to do now, is that it?'

The man stood his ground. He could see the man's mouth smiling at Mr. Angry. 'Save that tone for the wee lassies you want to scare.'

'So I don't scare you?'

'No, you don't. And if you want to leave this place in one piece, you'd better stick to the story.'

They all heard more feet on the stairs. Terry's friend poked his head into the stairwell. 'You stay up there. You can't come down here. Not while we're doing this.' He turned back to Mr. Angry. 'Get on with it. I'll be upstairs with him. Make it quick.'

After he left, Terry was alone with Mr. Angry, convinced the man was going to hurt him. He didn't though. 'You're going to read this. Make it sound like you're scared. If you don't make it convincing, I'll fucking slap you about for real. Got it?'

He brought out the recorder, and an index card. Mr. Angry nodded and Terry started talking.

'Please help me. He hurts me! I want my mum. Please help me!

CHAPTER 39

'You look rough, boss,' Martin Crawley said, handing Carl White a cup of coffee.

'Rougher than a badger's arse, Martin,' White said, taking the coffee. 'I had to get a taxi in this morning.'

'At least nobody will bawl you out for coming in a bit later.' Crawley smiled.

'The only person who bawled me out was my mother. That's worse than being married to Jill.'

'That's why I like being my own boss. At home anyway.'

'You know when people say, *Stay single?* Sometimes that's the best advice.'

'Has Jill moved on?'

'Tell you the truth, Martin, I don't know, and I really don't care. She was turning into a nag anyway. The only thing that kept us together for the longest time was Terry. I know that sounds clichéd, but it's true. Sometimes you just dig deep and knuckle down. I couldn't take it anymore.'

'It's a pity things didn't work out with Louise. I liked her a lot. She was always a laugh when we worked together.'

'Such is life, Martin.' White's mouth was parched and he had another sip of water from the glass sitting on his desk before Crawley brought him the coffee.

'So where's Cindy today, then? Wasn't she supposed to be on the late shift again?'

White looked at his salesman with bloodshot eyes and an expression that conveyed his total lack of knowledge. 'I suppose she is. I thought you guys figured all that out? Micro management, didn't you call it?'

'Yes we did. And she is supposed to be here by now.' He made a show of looking at his watch.

'Are you saying you're having to carry her?' White's face was getting redder and his voice was getting louder.

'I'm not saying that at all. I just wondered where she was, that's all.'

White jumped out of his seat as if he'd been bitten. 'So you think you'd come in here and give me a coffee, telling tales on your colleague? What the fuck is wrong with you? You make me fucking sick.'

'I don't have to take this shit off you. Stick your job up your fucking arse.'

'Really? If you leave here now don't bother coming back. Ever.'

'Fine by me.'

'You won't survive without me, Crawley.'

Crawley turned to the door and opened it, stopping before he stepped out. 'Louise offered me a job, anyway. I told her I'd think about it, and to be honest, I was happy here. Now I'll tell her I'm more than happy to accept.' He walked out and down the stairs to the showroom floor.

White slammed the door behind him.

There were a few customers in, and Crawley walked over to his desk and started to clear things out of the drawers.

'What the hell happened here, Martin?' one of the other sales consultants asked.

'I just got fired, Pete. I only made a comment about Cindy being late, that's all. I mean, I wasn't dropping her in it, I just wondered if she was coming in or not.'

'Carl's been through a lot. Maybe he didn't mean it.'

'Oh he meant it alright, and I meant it too; I'm going to take up Louise's offer.'

Pete gave a short laugh. 'Maybe I'll be joining you. Carl's a train wreck right now, and who knows, we could all be out of a job by the end of the week.'

'I've been here the longest, so maybe you're right; he wants new blood in here so he can pay them less and tell his tales of how sad his life's been.'

'That's a bit harsh, Martin.'

'Is it? We've listened to his drivel for years now, and what thanks do we get for it? Nothing. Shown the door.' He finished putting what meagre items he had into his cardboard box and lifted it off the desk. 'I mean, I don't drive a company car. I bought my own. What sort of outfit is this anyway?'

'I'll be sorry to see you go, mate,' Pete said, holding out his hand. Crawley shook it.

'If you know what's good for you, you'll join me in Louise's new business. She's starting small but we'll make it big. Bigger than this dump.' He walked out of the showroom without looking back.

****

'Lena, it's me,' Jack said, as Lena screamed and ran full tilt into him, her hands pounding him. He grabbed her arms and stood her back so she could see him properly.

'Oh, Jack,' she said, and threw herself into his arms. 'In the bath. He's dead, Jack.'

'Go and get dressed, I'll call Frank.' He led her through to her bedroom and gently closed the door behind her.

'Promise me you'll stay there,' Lena said, behind the closed door, her voice breaking as she started sobbing again.

'I promise. I'll be right here.' He took his phone out and dialled his son's number, automatically going into detective mode. 'Frank? It's Jack. We've got a situation at Lena's house. We'll need all you've got, son. There's a life extinct in the bathtub.'

'What? Any ID?'

'No, this guy hasn't breathed any of God's fresh air for a very long time.'

'He's definitely dead?'

'I *was* a detective, son. He's decomposed.'

'Is Lena alright?'

'I got here and there was no answer, so I opened the door. She's here, but she discovered the guy when I arrived. She's pretty scared.'

'I'll get a team out there and call forensics. Keep your eye on Lena. And don't touch anything.'

'Again, I know what I'm doing at a crime scene, Detective.' He hung up and waited for Lena to come out. She had hastily pulled on a pair of jeans and a T-shirt. She had slipped her feet into a pair of trainers with the laces tucked into them.

'I need to have a look at this, Lena. Stay just outside the door. Don't look in again, but stay near me.'

'Okay.' She replied, still visibly shaken.

'Did you see anything else suspicious when you got here?'

'The front door was open. I thought at first somebody was in here, but I didn't see anything, so I thought I must have not shut it properly.'

'You should have driven away and called somebody. You know you can always call me.'

She put a hand on his arm and smiled a smile that only people who have been crying can smile. 'I know. Thank you.'

'If you hear anything while I'm in here, just shout.'

He walked into the bathroom and the smell seeped into his nostrils. The bathroom window had been opened and let some of the smell out, but it was still rank. Jack walked forward, careful not to touch anything, and looked down at the man lying in the tub.

He couldn't tell how old he was, but a lot of the skin remained on his face. As did his hair. The grin on his face was much wider than it had been in life, as part of the lower face had been eaten away, probably by insects. His clothes were remarkably well preserved. Jack had no doubt this was the man who Lena had seen being extricated from a shallow grave the night before.

He looked around the bathroom; there was no evidence of dirt, no remnants of plastic sheeting, nothing. Whoever dumped him here had tidied up afterwards.

He stepped outside the bathroom. 'There's nothing we can do here. Let's wait downstairs for Frank.'

They waited with the front door open. Miller had contacted Control and they had sent back-up from South Queensferry, just a stone's throw from Dalmeny. The patrol car shot along the road at high speed, and drove up Lena's driveway too fast.

Jack walked out to meet them and they rushed out of their car, maybe expecting to take Jack down, but he identified himself, the older sergeant recognising him.

'I thought we were going to have a bit of a belting going on there, sir,' the uniform said.

'Not today, Freddie. The corpse is upstairs in the bath and we're waiting for the cavalry.'

'Right you are then.' He looked at the young female in uniform standing beside him. 'What this man means is we're cannon fodder if anybody comes out shooting.'

'You've got too much imagination,' Jack said.

****

Miller turned up ahead of the forensics crew. Lena was glad to see him and Kim.

'What's going on here, Jack?' Miller asked.

'When you called me about Kim finding Lena's phone, I had a bad feeling. It just happened to be out in the open to be found? Not likely. I'll bet when you have it checked over, it's been tampered with.'

'I'll call them now.' While Miller dialled, Kim gave Lena a hug. 'I'm sorry. I shouldn't have left you alone.'

'There's nothing to be sorry about. I got my phone back, so how could they know where I live?'

Miller cut the call after thanking the man on the other end. 'The lab ran it. They said it was a two-minute job. No prints on it at all. As if it had been wiped. And the photos were wiped from the SIM card.'

Jack looked at his son. 'So, they found the phone, wiped the photos, got Lena's information from it and left it where it was.'

'It looks that way. I think they dumped this guy here as a warning.'

'So they're going to come after me. Brilliant.'

'You don't have to stay here, Lena. You can come and stay at our flat,' Jack said. Miller agreed, pulling on a pair of nitrile gloves.

'Let's see if this guy has any ID on him.'

He walked inside and up to the bathroom with Kim and Jack behind him. Over to the tub, realising he had forgotten his little tub of Vicks, but soldiered on, leaning in and gently pulling the remains of the jacket open. Searched the inside pockets. Nothing. Then the trousers, finding a wallet. He carefully pulled it out. Turned to look at Kim.

'Now we know where Brian Sewell disappeared to.'

'Who?' Jack asked.

'The caretaker at the cemetery when Terry went missing. Rosie just told us he left without any forwarding address. Now, we know why; he was lying buried in the caretaker's garden. So, we have to assume whoever killed Terry, killed Brian as well. Question is, why?'

CHAPTER 40

The young girl sped past the two high schools, oblivious to the pupils making their way out of the gates. Forty-miles-an-hour, in a thirty zone.

Chris Mason sighed inwardly and put a cross in the box marked for speed. The parallax view of the speedometer from the passenger seat showed she was doing "well in excess of thirty-miles-an-hour", the technical jargon he had been taught at the training school in Cardington.

As the car drove over the Fife railway line, the girl slowed for the speed camera on the other side, showing she knew she was speeding. Over confident. It had caused her to fail her test.

In the back of the car sat Adam Stuart, Supervising Driving Examiner. Mason's nemesis. He was doing a check test, a routine all driving examiners had to go through on duty, including contract driving examiners such as Mason.

'Take the next opening on the right,' Mason said, looking out the window. The rest of the test was going through the motions, giving the girl her money's worth. The parallel parking exercise, the turn-in-the-road exercise.

The girl smiled and looked at him. 'Okay,' she said, thinking that maybe the short skirt and flirtatious smile would get her through her test. Wrong.

Mason looked in the second rear view mirror positioned on the windscreen in front of him. Stuart's face was there. The hooded eyes with the thick eyebrows. The long, greying hair, trying to make him look young and failing miserably. The beginnings of a double chin. The fine veins in his cheeks, testament to too many years enjoying life's finer beer pumps.

How Mason hated the bastard. Ever since they'd met at Cardington, the agency's national training centre near Bedford, he'd got off on the wrong foot with Stuart.

Mason had been partnered with two women, Angela Dickson and Maria Hall, both of them in their thirties, very good looking, but Maria was married. Angela wasn't. It had been a pleasure to work with them, having a laugh when they stopped for coffee, flirting outrageously, getting too close and smelling the perfume.

The course was residential over four weeks, with the option of going home at the weekend. Mason didn't bother going home at the weekend, neither did Angela.

Mason and Angela had hit it off right from the word go. After the evening meal, all the examiners would gather in the hotel bar, to relax, and swap anecdotes about the day's training.

The examiners, who were seconded from their driving test centres to be trainers for the four weeks, inevitably appeared in the hotel later on. They too had the choice of staying in the big hotel in Bedford but decided to sniff out small B&B's so they could skim off most of their living allowance.

Stuart had tried pretending he was one of the boys at first. Mason had even bought the man a drink, knowing he was going to be working at the same test centre in Edinburgh. Stuart had seemed amiable, even appearing to be quite humorous after a few pints were down his neck, but his real motive soon became apparent.

Mason had gone with Angela and a few of the other trainees to a bar just down from the hotel where there was a disco playing. It was midweek, and this was an attempt by the landlord to draw punters in to an otherwise dead evening.

Angela and Mason were having a dance, showing off like the others. 'So what's Scotland like, darlin'?' Angela asked Mason.

'Just like London, only you can breathe fresh air. I think you'd like it.'

'I know I will. I want to come up and see it for myself.' She smiled and winked at him.

Then Stuart and two of the other trainers came into the pub, the worse for wear.

'There you are,' Stuart shouted over to Mason, but he ignored the man, kept on dancing, holding Angela tight.

'Come on then, let me in,' Stuart said, trying to pull the two apart.

'Now now, Adam,' Angela said, pulling herself away from the older man.

'Angela, there's no point in trying to play hard to get.' Stuart had stood with a stupid grin on his face.

'Go home, Adam,' Mason had said. 'You've had enough.'

Suddenly the grin was gone from Stuart's face, the drink flicking his angry button. Finger pointed, eyes blazing, blood rushing through his veins. 'I'll fucking decide when I've had enough. Right?'

Mason had turned away from the man. They had resumed their dance. In each other's arms. Once again, Stuart had tried to split them up.

'I don't like being ignored,' he said, grabbing Angela's arm. Mason had wanted to grab hold of Stuart and fuck the training. Put the fucker's lights out there and then.

Angela had moved quickly despite the drink in her. Before anybody knew what had happened, Stuart's arm was up his back and he was kissing the sleeping juke box, his mouth twisted against the glass, forced to read the tracks made redundant by the disco.

Angela whispered something in his ear. Stood back. Watched him leave the pub. Smiled as the others cheered. The other trainers left.

Mason had held her, kissed her. Asked her what she had said to Stuart. She wouldn't say. He had taken her to her room that night and made love to her. Then again. Spent the rest of the night with her. Made love to her in the morning.

Mason had thought Stuart would be embarrassed by what had gone on, but the man wasn't having any of it. He pursued Angela with a vengeance but was forced to sit up and take notice when she said she wasn't interested. Stuart suspected Mason was shagging her but he couldn't prove it.

Still, there were other ways to skin a cat. Angela's marks had gone from superb to atrocious. Everything she did was wrong. Suddenly she was making mistakes whereas before she was doing everything fine. Angela had been a driving instructor before this and knew she was right. Her trainer was one of the men in the pub that night. One of Stuart's gang.

She had cried to Mason, saying they had it in for her now. The bastards were like Nazis. Even the head of training, Arnold Dayton, had her into the office at Cardington, asking her why she had gone downhill. She had started to say there was somebody who had it in for her, but Dayton had dismissed this information as trivial nonsense.

All the trainers acted as expected and closed ranks. Dayton suggested to Angela that maybe she would do better if she spent her time studying in her room at night rather than going to pubs. He reminded her that it was a pass or fail course. The implication was there.

That night in the hotel bar, Stuart was creeping about like a shadow, trying to look cool. He had approached Angela when Mason had been at the bar and asked her to go out with him. She had told him to fuck off.

Mason had breakfast with Angela the following morning. Told her he'd see her at lunchtime where they all gathered to eat their packed lunches supplied by the hotel.

It was over quicker than an execution.

Dayton called her into his office after her first practise test of the morning, knowing within herself that it had gone well. Dayton told her the trainer was very disappointed in her. He was very sorry, but she could go no further.

Her head had been spinning. She told Mason on the phone later that she could hardly concentrate on his words. Failure. Pack bags. Home.

Short and not so very sweet.

Out of the training centre, driven back to the hotel, bags packed and on her way. Mason never saw her again.

They had both known Stuart the bastard was responsible. The man was evil scum.

Now, the evil scum was sitting right behind him.

Ever since Mason had passed through the training and arrived at the test centre in Wester Hailes, Stuart had antagonised him, asking him how Angela was doing, asking if he kept in touch. Making it clear if Mason fucked up, then Stuart would be right there to jump on him from a great height.

Mason thought he might just kick Stuart's fucking head in, but decided to ignore him.

Now, he directed the girl round the rest of the test route, biding his time until he told her she had failed.

Back at the test centre now. Engine switched off. Driving instructors hovering in the background.

'Well, that's the test over.' Mason looked at the girl, keeping his face neutral. 'I'm sorry to tell you that you haven't passed your test. Would you like me to explain why?'

The girl nodded, her face not so confident now. Mason told her about the speeding, about making an arse of the *reverse round the corner* exercise. Then he got out of the car, held the door open while Stuart climbed out of the back.

Inside the test centre, the others hadn't arrived back yet. They were alone in the office. Stuart smiled at Mason, but there was no humour there, just a shark swimming around him in ever-decreasing circles.

'I told you it would happen, didn't I?' Stuart said.

Mason had sat down at his own desk, about to start writing up his report on the back of the test sheet. 'What?' he asked, not in the mood for the supervisor.

'I told you I'd be there when you fucked up. Now you just have.'

'What are you talking about?'

Stuart grinned. 'You just got a wrong result there; that should have been a pass.'

'No it shouldn't. She completely fucked her test.'

Stuart leaned in close, close enough that if Chris Mason had half a mind to, he could have broken Stuart's ugly face. 'It was a pass if I fucking said it should have been a pass.' He stood up straight. 'Did you hear the news about Angela?'

'Angela? From Cardington?'

'The same one. Silly bitch got herself run over by a bus outside King's Cross. Died instantly. So did her baby.' He sneered at Mason.

'What?'

'You fucking heard. She was three months gone, apparently. Some bastard got her knocked up. Now she's dead.'

CHAPTER 41

DS Andy Watt was standing holding a cup of coffee and talking to Sticks by the loading bay doors just inside the mortuary. 'Full house today, boss,' he said.

Miller was always waiting for the other shoe to drop when it came to Watt. The detective was in his fifties, just like DS Tam Scott, one of the old school, and sometimes he had a bad attitude. Not because he was older and only made it to DS, but because he was used to doing things a different way, back in the day.

'Who's here, Andy?'

'The Prof, Kate Murphy and lover boy himself, Jake Dagger.'

'He's getting a bit of a reputation for himself, I hear.'

'Dagger makes up rumours about himself. He couldn't pull a soldier off a hoor, never mind pull himself a girl.'

'I wouldn't know, Andy.'

'You need to get out more, boss.'

'I do just fine. Just because I don't go out on the lash with you hooligans so much these days, doesn't mean to say I'm stuck in watching TV all the time.'

Watt smirked and put out a thumb sideways when he saw Tam Scott coming along the corridor towards them. *Under the thumb.*

'What have we got here, Tam?' Miller said, as they followed Watt back along the corridor and up the stairs to the post-mortem suite.

'The prelims are in for Cindy Shields, but they haven't gone over them with me. They're waiting for you.'

Kate Murphy was standing talking with Leo Chester. Norma Banks was also there.

'Ah, Frank, good to see you.' Chester was a small man, packing extra weight that he kept promising his wife he would lose before he found himself being dissected by one of his colleagues.

'Good to see you again, Professor.' He smiled at Kate. 'Doctor.'

'Hello, Detective.'

'I wanted to be here, as things have taken a turn,' Norma said.

'They certainly have. Sometimes cadavers are like buses; none around for a while, then three come at once. Come, we'll show you.'

Miller and Scott followed the two pathologists into the autopsy suite. Chester stopped at one of the tables. He pulled back the white sheet covering a cadaver. It was completely burned. 'I'll let Kate explain. She's the one who made the connection.'

'Connection?' Miller said.

'Yes. I was examining this female, the one from the house fire in Ratho, and it would appear she was dead before the fire got hold of her. Which isn't unusual. It seems she was up in the attic, had what I suspect was a kerosene lamp, tripped, hit her head going down the stairs and broke her neck. There's no soot in her lungs, so I know for a fact she was dead by the time she got to the bottom of the stairs.'

'What connection did you find?' Miller said, his interest piqued.

'I said it appears she was dead before the fire got hold of her. Sometimes appearances can be deceptive. I took a closer look at the break in her neck. To me, this has been done by a professional, somebody trained to do this sort of thing.'

'Like a soldier?' Miller said.

'Yes. It's clean, and the way the neck was broken, is front to back, and by that, I mean her head was snapped back, the front going up sharply, and the back of the neck being compressed rapidly. This caused the break.'

'So, her head snapped back, breaking her neck, but as she was found at the bottom of the stairs, wouldn't that tie in with her falling, catching her chin, and then the momentum of her fall would cause her body weight to break her neck?'

'That would seem plausible, Frank, but when I saw that, I wanted to look closely at Terry. He too has the same cause of death. His neck is broken. And then we just got Brian Sewell in, and although we haven't done his PM yet, we looked at his neck, and his too has been broken. The injuries are exactly the same. So when we have three connected victims, I would say all three of them have been murdered.'

'Even Terry?' Miller said, his voice low.

'I'm afraid so,' Chester said, his face sombre.

Norma was still looking at Cindy's body. Then she turned to Miller. 'It would seem that it was never their intention to let Terry go.' She looked at Miller. 'And Miss Shields' death was meant to look like an accident.'

'I'm sure they knew it would be discovered that they all died the same way, but that didn't bother them. The question we have now is motive; we know why Terry died, but not Sewell or Cindy. We have a connection between Sewell and Terry though.'

'What's that?' Norma asked. Her face unnaturally pale.

'He was treated by Dr. Robert Borthwick at the Royal Scottish for PTSD. He's ex-Army. And he had an affair with Jill White, Terry's mother.'

'Where does Miss Shields fit into all of this?'

Miller looked round at the pathologists. 'Excuse us for a moment, but I need to talk to the PF alone.'

The others nodded and went about their business while Miller walked back along the corridor, Norma at his back. They went into Kate's office and Miller closed the door.

'That hospital has everything to do with this. It's the main link, but I'm not sure in what way yet. Let me tell you what I'm thinking: Sewell is in there, gets treated by Borthwick, and is released. His caseworker is Jill White, who has a relationship with him. I don't know for how long, but I'll ask her. Jill works at the Astley Ainsley, but is also connected to the Royal Scottish. If Sewell has an affair with Jill, then surely he met her son, Terry. Rosie Davidson is on the patient council at the hospital. Borthwick asks her if Sewell can apply for a job at the council. She says yes, there's nothing stopping him, in fact they encourage people with disabilities. He gets the job as caretaker in Warriston Cemetery. Terry is kidnapped. A little while later, the house burns down. Sewell vanishes. So somebody killed Terry, buried him in the basement of that house, and now we know, thanks to Lena Finn, Sewell was murdered and buried in that garden as well.'

Norma let out a breath as if all the air had gone out of her. 'Where does Cindy Shields fit into all of this?' She sat down in Kate's chair.

'Let me back-track: Louise Walker works with Cindy at White's car dealership. She is also Carl White's girlfriend. Louise has her own place, a farmhouse in Ratho. It was in her family, apparently. White asks if he can move in with her. Turns out he's broke. He doesn't own the house in Barnton, his mother does. So Louise agrees and he moves in. She has a big, walk-up attic and he puts some of his stuff up there in boxes. After a while, they split up and Louise leaves the dealership, starting up her own car business. She's still friends with Cindy, and as Cindy is looking for a new place, Louise asks if she wants to move in with her. Cindy agrees, and moves in with her stuff. Now, Louise wants Carl White to get his stuff out of her attic, and she finds a box of his and it falls apart. Inside is a V5 registration document, belonging to the little red Vauxhall Nova used by the kidnapper.'

'Wasn't that car checked out at the time?'

'Yes, it was.' Miller started pacing about the small office, feeling the adrenaline rushing through him. 'It belonged to none other than Brian Sewell. He bought it from Carl White, who sells some of the cars people trade in. Then the kidnappers stole it. Louise also found a bundle of bank notes, which she thinks is from the ransom money.'

'Did she keep hold of them to show you?'

'No. She didn't want to take them as White would know she took them.'

'So what about Cindy?'

'My theory is Louise went storming into the dealership to demand White get rid of his stuff, and we happened to be there at the time, so we witnessed it. This panicked White, and I think he wanted to get rid of her. I don't think he did the deed himself, but sent two guys round. They got it wrong, and killed Cindy, thinking they'd killed Louise.'

'I think Neil got *The Caledonian* editor to report it *is* her. Later, we can say a mistake was made.'

'Agreed.'

Norma closed her eyes briefly. 'Do you think Carl White killed his own son?

'On the day of Terry's kidnapping, he had a solid alibi.'

'That could have been manufactured.'

'So could leaving that money in a box.' Miller stopped pacing. 'Maybe somebody wanted that money to be found eventually. Cast suspicion on White.'

'What about his wife? This Jill woman? Do you think she was involved, considering she was seeing Sewell?'

'I don't know. Both of them seemed genuine, but we both know how that goes.'

'I think you should bring them in for questioning, Frank.'

'I was thinking that myself. Ask them to the station.'

'What is your gut telling you?' Norma rubbed a hand over her face, as if she hadn't slept for a week.

'If I was to put money on it, I'd say it's a smokescreen. Somebody wants us to believe White was involved. Take the heat off them.'

'Any ideas who?'

Miller gave a grim smile. 'I think Doctor Borthwick has something strange going on. I'd like to give him a talking to, but we have to tread carefully with him.'

Norma stood up so suddenly Miller wondered if she was going to lunge at him. 'No we don't. Louise Walker was meant to die last night. Some poor bugger with mental issues overheard men saying he was going to die in that place, and now we find out a psychologist was fucking a man who just happened to be a patient of Borthwick's . No, you let me make a phone call to my husband. By the time I'm finished with Doctor fucking Borthwick, he'll be picking his stethoscope out of his arse.'

CHAPTER 42

The Retreat was a small, independently owned hotel on the outskirts of Edinburgh, tucked away off Lanark Road in the shadow of the Pentlands. It was a ten-bedroom affair, with a large garden for the patrons to sit in during summer, and spectacular views of the hills.

It was the hotel's bar Adam Stuart was interested in. Just the perfect place to get a few down his neck at lunchtime without anybody knowing who he was. It wasn't as if he was staggering all over the place, and he made sure his breath didn't smell, but he managed to get a few in before heading back to Wester Hailes for the afternoon. The other examiners knew he didn't come out with them on a test after lunch, because they thought he was in the back office catching up with paperwork, and nobody complained, because nobody wanted the supervisor to come out with them. It was a win-win situation.

Sometimes, on a nice spring day, he would sit out in the beer garden and relax. By himself. He wasn't one for idle chit-chat. Some blokes could talk to anybody, but not Stuart. He preferred his own company. Besides, if he got chatting, the inevitable next question would be, *What do you do for a living?* He hated that. That question was on a par with, *How many beers can you have without falling over?* and, *How many women have you had?* Stuart couldn't be bothered with any of that nonsense. He had one friend who he drank with in his local, but even he was a wanker sometimes.

Today he sat in the cool shade of the bar, reading that morning's copy of *The Caledonian*. Reading and drinking. Just a few pints, nothing gung-ho. Although sometimes he had to admit when the taste got hold of him, he could give the beer a bloody good belting. It was always the Irish stuff he drank, Kilkenny's, because it was so smooth, it went down like water. In fact, there were times when his wife had to drive him to work, and he'd told the nosy bastards he worked with that she needed the car that day. Then she would be mad at him because she had to pick him up again.

Stuart loved his wife, but she was an executive in The Scottish National Bank. *Follow The Money!* He cringed every time he heard the jingle on the radio, or saw the advert on TV. Yes, his wife earned good money – more than he did – and if truth be told, he was jealous of her success. He felt he should have risen to at least Assistant Chief Driving Examiner by now, but some other bloke had that position. He could have applied for Sector Manager, but that meant impinging on his drinking.

Well, what would Assistant Chief Driving Examiner have done? A voice in his head asked. That would have been different. Loads more money, and he would have curtailed his drinking 'til the evenings.

Whatever. He was earning good money, which was the main thing.

He looked at his watch. Time to go. Maybe he'd take off early this afternoon. After all, he was the boss.

He climbed into his car, putting his sunglasses on. Then he started down the narrow road leading down to Juniper Green. He was just reaching for the radio button when he felt it. The bump. He was jolted forward, and his head whipped back and forward and instinct made him hit the brakes.

Shit. That's all he needed. He looked in his rear view mirror and saw a black car behind him. *Have a mint, you daft bastard,* he thought, but too late, the driver of the other car was getting out. *Keep calm, you're not pished.*

He got out and walked to the back of his car, hoping it was nothing more than a scratch. It was a light dent where the bumper had been hit.

'Oh, shit, I am so very sorry,' the woman said to him.

Stuart looked at her; late twenties, hour-glass figure, large breasts. Everything his wife wasn't.

'Don't worry. Are you alright?'

'Yes, yes, I'm fine. The sun blinded me for a second, and then boom. It was all my fault.' She spoke with an accent he guessed was somewhere in the London region. Essex probably.

Stuart looked at the damage again. He was going to lose his license, lose his job, his pension, even though she said it was her fault.

'-police?'

'I'm sorry?'

'I said, would you mind if we don't call the police? I'd rather my husband didn't find out.'

'Sure. You do have insurance though?' *Play it cool. Don't let her smell your breath, and you're home and clear.*

'Oh, yes. This is a rental and I have full insurance on it. I'll say it was my fault. I'll even sign something confirming that.'

'Sure, that would be okay.'

She ducked back inside the car, reaching for something, and he checked her out as she bent over. Tight black skirt, tight white blouse, shapely legs. Then she straightened up and came back with a pad and pen, wrote on it accepting responsibility and signed it. She showed him her license with her name and signature on it. *April Morrison.* She also wrote down details of the rental company. He gave her his details.

'I really appreciate this. If my husband found out I'd been involved in a crash, he'd never let me drive his car again.'

'We don't want that, do we?'

'I'm only here for a few days, meeting clients and drumming up some sales leads. This is the last thing I expected to happen.'

'It could happen to anybody.'

'That's very kind, Mr. Stuart.'

'Call me Adam.'

'April.'

They shook hands.

'Listen, Adam, I'm at a loose end tonight, and this is my first trip to Edinburgh. Would you let me buy you dinner? Just to say thank you for saving my skin?'

'I'd like that.'

'Do you know any good restaurants?'

'How about Torches? That's at the west end of George Street.'

'Sounds great.'

'How about I pick you up at seven at your hotel?'

'Sounds good. I'm staying at the Holiday Inn on Queensferry Road. See you then.'

Give me time to sober up a bit. Taking the afternoon off sounded good to him right then, and he made a phone call to the office.

Now all he had to figure out was what was he going to tell his wife?

CHAPTER 43

'You can't do this! I will not hear of this nonsense.'

Miller walked into The Royal Scottish and heard Robert Borthwick shouting. He was standing at the main reception desk, his face turning red with fury. A man, smaller in stature but not authority, stood in front of him.

'Oh, I can me old son, and I will.' Neil McGovern waved a piece of paper in front of the doctor.

'I don't care what warrant you have. It's no applicable in here. I'll be right onto the chief constable.'

'First of all, I'm not working under the chief constable. This warrant has been sanctioned by the Lord Advocate's office. I work for the government, not the police, and as such, I have the authority to direct any such police action I see necessary.' McGovern slapped the paper against Borthwick's chest and then turned to the teams of uniforms and detectives standing by in the lobby.

'Up you go. You've all been briefed.'

The teams moved swiftly into the hospital and once again, McGovern faced the flabbergasted doctor. 'You'll notice patient confidentiality doesn't count here. We'll be looking through files for both staff and patients.'

'You simply can't do this. I have never heard such nonsense in my life. You can't just go looking at patient's files.'

'Normally the Lord Advocate's office would agree, but we believe there's a conspiracy to commit murder here, and as such, although they are extraordinary measures, we need access to those files.'

'You are doing this completely against my will.' He looked and saw Miller coming. 'Oh, I might have known you would be behind this. First you kidnap one of my patients, then this. Well, I'll see you lose your job over this.' He took a step towards Miller.

DS Tam Scott was there, as well as the rest of Miller's team. 'Cool your jets there, Doc, or I'll have you in handcuffs, and we'll add assaulting a senior police officer to whatever else we find. *You'll* be the one who loses his job.'

Borthwick gritted his teeth but then thought better about what he was going to do and turned and walked away.

'So, the Lord Advocate approved this,' Miller said, under his breath, to

McGovern.

'Yes he did. He consulted with the Minister for Justice, and they both agreed to it. This normally wouldn't happen in a million years, but there are names in here that could lead us to young Terry's killer, and after I spoke with Shaun this morning, there are a group of them in here who want to kill him for some reason. That's good enough for me.'

They rode the lift up with Tam Scott and Andy Watt. 'Doctors think they're so far up their own arse, don't they?' Watt said. 'And don't get me started on the receptionists who work at GP's surgeries.'

'Andy narrowly missed out on being patient of the year at his own doctor's and now he's pissed off,' Miller said.

'I just hope the one you go to is a lot better than mine. I wouldn't let my doctor examine a dead dog.'

'Where do you go when you're ill then, Andy?' Scott said.

'I just grin and bear it. Then I'll go and see the old quack when I'm on my knees.'

'I usually just bribe mine with a bottle of whisky, but whatever works for you, Andy.'

'Oh, fuck off.'

'See what I have to put up with, Neil?' Miller said, as the doors opened.

'Andy's not half bad.'

Watt looked at the little Londoner as if he was taking the piss. 'That's right. I'm just misunderstood.'

'Piss off, Andy,' Scott said, as they all stepped out onto Borthwick's floor. Uniforms were filling the place, having been instructed by senior officers. McGovern walked over to a superintendent.

'Neil McGovern. I'm in charge of this operation, and Frank Miller is aiding me. If you come across anything worth looking at, give me a shout. We're going to take a look around.'

'Very good, sir,' the super said, eyeing Miller and wondering what the detective had done to get on board with a high-ranking government official.

'This thing is probably routine in Russia,' Miller said, as they walked towards the offices. Some of the nurses herded patients out and away into a common room. They asked the day patients to leave the hospital and reschedule their appointments.

'Have you spoken to Margaret White?'

'No, I've not contacted her at all. Why?'

'Nothing. She was onto the chief constable this morning, demanding her grandson back. Richard Sullivan fielded her questions, but she was threatening to have him struck off.'

'Does she have that kind of power?' he asked, as they went into an office.

'No. I spoke to the Lord Advocate myself earlier, and told him Sullivan is helping us with this investigation, and he's been a tremendous help, even though he's been under duress.'

They shut the door to Borthwick's office. The doctor was nowhere in sight. McGovern opened a filing cabinet and started flicking through the files, finding nothing of importance there.

'I've never seen Norma so angry,' Miller said, looking through another cabinet.

'She was raging down the phone at me. She said something about trained killers murdering a young woman last night in the same way as the young boy and a man who was a patient here. I was fucked if I was going to get in her way.'

After fifteen minutes of looking, they found nothing. They went back into the corridor. McGovern walked over to the superintendent again. 'Have you seen the doctor who's in charge here? Borthwick?'

'No. He didn't come up here.'

McGovern turned back to Miller. 'I wonder where he went?'

'Probably calling his own lawyer, trying to cover his arse.'

Andy Watt walked over to them. 'There's a room with a lot of files in it. We found the section listing who the patient council members are.'

'Right. Get them downstairs and back to the station. And get Borthwick. He's coming with us.'

'Nobody's seen him since we came in.'

McGovern walked over to the nurse's station. 'Can you call Doctor Borthwick for me? I need to speak to him. Tell him if he's not here in the next ten minutes, I'll have him arrested.'

The nurse looked flustered. 'Well, I'm not sure-'

'There's no need for that,' a voice said from behind McGovern. Borthwick was standing there, looking calmer now. The male nurse Miller had spoken to the night before, Brannigan, stood behind the doctor.

'Does Ross here have to come?' Borthwick indicated Brannigan.

'Not yet. Just you, Doctor.'

'Let's go then. Get this crap out the way.'

They made their way back downstairs and put Borthwick in the back of a waiting unmarked car. Miller drove him, with Scott riding shotgun. McGovern said he would meet him at the station.

****

There were different levels of interrogation rooms in the High Street, some of them small and darker, whilst other ones were brighter, for more of an informal chat.

Borthwick was in the former.

Between him and Miller sat the battle-scarred table, with nicks and grooves cut into the top, and even some graffiti on it, like an old school desk.

'This is being recorded, and your lawyer will get a copy when you leave.' Miller looked at the older man sitting next to Borthwick. Despite the fact he hadn't been charged with anything, he had requested the company of his lawyer, just in case there were any legal issues that might arise.

'You are also free to leave any time you like. We have you in here today to answer some questions for us, that's all.'

'Yes, I get it. Can we get on with this? I want my hospital to get back to normal as soon as. Some of those patients have real problems.'

'Very well. I want to ask you about a former patient of yours, Brian Sewell.'

'I can't talk about patients. You know that.'

'As we explained at the hospital, we can if that person was involved in the commission of a crime, or is believed to have been involved and is now deceased. Mental Health Scotland Act, twenty-ten. It was all part of the *Care in the Community* deal, remember?'

Borthwick made a display of taking a deep breath and letting it out, as if he was doing this under what amounted to, in his mind, torture. 'Brian was an infantry soldier. He served in Afghanistan and Iraq. The troop carrier he was riding in blew up after it hit a roadside bomb. Brian's nerves were shot after that. He served out the rest of his career in a hospital in England, although the mental scars were worse than the physical ones.

'He came up to Edinburgh because of family. His father lived here, but a couple of months after moving, his father died, adding to Brian's PTSD. He came to see me. He was admitted for a little while, where he felt secure and safe, and gradually, he was put on a day programme. That's when Jill White interacted with him. She integrated him. We both signed off on him as being fit to enter society again.'

'Was he cured?'

'There's no such thing as being cured, Detective. He was better prepared for the outside world, and we gave him a mental toolbox, as we like to call it, so whenever he came across a situation he didn't think he could handle, he could mentally reach into his toolbox and tackle the issue.'

'Did he give the impression he was fit to handle stress in the outside world again?'

'I wouldn't have signed off on him if I didn't think so. In fact, he wouldn't have been sent to work with Jill White until I thought he could make it on his own.'

Miller looked down at his notes, pretending he was reading. Then he looked at Borthwick. 'We think he was involved in Terry White's kidnapping.'

Borthwick didn't move for a moment, and Miller could see the mental wheels grinding in the doctor's head. 'I wouldn't know anything about that.'

'How often did you see him after he was released?'

'Not often. Jill was his liaison person. If he had a problem, she would deal with it, but if that problem became something more, then she would have come to me, and I could have had Brian admitted to the hospital again.'

'Just like you had Shaun Foxall readmitted?' Another quick change of pace. Miller watched the man's eyes, could almost see into his head to see how his thought process was working. Borthwick was digesting the question and formulating the answer before converting it to speech.

'Don't you think that was a good idea since he was shooting at you and your officers with a pistol?'

Answering a question with a question, buying himself time. Miller ignored it. 'There's one thing that's bothering us; Rosie Davidson was sent emails, supposedly by Shaun, but the account they were sent from was made up, on a public Wi-Fi, which is untraceable. The gun he had was a starting pistol. He told us he thought he was playing a game. How do you suppose he was able to conjure up an email account while sitting on a bus? Where did he get the gun and who are the people who told him he was playing a real-life game?'

Borthwick's face started going red. 'How the bloody hell do I know?'

'He's a patient at your hospital, Doctor. That's how I would expect you to know.' Miller kept his voice even, to make Borthwick's outburst look even worse.

'I know nothing about him getting hold of a gun.'

The lawyer sat forward. 'This is starting to sound like an interrogation, Detective.'

'Is it? I'm merely asking the doctor some questions about his patient.'

'Fuck it,' Borthwick said, suddenly standing and sliding his chair back with the back of his legs. Tam Scott jumped up, hoping there was going to be a fight, but nothing came of it.

'What's wrong, Doctor?' Miller said, remaining calm.

'Fuck you. You come belting into my hospital with your Nazi storm troopers and that little squirt, take things away and start barking orders at everyone. Well, no more. I'm answering nothing more and I want those boxes of files back this afternoon.'

'That's not going to happen. We have the warrant, which we executed and they will be returned to you, I can assure you of that, but after they've been gone through.' *And that little squirt could do so much damage to your internal organs, the trauma surgeon would think they'd been put through a blender.*

Miller stopped the interview and signed the tape, giving the copy to the lawyer. Then they both left.

McGovern walked into the room. 'Little squirt?' He had been behind the one-way mirror that was on the wall behind Borthwick.

'I told you people call you names behind your back.'

McGovern smiled. 'As long as you don't, is all that matters. I would hate to have to tell my daughter bad things about you.'

'She wouldn't believe you, McGovern.'

'Never underestimate a little girl's love for her daddy. Flesh and blood trumps every time.'

Miller laughed. 'And you could always have me taken to a little island in the Forth and have somebody talk to me?'

'What kind of accusation is that?' McGovern had a smirk on his face. 'Besides, we have abandoned airfields in the middle of England for that.'

Miller closed the file he had on the table and picked it up. 'Did you hear all of that?'

'Of course I did. He's full of shit.'

'Did you notice one thing, though?'

'What's that?' McGovern said.

'He wasn't surprised that Brian Sewell was dead.'

CHAPTER 44

Miller decided to go and see Jill White with Kim. He was feeling hungry, as they travelled to the hospital, having missed lunch. Jill was taking a class until two pm, and she would see them then.

'You hungry?' he asked Kim, as they drove up Bruntsfield.

'Yes, I am. Any suggestions?'

The chippie was near the King's Theatre at Tollcross, on the way to the hospital. Fish and chips, wrapped in brown paper. It was such a simple meal, but Miller knew how much he would miss it if he ever went to live anywhere else in the world. They parked the car and sat in Bruntsfield Links, finding an unoccupied bench. The sun was out and there was no breeze. They sat in the shadow of a tree.

'I know I've been diddling about on the issue of us moving in together, and I'm sorry about that, love, but it's not been easy.'

Kim reached a hand out and put it over his. 'I know. And it's even harder now they've found Terry. I do understand, and I don't want to push you away by going on about it. I'm prepared to wait.' She smiled at him, and he saw something there that he hadn't seen in a woman's eyes for a long time; true love.

'I've dealt with it, Kim. Now I want to start making plans. Talk things over; see what would be the best thing to do. I mean, Emm's at school down in Stockbridge, so would it be better if you moved in with me and Jack? Would that be wise, knowing it wouldn't be the three of us, but Grandpa Jack being there too? Or should I come and live at your place? How would all that work-'

'Frank, honey, we don't need to decide this afternoon. We have all summer to think about things. Just relax.'

Miller ate some fish, thought briefly about Carol, wondering what she would think about another woman living with him in their apartment. *There you go, thinking she's still alive. She would be happy that you're happy.* 'I know, I started rattling there.'

Kim laughed and ate some of her own fish. 'Life's what we make it, Frank. We can go through it feeling happy, or we can go through it feeling sad.' She looked at him. 'Don't take this the wrong way, but do I wish my marriage had worked? Of course I do. Who wants to have a young child and get divorced?

Nobody plans for that. I would have liked to have had a stable relationship, but Eric going away all the time and me not knowing if he was coming back, well, it did a number on me. I know it's a cliché, but that was what happened. I didn't meet anybody, I didn't stop loving him, I just thought my brain was going to explode. I got help, but by then, the answer was to walk away from it.'

'Eric must have taken it badly.'

'Eric's trained in a different way from most soldiers, so he kept it hidden, but yes, he took it hard. He loves his little girl, but he moved on, and now he's happy again, and they're expecting a little boy. I wish him all the best and hope his new wife can deal with it better than I could.'

He looked at her. 'Yet, knowing what I do about you, about the job you do and how you faced danger all the time, I would find it hard to believe you couldn't cope with all that.'

'It happens to the best of us. It was a dark period in my life, but I got things sorted. I don't feel that way anymore.'

Miller ate a few chips, and then felt his appetite suddenly fall away. 'Here's a question for you; what if you decided you wanted to be a stay-at-home mum one day, and I was going out to work, would it get on top of you do you think? Worrying about me when I was at work?'

'No. I mean, of course I would worry, but as I said, I learned to deal with it, Frank.'

He nodded and looked away, towards Arthur's Seat in the distance. *If she can deal with it now, couldn't she go back to Eric? If Eric dumped his new wife? Of course she could, but she's not going to.*

He smiled, leaned over and kissed her on the cheek. 'I do love you, Kim.'

'I love you too.' She scrunched up the paper and looked at her watch. 'Come on, let's go. Jill White will be champing at the bit.'

They drove up to the hospital making small talk, neither of them touching on the subject of moving in together again. Miller didn't want to think about it. Just the very idea made his guts feel as if he had been stabbed with an ice pick.

****

'So. You came to tell me you caught my son's killer?' Jill White had a whole new demeanour about her. *Combative* was the word he would have used if asked to sum her up.

'We were hoping you might have some information about that,' Kim said, pulling up a chair.

They were in the large room again, but this time the branches outside the window were still, as if they were holding their breath, waiting for the punchline, before leaping into the air and giving each other a high-five.

'What do you mean? You think I'm a suspect? That I would kill my own son?' She looked at Miller with a disgusted expression on her face.

'We're not saying that, Jill. We do want to talk about Brian Sewell though.'

Jill's shoulders seemed to slump. 'Oh yes, Brian. He was one of my patients.'

'He was also your lover, isn't that right?' Kim said.

'What? No, of course not. Who told you that? Oh let me guess; big mouth Carl.'

Miller said. 'We're not here to point fingers, but we do need to know all about him.'

'Brian was a patient of mine, not a love interest. If you listen to Carl long enough, he'll fill your head full of broken glass.'

'What can you tell us about Brian?'

'Why? Did you trace him?'

Miller locked eyes with Kim before answering. 'We found him, Jill. He's dead.'

Jill licked her lips and looked down, fighting back tears. 'How did he die?'

'We're not sure yet,' Miller lied, 'but he was discovered in a house near South Queensferry.'

Jill looked puzzled. 'Was he living with somebody?'

'No, we believe he was murdered.'

'Oh my God. No. Not Brian. No, I don't believe it.' Her hand went to her mouth and in that instant, Miller knew she hadn't killed Sewell. He'd interviewed dozens of killers, and every detective got a feel for somebody's reactions, and this wasn't the reaction of a killer.

Tears started streaming down Jill's cheeks.

'We're trying to trace his last movements. Who was the last to see him alive around the time of his death.'

'It wasn't me. I haven't seen Brian for years.'

That confirmed it for Miller, unless Jill was a brilliant actor, which he doubted. 'Brian's been dead for years, Jill. He was buried in the same place as Terry, in the garden by the caretaker's cottage.'

'What? He's been dead all this time?'

'We believe he was murdered and placed there.'

'I thought you said he was found in a house?' She looked at Miller, and then it dawned on her. 'Oh, no, don't tell me...'

'I'm afraid so. His killer dug him up and put him in somebody's house. As a warning, we think.'

All the air went out of her and her head slumped forward, touching her chest, and Miller thought for a moment that she had fainted, expecting to jump out of his chair and catch her falling body, but then she suddenly snapped her head up, her eyes bright.

'I want you to catch the bastard who did this. Brian and I weren't lovers, Detective Miller, we were more than that.'

'In what way?'

She sniffed back her tears. 'I've never met such a kind man in my life. He had problems, sure he did, but he overcame them. He was so gentle, and after all the things he'd seen in war, he could have gone off the rails and stayed there, but he didn't. With our help, Borthwick and me, we got him back on his feet. For the first time, I saw the man behind the mask. He got the caretaker's job, and was getting back on his feet. I even trusted him enough to introduce him to my son.'

'He met Terry?'

'Yes. Terry thought he was brilliant.'

'Was he ever alone with Terry?' Kim asked.

'What are you getting at?' There was fire in Jill's eyes now.

'It's a simple question, Jill. It's just something we need to know.'

Jill's breathing was fast as if her body was preparing to go into fight mode. 'Once or twice. Why? He didn't touch Terry, if that's what you're thinking.'

'We're just trying to build a picture, that's all, Jill,' Miller said, in a placating tone.

'I trusted him. He might have had mental health issues, but he was a great man.'

'When was the last time you saw Brian?' Miller asked.

Jill thought about it. 'Things weren't easy when Terry was taken. Brian was the one who was there for me, unlike Carl. Brian comforted me, while Carl told me to pull myself together. I wanted to go and see him in the house in the cemetery, but he said no, the press were hounding me, and they might take it the wrong way. So he and I would meet up at the Royal Scottish. Nobody even gave that a second thought. He was a former patient who came back for help. It wasn't on anybody's radar. Not even Carl's as far as I knew. Then Margaret White caught us in an embrace one day, while we were in a private office. She excused herself, and didn't mention it to me, but she told Carl. He brought it up to me one day when we were arguing. I told him it was nothing. That Brian gave me a hug because he was grateful for my help. I persuaded him it wouldn't be ethical for me to get involved with a patient, and then I got angry, saying he was one to talk. He backed off after that, but I don't know if he ever believed me or not. And since you're here, I guess he didn't.'

'So the last time you saw him was...?' Miller said, repeating his question.

'It wasn't long after Terry was taken. The house caught on fire. It was a chip pan left on the cooker, the fire investigator said. Brian must have put it on and forgotten about it.'

'Did they think he set it on fire deliberately, since he wasn't there?' Kim said.

'They might have, but the investigator was told about Brian's mental health issues, and they didn't pursue it. They marked it as an accident.' She looked at Miller. 'Did he die after the fire?'

'That's the theory we're working on. In fact, we don't even know if he caused the fire. It might have been set to make it look like Brian was responsible, even if it *was* an accident, and nobody would question why somebody with mental health issues would leave.'

'All this time, I thought he had gone, forgotten about me, and here he was, buried in the ground.'

'Do you know anybody who would want to harm him?'

'Brian didn't have any enemies, as far as I know. He had a few select friends, and they even made a point of coming to the hospital to visit him.'

Miller's eyes shifted to Kim's for just the briefest of moments before turning back to Jill. 'Who are these friends, Jill?'

'I don't know. I saw him coming out of a room one time over at the Royal Scottish, and there were other men in there. I saw the backs of two men, but there were others in there. I could hear them laughing and talking. I asked Brian who they were and he said they were just some mates of his from his Army days.'

The big room suddenly felt stifling, as if all the air had been sucked out of it. 'Did Carl know these men?' Kim asked.

'I don't think so. If he did, he didn't say, but he wasn't in the Army, so it would be unlikely.'

'Have you seen these men recently?'

'No, I didn't see them again.'

'If anything comes up, can you please give us a call?' Miller said.

'I will.'

They all stood.

'I'm here for you if you need me,' Miller said. 'Kim too, if you want a shoulder to cry on. And if Carl bothers you, let me know and I'll have a talk with him.'

'If he bothers me, Davie will have a talk with him.'

'Who's Davie?'

'Davie Raeburn. He's a friend of mine. He had a lot to do with Brian's recovery too, but more in a social way. With Davie, what you see is what you get. He's such a nice guy. He's been there for me over the past couple of years. He's very protective towards me, and that feels good after what I went through with Carl.'

'Can you tell me his address?'

'I don't have it. We don't socialise, just see each other sometimes when he's at the hospital.'

'How did he know Brian?'

Jill looked at him. 'They were in the Army together.'

CHAPTER 45

'Here he comes; Postman Pat.' One of the young assistants on the second floor thought she was a comedian, and every day would announce Davie Raeburn's arrival for the two o'clock pick up.

'I think I might have heard that one before,' Raeburn said, with a smile. *Grit your teeth. Let it wash over you.*

'See that's the thing, Raeburn, you're not paid to think. That's why you work down in the mailroom.'

'Janice, really,' the department boss said, an old matronly woman who barely managed to garner any respect herself.

'Just telling it like it is,' Janice said, walking up to Raeburn as he put the mail from his cart into the individual department slots. 'Tell me, I've heard that men who are,' she lifted her fingers and made air quotes, '*special*, are well hung. Is that true?'

'Oh, I'm sure you've been out with more than your fair share of *special* men to answer that question yourself, Janice.'

Some of the people in the department let out a laugh. Overhearing the remark in the open plan office, other adjoining departments joined in.

'Just give me the mail,' she said, snatching the envelopes out of his hand. She stormed away to her own desk.

'Pub after work, Davie?' one of the department guys asked.

'Not tonight, I have to take the missus to yoga, or some other such crap. Somewhere that she jumps about and sweats a lot.'

'Haha. Okay, mate, but defo next week, right?'

'You got it, big man.' Raeburn walked away with his cart, heading for the next mail station. *Why did fuckers like Janice even get to breathe God's fresh air?* He wondered, as he rounded the corner.

'Ah, just the man I've been waiting for.'

Oh, fuck. 'Caitlin, light of my life. How can I do you? I mean, what can I do you for?'

She giggled and covered her mouth. 'Saucy. My mother told me about men like you.'

'Handsome. Debonair. Witty. Charming. Your mother was a very astute woman, let me tell you.'

'How awful you are.' Caitlin giggled again. 'Anyway, my boss is sending two boxes of stationery over to New York for a conference. Can you deal with that?'

'Hey, if I was any more super, I'd be wearing my underpants over my trousers, know what I'm saying? Of course I can handle that. I'll just call FedEx, they'll pop round, pick it up, and then Bob's your Aunt Fanny.'

Caitlin started laughing again. 'You really need to come out with us more often, Davie. How about tomorrow night after work? Your wife wouldn't mind, would she?'

'I'll tell her I'm going, and that'll be the end of it. I'll say to her, *I'm going out with the crew at work, and if you don't like it, then you know what you can do.* Then I'll hang up on her.'

Caitlin let out a cackle again. 'You're so funny, Davie.'

'It's working with you that keeps me off the bridge, Cait.' He winked at her. 'Now, just you let me know when you want those boxes picked up and I'll drop everything and come running. Well, not everything, you understand.' He looked down at his trousers.

Caitlin went away giggling, hardly able to contain herself.

It didn't do any harm to let them think he was married. He'd bought the ring in a pawn shop for a few notes. It wasn't flashy, just a cheap band of gold, but some women liked shagging married men. First, some just wanted a wee fling, and a married man offered that opportunity. Secondly, they could trust a married man, not like some single loser who still lived with his mother and secretly watched Sponge Bob on a Saturday morning. Not that he himself lived with his mother or watched cartoons, but the ring had helped him pick up some married women. Even single women like Caitlin could be up for a bit of fun. He knew exactly which buttons to push.

Raeburn finished the rest of his round, picking up the outgoing mail, and depositing the last of the incoming for that round. The bulk of the mail came in from Royal Mail at seven in the morning, but the internal mail was dropped off and picked up several times a day. It kept them busy. The mailroom comprised two supervisors and three mail staff, and it didn't take a degree in rocket science to see who worked the hardest.

Tom Hardy, one of the supervisors, was on the phone when Raeburn went back down to the mailroom. 'Yes, he's just come in the door now. I'll ask him.' Hardy put a hand over the mouthpiece and looked at Raeburn. 'Can you stay late tonight? We have a package coming in by special courier. It won't be here until about eight or so. I'll make sure you get taken care of for doing it.'

'Yes, of course I can.'

'He said yes. Okay, I'll talk to you later.' He hung up and looked at

Raeburn.

'Good lad. I would have stayed myself, but you know how it is. One of my daughters is sick, and the wife's knackered, so I have to go home and take over for a while.'

'No problem, Tom. Only happy to help.' *Sick daughter, that's a new one. Probably going to one of those wank clubs, where you pay a fortune for a drink, then even more dosh to have some manky fanny sit on your lap and grease up your fly while you have to keep your hands to yourself in case a bouncer breaks them. Tom Hardy, The Scottish National Bank's resident pervert.*

'You're one of the good guys in here.'

I fucking bet I am. Nobody else would put up with your pish. 'That's good of you to say so, m'man.'

'Don't think this will be forgotten when it's time to offer out supervisor posts. I'll make sure you're given one. You can count on it.'

I'd rather put a bullet through my fucking brain, Raeburn thought. *Or yours.*

****

Paddy Gibb stood in front of the white board, pacing back and forward, looking like, as Andy Watt put it, a demented leprechaun. Not to his face though.

'Right, we've got all this collated, so I want to see notes being taken. Got that?'

A mumble rumbled through the room. Miller stood near an open window at the back, trying desperately to feel a draft, any little draft, but the trouble with this old building was, it was freezing in winter and roasting in summer. Kim stood beside him, hardly sweating at all.

It's mind over matter, she said.

No it's not, he had started to argue, but then he saw her smile and knew he wouldn't win, so he just shrugged and moved closer to the window.

'Right. So we have Brian Sewell in the mortuary right now. He was the caretaker at Warriston Cemetery when young Terry was kidnapped, and then the house caught on fire and burnt down. Chip pan fire. Only now, we know he was murdered, and buried in the garden, when everybody thought he'd pissed off somewhere. He had been under the care of Jill White, and she too thought he had just upped and left. Sewell had bought a car from Jill's husband, at one of the offshoot dealerships he has, and that car was subsequently stolen and used in the delivery of the ransom money as per the kidnapper's instructions to our late colleague, Carol Miller. White was a person of interest back then, but he had an alibi for the day Terry went missing. Any questions so far?'

Nobody said anything.

'Okay then, moving on. Terry's body is uncovered by a demolition team. Then the same night, a pair of men dig up another body from the same location. Turns out to be Brian Sewell. They were spotted by *The Evening Post* crime editor, Lena Finn, and they then left Sewell for her to find in her bath. We think it was a warning to her; *we know who you are.*'

'How did they know where she lived?' one of the younger detectives asked.

'She dropped her phone, and when she went back to look for it, it was still there, but they'd tampered with it, and found her address on it, she thinks from a receipt sent in an email, which could be read from her phone.'

Gibb ran a cotton hanky over his forehead. 'Last night, our boys were busy, and I mean the two jokers who dug up Sewell. Before going to the cemetery after dark, they went to Louise Walker's house. She used to date Carl White; he lived with her, and put some of his crap up in her attic, a big, walk-up affair, apparently. So they split up, and Louise goes to the dealership he owns and tells him to move his shit. Miller was there with some of the team and witnessed it. As she's moving some of the boxes herself, one falls open and the registration document for Brian Sewell's car is in there, and a bundle of money, which we believe is from the ransom money.

'We think by going to the dealership, Louise alerted White. He was well pished last night, and we tracked him on the council's CCTV, so he really was at the pubs he said he was at, around the time he said he was, which means he couldn't have been out at Ratho setting fire to Louise Walker's house. However, he could have sent two men to do it. They obviously don't know what Louise looks like, because they killed her housemate, Cindy Shields, who also works at White's dealership.'

'How do you know there were two of them at the house?'

'We got local CCTV and it shows two men in a grey van driving away from the direction of the house. We ran the plates and they're false, so we're pretty sure these are our two guys. We didn't get a clear picture of them however. The two men chased her, but she hid and then she saw them leaving.'

Tam Scott put his hand up from near the front. 'Do we think these two guys are the kidnappers?'

'We're not sure yet, Tam, but it's looking likely that they were involved somehow. We want to know why Sewell was killed. And if they killed Cindy thinking it was Louise, then we know they are thoroughly ruthless and will go to any lengths to cover their tracks.'

'So there's still the possibility Carl White is involved in his son's kidnapping,' Miller said. 'We spoke to him, and to be honest, I personally don't believe he was, but I'm not discounting it. He might just be clever enough to cover his tracks, and make sure he had an alibi for every time he needed one, including the day Terry was taken.'

'How about Jill White?' Scott asked. 'She was involved with a guy who was in charge of the very place where her son was found.'

'Again, we're keeping an open mind about her, although she says she wasn't romantically involved with Sewell like Carl White thought she was. I tend to believe her.'

'As for today's jaunt to the Royal Scottish,' Gibb said, getting all eyes on the front of the room, 'we took every name from the patient council, and drafted some of our colleagues in Gayfield Square CID to check them out. There are twenty-eight members of the council. All of them checked out. They come from all walks of life, and we concentrated on the males, as Shaun Foxall said he heard men saying they were going to kill him. That narrowed it down. So we checked out the eight members who were at the hospital when Foxall was taken there last night, five of them men. We tracked them down, and have since discounted them. Two are in their sixties, one in his fifties who happens to be a minister in the church, and the other two are a no-go. One is disabled and walks with a stick, which in itself doesn't mean anything, and the other guy has been personally vouched for by Jill White, a guy named Davie Raeburn. She's known him for years. None of them have a connection to each other. Subject to further background checks, we've discounted them. So that means, whoever Foxall overheard, weren't at the hospital on official business.'

'Then what were they doing there?' Scott asked.

'Listen to Frank's theory.'

Everybody in the room looked at Miller.

'I think Robert Borthwick is up to his neck in this. I think he has some of his friends round to the hospital. Nobody asks questions, because he runs the place as head doctor. These men are known to him. It just so happens that Shaun saw them before, or one of them, and now they want to get rid of him. They think he saw or heard something. So they concocted an elaborate plan to get him back to the hospital, by making us think he was extorting money from Rosie Davidson, who is also on the patient council. Then they could take their time over the next week to make his death look like an accident.

'There are four killers going in and out of that hospital unnoticed. And that's where they all meet. We just don't know who they are yet.'

'So we keep our eyes on Borthwick. We have him tailed and he'll be followed everywhere.'

'No can do,' Gibb said. 'His lawyer's already made a complaint to Dennis Friendly, who is now saying we've put Borthwick through enough. If we find anything concrete on him, then fair enough, but until such times, feel free to follow him if you want your next promotion to be a lollipop man.'

'If these guys are just walking into the hospital unannounced, then we won't know when he meets them,' Scott said.

'It's the best we can do, Tam. Sooner or later they'll slip up. Andrew Borthwick could walk along Princes Street with a machine gun and nobody's going to blink an eye. It's almost as if he has a free pass.'

CHAPTER 46

'Torches, eh? I'm impressed,' April said, as the waiter handed her a menu. 'Do you bring your wife here, or just your girlfriends?' She gave a little laugh and her eyes sparkled, having fun with him.

'Neither. I reserve it for beautiful women who run into my car,' Adam Stuart said. 'So, this is your first time in Edinburgh?'

The waiter brought the sparkling water April ordered and a glass of wine for Stuart.

'It is. I'm usually down south all the time, going as far as Reading, or Milton Keynes. Just wherever my boss drums up leads.'

'What sort of business are you in?' He clinked glasses with her and looked at the expensive blouse she had put on. Or maybe it was from Marks and Sparks, he couldn't really tell, but it *looked* expensive, and that was what counted. Nice red skirt, bit of red lippy, just the right amount of eye shadow that hinted at sophistication, not trashy.

'Diaries.'

'I beg your pardon?' Stuart thought he'd misheard for a moment.

'I'm a travelling sales person for a diary company.'

'Interesting,' Stuart said, hoping his voice didn't betray the surprise in his voice, a tone that said her job was anything *but* interesting. 'So you have a lot of dates, then?'

'Not really. I'm married-'

'It was a joke,' Stuart said, interrupting her. 'Dates, diaries. I know, I can't believe that came out of my mouth.'

'Oh, now I get it.' She laughed, and Stuart was hoping his fake-o-meter was working tonight, as she really didn't seem to be faking her laugh. She could be faking something else later on tonight if she liked, he didn't care about that, but he liked it when women genuinely thought he was funny. Most of the time he was.

'Isn't this a quiet time for diary companies?' he asked.

'No, this is the *busiest* time. We have to get all the orders in for the companies who want personalised diaries, so we can get them all printed and ready for shipping by December. There's a lot goes into the production.'

'Oh, that makes sense,' Stuart said.

'So, what do you do, Adam?'

This was the hard part, the *let's get this lie off my chest* time, *and see if it lands without me taking a beamer.* He'd practised many times, especially at Cardington where he'd used his wit and charm on unsuspecting female candidates. But sometimes a woman could see right through things, and if he thought she had, he'd probably take a beamer.

'I'm an accounts executive with a bank.'

'Really? That sounds exciting.'

She smiled at him. And he could tell she had taken it in. Now, if she pushed him further, which they sometimes did, he had already planned out the lie in greater detail. It helped that it was one he'd used before, and he kept polishing it, refining it the way somebody might refine an oil painting they weren't happy with. This one was certainly a Van Gogh, whereas sometimes they were Edward Hoppers. He'd even known them to be Andy Warhol's when he'd had too much to drink.

'It means I'm in charge of a department, and we deal with overseas clients. I really can't go into too much detail, just as a matter of privacy, you understand.' Brilliant. He had slipped in there that he wasn't some dummy, that he must be earning a few notes if he was in charge of a department, and he added the *Please don't ask me any more questions* clause, just in case he did slip up. Of course, he had more on the subject, if the female he was with turned out to be a pushy cow, but April seemed to be all right with his answer.

'Sounds all very secret agent,' she said, drinking more of the water.

'Not at all, just clerical stuff.'

'How many people work under you, then?'

Shit. Plan B! Plan B!

The waiter came along and asked if they were ready to order. They were, and Stuart rattled off his usual; Steak, rare. He thought April was a bit too sophisticated to hear his *Just cut off the horns and wipe its arse* quip, so *Rare* it was.

'You don't want to hear about my boring job,' he said to her, indicating for the waiter to bring more drinks, which he did.

'I like you, Adam. It's nice to have a friendly face to talk to when I'm on the road, but to be honest, most of the time, I have a McDonald's and sit in my hotel room watching Corrie.'

'Nothing wrong with a bit of drama.'

'What about you? What do you normally do for a bit of fun?'

'Just go out for a few pints with my mates.'

'Don't you go out much with your wife?'

'We've been married that long it's nice to get out away from her sometimes.'

'I know the feeling. My husband likes to go out with his mates, and I'm glad. We're celebrating twenty years next year. I told him I would have been out of prison by now, if I'd knifed him.' April laughed again, to show she was just joking.

'Won't your husband be expecting you to phone him tonight?' Stuart asked.

'Not likely. He's away playing golf with his mates in Spain.'

Oh yeah, Shagaluf. Once Stuart thought he might take up golf, just to get away from his wife, but his handicap was, he couldn't hit the ball in a straight line. He'd given up the idea and sold his clubs quicker than he'd bought them.

The lies flowed more easily the way the wine did, but Stuart was careful how much he had. He didn't want to have to resort to a little blue pill if things were looking like they were going in that direction. Wine was fine, but he wanted to watch his intake. April didn't seem to need the wine to have a good time.

A couple of hours later, she called the waiter over for the bill, and brought her purse out.

'No, April, this is on me,' Stuart said, not making a beeline for his wallet any time soon.

'Adam, don't be silly, I said this was on me tonight. For keeping this between ourselves. I insist.' Before any more arguments could take place, she had put the card in the plastic wallet the waiter had left with them, and he had swooped in to take it away before either of the customers got an idea to do a runner.

After everything was paid for, Stuart saw his night ending with him watching a rerun of the X-Files or maybe he'd put on a *Family Guy* DVD, a show his wife hated. The very idea of a talking dog and a swearing toddler. Better than the highbrow stuff she watched, he thought. He could imagine Stewie walking up to the doors of Downton Abbey, and his dog running in ahead of him, the sound of *Brian, come here you bastard!* echoing round the great reception hall.

'What's so funny?' April asked him, smiling.

'Just thinking about how we met this afternoon,' he said, notching up another lie to his mental bedpost.

'We could go and get a drink if you like, or...'

'Or?'

'Or we could maybe have a nightcap in my hotel room.' She was wearing a light jacket now, as the temperature had dropped a little, even though it was still light out.

'I'd like to go to your hotel. I'm really enjoying your company, and it would be nice to spend a little more time with you.'

John Carson

It wasn't that far to walk on a nice summer's evening, but Stuart knew he'd be needing CPR by the time he got to the hotel, and it was best if he saved what little energy he still had left. He'd already cut back on the booze, skipped the dessert and brushed his teeth with his finger in the toilets, so he reckoned he was good to go. He hailed a taxi, and all but told the taxi driver to *get the fucking boot down* as he sat back with April.

He sighed with relief as she made the first move. There was going to be no diddling about as they got to reception, no, *Should we get a nightcap* and him wondering if he had gotten the wrong signals and was about to get a slap in front of witnesses. April kissed him on the lips and made the appropriate noises as the driver got them up the road to her hotel in record time.

Stuart gave him a big tip and April giggled as she walked into the reception and got her key. Stuart hovered round the lift doors and they made it up to the fourth floor.

He thought he might start slowly, build up his prowess, but April had other ideas, and started stripping him off as soon as he had closed the door. She knew how to manipulate a man, and there was no need for his *In case of emergency, pull the handle* little blue friend.

April did things to him that his wife would have divorced him for if he'd even suggested they try, and she kept the momentum going. They lay side-by-side with only a side light on, and she had held him, until a little while later, she got him going again.

After an hour, he was spent. He was running through all the one-liners he'd used in the past on how to exit without it seeming as if he'd only come here for sex, when April gave him his way out.

'I know you must have to be up for work tomorrow, and I have a long drive in the morning, so if you want to go, that's fine.'

'I hate to run.'

'It's fine. I had a great night.'

'Me too.' He dressed quickly whilst trying not to show he was enthusiastic about leaving, and April had pulled on a bathrobe that had been hanging in her bathroom. She pulled him close and kissed him.

He left, and neither one of them asked for the other's phone number.

When Stuart had gone, April got dressed quickly. The mirrored wardrobe door opened silently on its tracks.

'Did you get it?' she asked the man who stepped out, holding the small video camera.

'Oh yes, it was perfect.'

'Good. Now I'll take my payment, and you can do your own thing. As long as you didn't get my face.'

'Some of the time I did, but I'll get our guy to edit those parts out.' He pulled an envelope out of his pocket and handed it over. 'Good job as usual.'

'Thanks.'

'So, what were you tonight?'

'A travelling salesperson.'

He smiled. 'Somebody's got to be, I guess.'

The woman who wasn't April Morrison walked out of the hotel room and paid her bill with the same fake credit card she'd paid for dinner with.

CHAPTER 47

Miller rang the doorbell and put his hands into his pockets, trying to get them deeper into the coat. He hunched his shoulders against the cold as rain rattled down on him. Wind rushed through the bushes in the garden like an intruder.

Summer in Scotland. Sunny one minute, pissing down the next. They don't mention this in the tourist brochures.

The house he was standing at was a semi-detached, with a well-kept front garden. This was Fox Covert, in a part of Corstorphine that sat in the shadow of Corstorphine Hill and the zoo next to it. Miller remembered getting a call years back when a wallaby had escaped from the zoo and a bus driver had reported a kangaroo running about on the road.

The rest of the afternoon had gone by in a blur. Dinner had been an uneventful affair, with Miller trying not to talk shop and failing miserably. Jack was going for a drink with his new friend, Samantha, and Miller had been up and down from his armchair, unable to settle. Then he got the phone call.

'Frank, it's George.' The voice was older, sounding a little frailer, but still instantly recognisable.

'Hey, George, how are things going?'

'I was wondering, if you had a minute, could you pop round?'

'Yeah, I could do that. What night were you thinking of?'

'Tonight, son. It's about Terry White.'

He had picked up his lightweight jacket and then the rain had started splattering the windows. He took a lightweight waterproof instead. Now the sky was filled with rain and it was overflowing. The outside light came on and he took a deep breath as if expecting the occupant of the house to lay a punch on him, bracing himself for what was to come.

The door opened inwards and an old man stood looking out at the figure standing on his doorstep, his eyes searching the face for a clue.

'How are you doing, George?' Miller swallowed hard as his eyes found the old man's. They were old, the fleshy hoods of his eyebrows coming together to form a question, as if he'd forgotten Miller was coming round.

Then it came to him.

'Frank?' The voice gravely from too many smokes.

Miller nodded.

'Come away in, son.'

Miller stepped into the hallway of George West's house. *Or Detective Chief Superintendent George West, as he was known back then.* He could smell the booze on the old man's breath.

The white painted walls brightened up the hallway. Small prints hung on them like blemishes on a perfect face.

'In you go,' West said, after closing the front door. Miller walked into the living room where a real fire burned away in the fireplace. The rain had brought with it a cold wind. *Four seasons in one day, that was Edinburgh.*

Miller wasn't usually stuck for an answer but he had difficulty forming the words he knew had to be spoken. 'How have things been, George?' he said at last, sitting down on the settee. The fire crackled and spat in the intervening silence.

The old man sat in a chair opposite and Miller could see *The Edinburgh Evening Post* folded in half sitting on the other chair. That night's headlines looked back at him.

'I don't get out so much now, Frank. The joints are just that bit tight for dancing. You know how it is.'

Miller nodded. How could he know how it was? He didn't want to think about getting old. Not this way at least. On his own.

'Would you like a drink, son?'

'Not for me, George, I'm driving.'

The old man pushed up out of his chair and went over to the old display cabinet sitting in the corner of the room. The glass shelves that used to show off ornaments now held only glasses and bottles of booze.

The TV was on but muted. A soap played out its storyline behind a screen that had seen better days. This room had been painted white as well; it was cheaper to get a man in to slap on a bit of emulsion than having every room different he assumed.

West poured himself a measure of Bell's. 'Here's to us,' he said, saluting with his glass as he sat back down. Miller silently saluted with a nod of his head.

'How's Jack these days? Enjoying retirement?'

'He's great. He and retirement are suited just fine. He's got a new lady friend just now, but they're just friends.'

'Aren't they all?'

'He only met her yesterday, but they seem to have clicked. She's a crime writer.'

'Really? What's her name?'

'Samantha Willis.'

His eyebrows raised as if they were alive. He put his drink on a side table next to his chair and reached over the other side, raking about in a magazine rack for a moment, moving magazines out of the way until he found what he was looking for; a dog-eared copy of *Out For Justice.* 'I like this guy, DI Callahan. I thought the name was a bit Hollywood for an Edinburgh detective, but he kicks arse and I like that.' West held up the copy for Miller to see. 'You read any of her stuff?'

'Not yet, but I will. I don't read much these days.'

West was looking at the cover again, ignoring his guest. Miller thought the older man must be in his early sixties now, and he didn't know where the time had gone. He was the head of CID when Miller started out as a wet-behind-the-ears detective.

'Here, take this one. I'm done with it. I read a lot these days. Nothing else to do with my time except get pished and read books.' West handed the book over. 'Who would have thought it? Jack Miller going out with a writer.'

'I don't know if they're going out, George,' Miller said, putting the paperback into his jacket pocket.

West waved away Miller's denial and smiled. 'This is Jack Miller we're talking about. I've had a few beers with him in the past two years since he retired. I know what he's like. He's what, fifty-five now?'

'Just turned fifty-six.'

'Good for him. He needs to have a good time while he's still here. I'm sixty-two now, and just buried three of my old muckers from the old days, all in the space of two months. Two heart attacks and one from natural causes. Poor bastard went to bed one night and didn't get up. Dropping like flies, we are. I'm fucking scared to go to sleep. I'm glad for Jack. Get it while you can. I wouldn't mind stepping out with a young thing myself. Bit of dancing, bite to eat and then give her a good seeing to.'

Miller thought the unsuspecting female who agreed to *step out* with George was in for a big surprise. No waiting for the third date with him. Maybe he didn't think his heart would last until the third date.

'You said you wanted to see me about Terry White?' Miller said, at last, when it was obvious the conversation was going to flag.

West nodded. 'Was there any sign my little boy Peter could be found in the cemetery?' he asked.

'No. Not so far, George. I don't want to give you false hope. They're still looking but we don't think there's a link between your son and Terry.'

'His name's Peter, Frank. You can say his name out loud.'

Miller noticed the older man used the present tense, as if he would never give up the idea that his son was still alive and out there somewhere.

'I will let you know if we find Peter. I'll come and tell you personally, I promise.'

'Nobody's looking for my little boy anymore because it happened such a long time ago.'

Miller didn't have an answer, because he knew West's words rang true; nobody was looking for the boy anymore.

'You know, Frank, there isn't a day goes by that I don't speak to him. I hear his voice in my head all the time. The way I remember him the last time I left the house to go on duty. He was eating breakfast.

'If I'd known I wouldn't see him again, I would have held him so tightly and told him I loved him, but I didn't, because I thought I'd see him at dinner time. You never know what's round the corner. Do you know what I mean, Frank?'

'I do, George: I gave Carol a hug in the back car park, and watched her drive up through the tunnel to the High Street not knowing that was the last time I'd ever see her alive.'

'Of course you do. I forgot there for a minute. Sorry, son.'

'It's okay, George.'

'He would have been forty-two now.' West swallowed the rest of his whisky and got up to pour another. Adding a little water this time and sat back down. 'That wasn't the only reason I asked you round, Frank. To talk about Peter. I did say it was about young Terry.'

'Okay.' Miller sat looking at the older man who looked far older than his years.

'I have a theory, Frank, one I've had for a couple of years now. Ever since Terry was taken.'

'What's that?'

'You haven't heard it, have you? My theory?'

Miller wondered if his old boss was actually all there, if the trauma of losing his son many years before had done something to his mind. 'No, I haven't.'

'I knew it. They didn't take me seriously, at the time, but I've been thinking more about the Terry White case.'

Miller sighed inwardly. This happened a lot with retired detectives; they couldn't let the job go, and were always coming up with a theory, how they could solve the crime now. He thought this was going to be one of those deals now.

'What's your theory then, George?'

'I'm not saying Peter's kidnapping was in any way linked to Terry White's. Of course it wasn't. The man who took him was caught and died a long time ago. It's just that the M.O. is similar, as if Peter's disappearance was a blueprint for Terry's. Like they do reconstructions on TV of a murder or something. That re-enactment is almost the same as the real thing, and that's what they were going for. It was almost as if Terry's kidnapping was a re-enactment of Peter's.'

Miller had to admit if he was at the station and somebody walked in off the street and started talking like this, he would dismiss them. After Terry was taken, they had had more than their fair share of nutters calling and coming into the station, with all sorts of stories and claims to be the kidnapper. George was borderline, but since he used to be one of the best cops he knew, he was going to hear him out.

'Go on, I'm listening.'

'I told them, this is more than similar: the boy is taken; the money is asked for, although in my case, it was only a few grand; a female cop is asked to do the ransom drop and he claims to know her; she gets bounced from pub to pub.'

'What pubs did he use?'

'The White House. The Grey Horse Inn. Bouncing her between pubs, then getting her to dump her police radio. Then getting her into another car. There weren't mobile phones then, so the lassie was working blind. He told her to go out of the pub and make her way to a blue Vauxhall. When she hung up the phone, she radioed this information in. Then she dropped her radio into the wastebasket. At least they would know what car she was in.

'When she got to the car, there was a note on the windscreen, directing her to a red Ford Cortina round the corner. The keys were on one of the tyres. Inside, there was a note telling her where to take the money. To a pub down Leith. When she got there, she got a call on the payphone in the pub. He told her where to go to pick up her next car. She called it in. When she got outside, looking for a car, she was bundled into the back of a van. She was tied up, driven away before her colleagues got there, and the van went into the docks. He bundled her out and took the money. He didn't harm her, just left her there. She was found by a security company doing a patrol later on. We went mad, not knowing where she was. We thought he'd killed her. But he just took the money. And I never got my son back.' He looked Miller in the eyes. 'Now do you see the similarity?'

Miller was fully awake now; hanging on West's every word. 'Now, the kidnapper was eventually caught, and he died in prison, isn't that right?'

'That's right. They're not connected, but as I said, I think somebody used that blueprint to take Terry.'

Miller had to admit West was making sense. 'The thing is, George, and I'm playing Devil's Advocate here, even if it was similar, how would that have helped Terry's kidnappers?'

'I'm not saying it would have helped them. That's not my point, Frank. Some similarities in there were never published in the papers. Like the young WPC having to dump her radio, and him making her take a different car from the pub from the one she went in. That's never been released. At least, I've never read about it.'

'So what are you saying?' Miller asked, but he knew damn well, what West was getting at.

'I'm saying, whoever was involved in Terry's kidnapping, had inside information.'

Miller sat back, taking a breath in through his nose and letting it out slowly. 'You're suggesting he's one of us.'

'I'm not suggesting it; I'm saying it. You've got a dirty cop working with you now. They thought they'd got all the dirt bags who were taking back-handers, but one slipped through the cracks.'

'Who did you tell your theory to, when Terry first went missing three years ago?' Miller asked.

But in his gut, he knew who George West had gone to. And he was right.

CHAPTER 48

The rain spattered the windscreen of the car like blood from a murder victim. It was coming down heavy now, just as anybody who lived in Edinburgh would expect.

Miller drove the car away from George West's house, and chose to go up and over Clermiston Road, towards St. John's Road. It had been a while since he had been in Corstorphine. One of Carol's favourite pastimes was raking about in charity shops, which the main drag had. He especially liked going in and finding a book that was in decent shape and was neither dog-eared nor yellowed. Unlike the paperback he'd put on the passenger seat.

Out For Justice. It wasn't the first in the series of detective novels Samantha Willis had written, and although she said on her website you didn't need to read them in order, he liked to start a series from book one. Especially when there were recurring characters. Some writers knew how to develop their characters, allowing them to follow a natural arc, like getting married, having kids, doing normal stuff as well as solving crimes. Other writers should take up gardening for a living, he thought as he stopped at the lights at the bottom of the hill, waiting to turn left.

He wondered how real the books would be. He'd read somewhere that some readers wanted perfection when reading a police procedural. Miller didn't want that. If he wanted to read exactly how to run a murder investigation, he'd go back to reading the police manuals. He wanted to be entertained when he was reading a book. He didn't know how to defuse a nuclear bomb, and if a writer was describing how it was done in a book, and it was bullshit, then as long as it sounded as if he knew what he was writing about, then that was good enough.

He turned when the light changed and headed towards Haymarket.

He turned the radio on. A station was playing oldies. *Every Day. Steve Hackett.* Miller was a Genesis fan. Ever since he put the radio on one day and a Genesis track was playing. He'd bought all their stuff and always had a CD ready to take to the car. Except tonight of course.

He knew he was thinking about other things when he really should be thinking about George West's thoughts; *Gary Davidson kidnapped Terry White.*

Maybe not on his own, but that bastard had a hand in it.

As soon as West had said he had gone to somebody at the time of Terry's kidnapping, Miller knew in his heart it was Gary. He hadn't thought it before. Before Gary had died and told Miller he had taken the ransom money, Miller hadn't thought Gary had been involved. Now he was certain. He had to get back to the station and check through the files. He also knew Jack would remember that night. He too had been on the team. Carol's father, Det Sup Harry Davidson had led the team, while Jack had been DCI. Gary was a DI just like Miller. Carol was the DS who had been told by the kidnapper to deliver the money. Five members of one family in the police force who were dealing with the kidnapping, and one of them was a double-crossing little bastard who had gone behind everybody's back and was in on the whole thing.

Didn't you already suspect though, Frank? When Shaun Foxall said Gary was a bad man?

Maybe in his subconscious he felt Gary might be more involved than he was prepared to believe. But West was a retired detective, and although he might not be the sharpest pin in the box right now, he had been a bloody good detective when he was on the force.

He used the Bluetooth connection in the car to call his father.

'You busy, Jack?'

He heard background noise from his father's phone. 'I am, actually.'

'What are you doing?'

'I'm having a refreshment with a lady friend.'

'Refreshment? Lady friend? You mean you're in the pub with Samantha.'

'Hey, can't a man have a wee refreshment now and again?'

'Stop calling it that.'

'It's better than saying I'm having a wee swally.'

'I need your help, Jack.'

Miller heard his father talking to somebody – Samantha he presumed – before Jack came back on the line. 'Fuck me, Son, is this some kind of conspiracy? This lassie will be getting a complex. It seems every time I ask her out for a drink, I get a phone call.'

Roseburn flashed by, Murrayfield rugby stadium lit up in the background, the rain sizzling past the spotlights. 'I knew you were after more.'

'That's it, make me sound like some fucking deviant. We're just neighbours having a drink in the pub.'

'I think it's past that, don't you?'

'It might be for you, you dirty-minded little sod. I knew I should have skelped your arse more when you were wee.'

'I'm a red-blooded man just like you, big man.'

'Try and have some respect for your father for once in your life.'

'Anyway, as I said, I need your help.'

'As much as I hate to say it, I need you to bugger off.'

Miller liked having a banter with his father, but there were times when he really did need his help. 'It's about Terry White, Dad. I think I know who one of his kidnappers was.'

Silence for a moment, except for the background noise. 'What do you need?'

'I need you to meet me in the station.'

Silence again. 'Okay, but Sam comes with me.'

'Fine. I'll make sure you both get access.'

'You owe me a pint.'

'Love you too, Dad.' Miller hung up, and hit the blues and twos. If he knew his father, he'd have taken Samantha to The Rebel or Logie Bairds. A quick pint then back to her place. He laughed inwardly. He was giving his father a bad rap. If anything, Jack was a gentleman. He'd always treated his wife – Miller's mother – with respect, and as far as he knew, hadn't cheated on her.

He blew through Haymarket, the traffic parting for him, slipping past a tram as it made its way into the city centre, Gary Davidson back on his mind.

****

Jack Miller hung up his phone and put the infernal thing back into his pocket. 'Just my boy,' he said, walking back to the table.

'What time do you have to go?' Samantha asked him.

Jack could feel his cheeks going red. 'Everybody needs me, when it suits them.'

'Don't worry about it. You go if you need to go.'

'*We're* going.'

Samantha looked puzzled. 'Where?'

'Frank said he needs my help on the case they're working on just now, and he wants me to meet him at the station. Like I would just drop everything. I told him if I come, it'll be with you. He said fine. So, would you like a brief tour of my old workplace? Although I'm sure you've seen the inside of an Edinburgh police station before.'

Samantha laughed. 'I'd love to. And yes, I've had a tour of the West End station before. Where Jimmy Callahan is based.'

'The High Street is much better than the West End. We used to knock seven bells out of them at the darts night.'

'Not just a pretty face, then.'

'I have many hidden talents, my dear. Some of which I may, or may not, reveal to you.'

'Man of mystery. I like it.'

Logie Bairds was busy, filled with office workers who had congregated to celebrate pay day, or maybe just because it was Thursday.

'I need to go and use the facilities before we walk up the road,' Jack said.

'I'll be here.'

The toilets were downstairs, in what were probably vaults or something a long time ago. Jack walked down and used the Gents. He was the only one in the room and was washing his hands when a man came in and stood barring the door.

Jack turned to leave and instinct kicked in. If this guy was a mugger, he'd chosen to be in the wrong place at the wrong time. However, Jack was prepared to give him the benefit of the doubt.

'Excuse me, mate.'

The man gave a humourless grin and nodded his head up and down slightly, as if he was the only one privy to an unspoken joke. 'Oh, I don't think we're going to be mates.'

Jack sized him up in only a few seconds: aged around forty or so, bulky but not fat, like he worked out; around six two, three inches shorter than Jack; a nose that had been broken before; eyes that were sharp and didn't flinch. He was holding a cigarette. He took a drag and blew the smoke in Jack's face.

He had met many men like this joker over a good many years, and hadn't ever backed down to any of them. Not one time.

'Son, I'm only going to tell you this one time: move your arse.'

'I'm only going to tell you this once as well, old man; stay away from my missus.'

Samantha's husband.

'I'm prepared to forget this ever happened,' Jack said.

'I don't give a fuck what you're prepared to do.' He stuck the cigarette in his mouth and grabbed Jack by the front of the shirt. 'I see I'm going to have to teach you a little lesson.' The cigarette bobbed up and down as he spoke around it.

Jack had spent too many years dealing with pond life to walk away. Besides, as soon as the guy grabbed the front of his shirt, he went into auto pilot. He'd seen too many men lying on the pathologist's slab to want to be one of them.

His left arm came up and over both of the man's arms and his right hand came round from the other side, grabbing the cigarette and shoving it up the man's nose. Jack then squeezed the nostrils shut.

The man let out a scream as if he was dying, let Jack's shirt go, and then Jack slapped him across the face with a cupped hand. Hard enough to make it sting, and take it like it was meant to be taken; as a little warning.

Ralph fell back against the door, still screaming. Jack leaned down and pulled the man's hair, moving his face close to his assailant's.

'If you don't know who I am by now, you'd better find out. But if I were you, I'd piss off and not come back. You want a war with me, you got it, but remember one thing; I have a big Army behind me. We're not constrained by rules and regulations anymore, boy. Take a fucking telling. You got that?'

Ralph nodded.

'And if I hear you've been bothering Samantha, then you and I will be having another wee chat. No witnesses, just like this, only next time, you won't be walking away from it.'

He walked out and back upstairs, where Samantha was just finishing her drink. 'Everything okay?' she asked.

'Yes, I'm fine. Why?' He smiled at her.

'You just seem a bit flustered, that's all.'

'My damn zipper jammed. I thought I was going to come up here with my barn door open.'

She laughed at him. 'Come on, Mr. Detective, show me your police station.'

They grabbed their coats, and walked out into the rain.

CHAPTER 49

The bank had been chosen not only because of its location, but because of the type of sorting it did. The Scottish National Bank wanted to prove to the other big national banks that it was better in every way, certainly more convenient for the customer.

That's why some of their branches, called Neighbourhood Branches, stayed open until eight o'clock on a Thursday evening. The branch in Morningside was also a business hub. *We mean business!* was the slogan they used to attract commercial customers, and so far, it was working.

At a time when other major banks were closing branches left and right, The Scottish National was going in the opposite direction, attracting customers, taking more of the market share and keeping the shareholders happy.

The Morningside branch was doing big business. The manager made sure the staff were on top of customer service, treating people like they were human and not just another number.

In the basement was a small sorting office, sorting coins by denomination, and machines counting notes into bundles, all ready for the pick up on Friday morning.

Except tomorrow, there would be nothing to pick up.

The four men stood in the small staff canteen along the corridor from the sorting room. They had parked their van - complete with new plates - in the small car park, and slipped in unnoticed through the back basement window.

Many years before, when the branch had been a very large house for a local merchant, iron bars had been added to the outside of the basement windows for security.

The night before, Number Three and Number Four had come along and cut through the bars, putting them back in place with black duct tape, which wouldn't be noticed from the outside, unless somebody looked closely.

Thursday night had gone like clockwork. Pull in with the van, the driver fiddling about with papers in the front to make it look as if he was sorting things out before they went in, his long hair wig in place. The magnetic sign on the side advertising that the van belonged to a building company. Should anybody call it, they would get a voicemail telling them they were closed and to call back in the morning. That's what throwaway phones were for. So far, nobody had called, but so far, they hadn't turned this bank over. You could never over-plan something.

Number Four cleared his throat for a second. Although they were all wearing balaclavas, Three looked over at him, and his eyes showed the anger in there. He didn't have to use any words. *No fucking noise.* Four looked away.

Three wasn't their main leader, but he was the team leader tonight, and nobody argued. Three walked past them all, looking them up and down. Nothing was showing except their eyes, and what little of their faces that did show, was starting to sweat. They had already pulled the masks down, but luckily, this building had air conditioning.

'The bank is now closed,' he whispered. 'They'll be down shortly. We know what we have to do.'

The other two nodded. They waited patiently until they heard the voices approaching, footsteps coming down the stone steps, into what was once probably the servant's quarters. There should be six. They heard the first two come down.

This room was in darkness, and though it was light outside, there were no windows in here. If anybody went into the room they had entered through, they would be dealt with. The belting rain outside making it seem unnaturally dark anyway.

Three held up one gloved hand. Four fingers. That meant there were still four of them upstairs. Dealing with customers? They would wait for a few more minutes. Waiting was something they were good at. Two and Three had spent time in an Army unit that specialised in waiting, poised to strike like a cobra. They had patience in spades. Number Four didn't have their training, but they would make sure he didn't jump the gun.

Two more set of footsteps. They waited for the next two but they didn't come. That meant only four had come down so far, leaving two upstairs. They couldn't wait any longer.

They each held their sawn-off shotgun at their side. Three closed his eyes for a brief moment, and in his mind's eye he was back in another country, in a different time. He missed those times so badly. This helped to make up for things.

He opened his eyes. Nodded once. *Let's do this.*

****

Davie Raeburn looked at his watch again, maybe for the fourth or fifth time in the last few minutes and walked along to the marketing department. The security guard who was on duty would be on until ten when the relief guard came on to do the night shift.

'Hey, Davie, how's things, my friend?'

'Not so bad, Willie.'

'You're working late tonight. You not got a home to go to?'

'We're expecting some stuff coming in, but the courier won't be here until about eight. Make sure you keep your eyes peeled on those screens of yours.'

'Captain Monitor, that's what they call me.' Willie smiled.

'I thought they called you Shagger? Because of all the women who're after you in here.'

'What? Away with yourself.'

'Seriously, mate. Take the manager in marketing. I overheard her talking about you just the other day. You forget that I'm walking about here, invisible.'

Willie shoved another doughnut in his mouth. 'Really? That woman who wears those big earrings?'

Raeburn pointed a finger. 'That's her. She recently got out of a messy relationship, and her pal asks her if that put her off men. Manager says, no, but she'd like to meet somebody like that sweet guy Willie in security.'

Willie wiped the back of his mouth. 'Really?' He stood up.

'Really. I heard it for myself.' Raeburn walked further in to the small control room, a bank of monitors in front of a control desk, and servers blinking away on the left hand side, status lights for alarms changing in each area as staff moved from one section of a building to another.

One server controlled the alarms for the branches. Morningside was still green. The branch was still open. The light would go red when the branch closed and the manager put the code in to secure the building.

'That would be great. I'd love to go out with her.' Then Willie looked puzzled for a moment. 'She never talks to me though, Davie. She's never shown any interest.'

'As I said, big man, she was in a relationship. He was a cheater or something. She doesn't want to give up men though, so now she's in the market for a new boyfriend.'

Willie pulled himself up to his full height and tugged on his belt. 'And you really think she would go for me?'

'Heard it with my own ears.'

Willie picked up his travel mug and finished off the coffee inside, wiped his mouth with the back of his hand and burped. 'I could just imagine giving her one. I bet she squeals like a pig.'

I bet you'd squeal like a pig if I kicked you in the fucking nuts. 'That's another thing I heard when I was-'

'Eavesdropping?'

'Doing my rounds.'

'What did you hear?'

If you'd stop interrupting you disgusting twat, I'd get round to it. Raeburn looked around conspiratorially. 'I heard she likes a good workout.'

Willie pursed his lips together and pointed them out, as if he was imagining what she was like naked. 'I wonder what she would do to me?'

Probably give you a heart attack. 'Only one way to find out; ask her out.'

'I don't know, Davie.'

'Or I could put in a good word for you.'

'You would do that?'

'I certainly would, my friend. Now, any chance of a coffee and we'll talk strategy?' he looked at the clock. Almost seven forty-five.

'Sure. You can use Tony's mug.'

Slavering Tony? No thanks. 'That's too big, Willie. I'll be peeing all night if I drink that much. Just a wee mug if you have one.'

'I've got one here. Let me go and wash it out.'

'What about this lot?' Raeburn indicated to the monitors.

'This job does itself. Nothing will go wrong. I'll be away for two minutes. You can keep an eye on it for me.'

'That I will, my friend,' Raeburn said. He sat down and looked at the inactivity on the monitors.

Willie came back, drying the inside of the mug with a paper towel. 'Anything happen while I was gone?'

'I just saw a bunch of strippers walking about in reception, calling out your name.'

Willie let out a dirty laugh. 'Oh barleys, I wish.' He poured Raeburn a coffee from the pot sitting on the coffee maker. 'Milk?'

'I only take it black, my friend.' He accepted the mug from Willie and watched as the guard drank the coffee.

'So, how do I get this manager interested in me, Davie?'

'Chat to her. Nothing over the top, just a little small talk, introduce a bit of banter, make her laugh.'

'I'll make her more than laugh.'

Raeburn wanted to punch the man in the face. How any woman would look at him beggared belief.

For the next few minutes, Raeburn listened to Willie describe his previous conquests in great detail. *If that courier doesn't arrive in the next few minutes, I'll stab myself in the fucking eye with a Biro.*

'Oh, shit,' Willie said, clutching his stomach.

'What's wrong, Willie?'

'Oh, my stomach. Too many fucking doughnuts again. My stomach's acting all weird, Davie.'

'You alright? Your face has gone all red.'

'Oh, man, I think my stomach's going to explode.' He jumped up. 'Watch the monitors, Davie, there's a good lad.' Willie moved with great speed down the corridor.

The men's bathroom door squeaked open again a few minutes later. 'Holy crap,' Willie said, as he came into the control room. 'If you'll pardon the pun.'

Jesus. 'You okay?'

'I'm fine. It just happens now and again when I overeat. I'll be fine. And then Raeburn heard Willie's stomach growl. 'Oh fuck, here we go again.' Once again, the guard got up and rushed down the corridor.

'Davie!'

Raeburn turned at the sound of the female voice. *Oh shit.* Caitlin was walking along the marketing department, past the empty cubicle farm, heading in his direction. She was smiling and waving, a little unsteady on her feet.

Raeburn moved up out of his seat as quickly as he could without making it look like he wasn't pleased to see her.

'Caitlin! What are you doing back here?' the fake charming smile was in place.

'I've come to see you, Davie. Where's the other bloke?'

'If you mean the security guard, he's just stepped away to use the toilet for a minute. He won't be pleased to see you hanging around here after hours.' Raeburn smelled the drink on her breath, and noticed her slurred words. God in Heaven, this was all he needed.

'I work here. And I'll tell him I've come to see my friend, the one and only Davie Raeburn. Three cheers for Davie Raeburn! Hip hip!'

Raeburn gently put a hand on her arm before she could get out the *Hooray!* 'Come on now, Caitlin, let's get you out of here.' He walked over to the lift and pressed the button. *How did she get up here? The other lift on the other side of the building?*

Caitlin shrugged off his arm. 'I want to be with you, Davie.' She fumbled around in her handbag and brought out a condom. 'We can find somewhere quiet. I know you want me as much as I want you.'

'My wife would kill us both, honey,' he said. That was another good reason to pretend you were married; it was a get-out excuse for situations exactly like this.

'She'll never find out.'

Famous last words. Many a man should have the words engraved on his tombstone: *She found out.*

'I love the idea of being with you, and to be honest, I respect you too much to do this here.'

'Oh, pish.'

Okay, Plan B. 'I was going to ask you out when we went for a drink tomorrow night. Ask you to go out on a date with me, but if that's not what you want...'

'Oh, Davie, that's exactly what I want.' She stood looking at him, swaying slightly on her feet.

'So, I'll see you tomorrow then?'

'Oh, I'm going to be sick.'

As foreplay goes, it needs a little bit brushing up, Caitlin.

She tried putting the condom back in her handbag but the bag fell onto the floor, scattering the contents.

The lift arrived and dinged as the doors slid open. 'Go to the toilet and I'll pick up your stuff,' Raeburn said. *And fucking hurry up before Casanova gets back from the toilet or he'll have you bent over that console before you can say "Ride 'em cowboy".*

'You're a love,' Caitlin said, running along the same corridor Willie had run along, going right into the Ladies.

Raeburn put all the crap back into her bag, left it sitting on a desk and went back into the control room. Almost eight o'clock; where was the package? He didn't want to be here all night.

Caitlin came back out a few minutes later, her face white and her eyes red, giving her best *I don't really want a man to fancy me* look.

Raeburn handed her a plastic cup of water he'd poured for her. 'You'll get dehydrated otherwise.'

'Thanks, Davie, you're a love,' she said, drinking the water.

'You should go home. Get an early night so you're fresh for tomorrow.'

'You're right. You're a love, Davie. Let me pee first.' She staggered back along the corridor.

Willie eventually came back out of the toilet and walked up the corridor, groaning. He almost staggered into the control room. 'Fuck me.'

No thanks. 'Here, Willie, take this cup of water.'

'Water? Is there a wee nip in there?'

'Ha. No, my friend, but if you've just had what I think you've just had, then you'll get dehydrated. That can prove fatal.'

'Jeez, Davie, way to give a man a heart attack.'

Raeburn watched as the heavy security guard drank it down. 'I hate drinking water.' He held out the cup for Raeburn to take. Raeburn took it, and felt like ramming it down the security guard's throat. He tossed it into a bin nearby.

Then Willie looked at the monitors. 'Anything come up?'

'Just my lottery numbers, I hope.' Raeburn laughed, and clapped a hand on Willie's shoulder.

Willie swung round again, looking at his watch. 'You're one of the better guys who work here, Davie.'

'Nice to be appreciated, Willie.'

'Us lackeys have to stick together.'

Speak for your fucking self. 'That's true. Fanfare for the common man.'

'Exactly. You know that wanker in Legal?'

'Which one?'

Willie laughed. 'Oh, jeez, I have to go again.'

Raeburn didn't have time to tell him Caitlin was in the toilets.

CHAPTER 50

Nothing changes much, Jack thought, as he walked into the public reception of his old station. It was too hot in summer, and the small area felt claustrophobic.

The desk sergeant buzzed them through and Jack led the way along the back corridor.

'I can just imagine all the ghosts that live here,' Samantha said, as they started climbing the stairs, their footsteps echoing upwards.

'There's enough ghoulies here already,' Jack said, laughing.

'You're so bad, Jack Miller.'

'And proud of it,' he said, winking at her. Past the second level on the way up to the third, where the offices were, Jack suddenly stopped, thinking maybe he should tell Samantha about the confrontation he'd had with her husband.

Samantha looked at him before leaning forward and kissing him. Then she pulled away. 'Oh, God, I'm sorry. I don't normally kiss men I've just met.'

Jack smiled. 'That's good to hear. He kissed her back.

'You make me feel like a teenager sneaking out to meet up with the local bad boy,' she said, as they made their way onto level three.

They walked along the corridor and he opened the door to the investigation suite.

The main office was deserted, and Jack automatically looked over at the white board and saw Terry White's face looking back at him. Carol's too.

'She was very pretty,' Samantha said, nodding towards Carol's photo. Underneath her photo, somebody had written her name in red marker.

'I certainly thought so,' Miller said, coming into the room from his office.

'Hello again, Frank.'

'Hi, Samantha.'

'Call me Sam.'

He took the paperback that George West had given him out of his pocket. 'Can you sign this? An old copper friend gave it to me earlier.'

'I'd love to.' She took the proffered pen and signed the fly page. Handed it back. 'I hope you enjoy it.'

'I'm sure I will, but I want to start with the first one.'

'Good choice.'

'So what's so important, Son?' Jack asked.

Miller sat at a desk and indicated for his two visitors to do the same. 'George West had a theory about Terry's kidnapping.'

'Old George West?' Jack said. 'I haven't seen that old codger in ages. Last I heard he was losing his marbles.'

'Who told you that?'

Jack shrugged. 'Just one of the lads.'

'Maybe if that lad went round and visited the poor old bugger, he'd see for himself that George is just a sad, lonely old man.' Miller felt anger rising up but quelled it.

'I'm not disrespecting him, I'm just going by what somebody said, that's all.'

'Who's George?' Samantha asked.

Miller looked at her. 'He was my first boss when I became a detective. He was good at his job, but very bitter. Somebody kidnapped his little boy a long time ago. Before I was even born. They got the guy, but didn't get George's son back. They never did.'

'So what's his theory, Son?' Jack rocked back in the chair.

'He reckoned somebody used little Peter's kidnapping as a template to kidnap Terry White. There were a lot of coincidences, right down to bouncing a female cop from pub to pub. However, as far as we know, Peter's kidnapper was working alone, or if he wasn't, then it was never proved he had an accomplice.'

'That's interesting, but it doesn't prove anything.'

'This is just a theory, remember? So back when Terry was kidnapped, George had friends here who were still working, and although things were kept out of the press, he knew what was going on. And that's when it hit him, and he came up with his theory. And he went to talk to somebody in Serious Crimes. Gary Davidson.'

Jack stopped rocking and sat up straight. 'What did Davidson say to him?'

'That's just the thing; he said nothing. He didn't get back to George, and since George was head of CID at one time, he's no fool. That raised his suspicion level high. If Gary had sat down and gone through the theory with him, then maybe George would have thought nothing of it, but it was almost as if Gary was giving him the brush-off. Not the same way we do when we get the nutters coming out of the woodwork to confess to murders, but in a *yeah, whatever,* way.'

'It was a bad time for us all after Carol died, Son. She was Gary's sister after all.'

'I know that, Dad, but don't you think Gary would want to do everything he possibly could to get the kidnappers?'

'He stole the ransom money, remember. Maybe he just wanted it to all go away.'

'Maybe, but let's look at some facts; we know there was more than one kidnapper working this, because of the logistics.'

'We don't know for sure, but that was *our* theory.'

'Right, but let's assume there were a few of them. More than one anyway. We take the fact that Gary was at the hospital where Shaun Foxall said he heard men threatening to kill him. Put two-and-two together. Gary was working with those same men at the hospital. He was protecting not only himself, but those men.'

'It seems that the hospital is the centre of everything,' Samantha said.

Miller sat back in his own chair. 'We went through the records, and all the volunteers on the patient council are accounted for. So the hospital is the meeting place for these men.'

'And that means Robert Borthwick knows a lot more than he's letting on. There's only one way he'd let those guys in there; if he knew them.'

'You're right.' Miller stood up. 'Borthwick not only knows who they are, but he's one of them.'

CHAPTER 51

'Scream and you're fucking dead!' Two said, as they moved into the room with practised ease, pointing their guns at the bank workers. Four of them. Three women, one man.

An older woman's eyes went wide, and Two saw she was going to scream. He could read her eyes, and see the large intake of breath, ready to blow it back out with a scream. It was a natural reaction with some people, out of fear and confusion, but mainly fear.

He stepped forward quickly, and hit her on the side of the jaw with the gun barrel as hard as he could and she fell to the floor with a thump, dead to the world.

'Please don't hurt us,' one of the other women said, her bottom lip trembling.

Four stepped forward, brandishing his own shotgun. 'Nobody needs to get hurt. We just want the money. The sooner you give it to us, the sooner we get out of here. The sooner you can all go home.'

The young male banker glared at Four. 'We've seen the movies, pal. You're going to shoot us anyway.'

Two stepped forward and rammed the barrels into his gut. 'Well, if we do, I'll make sure you go first.'

Then he saw the fight go out of his eyes. Saw the shoulders slump slightly. Game over. 'Get the moneybags and start filling. You've got five minutes. If anybody tries to be a hero, you all die. Makes no odds to us. We just want the money. You lot getting out of here alive is your choice. Now move!'

They walked across to another room round a short corridor. There was a steel door barring their way, but one of the women hit the keypad and they all heard the door unlock.

In the main banking hall, where business deposits were made, the cash was put into a cylinder and then into a vacuum pipe running below the counter, each cylinder ending up in a large bin on wheels in this vault, where it would then be counted in a secure environment before being added to the lower main vault.

'Take all the paper crap out of those tubes and put the money in the bags,' Two said. They watched as the clerks bagged the money, throwing the deposit slips aside, sometimes fumbling the money. One dropped a small bundle and bent to pick it up.

'Leave it! Keep bagging,' Two said, lifting the gun higher. He turned to Four. 'Go and check on that woman. Make sure she's still breathing.'

Four left the room and walked along the short corridor, his shotgun by his side. He was sweating with the mask on, but felt he would be sweating more if he was standing in the dock in the High Court. He turned the corner and into the room where the group had gathered.

The woman was gone.

****

One and Three made their way up the stairs stealthily. Three moved with the silence of a shadow while One was quiet, but not as whisper quiet as his colleague. Three took the lead and remained in this position as they silently appeared in the banking hall from a doorway behind the main counter.

The bank was large, having been converted from a huge house back in the sixties, the ceiling adorned with elaborate cornices. It might have been a pleasant place to be in had it been the lobby of a hotel in the south of France, but such as it was, they didn't have time to notice the architecture.

What Three did notice was the wooden shutters that had been closed over the windows, a safety precaution brought in before the robberies had started. They didn't want prying eyes seeing workers still in the bank after closing hours.

'You two, do as you're fucking well told and nobody dies. Got it?' Three walked forward with the shotgun held at waist level, pointing it at the manager and the assistant. The final two members of staff, making the total six, which they had expected.

The manager gasped and his eyes went wide. The assistant held up his hands, his mouth dropping open.

'Right then, now we've established that, get through the back and start filling bags with money. Wrong move, you fucking die.' He swung his own shotgun about in an attempt to scare both men, succeeding with each swing.

The two bank employees moved slowly at first, but then walked faster when Three shoved his gun into the manager's back.

The back vault was large and the huge steel door open, but sitting behind a set of steel bars that had to be unlocked.

His hand shaking, the manager eventually unlocked the bars and they swung open, revealing the room inside.

'Get inside and start fucking bagging,' Three ordered. The two managers did as they were told, grabbed some bank bags, and started filling them from the drawers that held the cash from the day's takings.

Three looked at his watch. It was approaching five past eight, and he knew the call would be coming through shortly. 'You, get that fucking door locked. Make it look like the bank is empty and you're doing what you normally do on a Thursday night. And I know what the difference is between an alarm and a lock button. One, take him out and watch him.'

The manager stopped what he was doing, and walked into the area outside the vault, with One holding the shotgun against his back.

'The control box is here,' he said.

'Well, lock the bank, and if I even think for one moment you've pressed the alarm, I'll blow you away. Understand?'

The manager nodded. 'There are two locks. This one tells control the door is locked but we're still inside. Only when we leave do we set the main one.'

'Well, if you set the right one first time, you'll all get to leave tonight.'

The manager hit the lock that indicated the building was secure but they were still inside. 'There, it's done.' They both went to turn to go back into the vault when they heard the voice.

'I've tripped the alarm!'

The woman who had been knocked out downstairs hadn't been unconscious at all, and was now standing behind the counter, blood running down her face.

It was One who reacted first, turning round suddenly as he heard the voice, pulling the trigger on his shotgun.

The boom inside the bank was deafening.

****

'I really need to eat low-fat doughnuts or something,' Willie said, as his stomach growled. 'If the courier comes and he buzzes, tell him you'll be down in a minute, Davie. I've got a real dose of the shits tonight.'

Fuck me, I wasn't hungry for dinner anyway. 'Right you are, Willie,' Raeburn said, as the overweight guard sped off down the hallway, probably the quickest he'd moved all day.

Caitlin came out of the toilets a minute later. 'I feel awful, Davie. I don't usually have a drink, but I had a wee drop of Dutch courage. I was a little nervous at coming to see you, I have to admit. Not now I'm not.' She smiled at him, her eyes even more bloodshot now, and there was vomit on the front of her shirt. 'How about we go find somewhere quiet?'

And do what, you manky cow? 'I can tell you've forgotten what I said already, you wee rascal,' he said, smiling and trying not to grit his teeth. This woman was causing him all sorts of grief and she wasn't even his girlfriend. That would be the last time he flirted with her.

'What did you tell me already? That you love me?'

'No, that we were going for a drink tomorrow after work.'

'Make love to me now, Davie.'

Not even at gunpoint. 'Honey, I'm a gentleman, and I don't want to take advantage of you. I like you too much for that.'

She looked at him and smiled before staggering sideways. Raeburn caught her by the arm before she toppled right over. 'You're such a wonderful guy, Davie Raeburn,' she said, and then she toppled again, this time right onto the console.

Raeburn missed her arm.

****

Downstairs in the branch, they all heard the shotgun blast.

'What was that?' the young bank worker said, his face going deathly pale.

'Shut it,' Four said, knowing what the sound was. He nodded his head sideways at Two: *Get up there and find out what's going on.*

Two ran full tilt, getting up into the banking area, seeing the woman lying dead, a bloody mess where her guts had just been.

'It was me,' One said.

'Never mind,' Three said, in complete control. He turned to the manager. 'Get the automatic locks on. You have one minute and then you all start dying.' He spoke to the managers. 'Drag her into the safe and lock it.'

Both the managers looked at him to see if he was being serious or not. He was.

'Do it now, or there will be three funerals to arrange.'

With a look of fear and trepidation on their faces, the manager and his assistant grabbed an ankle each and dragged their colleague into the steel room. Then the manager took one last pitiful look, and closed the door on the dead woman.

'Grab those bags; don't do anything stupid and your loved ones won't be reading about your murder in tomorrow's *Caledonian*.'

The fight, if there had been any there in the first place, was completely gone from both the senior men. If there had been any doubt that the robbers would actually shoot them dead, it was gone now, to be replaced by complete certainty. They both grabbed as many moneybags as they could manage, and One grabbed the remaining bags whilst Three followed the two managers.

Downstairs, there was what seemed to be a sea of worried faces looking at them all as they entered the back room where more moneybags had been collected.

'What happened?' one of the women asked, looking at the ashen face of the manager.

'Just do as they say and we'll be safe. Please.'

All the bank workers knew something was wrong but didn't say anything about their missing colleague. Nobody voiced what they were all thinking.

The four robbers gathered up the bags in the outside corridor and they closed the heavy steel door behind them.

'What the fuck happened?' Two asked.

'One got careless with the gun and let one of them have it,' Three answered.

'What? Oh fuck me. That escalates everything.'

'Well, it's not as if you pair of mental bastards will have a problem with that,' One said.

Three turned on him. 'We do what's fucking necessary. Don't forget that.'

'Once a killer, always a killer, eh?'

Three lifted his own gun and pointed it at One.

Four stepped forward. 'We don't have time for this. Let's get the bags and get the fuck out of here.'

One more check that the door was locked and they started carrying the bags to the back room they'd entered through earlier. They took their masks off, knowing they couldn't be seen by anybody at this point. The side door to the van was unlocked, and they threw the bags in, closing the door after them as Three got behind the wheel. The others were shut in the back, sitting amongst a lot of tools and boxes, the moneybags and guns with them. If they were stopped, they had their story sorted out, but the guns were there to stop any nosy copper doing a search.

Three pulled away and then they were on the road.

****

'What the fuck's happening, Davie?'

Raeburn wasn't startled easily, but he felt disappointed that he hadn't heard Willie coming back from the toilet. Back in the day, if anybody had been creeping up on him, that man would have been dead before he'd come within ten feet.

You're slipping up, Davie, he told himself.

'What do you think I'm doing, Willie? Pouring coffee into your console?'

Raeburn was standing holding a fire extinguisher, not yet used, but in his hand should there be a sudden appearance of flames.

'Are you taking a fucking turn or something?' Willie said, taking a step forward.

'Relax, man. It was Caitlin who toppled onto your console, knocking the coffee into it.'

'Caitlin?'

'Lassie from accounts. She says you were giving her the eye or something and came here to see you. She wouldn't go and then she overbalanced in here. Only then did she leave.'

'Aw, man, away t'fuck. They're not going to blame her for this, they're going to think I did it. Just a wee one-man protest to management. Then I'll get my arsed kicked out of here. What am I going to do now?'

'I don't have the answer, buddy, but here's the courier's van now. I'll go sign for this and see you tomorrow.'

But Willie wasn't listening. He was too busy rushing back to the toilets.

CHAPTER 52

The safe house was a detached house in Juniper Green on the West side of the city. Its location chosen for its close proximity to the Edinburgh bypass, and the airport, as well as the M8, the main artery linking Edinburgh and Glasgow.

Miller looked at the unobtrusive house, knowing it was probably ringed with all sorts of sensors and covert cameras. There was a large stone wall on the perimeter, closed off by two steel gates. The back of the house overlooked the bypass, so anybody coming in would have to come in this way.

Miller sat in the passenger seat of Kim's Audi TT, and they waited for the gates to open, which they did, as if by magic.

'This place doesn't stick out,' Kim said.

'That's the whole point, I suppose,' Miller said, looking over to the lawn on the right hand side, as Kim drove round to the garages. The front of the house faced north, towards Corstorphine Hill in the distance, and Fife farther on. There was a rumble of traffic from the bypass, which was over the east wall.

The front door opened electronically, and they stepped inside, where it closed behind them. They were in an anteroom, and the door in front of them only opened when the front door shut. Both were made from three-inch thick steel, designed to withstand a round from a NATO issued rifle.

'Come in,' Neil McGovern said, from the hallway. He was dressed casually and had a glass of whisky in his hand. 'Can I get you both a drink?'

'Coffee for me, Neil, thanks,' Miller said.

'How about you, sweetheart?' he asked his daughter, as she pecked his cheek.

'Coffee as well, Dad.'

'Come away through then. Louise is through there and Shaun's in a back room.'

Foxall was playing a video game on a large screen TV in a back room that looked onto a large lawn. 'Hi, Mr. Miller,' he said, pausing the game for a moment.

'Hi, Shaun. How are things?'

'Great. I get to stay up later than when I'm staying with my granny.'

'Come on, come away through to the kitchen,' McGovern said, leading them through to the back where Louise was sitting at a large kitchen table, holding onto a cup of coffee. One of McGovern's men was pouring coffee into another two cups.

When he was done, he left the room and they sat at the table.

'How are you doing, Louise?' Kim asked.

'I feel sick, if I'm honest. I can't believe Carl would want me dead.'

'I don't think he did,' Miller said. 'I think some people wanted it to look that way.'

She put her mug on the table before looking at Miller. 'Why, though?'

'These are dangerous men, Louise, and if they think you're getting close to discovering things about them, then they'll take drastic action.'

'I'm scared.'

You should be. 'You'll be safe with Neil and his men, but we need to catch them before we can let you go back to your normal life.'

'At least I'm alive. Not like Cindy.'

McGovern got up from the table and indicated for Miller to follow him. They went into an office upstairs and McGovern closed the door behind them.

'Do you think Gary Davidson was working with anybody in your station?' he said to Miller, as he sat down behind the desk with his coffee.

Miller stood with his back to McGovern, and looked out the window, drinking the brew. As usual, it tasted superb. The view was uninterrupted, and the landscape fell away as it headed north, laying before it West Lothian and beyond. He turned back to McGovern.

'Don't worry,' McGovern said, 'they're bullet-proof. Now, Davidson.'

'To be honest, Neil, I don't think he was, but I can't even be sure of that. These guys are highly skilled if it's the same ones who set fire to Louise's house and managed to get a decomposed corpse into a house without anybody seeing them.'

'Are you saying there's nobody like that on Police Scotland's payroll?'

'You obviously think so.' He sat down opposite the older man, laying his cup on the desk.

'I can't help it, Frank, me old son.' Despite being dressed in a casual shirt and trousers, McGovern still managed to give off an aura of power.

'So do you want to tell me how you really managed to haul away all of Robert Borthwick's patient files? There's no way on God's Earth that we could have just walked in there and taken that stuff. I mean, even if we did find something and it wasn't a legal search, then it's all over.'

McGovern had one of those cheeky smiles that managed to make the owner look like he was a little rascal, no matter what his age was. 'Everything was above board, Frank. I was able to authorise taking those files because in this day and age, the *T* word trumps everything.'

Miller sat quiet for a moment, to see if McGovern was joking. He wasn't. 'Terrorism?'

'Don't look so puzzled. If those guys are ex-military, then they know what they're doing. If they kidnapped Terry, and Gary was part of their little gang, then them being military brings it into a whole new ball park. One theory I put forward is that they could be doing this to support terrorism. Then I got the green light.'

'I'm sure if I went to Paddy Gibb with that story, he'd kick my arse all the way from here to Dublin.'

'Paddy's a great copper but his ideals are based on the old school way of thinking. Bobbies on the beat, give somebody a good smack and bang them up for a while. Not slagging the guy off, but maybe he should think about retiring. We have many more threats nowadays, and everybody needs to keep their finger on the pulse.'

'We're not thinking terrorism, though, are we?'

'No, but sometimes we need to take a shortcut. It's all very well protecting people's privacy, but that privacy is also protecting some dangerous people, and you know me, Frank, I don't take kindly to somebody taking the piss.

'I'm planning to go round to the hospital tomorrow with an armed response team and take Borthwick in for questioning. If nothing else, it will put the heat on him and maybe he'll make a mistake. I also want to get somebody in there undercover.'

'You've obviously run a criminal background check on Borthwick.'

'I have. He's clean.'

'I did a check on him too. A military background check, to see if his name popped up. And it did.'

'Really? Tell me he's a dirty bastard who got kicked out.'

'Far from it. He was a doctor in the Army. Quite the hero he was. Saved a few lives in the Middle East, and he's not even a surgeon. Just like he is now, he was a shrink over there. Quite a few of our lads need a little help in the mind department, and I don't blame them, and Borthwick was one of the boys who helped sort them out. By all accounts he was a good guy, who made the transition into civvy life quite easily.'

'Yet he's in a hospital where there are apparently men who want to do harm to one of his patients. So much for his Hippocratic Oath.'

'He might have been squeaky clean back then, but he's not now. Something happened along the way to make him who is today. He's hiding behind his position, and allowing those men to come into the hospital.'

'I know. I think he's one of them, Neil. I'm working on connecting those dots, although when we bring him in for more questioning, I doubt he'll crack under pressure. I already checked, but I'm not allowed access to Borthwick's service history. Something to do with the mental health issue of the soldiers he treated, so I can't get access to the men he served with.'

'And you want me to screw over my own career by making a phone call and breaking all the rules just so you can get some info on him?'

'Pretty much.'

'Sure. I'll make a call tonight and get back to you.' McGovern was silent for a moment before looking Miller in the eyes. 'Look, son, I might be out of line here, and don't for one minute think Kim has been talking out of turn, but I overheard her talking with her mother. I know you've only know each other for a few short months, but she's fallen for you, m'boy. When she was married to Eric, I never saw her this happy.'

'I'm glad. She makes me happy, too.'

'She mentioned to her mother that she wants to move in with you, but she feels there's something holding you back.' McGovern picked up a pencil and twirled it round his fingers. Miller had no doubt the older man would know how to use it to kill him with the minimum of fuss and effort.

'I won't pretend it's been easy. I didn't think I'd ever get over Carol, but things got a little easier. Each day was more bearable, but then when I found out who had been involved in her death, it hit me hard. It just brought back feelings for her. I feel guilty about letting her go on the run that night. Which stirred up other feelings. Am I making sense?'

'You are,' McGovern said, putting the pencil back down. Maybe the urge to kill Miller with it passing as quickly as it had arrived.

'I see a future with your daughter, but I don't want to rush things. I want it to be right. It's like running into the railway station and jumping on the wrong train because you were in so much of a hurry, you wanted to catch the right train. I now that's a stupid analogy, but you get my meaning. Kim has a little girl, so she has to feel comfortable too.'

'She does, believe me.'

There was no need to ask if he'd asked Emma. 'Kim means a lot to me, and so does Emma.'

'I'm going to be blunt, Frank; do you love my daughter?'

'Yes I do. I can see me spending the rest of my life with her. Carol would have liked her, I know she would, if they were colleagues, and I'm sure they would have become friends. Believe it or not, that makes a difference.'

McGovern took the answer on board and answered after a few moments. 'You know that her ex is in the military, right?'

'I do.'

'She might not have come right out and said it, but he's a serving soldier in the SAS. He went through the Para's first, and joined the Regiment after that. He's a hard man, Frank, but I told him one thing; I don't care how hard you are or how many friends you have, if you hurt my daughter, the war for you will definitely be over. So I'm saying the same thing to you, son. If you think you'll hurt my daughter in the future, you need to walk away now.'

'I appreciate that, Neil, but I'll never hurt your daughter, and if anybody else does, you'll have to wait in line to deal with him.'

McGovern smiled and stood up. 'That's what I want to hear. Luckily for Eric, their split was amicable. Now, I'm not forcing you into a hasty decision, but remember one thing; if you don't snap her up, somebody else will.'

They went downstairs, McGovern's words echoing through Miller's head.

'Have you heard from Margaret White through Sullivan?' Miller asked.

'Oh yes. She's threatening all sorts of shit, but fuck her.' McGovern stopped at the foot of the stairs and turned round. 'I'm not saying she shouldn't be concerned about her grandson, but he was emailing people right under her very nose, and he has mental health issues. What does that tell you?'

'That tells me he really shouldn't be living with her.'

'I agree, but the British mental health system being what it is, he's lucky to be living with her. This whole country needs an overhaul. It's the same the world over though; they close down the asylums and then what? It's all so the political arseholes can line their own pockets, but don't get me started going down that road, Frank.' He turned and walked down the hall and the detective followed him, feeling McGovern had a point.

Miller left with Kim shortly after that, heading through the town, unaware of a chain of events that were about to be put into play. And one event that was going to change Miller for the rest of his life.

****

Miller didn't know where Jack and Samantha had gone after they left the station, but if he knew his father, it would no doubt involve consuming copious amounts of alcohol. Or maybe that was being unfair, but he had known his father to put a fair amount of booze away in his time, mainly because he had been right there at his side. After Carol had died. Now he had a pint with his dad when he could, and couldn't remember the last time he'd had to do a commando crawl across the bedroom floor to get into bed.

The light had died a sudden death but the night was promising to be a warm one. Revellers were out in the High Street, the young men wearing T-shirts, either to show how hard they were or how ignorant they were. Miller had arrested a few in his time, and gotten into a brawl into the bargain. While he was in uniform.

'I like it up here,' Kim said, and Miller knew she was hinting that she didn't mind the relocation, if they chose his flat to settle into.

'I do too. Work just up the road, a pub across the street, and a supermarket that will deliver the groceries. There's only one thing missing.'

'Oh? What's that, Miller?'

'A decent chippie, of course.'

'I can see I'm going to have to recruit Jack to have a word with you.'

He laughed as they made their way upstairs.

'It's strange, not having a little girl running to me when I get in,' Kim said.

'It's only for a short time,' Miller said. 'She'll be back before you know it.'

Kim hung her jacket up, took out her mobile phone and hit a few buttons. Spoke to her daughter and tried not to let the anxiety creep into her voice.

'Okay, honey, get daddy to read you a story in bed.' Kim listened to the phone as her daughter spoke to her.

'I'll tell him. Night night. Talk to you tomorrow. Love you.' She hung up, put her mobile phone into her pocket and walked from the kitchen through to the living room.

'How is she?' Miller asked, slouching back on the settee.

'She's great. She says hi to you.' Kim sat beside him and Miller straightened up, picked up the remote and aimed it at the flat screen, muting the sound.

'She's a great little girl.'

'I miss her, Frank. I know she has to be with her dad, but I feel like she's all mine. I know that sounds selfish, but I can't help it.'

He put his arm around her and pulled her in close. 'It's not selfish. Your marriage didn't work out and now you are her main provider. To all intents and purposes, she *is* all yours.'

She sat up straighter and stretched her back. 'I can't seem to relax.'

Miller knew it was more than just her daughter being in London with her father that was bothering Kim; *he* was screwing her up mentally, too.

'I know I've been a real pain recently, dithering about making a decision as to when we should move in together, but my head was all over the place. We should do it soon. When Emma gets back from visiting her dad.'

'Really?'

'Really. She should be a part of it all.'

'That's wonderful, Frank. I promise you I'll do all I can to make this work.'

'We'll both make it work.' He kissed her then, feeling more relaxed than he had in a long time.

They sat and talked about their plans for the future.

As did five men in a house not three miles away.

CHAPTER 53

Five actually smiled as he closed the living room door behind him. He observed the other four men in the room, looking each of them in the eyes.

'Two of you at least have the decency to look embarrassed.' He looked at One and Four. Two and Three gave a *couldn't care less* look, which was to be expected.

'We got the money,' One said, his face red.

'Well, that's something, I have to say. I mean, we went over this plan many times, so I have to admit it came as a bit of a surprise to hear somebody had died.'

'It was just a reaction. She came at us shouting that she'd tripped the fucking alarm.'

'Truth is, you panicked and shot her, elevating this robbery to murder.'

'It's not as if we're going to get caught, is it?' One said, glaring at Five.

'No, you're right; we're not going to get caught. That's not the point. We're better than this.' Five still hadn't raised his voice. The others knew this wasn't a good sign, going by past experience.

Two walked through to the kitchen and came back with a bottle of water in his hand. 'We need to do damage limitation now, not start blaming each other. That way we won't fuck up and get caught.'

'Who made you boss?' One said to him, his face going red.

'What did you fucking say?' He took a step towards One and the two men faced each other off.

'Enough,' Five said, in a tone that wasn't to be argued with. 'All of you sit down. Two is right. We need to go through this step by step and dissect what happened so it won't happen again.'

Five walked over to the window and looked out as the other men sat down on the old furniture. Darkness had fallen and outside all was dark around them. The house was isolated, far enough outside Edinburgh to be called country living, but not so far that it couldn't still be classified as Edinburgh.

Nobody had lived in the place for a long time, and it was starting to smell, but that was to be expected with three out of the five living here. The van was tucked away in the large, detached garage, so no prying eyes would see it.

He had another set of plates for it, but it would stay hidden until they had another job to do. Their other cars were also in the garage.

He pulled the curtains shut and turned round to face the others in the room. It was just like the old days. Their old *Army* days. 'Three, put the kettle on and make us a brew, will you?'

Three got up and went through to the kitchen. Arguably the hardest man in the group, he never failed to show respect to the boss. Five was a hard man himself, and they'd all seen battle, and each of them had killed men overseas when a good kicking would have sufficed. That was war for you; kill or be killed, that was the motto that got them all through.

It was what would get them all through this now.

'Right, now Aunt Sally has the kettle on, we'll get down to business.'

'I heard that,' Three said from the kitchen doorway.

'You were meant to, now have a seat with the others until you hear the kettle click off. You have my permission to get up when it does. You know what we all take.'

'Yeah, you be mother,' Two said.

Three flipped him off.

'Right, ladies, we need to get this sorted. They're going to step this up a gear, so we need to be prepared for this.'

'We're still not on their radar,' Two said.

'Not yet, but they're going to come close. As long as we don't panic, we'll be alright.'

Some of the group laughed at that, but number One remained passive. Panicking wasn't in their repertoire. They'd seen things in war that no sane man could handle, and done worse.

'He's talking about you,' Four said to One.

'Fucking shut it. You know I don't panic.'

'A dead woman lying in a bank vault might argue that point, if she was still breathing,' Five said.

'That wasn't panic. That was just taking care of business.'

Five looked at him. He was starting to get a headache, nothing a few Paracetamol wouldn't take care of, but listening to this drivel would make it worse if he let it.

'You panicked, old yin, and that's it, plain and simple.' One was the oldest of the group, and instead of commanding respect as Five did, he was ridiculed.

'Pish,' One said. 'I let her have it. What if she grabbed the gun and shot one of us?'

The others laughed.

'You do tell a good story, I'll give you that,' Five said. 'However, we all make mistakes, and tonight, that was a mistake. We just need to talk it through so we can go forward with our plans.'

'I wish Gary was still here,' Four said. 'Having a copper in the group was a real bonus.'

'I hear you,' Five said. 'He is sorely missed, but he fucked up and Frank Miller got to him.'

'The inimitable Frank Miller,' Three said. 'Gary told me all about him. He didn't like him at all, and now I can see why. Coming into the hospital and messing things up for us. Maybe you should let me take care of him.'

Five was no longer smiling as he rounded on Four. 'Don't you ever let me hear you talking like that again. If a copper ever needs to be sorted, I'll be making that decision, not you. Is that clear?'

Four clearly wasn't happy, but he nodded. 'Clear.'

The kettle clicked off. 'Go make the tea.' He watched as Three walked through to the kitchen.

'There was a death tonight, and that was unfortunate. If we go around killing coppers, then they will stop at nothing to find the killer of one of their own. You know what they're like. So we carry on as if nothing happened and hopefully we'll have learned a lesson from our mistake tonight. You hear that, One?'

One looked over as if he was going to make a comment, and then he thought better of it. 'Lesson learned.'

'Good. Now we can move on and go over the plans for the big job.'

Three came back into the room carrying a tray with five mugs on it, four coffees and a cup of tea. They were all black.

'Now, did any of you take your gloves off?' Five asked, sipping the black liquid.

'No,' each of them answered in turn.

'Mask off?'

'No.'

And he went through the checklist as they had every other time. Sometimes a mistake was made by so-called pros, but they ended up making a mistake they hadn't noticed and were caught.

'Shoot anybody?' Three said.

'Fuck off,' One said, and the smile disappeared from Three's face.

'Ladies,' Five said, throwing Three a look. He had no doubt that if the team did have any women in it they would behave a lot better than this bunch of reprobates.

'We should be listening to the news,' Four said. 'That way we'll know when they find the woman.'

'And we will,' Five said. He was starting to feel more relaxed. This was like they were all on a mission in Iraq, ready to go out and kill a bunch of insurgents using any method they could. He felt sorry for a Royal Marine who was jailed for life in Britain for killing a Taliban in Iraq. The judge said the Marine could have taken the man prisoner instead. Well, how about you get your fat arse off the bench and go over and join them, Judge? Instead of sitting in your Ivory Tower where you were safe from the war. Five felt his blood boiling and forced himself to remain calm.

The men were talking among themselves, and it was almost as if they were back in their barracks. He tried to think of what time together he'd enjoyed the most, but they had done so much killing, it was hard to pinpoint an exact time when one had been more exciting than the other.

That was the thing about being in a Black Ops unit in the British Army; no holds barred. The ironic thing was, they had done a lot worse than that poor bastard Marine, yet here they were, walking about free. However, he knew if any prosecutor got a bit zealous, he would be paid a visit by them, then a man from the government would have a talk with the prosecutor. The great British public didn't know the half of what went on, but it was all in the name of keeping them safe in their beds at night.

Five remembered being deployed to Northern Ireland, but that wasn't such a fun time. It was so much better killing somebody with a foreign tongue than someone who spoke English. Needs must, though, and it had been good practise for their war overseas.

It was all going to end soon though. It had to. The bank jobs they were doing couldn't keep going on forever. If everything went according to plan, Sunday's job would be the last they would do for a long time and they would go their separate ways.

'You okay, boss?' Two asked.

'I'm just fine, my friend. Now, get the TV on and get it over to Sky News. I want to know when they start reporting the murder.'

CHAPTER 54

Miller knew he had made the right decision, but when he thought about it, there was a thud in his chest. *It's just nerves, you big poof,* he told himself. He thought he might have the same feeling if he were about to jump out of a plane with a parachute on his back, wondering if he'd picked up the right backpack.

Was he nervous because there was a little girl going to come into his life very shortly, or was it because of the image he could see in his mind, of his dead wife standing at the foot of the bed, staring at his new girlfriend?

Or was it because when he found out who had really killed his wife, he wished he could go back in time and change things? He knew he would if he could, but Harvey Levitt had told him a long time ago he couldn't go back, and the only thing he could do was not make the same mistake in the future.

'You want a coffee, honey?' Kim said, from the recliner chair. They were watching TV, some crime show that didn't even remotely reflect real life, but then again, wasn't that the whole point? Who wanted to watch real-life cop drama?

'No thanks. I might have a beer in a wee while.'

Kim got up and went through to the kitchen. She seemed to be able to drink coffee at any time of day and not have it affect her sleep. He supposed it all depended on your body's tolerance level. He knew if he had some, he'd have a nightmare and have to get up to the bathroom at three o'clock.

He got up and took his laptop from one of the shelves in the coffee table. Being a copper, he supposed he should do more to hide it should there be a break-in, but the usual places like the laundry basket and under the bed were a foregone conclusion for a housebreaker, so he figured if they found it easily, they wouldn't trash the rest of the flat in their hunt for it.

He booted it up and went to iPhoto. Carol was the big photo taker, and he couldn't imagine how people like his dad had got on with holiday photos on film. Miller was just getting into cameras as a teenager when digital cameras started to come onto the market. He wondered how many people had lost their job as a result in the decline for the demand for film.

'What're you doing now?' Kim asked, coming back into the living room with a coffee. It was said innocently enough, but Miller felt as if he'd been caught looking at porn.

'Just looking through some old photos.'

'My granny used to do that, but back in the day, it was called a photo album.'

Miller smiled. 'And I'll bet she used her phone for making phone calls as well.'

He opened up an event and looked through the photos. It was from the wedding of a colleague. Carol smiling, looking beautiful in her new dress, he, Miller, getting drunker as the night went on, the knot in his tie getting looser and looser until it finally disappeared from around his neck.

That had been a great night, and he knew he'd always have the photos backed up, to look at whenever he wanted to, but more importantly, he had the memories in his mind, something that nobody could ever take from him.

He closed the computer down, and patted the settee beside him. 'Come on, sit with me for a while. Then we can have an early night.'

Kim got up and sat beside him, and he held her then, his hands wandering over her body.

Then somebody decided to ruin his plans.

His phone rang.

He listened for a few moments then hung up.

'Come on, Kim, somebody's held up a bank in Morningside.'

Kim grabbed her jacket. 'Aren't the team who are working on the robberies going?'

'I suspect they will be, but right now, they have a murder scene as well.

****

One side of Bruntsfield Place had been cordoned off when Miller pulled up in his car. A swathe of blue flashing lights cut through the dark. Miller got out and stepped under the blue and white striped crime scene tape held up by a uniform. He walked across the gravel car park to the main entrance of the bank where another uniform stood guard.

There were photographers already on scene and Miller supposed the TV news stations would be on their way.

A screen had been erected just inside the bank, keeping the view inside hidden from the prey outside. A blast of white flashes came from farther in as Miller put on polythene shoe covers. The police photographer was busy at work.

A two-man team from an ARV were standing holding their Heckler and Koch's, but it was clear the robbers were long gone.

'What have we got here, Tam?' The sky was clear and a chill wind built up as darkness came down.

'A robbery gone wrong,' Scott said, as he led them inside. Detectives from the robbery team were there, and acknowledged Miller and Kim as they were led through to the back. When they rounded the teller's counter, Miller saw the huge amount of blood, and the trail that led to the vault.

Inside the cold, steel room lay the body of a woman, almost her entire front blown away by the buckshot. Her face pale, the blood loss having kicked in rapidly. Jake Dagger leant over the body in his white suit and turned when he heard Miller come in.

'She was lucky, I'd say,' Dagger said. There was no humour on the pathologist's face as he said it.

'How come?' Miller said.

'Death was instantaneous. The buckshot ripped through her insides. She would have dropped like a stone.'

Miller turned to Scott. 'Who found her?'

Scott looked at his notebook. 'Seems that the manager and his staff were kept locked in here after the robbery. The manager's wife called him after she started worrying when he didn't come home. If he was going to be late, he always called, apparently, so she called here. No answer. So she called his phone. No answer. She called the security room, but again, there was no answer. She then called treble nine. They sent a patrol car and they were met by a mobile security guard. That's when they came in here and discovered this.'

Miller shook his head. 'Where's the manager?'

'We're holding them downstairs. He's there with four other members of staff. There were six altogether.'

'Take me to them, Tam.'

Scott walked them downstairs to their canteen area. Five lost-looking souls. Only the manager was looking less shocked than the others, maybe feeling he was the captain of the ship and knew he had to keep control of things, but Miller couldn't help wondering what this captain felt, considering they'd just hit an iceberg.

DS Andy Watt was there, along with DS Hazel Carter.

'Evening, boss,' Watt said.

'Andy,' Miller said, nodding to Hazel. The five people in the room looked as if they'd been in a war zone. Somebody had made them a cup of tea, and they held onto them as if they would explode if they put them down.

Watt stood behind one man in particular, silently indicating to Miller this was the boss man.

'What's your name?' Miller asked the man. The others just stared at him, a mixture of fear and relief on their faces.

'Michael Anderson. I'm the manager.'

'Well, Mr. Anderson, why don't you tell me what happened earlier?' He was expecting the man to complain that he'd already told his story, but he didn't.

'Me and Johnny, my assistant, were busy closing out up here while the others went downstairs. A little later, two masked men came from nowhere, carrying shotguns and shouting.'

'Did they come in through the front door?'

'No, they came from down here. God knows how they got down here without being seen.'

'Then what?' Kim said.

'They wanted us to put money in some bags. The vault was still open at this point. We did what they told us to, then Sandra came up, shouting that she'd tripped the alarm. One of them shot her.' The manager looked away, trying not to let his face crumple.

Miller knew it wasn't easy being around guns if you weren't used to them. He'd been shot months earlier, and knew a firearm being pointed at somebody could render even the most hardened man into a wobbling bowl of jelly.

'I know it's not easy, Michael, but I need you to focus right now. Tell me what happened next.'

'They made us drag Sandra into the vault then lock it and bring out the bags we'd filled. Then they took us down here where the others had filled more bags. Then they locked us all in this room.'

'Did they use any names when they were talking to each other?'

Anderson looked at him. 'That's what was funny; they called each other by numbers.'

'Numbers?'

'Yes. One, Two, Three and Four.'

Miller looked at Kim and a shiver ran down his spine. He thought back to Christmas Day a couple of years back. He'd been round at his father-in-law's house, his first Christmas without Carol, and although he hadn't felt like celebrating, the family didn't want him to feel he wasn't part of the family anymore.

Gary, his now-dead brother-in-law had been there, along with his wife Rosie and their young daughter. Harry Davidson, Carol and Gary's father, was almost a broken man after losing his daughter, but his other daughter, Julie had been there, and she had made sure nobody was on a downer. They were to celebrate Carol's life, not dwell on her death.

Miller had drunk too much, and despite only losing Carol weeks earlier, they enjoyed their Christmas dinner, knowing they had to be there for each other. Miller couldn't eat much, but the alcohol was flowing.

After dinner, he got up from the table and went through to the kitchen for a glass of water.

Gary had been standing by the sink. He didn't hear Miller come in at first. He had been on the phone.

'It's me. Six,' he had said. Then he heard Miller and hung up. He had spun round. 'Jeez, I didn't hear you coming in there, Frank.'

'I just need a glass of water, or I'm going to get blootered, and I promised Jack I'd have a few beers with him later.'

'Sure. I'll get it for you,' he said, putting his phone away.

Miller wondered if Gary had been ordering something, and had told the caller there were six of them here, but then nothing happened after that, and Miller didn't mention it. It was only because he had been thinking about Gary recently, and the illegal activity he'd been caught up in that he remembered that little snippet of conversation.

When Gary said *Six*, he hadn't been ordering anything. He'd been telling the person on the other end who was calling.

The four men in the bank tonight were numbers One through Four.

Gary Davidson had been Number Six.

CHAPTER 55

'What's wrong, Frank?' Kim asked, as Miller walked to the door of the room.

Miller indicated for her to step out into the corridor. 'I've been thinking that Gary Davidson was part of this whole kidnapping thing, and I know I'm right now. Those men call themselves numbers so they won't slip up and blurt out somebody's name. It's a technique used by Special Forces. I know now that Gary was Number Six. I heard him use it one time but then I didn't know the significance.'

'Six? So who's Number Five I wonder?'

'We need to get these scumbags, and soon, but we're not playing with your average Joe here. These guys are professionals and they know what they're doing. Most of them, anyway. Hold on, I want to ask the manager something.'

He walked back over to the door. 'Michael. Do you know the number of the man who shot Sandra?'

Anderson looked at him. 'I'll never forget. Number One.'

Just then, DI Maggie Parks walked along the short corridor behind Miller. 'Frank? We know how they got in.'

Miller turned. 'Show me.'

They walked back into the room used as a canteen. 'The bars on the outside of the window were sawn through and then taped back in place. They got in that way. Then when they left, they taped them back up so it wouldn't be obvious to anybody who gave them a quick look.'

'Clever.'

'Dangerous, more like. Whoever these guys are, we need to get them off the streets as soon as.'

'They just stepped up the game, but we have a few suspects, Maggie.' He turned and walked back through to Anderson.

'Is it unusual for the security room not to answer the phone?'

'I wish,' Anderson said. 'There's a guy in there called Willie. Eats too many bloody doughnuts. He's been caught sleeping before, but he had some mental health issues a while back and the union saved his job. God knows what his excuse is going to be for tonight.'

Miller looked at Kim. 'I was going to send a patrol car round to speak to him, but I'm going to go with some uniforms myself and chew him a new arsehole.'

'I'll come with you.'

Miller turned back to the manager first. 'What was the dead woman's name?'

'Sandra Robinson.'

'Does she have any family?'

'She wasn't married. Lived alone.'

Miller turned to Watt. 'No names released until we find a distant next of kin.'

Watt scribbled in his notebook. 'Got that.'

'Her family details will be held on file at HQ. Somebody can get it for you tomorrow,' Anderson said.

Miller took Tam Scott outside the room and into the canteen area along the corridor. 'I want you to run their names through the database. I think they probably would have had a security check done on them before they joined the bank, but you never know, they might have been up to something since they started.'

'I'll get onto that now.' He walked out of the room while Miller went back to the manager.

'So, Mr. Anderson, I believe your wife started the ball rolling.'

'What do you mean?'

'She was the one who alerted the bank that you were late, am I right?'

'Yes.'

'Is that something she normally does when you're running late?'

'No.'

Miller seemed to think about it for a moment. A tactic designed to put the interviewee on edge. 'So why did she do it tonight?'

'She knew I was running late so she called my mobile, and when she got no answer, she called security. You don't need me to tell you the rest.'

'How long was it before she started to worry?'

Anderson stared at his mug of tea for a moment. 'I know what you're doing,' he said, before lifting his eyes to Miller.

'Oh? And what's that?'

'You think I'm in on this. You think I'm part of the gang who did this, that I'm partly to blame for Sandra's death.' His voice was getting louder. 'Well, I'll tell you right now, I had nothing to fucking do with this.' He suddenly stood up.

Watt put a hand on his shoulder to restrain him, and silently asked Miller if he wanted the manager taken care of. Although Miller's idea of restraining Anderson would have been to put speed cuffs on him, Watt's idea might have been to body throw him onto the table. He shook his head.

'You have to realise we won't be cutting any corners on this, seeing as a woman was murdered.'

Anderson shook off Watt's hand and sat back down.

'Where's this control room located?'

'At HQ. They have one of the new buildings over at Fountainbridge.'

'Near the big insurance building at Grove Street?'

Anderson nodded.

Miller walked out of the room followed by Kim. He stopped at the two armed officers.

'You two, come with us. Bank HQ at Fountainbridge. Something's wrong.'

'Yes, sir.'

Outside, TV crews had turned up, followed by more members of the press.

Miller drove away from the crowd of reporters, looking for Lena Finn's face but then he remembered she wouldn't be there.

'I have a bad feeling about this, Kim. I think we've been underestimating this crowd right from the beginning.'

'I know. When Shaun Foxall said they were going to kill him, we should have expected something like this tonight.'

He looked at her in the dark. 'And they're not going to stop until *we* stop them.'

CHAPTER 56

The Headquarters for The Scottish National Bank was unimposing, and could have been one of any number of indiscriminate buildings anywhere in the city. Miller pulled the car up to the front door and waited for the ARV to pull in behind him.

The entrance had floor-to-ceiling glass walls, with a set of doors either side of a revolving door.

'Bloody Willie,' the security man said, as he pulled out a set of keys. 'Probably fell asleep again, but this time he'll be for the high jump, what with one of the banks getting turned over.'

Typical of Edinburgh, the sun had gone and left behind it a sharp wind, which blew the security man's hair. He opened the lock on the left hand door and they all walked in, the guard locking the door behind them.

'So, are you a mobile guard all the time?' Miller said, as he and Kim walked beside the guard, the two uniforms following.

'Yes I am. I was inside for a while, but I prefer to be out and about.' They reached the lifts at the back corridor.

'Where were you earlier tonight?'

The doors slid open and they stepped inside. 'What? Am I a suspect?'

'Everybody who works for the bank is a suspect until we eliminate them.'

The guard looked flustered as he eyed up the machine guns. 'I was doing my rounds. You can check at whatever time you need to check. There's a little box at each bank, and we have a time-stamp machine that records what time we were there.'

'So it records *somebody* being there,' Kim said.

'I'm sorry, what did you say your name was again?' he said to Kim.

'Special Investigator Kim Smith, Procurator Fiscal's office.'

'So not a copper then?'

'She can fuck you over a lot worse than I can,' Miller said, in a low voice.

'I can assure you I was at every one of those checkpoints.'

'We will be doing a thorough investigation, considering a woman was murdered.'

'Good God, I have nothing to hide.' The lift doors opened. 'When I see that lazy bastard, I'm going to kick him square in the fucking nuts.' He looked at Kim. 'If you'll pardon the French.'

They followed the guard along a short corridor and turned right, past the toilets and up to the security room.

Where they found Willie slumped over his console, the smell of smoke still in the air, and all the monitors blank.

One of the uniforms stepped forward, but Miller held up a hand. 'Call it in. I just want to check for vitals, then we'll regard this as a crime scene until we know better. Cover our backs in case this isn't what it looks like.' He turned to Kim. 'If you don't mind, could you give him the once over?'

She stepped forward and put a couple of fingers on Willie's neck but couldn't find a pulse. She gently moved the big man and saw his lips had turned blue and his face was white.

'He's dead.' She looked at her watch and gave a time of death.

'Shouldn't a doctor be doing that?' the mobile guard said.

'She is a doctor,' Miller said. 'Any idea how long?'

'I'd say between two and three hours, just by looking at the pallor of his skin and how cold he is. That's just a ball park figure.'

'Get a pathologist over here,' Miller told one of the uniforms. 'I want to have a look around.' He snapped on a pair of latex gloves.

There was still some of the spilt coffee on the console, what little hadn't seeped through into the wiring and fried it. Miller looked at the drawers next to the console and opened the top one. He found a little polythene bag and took it out.

'Look what we have here.'

'What is it, sir?' one of the uniforms said.

'Whatever it is,' Kim said, 'it's certainly not prescription.' She took the bag from Miller after putting her own gloves on.

'Could be Rohypnol. See that manufacturer's name on there?'

Miller looked in disgust at the man. 'He certainly doesn't look like boyfriend material. He probably used them on women he normally wouldn't get close to.'

'He had that reputation,' the security guard said. 'Manky bastard. If you can't get a woman, just help yourself. That was his motto.'

'Do you know if he had any family? I'm assuming he wasn't married.' Miller said.

'You assume correctly. He didn't talk about any family that I know of. I had the misfortune to be stuck with that bastard in here at one time, until they cut back. Well, I hope they're happy. Now Doughnut Boy there is off to the big Krispy Kreme in the sky and one of their banks was ripped off, maybe they'll spend a bit more of their profits and hire two guards at night again.'

'I get the feeling you're not too happy at your work,' Kim said.

'Long hours, crap pay, taking shit off people. Just like being a copper, I would imagine.' He looked at Miller for confirmation.

'We do have a lot of morons to deal with, that's for sure.'

One of the uniforms came back. 'I've done a quick sweep of this level, and there's nobody about, including in the toilets.'

'Good. Get more uniforms here though. I want this place gone over.'

'Don't you think this was natural causes, then?' Kim said.

'This guy dies just at the same time as the bank's robbed? If this is coincidence, then I'm a Boy Scout.'

Miller walked round the floor, peering into cubicles as the lights came on automatically, sensors tracking his movement. It was the usual office-building deal; cubicle farms with desks and chairs, each one adorned with family photos, and other private paraphernalia.

The uniforms started arriving shortly afterwards, and Miller gave them their instructions; go through the whole building, and look for anything unusual.

A short while after that, Kate Murphy arrived, looking as if she wanted to be anywhere else but here.

'What have we got here, Miller?'

'Sudden death. Life extinct, as pronounced by Dr. Smith.'

'Ah, yes, the inimitable Dr. Smith. And what is your diagnosis?'

'Lips are slightly blue, so I would say a doughnut exploded in his gut causing mass eruption of the abdominal aorta.'

'What?' Kate screwed her face as if she had sucked on a lemon when she meant to suck on an orange.

'Heart attack, Dr. Murphy. Obviously.' She thought she heard the pathologist utter the words *Fucking cow* under her breath but couldn't be sure.

Kate looked at Willie, examining him closely before standing up and looking at the faces watching her. 'Show's over, kiddiewinks. I think the good doctor has earned her Blue Peter Badge on how to interpret a dead body. I'll have him shipped off to the mortuary and cut him open, maybe tomorrow.'

'Can I have a word with you, Doctor?' Miller said, walking down the corridor. Kate followed him and they rounded a corner, where Miller found an unused office.

'What the hell is your problem?' he said, rounding on her.

Kate didn't flinch. 'What? You want to invite me round for tea and we can all have a good chinwag? Get to know each other better so we can all be friends and sit round the campfire singing Kumbaya?'

'Oh get off your fucking high horse, Doctor. You waltz into this job and start talking to people as if they're a piece of shit. If you don't want to make friends with anybody, then that's your prerogative, but I won't have you talking to other officers as if they were something you scraped off your shoe.'

'Oh yes, I forgot your sleeping with little Miss Goody Two Shoes out there.'

'My private business is none of yours. If you think you can do this job alone, you're going to find out your career isn't going to go that far.'

Kate looked as if she was going to say something, her cheeks going red, but then she held her tongue, opened the door and stepped into the corridor. 'I'll contact the mortuary assistant who's on duty and have the security guard taken to the Cowgate.' It was said in a quieter voice, one that was resigned to her lot in life. Then she walked away and into the lift.

Miller walked back into the security office area.

'Well, she's charming,' the mobile security guard said. 'I wonder if her finishing school burnt down or something.'

'She's under a lot of pressure,' Miller said, not sure why he was defending her, but not wanting the guard to slag her off.

One of the drafted uniforms came up to him. An older sergeant who was in charge of the crew who checked the building. 'Nothing looks out of the ordinary. There was just a package that had been delivered around eight o'clock.'

'Did he sign for it?' Miller indicated the dead man.

'No, sir, it was somebody called Raeburn. D. Raeburn.'

'Okay, thanks.' He turned to Kim. We'll try and find out who that is and what he knows about Willie here.'

'I might know a guy who can help with tracking down Willie's address,' the guard said.

Miller walked over to Willie's corpse and patted down his trouser legs, finding what he wanted in the right pocket. A wallet. He slipped out a driving license. 'Got it right here.'

'There's always that too, I suppose.'

Miller did more searching but came up empty. 'He doesn't have any keys on him. Does he have a locker?' he asked the guard, who shook his head.

'Come on, Kim, let's go and have a look around.' He turned to the sergeant. 'Somebody from the mortuary is coming to pick him up. Can you supervise that?'

'Yes, sir.'

'And you two come with us,' Miller said to the ARV team.

Downstairs in the car, Miller looked thoughtful as he started the engine.

'You don't think he just had a heart attack, do you?' Kim said.

'No. It's too much of a coincidence. There's somebody else here in the building who signs for a package around the time you think the guard died, and at the same time, a bank's being turned over. No, this whole thing stinks.' He started the engine and pulled away.

'Let's go and see how Willie lived his life at home.'

CHAPTER 57

'You think we're going to need the ARV?' Kim said, as Miller floored it leaving Fountainbridge. He hit the siren and their blues cut through the dark as he headed along Dundee Street, the ARV unit right behind.

'Something's ringing alarm bells in my head, Kim. Willie dying at the same time the robbery's going down is not coincidence.'

'If it's a heart attack, then it's just that, Frank; a coincidence.'

'I want those armed boys with us in case there's something else going down.'

At full speed, they made it over to Willie's house in Hailesland, on the west side of the city, in ten minutes. Kim had spoken to the duty sergeant at Wester Hailes station and a patrol car was waiting for them. Miller got out of the car and walked up to the patrol crew as the ARV stopped behind them.

'I need you to breach a door,' Miller said, to the sergeant who had come round in the car with a female constable.

'Lead the way, sir,' the man said, as the young woman took the battering ram from the boot of the car.

The driver of the ARV sat with the car while the two armed officers went into the stairway first.

Graffiti lined the interior walls, but it didn't smell like Miller thought it would. One of the flats on the ground floor was empty and boarded up. Willie's flat was on the top floor, which was two flights up.

The uniform stood ready with the bright red Enforcer, basically a heavy steel pipe with a grip handle on it, known by the force as a *big key*. When Miller gave the nod, she swung it at the lock on the door, hard, and as the door swung open, the two armed officers walked in, announcing their arrival.

One of them came back out. 'It's all clear, sir.'

Miller walked in with Kim, the uniforms following. 'Get your gloves on, people, I don't want any unnecessary prints deposited.' He started switching on the lights in the flat. Interestingly, no neighbours came out at this point, and Miller wondered if this sort of thing was routine round here nowadays. Things had improved over the years, but there was still an element of social unrest.

'Are we looking for anything in particular, sir?' the sergeant asked.

'We have a life extinct at the Scottish National Bank's HQ in Fountainbridge, and he didn't have any keys on him.'

'Is it linked to the robbery that went down in Morningside earlier?'

'That's what we're here to find out.' They split up to search the other rooms.

The flat was tidy enough for a single man to live in, but not tidy enough to bring a woman round, especially if he wanted to impress her. The air didn't hold any previously smoked cigarettes. A couple of newspapers lay about on the settee, an old piece of furniture covered in a rough fabric with a leaf pattern. An old large-screen TV sat in one corner of the room, with a cable TV box balanced on top.

An old-fashioned clock sat on top of a gas fire. It was after eleven pm, but Miller wasn't feeling tired, adrenaline coursing through his veins.

'I don't know what the guard spent his wages on but it certainly wasn't new furniture,' Kim said, looking in a china cabinet that sat against the back wall. There were little china ornaments that had a woman's touch, but not a young woman.

'Sir, we have something in here,' the female uniform said, from the living room doorway.

Miller and Kim walked through to one of the three bedrooms where the sergeant was holding an open box.

Miller walked over and looked inside. There was a roll of money, a black balaclava, a combat knife and a throwaway phone still in its packaging. He took the box, laid it on the bed and started examining the contents. Also inside was a piece of folded paper.

'What's that?' Kim asked.

Miller read through the note again. 'Not only does it look like our boy was involved with the robberies, he left the plans for the next one.'

'And if he hadn't died tonight, then we wouldn't have found this stuff.'

'Looks as if they're going to hit another bank, and soon.'

'Except Willie isn't going to be a part of it this time.'

Miller called for a forensic team to attend, and a short time later, DI Maggie Parks showed up with some of her squad.

'You're up late, young man,' she said to Miller, winking.

'My dad says it's okay.'

'Don't make a habit of it though, my lad. You need your beauty sleep.'

'I'm not sure if that's an insult or not.'

'Hi, Kim,' Maggie said. 'See what you've got to look forward to?'

Kim smiled. 'I think I can handle him. He's just a big teddy bear.'

Miller rolled his eyes. 'Well, now that my reputation as a hard man is in shreds, we can move along to the matter at hand.'

Maggie laughed and put a hand on his arm for a moment. 'Show me what we're dealing with here.' She turned to look at her team for a moment, but they were already well-practised in what to do at a crime scene. The photographer was looking at his camera as if it was his first new-born, ready to bring it into the world.

'We have a dead guy in The Scottish National Bank HQ. He was a security guard there, but when Kim examined him, he showed signs of having had a heart attack.' He paused for a moment. 'You heard about the bank being robbed earlier tonight?'

'Yes. That poor woman. The other team were in attendance. I got the call to go to the security room but we were diverted here first. We were at the lab in Howdenhall. I tell you, my husband thinks I'm having an affair. I'm more out than at home.'

'What did you tell him?'

'I told him chance would be a fine thing.'

'So the security room has a link to CCTV cameras in the banks. There was no communication from the control room, so when we went round there, we found him dead. We get here, and find this stuff.' He showed her the box in the bedroom.

'Looks like our security guard was in on it.'

'Could be but we need a definitive answer.'

'Leave it with me, Frank. We'll go through this whole house, and there will be a report on Paddy Gibb's desk in the morning.'

'Thanks, Maggie.'

Outside, the wind from earlier had gone, leaving a coolness in the summer air. He looked at his watch. It was fast approaching midnight, and he felt a sudden tiredness kick him.

'I'll drive,' Kim said, when she saw him yawning.

He didn't argue. Their bed was waiting for them, and Miller didn't think wild horses could induce his sex life that night.

CHAPTER 58

The next morning, Rena Stuart yawned as her BMW 5 Series crawled along behind the other cars. More than once she thought about getting a bus pass, but the bus would only take her as far as the Gyle Centre, then she would have to wait on the staff bus to take her to the Operations Centre at Gogarburn.

The new HQ building was up and running now, and they were only just putting their own touches on the campus. Another bank had sat here for a few years, but they had gone down badly in the crunch, and The Scottish National Bank had jumped in and taken it over. Nothing could be done about it, as they were ninety percent owned by the government, and it was Westminster who was selling.

Rena was pleased at the thought. Before, they'd had their operational HQ over in Dunfermline in Fife, but as they'd grown, more rapidly than anybody thought, due to some very aggressive buyouts, they'd moved their HQ over to Edinburgh, in a new building that had come up for lease in Fountainbridge. Technically, it was still their HQ, until she, the Operations Director, said they were ready for the transition. Which would be any day now. Depending on if she could actually get her fucking BMW to the car park.

She yawned again. Turned up the radio and listened to her favourite DJ take the piss out of somebody with his prank phone call. He was talking to a woman in a call centre, explaining that he was actually a seventy-year-old woman who wanted to know how to calm down her eighty-five-year-old husband who had taken two Viagra's instead of one.

She took her travel mug out of the cup holder and took a swig of the extra strong coffee. She'd been up late arguing with her husband, Adam. Little bastard. He'd come in late again, saying he'd met up with a workmate and they'd gone for a couple of pints. Which she knew right away to be a lie. First off, he didn't *have* any fucking mates. And secondly, the perfume the piece on the side he was shagging was strong, and despite Adam hopping into the shower as soon as he came home, he failed to get rid of the smell from his shirt.

Her mother had warned her about the cheating little bastard. Adam had gone with another woman when they were engaged, and he'd promised her he would never do it again. And he hadn't, not that she'd known of. Yes, her girlfriends all said he would do it to her again, and despite her having suspicions on more than one occasion, she never found out for sure that he had been cheating on her.

She'd confronted him about the perfume on his shirt, and he'd said some drunken cow in the bar had come across to him, wanting to dance just because there was music playing, but he'd told her no, he was married, and he wasn't interested.

She'd been too tired to argue any more with him after that, and five minutes after the last shouting match, he'd been fast asleep, snoring his head off.

The lights at the Gogar Roundabout turned green and she floored it, the diesel engine pulling the car forward like a train. God, she would miss her car if she had to sit on a bus. Both vehicles had diesel engines, but the bus didn't have heated seats in the winter, or air conditioning in the summer. Maybe more people would travel by bus if they actually made the damn things more comfortable.

Most of the traffic was coming into Edinburgh along the A90, flowing in the opposite direction to her. She looked at the digital clock in her car; 8:19. Her official starting time was nine, but it wouldn't do for the boss to be late. Well, the real boss, the big chief himself, it was alright for him to be late. Nobody would be breathing down *his* neck, looking at their watch in front of him, silently asking, *Where the fuck have you been?*

One of Rena's earlier bosses had done just that one morning, back in the day when she was an upcoming manager. She had casually picked up the cup of coffee and smiled at him. Handed it over. The coffee shop was busy, she had told him. Then he remembered he had asked her to bring a cup in for him that day. Wanker.

Rena turned off the A90, following somebody in an Audi A6. Peterson from accounting, if she remembered correctly. He'd turned his nose up at her for driving a Beemer, but fuck 'im. If he opened his mouth to her, she'd fuck him over big time. You didn't get to the top by pissing yourself every time some knob in glasses looked down his nose at you. And she was fucked if she was going to drop a button for some guy.

Luckily, her parking spot was reserved for her now, and it was closer to the door than Peterson's.

She made her way across the sun-drenched car park, having put her blazer on. The building was all glass-and-steel, an edifice she would have thought gaudy had it not been for the fact she was instrumental in acquiring it. The faces looked glum this morning. Maybe it was the early hour, although 8:30 could hardly be called early.

On the fourth floor, she said good morning to the receptionist there. Not just anybody was allowed to walk up on this floor. This was where the management were. The receptionist wasn't smiling.

'Don't look so glum, dear. It's a bright morning, we're-'

'The police are here,' the young girl said, cutting off her boss.

Rena looked confused for a moment, then found her voice. 'The police? What do they want?'

'I don't know. They're waiting in your office.'

Rena walked along the corridor and saw a man and a woman in her office. The room was large, as was befitting a woman of her stature. It sat in a corner of the building, facing the back where trees and manicured lawns were. She saw some people sitting at the picnic benches, enjoying the day before it had even begun properly.

'Can I help you?' she said, striding into the room.

'I'm DI Miller, this is Investigator Smith with the procurator fiscal's office. May we have a word?'

She slipped her blazer off and put it on a hanger. 'Of course,' she said, turning back to face them. 'Would you like a coffee?'

'Thank you,' Miller said, as Kim nodded to him.

Rena called through to one of the assistants and ordered a pot. 'Please, sit down.'

Miller and Kim both sat on one of the leather chairs opposite Rena's desk.

'What can I do for you, Inspector?' She had a feeling her husband had gotten himself into something he couldn't get out of now, and she was the one who would have to bail the little bastard out.

'It's about the robbery and the murder last night.'

Rena looked at both the detectives as if they were a prank-a-gram or something, waiting for the punchline, but none came. She knew in that moment, her career was going to go off on a tangent. There was something in the copper's face that told her she should know what the fuck he was talking about, but she didn't. There had been a robbery and a murder, and they were here, in the Operations Director's office, and it didn't take Stephen Hawking to work out one of her banks had been fucked over again. This time with horrendous consequences.

'The extended hours branch at Morningside was robbed by four men last night just after closing, and one of your tellers was shot dead,' Miller said.

'Jesus,' she said, her face going pale. 'I was working late on some papers, and I didn't have any TV on so I wouldn't get distracted,' she said, then wondered if it was a good thing to lie to a copper. Not that she'd robbed the bank, but by starting off on a lie when you were getting questioned in your office didn't exactly scream innocence. Still, as excuses went, it sounded like a pile of made-up shit.

'And I overslept this morning, so again the TV wasn't on, and I listened to a little bit of radio, but not much.' *And not one fucker from the management team called me, the bastards.*

'We're not here pointing fingers, Mrs. Stuart, but we need some background information on one of your security guards.'

Please don't tell me one of those useless twats was involved.

'We think he was involved,' Kim said.

Fuck. 'I can certainly help you with that. What do you need?'

'All the background info you have on a man called Willie Cruickshank. He was a guard who worked at your old HQ.'

'Worked?'

'Yes, he was found dead in the control room last night. A post-mortem is being held today. Meantime, we need to know everything about him.'

'I'll get that for you.' She picked up the phone again as the coffee was brought in, and Miller poured. Rena hung up and looked at the cup in front of her as if it would bite her.

'Somebody from human resources will be along with his file in a few moments.' She took some of the coffee, and added a drop more milk.

'I've always been curious why personnel became human resources,' Miller said, taking more of the coffee, which was excellent.

Fucked if I know, Rena thought, wishing she'd listened to her husband a long time ago and bought herself a swear jar. It would have paid for itself in no time. 'Progress, Detective Miller,' she said, hoping she didn't sound like Margaret Thatcher.

'How well do you know the security staff?' Kim asked.

Rena took a few seconds to think about the answer. 'Not well at all.'

'You're in charge of everyday operations, is that right?' Miller asked.

'Yes. Did you get that from my title?' It was meant to be said in a lighter tone than actually came out.

'No, I got it from your boss.' He took another sip of coffee. 'I have to say, your coffee is better.'

'Oh, Ian's in, is he? I didn't see his car in the car park, but then he drives some Japanese thing.' She gave a brief laugh and put on a smile that might be the same one used when confronted by an axe-wielding serial killer. *You're not really going to use that thing, are you?*

'Oh yes, he's in. In fact, he was here before we got here, and we started work at seven this morning. Not that we were *here* at seven, you understand. No, we had to pull the team in early, not because somebody died on your property, no wait, *two* people died on your property, but because we have at least four killers on the run, we don't know where they're going to strike next, and one of their team didn't make it home.'

'Are you sure he was involved?' Rena asked, as a woman knocked on the door and came in with a buff folder.

'That's the file you asked for, ma'am.'

'Thank you,' Rena said, and took it from her. Then she raked about in a drawer and brought out a pair of reading glasses. Checked the details before handing it over to Miller.

Miller held it open so Kim could see it as well, and they read through his file. 'I see here there was a disciplinary hearing six months ago.' He looked at the executive.

'If it says so there. I don't deal with that side of things. That would be personnel. Human resources.'

'It says he was absent from his post when a security alarm went off at the cash centre in Sighthill. Turns out he'd fallen asleep on the toilet.'

'Ah yes, there was an occasion when one of the staff was reprimanded for dereliction of duty. If he wasn't disabled, he would have been out the door, but he was on some kind of medication, if I remember correctly.'

Miller looked at the file again. 'Yes, you do remember correctly. Other than that, there's nothing to write home about.'

'Well, are you sure he was involved in last night's robbery?'

'We're following lines of enquiry right now, but that's why we need to look into every aspect of his life.'

'Can I ask you why you think he was involved?'

'We're not at liberty to reveal that at the moment, Mrs. Stuart. I'm sure you understand.'

'Oh, I do.'

There was a sudden knocking on the door, as if somebody was coming to tell them the place was on fire but the alarms weren't working. The door burst open. It was the CEO's assistant.

'The boss wants to see you,' she said.

'Can you please tell him I'm busy with the police?'

'He says right now.'

Rena looked across at the two detectives and Miller nodded. 'That's fine.'

She got up and left the office and went along the corridor, slowly seeing her pension slipping away, and having a feeling she would end her days working in a school canteen. The door to the chief exec's office was open and he called her in when he saw her.

'I want you to see this,' he said, pointing a remote at the TV sitting in the corner of his office.

'What is it?'

'You tell me.' His face was red as if he was about to explode.

The TV burst into life and Rena couldn't believe what she was seeing and let out a horrendous scream. A few seconds later, Miller came running along, followed by Kim.

On the screen was a naked couple on a bed. Only the man's face was visible, grinning as he was obviously having a good time.

'What's this?' he asked, looking at the CEO.

Rena answered for him. 'That, Detective, is my husband.'

CHAPTER 59

'I would have killed my husband if he did that to me,' Kim said, as they walked across the car park to their Vauxhall.

'Message taken on board, ma'am,' Miller said, smiling.

'I trust you, Frank. Besides, I think you're too clever to be caught out like that.'

'As long as you're aware that I know what a Honey Trap is.'

'If I thought I needed to go down that road, I wouldn't be moving in with you, Frank Miller.'

The wind blew across the open car park and Miller wondered where the main part of the psychiatric hospital was. It had been torn down years ago and this multi-million pound building built on the land.

'So what about Willie Cruickshank?' Kim asked, as she started up the car.

'I'm not exactly sure, but now my instinct says he was set up to look like one of them.'

'What makes you say that?' she said, heading for the exit.

'Look at his file. He fell asleep when he was on meds, because he's disabled.'

'Did it say what disability he had?'

'A back injury. He had a torn disc in his lower back.'

'Did it say how he got it?' She sped up as she saw a gap in the traffic flow and joined the commuters still heading into the city centre.

'Yes it did. This is where it can go either way; was he involved or not?' He looked at her. 'He was medically discharged out of the Army.'

Kim kept her eyes on the road, slowing down behind an airport bus. 'I'm going to guess here, but the doctor who discharged him was Andrew Borthwick.'

'Correct. Not only that, but he was at a pain management class.'

'With Jill White?'

'Correct again.'

'Think we should go pay her a visit again?'

'That's exactly what I was thinking. Hit the lights and hit the bypass.'

She weaved the car past the bus and cut a swathe through the other cars and before they knew it, they were on the city bypass.

****

'I can't believe you lot went into Andrew's hospital and took the patient files.'

Miller loosened his tie a little. There was no air conditioning in the hospital, and the room felt stuffy and cloying.

'We're searching for Terry's killer, Jill. There were people using that hospital to meet and they might have plotted your son's kidnapping there for all we know.'

Jill White went around the room, adjusting chairs that didn't need to be adjusted. 'You need to look closer at my ex-husband. Him and his bloody mother. If she didn't have such a hold over him, then maybe our marriage would have survived.'

'Margaret's an old woman.'

'An old woman with plenty of money. And when you're somebody like Carl White, trying to spend as much as you can, then you have to go cap in hand to get more. I thought he was a self-made man when I married him, but then I found out the truth.'

'We need to ask you about a man who was a patient of yours,' Kim said.

'You know I can't break patient confidentiality.'

'He's dead, Jill,' Miller said.

'Dead? Who are we talking about?'

'Willie Cruickshank. He was a security guard-'

'With The Scottish National Bank, yes I know.' She sat down on one of the chairs. 'Willie's dead?'

'I'm afraid so.' Miller let it sink in for a moment. Outside the window, one of the hospital's gardeners pushed a lawnmower back and forward, oblivious to what was going on behind the window in front of him.

'How well did you know Willie, Jill?' Kim asked.

Jill looked as if she didn't know where she was for a moment then squeezed her eyes shut before opening them again. 'He was a nice guy. He would do anything for you.'

'What was he like around women?'

'He was a bit of a loud mouth. He talked the talk with the guys but he never could keep a relationship going.'

'Did he ever get funny with a woman?' Kim asked.

'What do you mean, *funny*?'

'Did he try and force himself on a woman?'

'No, of course not.'

'How can you be sure?'

Jill stood up again. 'I would vouch for him anytime. Why are you asking this?'

'We found a bag of roofies in his drawer at work,' Miller said.

'What? No, Willie wouldn't use that sort of shit on a woman.'

'Sometimes when you're disabled, it can be frustrating. Sexually, I mean,' Kim said.

'I know what you mean, but you're wrong. Willie met Terry. Even looked after him one afternoon when I was at work. I would have trusted Willie with my life.'

Miller saw that the conversation could go awry and needed to keep Jill focussed. 'What was he like in your pain management class?'

Jill slowly walked over to the window and watched the gardener for a moment. 'He was like everybody else.' She turned back to look at them. 'He was a man in pain, and he needed help in controlling it.'

'He was in the Army with Andrew Borthwick,' Kim said.

'I know. Andrew discharged him. He got a back injury, and then he couldn't take it and had mental health issues. Then they met again a year later, after Andrew was out of the Army. Then Andrew put Willie my way and he came to my class. I showed him how to take charge of the pain. Me and Davie.'

'Who's Davie?'

'Davie Raeburn. He's on the patient council. I told you about him already and I vouched for him when you wanted a list of volunteers.'

'Oh yes, I remember now.' Yet, the name came back to him in a different context and he struggled with it for a moment, as he might struggle with a crossword clue. Then it came to him.

'Is that the same Davie Raeburn who works at the bank? With Willie?'

'Yes. Davie put in a good word for Willie. Got him the job in security. How do you know that?'

'Raeburn was working late at the bank last night. For all we know, he might have been the last one to see Willie alive.'

CHAPTER 60

'You and I are finished, you know that, don't you?'

'What are you talking about?' Adam Stuart said to his wife, but he knew in that instant his little illicit meeting was out of the bag now. Her voice was sharp as her words came through his mobile phone.

He was at the test centre, having a cigarette before going in. The other morons were already inside, preparing their tests, and some of the candidates were standing outside with their instructors, looking as if they were about to be taken to the gallows. Stuart knew the feeling.

'They all had a good fucking laugh at the DVD that bitch sent to my boss.'

'What DVD? What bitch?' Keep up the denial right up until the firing squad had their fingers curled round the triggers, then come out fighting.

'When you were shagging her in whatever room it was, somebody was obviously filming you two getting it on. Had it not been my husband lying there getting his brains fucked out, I might have stopped to admire the quality of the movie. Obviously he filmed it in 1080p, it was that clear.'

Shit. Now he was looking into the eyes of the firing squad, and now was the time to come out swinging, especially since Rena wasn't raising her voice.

'Look, you were always knocking me back whenever I wanted to be with you. How do you think that makes me feel?' He turned away from the test candidates and walked further along, standing outside a bookies.

'Oh, don't give me that fucking crap. Poor, hard-done-by Adam, can't get a shag with the wife so he has to go and cry on a hoor's shoulder, only this time, there wasn't any crying, was there? Tell me, Adam, was she any good?'

Don't answer that, for fuck's sake.

'Cat got your tongue? Or is it still stuck in that trollop?'

The firing squad wasn't hanging about and had not only pulled their triggers, they were about to run over and stick their bayonets into him.

'You know what, blame me for all of this, but you have to shoulder some of it too.'

'No I don't, you little bastard.'

Stuart could hear his wife's heavy breathing, and her voice echoed, as if she was in a bathroom stall. 'I didn't know she was going to have it taped,' he said, as if this was the best excuse he could come up with.'

'This is how it's going to go down now; you are going to go home at lunchtime and you will pack your bags. You will leave with your belongings, and we will talk over splitting the rest. I am going to file for divorce and you are not going to contest it. If this goes smoothly, then I just might not take a meat cleaver to your little manhood. Do we understand?'

'Go fuck yourself, Rena,' Stuart said, hanging up with what little dignity he had left. He walked into the test centre and the first person he clapped eyes on was Chris Mason. Smug bastard.

Well, Mason's day was about to go from bad to worse. If Stuart couldn't batter Rena, he could certainly fuck up Mason's career. Suddenly, everything didn't seem so bad.

****

The mailroom was in the bowels of the building, where Miller suspected it might be. Right next to the back door for easy access to the delivery trucks. It was a windowless room, almost as if it was shoved down here as an afterthought.

'I can't believe he's dead,' Davie Raeburn said, grabbing another pile of mail from one of the sacks that lay about.

'Can you tell us how he seemed before you went home?'

'Willie is a big talker.' Raeburn put the mail down and stood facing Miller and Kim. 'You know the sort; has trouble getting a girlfriend, but talks like he's God's gift.'

'How was he acting?' Kim said.

'In what way?'

'Physically. Did he seem as if he was coming down with something?'

'Actually, he and I were talking when he had to get up and go to the bathroom. Said his stomach was bothering him something fierce. He was back and forwards a few times when I was up there. He said it was too many doughnuts.'

'You knew Willie a long time,' Miller said.

'I'm on the patient council at the hospital, and Willie had problems. So I helped him through it, with Jill's help. He was brand new afterwards. He just needed a little support, like a lot of guys returning from the war.'

Miller looked around the room. There were two other people there, both of them mailroom staff. The female was the supervisor. 'Did you ever see Willie take any medication that hadn't been prescribed to him?'

'Willie? Nah. He wasn't the type. Why?'

'There was a little bag of pills in his drawer in the control room.'

'What? What kind of pills?'

'They were roofies,' Kim said. 'Used to drug-'

'I know what they are. They couldn't have been Willie's.'

'Why not?'

'Well, Willie was harmless.'

'Not that harmless, I can assure you,' Miller said.

'What are you getting at?'

'We think he may have been involved in other things.'

Raeburn looked away for a second, before looking Miller in the eyes. 'You don't think he was touching women, do you?'

'We can't be sure.'

'Look, I've known Willie for a while, and when I said he was talking about going with women and what he'd like to do to them, I just thought it was bravado. I didn't know he was actually taking advantage of women.'

'It's called raping them, Mr. Raeburn,' Kim said.

'Yes, yes, of course. I just find it hard to believe Willie would be involved in any stuff like this.'

'When you were talking to him, did he call anybody? Or did anybody call him?'

'No. I didn't see anything like that.'

'Can I ask you why you were working late last night? Is that normal for you?'

'Sometimes we get asked, if there's a package coming in and we have to deal with it. There's only the security guard on, and he's not allowed to leave the control room. So one of us has to be here, and the boss asked me to stay late.'

Raeburn looked over Miller's shoulder, as if a thought had just occurred to him. 'When he was in the bathroom, he was there for quite a while. I didn't think much about it, but when I heard about the robbery, and it happened around the time Willie died and the CCTV console was wrecked, well, it makes you wonder, doesn't it? What if he *was* involved?'

'It certainly does,' Miller said. 'That'll be all for now, Mr. Raeburn. If we need to ask you any more questions, we know where to find you.'

CHAPTER 61

Bastard. Adam Stuart sat at his desk looking across at Chris Mason filling in his test sheets. It had to be him. Who the hell else would set him up and send the fucking video to his wife? Nobody else was in the frame.

'I'll be going out with you all on some check tests today,' Stuart said to Mason, who looked up at him.

'Why?'

'Don't question me.'

Mason looked across at one of the other examiners who was filling in his own sheets. The man just shrugged his shoulders.

'There's no point looking across at him,' Stuart said, trying hard to keep his temper in check. It would be so easy to shout at the man, to lay the blame at his door, but all the coward would do is deny it was him who sent the video. Well, he had a better way of dealing with the situation.

He was going to fuck Mason over once and for all.

'Right. Let's get the first tests started. Let's not keep the poor sods waiting. Mason, I'll be in the car with you.'

'Course you will.'

'Let's get on with it.'

Outside, in the waiting room, the candidates who had been outside and had witnessed Stuart raising his voice on the phone, were now hanging around wondering if that was a bad omen.

After the three other examiners checked the provisional license of the candidates, Stuart followed Mason out to the car. The girl said goodbye to her instructor and Mason told her they would be accompanied by a supervisor today, and not to worry, it was routine. She didn't look convinced, but got in behind the wheel anyway.

They headed out of the car park and up towards Barberton Mains.

'Turn right at the roundabout and follow the road ahead,' Mason said, and had a look in the rear view mirror the instructor usually used. Stuart's glaring face looked back at him.

He took her round a set route, going through some quiet streets at Colinton village, getting her to do a turn in the road and a parallel park, before heading back towards the test centre. Everything was going well until they were heading back down Wester Hailes Road.

Maybe it was over-confidence, maybe it was her nerves getting to her, but whatever it was, the young girl approached the large roundabout at speed. Traffic flashed by up ahead. Still the car carried on its relentless pace.

Christ Almighty, she doesn't see it, Chris Mason thought to himself as the girl stared out the windscreen, fingers turning white as her hands attempted to pull the steering wheel free from the mounting.

Right Chris, steady yourself, wait for it, wait for it, get your foot near the brake, not too early, make sure she's definitely not going to stop, easy now, getting closer, watch the traffic on the roundabout, wait, wait, wait. Now!

Mason brought his foot down hard on the twin brake in the passenger foot well, his heart hammering in his chest. The car came to a sudden stop, the engine dying. He didn't bother dipping the clutch; his only concern was stopping the car.

He looked in the mirror, saw Stuart looking out of the side window.

'The car's stalled,' the girl said.

'That's because I've had to use the foot-brake,' Mason said, the cross going down on the test sheet.

'Oh shit,' the girl said, knowing any intervention on the examiner's behalf, either vocal or physical, meant an automatic failure.

'Carry on when you're ready,' Mason told her, as the engine was re-started. The traffic that had built up behind her started overtaking onto the roundabout. They moved off, this time when the road was clear.

Back at the test centre, the girl pulled the car into the side of the road.

'That's the end of the test. I'm sorry to tell you that you haven't passed.'

'Tell me something I don't already know,' she said, getting out of the car and slamming the door. Mason got out followed by Stuart.

Inside the office, they heard one of the other examiners in the back making coffee.

'That was a bit harsh, wasn't it?' Stuart said, putting his checklist down.

'What was?' Mason replied, stopping half-way to the kitchen.

'That test. The girl was about to put the brakes on herself but you jumped the gun.'

'I don't think so.'

'I was in the back.'

'And I was in the front, remember? How could you possibly know what was happening when you were busy looking out the window?'

'If I had been concerned, I would have been pulling my fucking hair out, but I wasn't.'

'She was approaching at a speed that indicated to me she wasn't about to stop at the give-way line...'

'Rubbish. They're not advanced drivers like you, Mason. You've got to cut them some slack.'

'Some slack? Would you rather we ended up under a fucking truck?'

'Don't dramatise, Mason. She was going to stop that car and you fucking jumped the gun. Christ, I wouldn't be surprised if that girl wrote and complained, demanding another test.'

'Well let's hope she doesn't get you then.'

Stuart stood and looked at Mason's departing back. That was all he wanted; now he could write up a report and hopefully get Mason fired out of here.

CHAPTER 62

Miller felt dog tired as he poured himself and Kim a coffee from the pot in his office. Paddy Gibb came in.

'No, no, I'll crack the window meself, just you sit there,' he said to Miller, crossing the room and opening the window. The sun streamed through the blinds, promising a nice day ahead.

'You want a coffee, Paddy?' Kim asked.

'Cigarettes, coffee. You'll be offering me a doughnut next.'

'I don't have any doughnuts,' Miller said.

'Oh well, two out of three ain't bad.' Gibb sucked on the cigarette as if it was the last one before the government banned them. 'Make mine black, Kim, please. He always has milk that's gone bad.'

'You could make your own coffee,' Miller said, 'or better still, put your hand into your wee purse and splash for Starbucks for us.'

Gibb took another draw and nipped the cigarette, putting it back into its packet, beside its brothers and sisters. 'First of all,' he said, closing the window and wafting any secondary smoke around the room in the hope of dissipating it, 'it is not a wee purse. It is a coin carrier. It holds all my change and I flip it out when I need to get at said change, instead of raking about in my pocket, looking like I'm some pervert.'

'So basically it's a purse. You have a purse, don't you, Kim?' Miller said, with a straight face, taking a sip of his coffee and handing Gibb his.

'If you think you and I are still going off on a hooly to Blackpool now, son, then you're sorely mistaken.'

'Come on, you know I'm only joking.'

'And those Ginger Snaps in the tin through in the squad room? Keep your filthy mitts off them. I'm going to count them, and if I see so much as one Ginger crumb on your face, you'll be off my Christmas Card list before you can belt out the first line of *White Christmas*.'

'Well, that's me told then.' Miller sat down behind his desk, put his coffee down, stretched his arms out and yawned. 'Oh man, I'm having a lie in this weekend, that's for sure.'

'You and me both,' Gibb said, sitting in another chair. 'But not in the same house, of course.'

'Did you get any results regarding Gary Davidson and George West's theory?' Kim asked.

'That I did, Kim, that I did. Now, you both know that sometimes Andy Watt is about as useful as non-alcoholic lager, but this time he seems to have come up with the goods. He does indeed remember Davidson getting a visit from old George. He heard them talking, and when he asked Davidson about it, Davidson just dismissed it out of hand. When Andy pushed it, Davidson snapped at him. They were so busy at the time that Andy forgot about it after that, until I brought it up.'

'I think Gary was in on the whole thing. As I said to Kim, I heard him talking about something on the phone a long time ago, and I think he was number Six.'

'What do you mean?'

'Like the robbers, they only went by numbers, One through Four, then Gary was Number Six.'

Gibb took a sip of his coffee. 'Then who would be number Five?'

'I don't know, but I could have a guess; Andrew Borthwick.'

'You really think he's involved in all of this? A doctor with everything to lose?'

'I do. Sometimes it's not the money, it's the thrill. Borthwick is arrogant, conceited and shows narcissistic tendencies.'

'Okay, so what do we think then, Frank?' Gibb said, holding his coffee tighter as if somebody was about to steal it. 'That Borthwick is the leader of this band of not-quite-so-merry men?'

'I do. He has the personality for it. We know he was at the hospital the other night when Shaun Foxall heard those other men say they were going to kill Shaun. Foxall also remembers Gary being there a few years ago, and how Gary was seen with those men.'

Kim took some of her own coffee. 'And now he's got his lawyer to complain, we've backed off, giving him some breathing space.'

Gibb sat and thought about it for a moment. 'Fuck 'im. Go get him, Frank. It doesn't have to be heavy-handed and you won't have that psycho McGovern with you,' looking at Kim, 'no offence-'

'None taken.'

'but you will have my authority to bring him in for questioning. I'll give him number fucking Five.'

'What about Dennis Friendly?'

Gibb looked at Kim. 'I know somebody's mummy who Friendly is a little bit scared of. I don't think he'll have anything to object about. Anybody else, well, we can deal with that fallout when it happens. Meantime, go get yourself a bad doctor, Inspector.'

Before Miller could leave, there was another knock on the door, and Maggie Parks came in. 'So this is where you all hang out?'

'Come in, Maggie,' Miller said, about to stand up.

'Stay, Frank. I just wanted to give you this report. You might find this interesting.' She looked at Gibb. 'You've been smoking again, haven't you?'

'Now, now, Inspector, that's a sackable offence. We won't have any arrows slung around this office.'

'Don't worry, your secret's safe with me, but there's no fooling my nose.'

'No wonder, it's big enough,' Gibb said, under his breath.

'I'm sorry, what?'

'I said, that's big of you.' He got up and stretched. 'Well, if you want me, you'll know where I'll be.'

'Bookies? Pub?' Maggie said.

'Oh, my dear Maggie, I do wish. Perhaps you could take the rest of the day off and we could go bar hopping? Tell them upstairs that I said it was alright.'

'Paddy, I was hoping one day you'd get around to asking me out.'

'Were you?'

'No. And stay here, you'll want to hear this.'

'Yes, ma'am.' Gibb drank more coffee.

'We went through Willie Cruickshank's flat with a nit comb, and we not only found more money shoved into a box in his wardrobe, we found a little notebook. It outlines last night's robbery, and it also mentions somebody by name.'

Gibb perked up. 'Oh yeah? Who?'

Maggie turned to him. 'Adam Stuart. He says in his little book that he's been doing some planning with Adam Stuart.'

'Adam Stuart?' Gibb said. 'Do we know him?'

'I've heard of him,' Miller said. 'I went to speak with the operations director of the bank first thing this morning. Rena Stuart. She was pissed off, because somebody had sent her boss a DVD of her husband in a room with some tart. Her husband's name is Adam Stuart.'

CHAPTER 63

Adam Stuart told the others he had a meeting to go to and would be going down to Cardington as a trainer again, the following week.

'You remember that, don't you, Mason? You and that chick you were banging. What was her name again? Angela something wasn't it?'

Mason looked at Stuart with contempt. 'You're pathetic.'

'Really now? Will that still be your opinion when the area supervisor comes round asking for a performance check? When I tell him you couldn't test a sausage with a fork. Then we'll see who's the pathetic one.'

'Well, at least we know if you can't cut it as an examiner anymore, you could always move into the movie business,' Mason said, and the others started laughing.

'What did you say?' Stuart felt his face turning red.

'Your wife called here asking us if we knew about you having it away with a hooker in a hotel room.'

'You're a fucking liar,' he said to Mason. 'I knew it was you all along.'

'She did call up, boss,' one of the other examiners said. 'I heard her on the speaker phone.'

'Shut up, you. Nobody asked you.'

The man shrugged while Mason sat smiling.

'I'm leaving, and I'll damn well make sure you lot get what you deserve.' He stormed out of the test centre and jumped into his car.

He drove away out of the car park near Wester Hailes station, and thought about how his life had come to this. Maybe some other guy would be happy with a nice house and a nice wife and boring sex, but he needed that little bit of excitement. It was like a drug. He couldn't help himself.

Now his life as he knew it was over. Rena would never give him another chance. His job sucked, and the only exciting part of that was going to Cardington, where he could probably get away with fooling around with another candidate.

He hit the Edinburgh bypass and headed for the Forth Bridge. The traffic flowed freely for a change. Over to his left, the new bridge was taking shape, getting bigger every day. Queensferry Crossing it was going to be called. He drove faster, and only slowed down when he reached the Dunfermline interchange. There was something about Fife he loved. It was almost as if he was coming home.

He took a country road, driving faster. A tractor pulled out from what seemed like the middle of a hedge. Stuart flew past it and left it behind. For the next few miles, there were no distractions at all. Being an examiner meant he'd had to take an advanced driving course, which he had passed with flying colours. He'd always loved driving, and could fly along a tight B road with the greatest of ease. It was all about observation, predicting what the motorist in front of you was going to do, and keeping an eye on the van behind you.

The dark-coloured van.

This one had his lights on, full beam, and it was coming up fast. Shit, for a van it could move. Stuart floored his car and it shot forward, but the van had no problem keeping up. He was obviously an advanced driver.

There was nothing else on the road. Just Stuart and the van.

He gave it more gas then let all his training kick in. Approaching a corner fast, faster than a normal driver might have been able to take it. And still the van hurtled behind him, getting even faster.

Then it caught up with him, its full beams catching his mirror, and then all of a sudden they made contact.

No matter how well built Stuart's German car was, how good the reliability, the quality, the design or the performance, it just didn't like being under water.

The front of the Ford Transit was built to take dings and bumps easily on a building site, whereas the German was designed with fancy duds, to take a couple out on date night, or a power businessman to a meeting where the car, watch and shoes did the talking before he did. And despite all the accolades from car journalists, it couldn't swim. The airbag went off as it was supposed to, as the weight of the engine pulled the front of the car down and it hit the deep river solidly.

Adam Stuart screamed as he first saw the fields in the distance, as if he was in a light aircraft and he was taking off, then the car's weight shifted, and the big engine was hauling him down and his view changed from blue sky and green fields to dirty brown water. He knew what was coming and was powerless to stop it.

The river was a good way down from the road, surrounded by trees and uncut grass, weeds and bushes. The bushes had done their stuff on the front paintwork, but that was the least of Stuart's problems.

Hitting the river was like hitting a wall. The airbag broke his nose, which erupted like a volcano. Blood spattered the airbag and hit the side window. It stopped him from screaming more.

The heavy vehicle sank fast, but it wasn't deep, which might have been lucky for Stuart had the two men from the van not come down the embankment after him. He was dazed and didn't see them, but then the door was being yanked open.

'Thank...God..' he started to say, then he recognised a face. 'What...are...you...doing?' he asked, not quite grasping what was going on until the bottle of whisky was put into his mouth and poured.

Stuart spluttered and spat some of the fiery liquid at his assailant, who promptly poured more of the liquid into Stuart's mouth. The examiner had no choice but to swallow it.

'Help me,' he said, the blood running down his face and into his mouth where it joined the whisky. A blood chaser. His words were no good, he realised, but it was his desire to live that made him utter them.

Then his arms started flailing. 'Three. Give me a hand, will you?' Number Two said.

'Sure,' the other man said, wading through the water to the passenger side. The flow of the murky water making it difficult to open the door, but he managed it. 'Although I think we're past using our code names now, Chris.'

Stuart looked across at him. 'Who...are you?'

'You don't need to know my name,' Ross Brannigan said.

'I...don't understand.'

'It's simple; we're going to kill you.' The big ex-soldier grinned at him.

'No, please. Why are you doing this?' He looked back at number Two. 'We can work this out, Chris. There's...no need for this.'

'Believe it or not, it's nothing personal,' Chris Mason said, 'but we need you to die right now. You were part of our plan all along.'

Before Stuart could protest any further, Mason reached in and pushed Stuart's head under the water.

The two men went back to the van where they changed into dry clothes. Soon it would be over. As long as the others played their part.

CHAPTER 64

It didn't take long to find out where Stuart worked. His wife was only too happy to give the police the information.

Now, Miller was pulling into the large car park at Wester Hailes Station. A train pulled in, a commuter job, heading into Edinburgh Waverley.

'I remember being sent here when I was in uniform,' he said, getting out of the car. Despite the sun being out, a wind whipped through the open area. 'They needed more uniforms at the weekend, because of the hotel over there.'

Kim looked over to where Miller was indicating. 'Why did a hotel need more manpower?'

'This is Wester Hailes. The women were fighting at the weekend. Battering the bouncers before turning on the customers who were there having a quiet drink.'

Kim looked around her. Besides the entrance to the hotel, an Odeon cinema took pride of place opposite the driving test centre, and a few shops were along from the entrance to the Wester Hailes shopping centre.

She had been in many areas like this, and every time they exuded an air of fear. The police were often called to the centre, and cars were broken into as patrons watched a movie, presumably for the last time at that theatre.

'Where's the police station round here?' she asked, as he locked the car.

'Five minutes down the road. They're kept busy.'

The test centre was a one-storey anonymous building, with white stucco walls and a grey tiled roof. It might have passed for a bookies or a dive bar had it not been for the driving test centre sign out front. They walked past a few driving school cars as the test candidates were waiting to go into the Lion's Den. Miller led the way into the centre as the train pulled out of the station.

'We're not ready for candidates,' one of the examiners said, as he saw Miller coming in.

'DI Miller, Police Edinburgh. Special Investigator Smith. We're here to talk to Adam Stuart.'

'He's not here.'

'And you are, sir?'

'Kevin Pearce.'

'And where is Mr. Stuart?'

Pearce was playing around with papers on his clipboard. 'Who knows? He's an enigma. Rules this place with an iron fist, then goes swanning off God knows where whenever he feels like it.'

'Have you ever heard him talking about a man called Willie Cruickshank?'

Pearce made a show of thinking about it for a moment but was probably thinking about nothing more than having a few beers after work. 'Nope. Never heard that name before.'

'Please think hard about this, Mr. Pearce.'

Pearce took a deep breath and blew it out. 'No, sorry. To be honest, Stuart never talks about his personal life, except when he came in one day gibbering about a new life insurance policy his wife's bank had going. Nobody took him up on the offer, and he went in a huff for a wee while. The guy's just a tool, if you ask me, and that's not just my opinion. Everybody hates him. If you don't kiss his arse, then he makes life hell. Like that poor sod Chris.'

'Chris?'

'Chris Mason, one of our other examiners. Stuart was on his back all the time. Never let up.'

'In what way?'

'He was always going out on a supervising check with Chris. I mean, we all got them, but he was relentless And he always said Chris got the wrong result in a test.'

'Where's Chris Mason now?'

'He left.'

'When will he be back?' Kim asked.

'That's the thing; he won't be. He left for good. He said he was sick of Stuart being on his back all the time and he would look for another job. So he just walked out.'

'Do you know how to get a hold of him?'

'No. We never socialised.'

'Who else works here?' Kim asked.

'Just a part-timer, Charlie. He's just biding his time until he retires. He's part-time because a test candidate ran him over and smashed his ankle. Now he walks with a walking stick.'

'And I don't suppose he socialises with Stuart or Mason either?' Miller said.

'I would doubt it. Charlie is a real home bird. He and his missus love nothing more than to stay in and watch a good movie on Netflix.'

Miller took a business card out of his pocket and handed it to the examiner. 'Do me a favour; when Stuart gets back, tell him to call me. If I don't hear from him, I'll be coming back here to speak to him.'

Pearce took the card. 'Will do. Although I think he'll be red-faced when he comes back. Did you hear about what he did to his wife?'

'Yes I did. How do you know?'

'She called us up to tell us. What a laugh we had behind his back. I'm not surprised though. He was always saying how much he hated her and how his wife was going to get what was coming to her.'

Miller and Kim both looked at the man.

Miller: 'What did he mean by that?'

'She's a real bossy boots. We met her a few times at bank do's. The way she spoke to him was awful. I would have walked out on my wife years ago if she spoke to me like that, but I guess he knew what side his bread was buttered. She earned a lot and has a far more powerful position than he does. On more than one occasion, he said she was going to get what was coming to her.'

'Did you hear him say this?'

'No, not exactly.'

'How did you hear this?'

Pearce snapped his fingers. 'Wait. You said Willie Cruickshank?'

'Yes,' Miller said, not wanting the other man to lose concentration.

'I didn't hear Stuart trash talking his wife, but Chris told me. He said that Stuart was really angry one morning, while me and Charlie were out on our tests. It was quiet that day, so Chris was left behind in the office. When I got back, Stuart was gone for lunch, and Chris said Stuart was talking not only about getting back at his wife, but getting back at the bank too. For hiring her. They were both going to be taught a lesson.'

'What about Willie Cruickshank, Mr. Pearce?' Kim said, keeping her tone level.

'I remember Chris answering the phone a few times. Me and Charlie never did. That's what the new guy's for, am I right? Even though he's been here for six months, he's always going to be the junior guy until a new guy joins. So Chris answers the phone, and I remember him telling Stuart that a Willie Cruickshank was calling for him. After the third time I think it was, Stuart went mad. Got all angry like and shouted at Chris, *I don't know any fucking Willie!*' And that was the end of that, except Willie called a few times after, and Chris asked what he should do? Tell Stuart or not? And we said to leave it. So he did.'

Pearce looked at his watch. 'If you'll excuse me, I need to go on a test.'

'Sure. Thanks for the information.'

'Anytime. I like to see Stuart getting it shoved up him.' Pearce walked into the waiting room where a young man of about seventeen was waiting to go on his driving test, looking like he was waiting to go to the guillotine.

Miller walked past with Kim and they went back to their car.

'Stuart seems like a real barrel of laughs,' Miller said.

'I'd rather be self-employed than work for some monster like that.'

'Seems as if he and Willie did have a friendship after all,' Miller said, as they got back in the car.

'And he didn't want anybody to find out about it. Maybe that's why he hounded Chris Mason, to make him quit.'

Miller started the car and they drove out of the big car park, turning right onto Wester Hailes Road. 'That way, if Mason quit, then he wouldn't be around to take a call from Willie Cruickshank. Although it does seem a bit strange why Cruickshank would call the test centre.'

'Well, if we know he used throwaway phones, and if he was using one to call the test centre, nothing would be registered on Stuart's phone, so it makes sense that way.'

Miller looked across at her. 'Very true.'

'Where are we heading now?'

'I want a word with Stuart's wife again. I want to give her the news that I think her husband is one of the bank robbers.'

CHAPTER 65

Rena Stuart was in a meeting with department managers, but she was just chewing on the end of a pencil, looking out the windows into the grounds of the bank.

The other people in the room were cutting her some slack because they had all heard the news. That, and she was above them in pay scale and would fire any of them on the spot if she could get away with it.

How could he do that to her? Was their sex life as good as it was when they were dating? Please. Of course, it wasn't, but after a while, you just became comfortable with each other, to a point where sex became a part of the marriage, not the reason to stay together. She didn't enjoy it as much as she used to, preferring to dine out at a nice restaurant than go the whole nine yards with her husband, but they had their moments. If he would stop drinking so much, and keep his eyes on her while they were out, that would be nice.

Now she was thinking she would have to put in for a transfer after this. How could she look the CEO in the eye again? That twat didn't know half the damage he'd caused.

'Is that alright, Mrs. Stuart?'

Rena was looking at the man as if he had two heads. 'Sorry, what?'

'The idea for marketing. Maybe we could get them on board with an updated app for home banking?'

'Yes, talk to somebody who's in charge of home banking.'

'Well, that's you.'

'Well, somebody else then. My assistant. Somebody else for fuck's sake.' She shouted the last sentence, and could positively feel her face going red. She stood and was about to launch into a tirade, about what a bunch of lazy slackers they all were, but she left the room instead. She felt the heat creep up inside her head until it was going to explode and throw her brains all over the walls of the corridor.

She stopped at a water cooler, grabbed a little pointed cup and filled it three times, each time gulping the liquid back as if it were nectar.

'Oh there you are,' her assistant came up to her, a worried look on her face. 'I've been looking for you. There are some police officers here to see you.'

Rena fired the little cup into a trash bucket. 'Not again. Haven't they messed me about enough?'

'They said it was urgent. They've come over from Fife.'

'Fife?'

'That's what they said.'

'Where are they now?'

'In your office.'

Rena walked along the corridor, keeping her eyes fixed ahead and moving as fast as her heels would allow.

A man in an ill-fitting suit with a badly trimmed moustache stood by a man in a police uniform, looking like a sketch from Monty Python.

'Mrs. Stuart?' suit asked.

'Yes.'

'I'm DI Abercromby, Police Fife. Would you like to take a seat?'

Where to? She almost blurted out, but this was no time for levity. Adam was dead. She could tell. 'No, I'm fine standing. What's this about?'

'I'm sorry to tell you this, but we found the body of a man in a car that was registered to your husband, Adam Stuart.'

The words hit her like electricity coursing through water. A conflict of emotions shot through her, and her mind tried to sort them all out, but she couldn't quite get the syntax going.

'Are you sure you don't want to take a seat?' Abercrombie said, grabbing her arm as she swayed.

Rena sat down in one of the office chairs as her secretary said she would get a glass of water. Then she looked at the man standing before her. He wasn't smiling, or coming out with some wisecrack. This was no sketch. There was no punchline. Any thoughts she'd entertained of giving Adam a second chance were gone. She looked at the buttons on the detective's suit, feeling if she looked right at him now, she'd faint.

'How did it happen?' Her words were a croak, sounding alien to her, as if she had a bad cold.

Abercrombie had let go of her arm, and her assistant came back with more water, which she just held without drinking.

'His car was found in a river outside Milton of Balgonie, near Glenrothes.'

'Was it...a mess?' she asked, her lip trembling.

'No, but the diving team brought him up from under the water. There was also a half-empty bottle of whisky found in his car. We suspect he'd been drinking and driving, but we can't make a proper determination until the PM report.'

Now Rena looked at him. Noticed he didn't say *half-full bottle of whisky.*

Half-empty sounded more dramatic. 'There's something not right about this, Inspector.' Rena stood up. Now she looked at the man's moustache, which would have seemed comical were it not for the situation she found herself in.

'What do you mean, Mrs. Stuart?'

'I don't know why there would have been a bottle of whisky in his car. My husband didn't drink whisky. We often joked about him not being a true Scotsman, because on the one occasion he did wear a Kilt, he wore bike shorts underneath. That and the fact that he hated whisky.'

'Maybe he drank it today to...' Abercrombie turned to the uniform for a moment as if to say, *Come on then bright spark. You want into CID, you throw something out there.* The uniform stood as if making some sort of suggestion as to why Stuart would have a bottle of whisky in his car was well above his pay grade.

'What, Detective? To kill himself? He was too much of a narcissist to do that.'

Rena was aware of a man and a woman walking along the corridor towards her office. The blinds on the glass walls partly hid their identity, and at first, she thought it was more of Abercrombie's cronies, but then she saw it was the same detective who had visited her earlier that morning. Miller. She forgot the woman's name.

Abercrombie looked over at the other man in the suit and knew he was one of their own.

'DI Miller. I'm here to speak to Mrs. Stuart.'

'DI Abercrombie. Are you here about the death of Mrs. Stuart's husband?'

'No, I was here to ask her where he is. I was going to arrest him for armed robbery.'

This time Rena fainted.

CHAPTER 66

Louise Walker stood and looked out the window facing the back garden. She had been feeling antsy now, antsy and scared. McGovern said he had put a manager in place in her dealership, and he was making a good job of it, but Louise had always been what was known these days as a control freak.

And why not? she asked herself. She was building the business up nicely, giving some of the big names a run for their money. And her cars were lightly used luxury cars, just like Carl White's. Only hers were better quality and she made sure they ran well. She'd had one or two problems with people bringing their cars back, and had given them a loaner car, and fixed the problem free of charge. Her reputation was going to see her get ahead of Carl White.

She turned when somebody walked into the room. Neil McGovern.

'Hi, Neil.'

'Hi, Louise.'

'How are things coming along?' *Have you caught the bad guys?*

'We're still working on things right now, but we feel the net is tightening.'

'That's good.' She walked over to him. 'These men are so dangerous, aren't they?'

'I'm afraid so. You'll have to stay in the safe house until we get them.'

She closed her eyes for a moment. 'How safe is my place of business?'

McGovern smiled. 'I would love one of those jokers to visit down there. I have three of my men working for you now. Two salesmen and a mechanic. And believe me, they are even more dangerous than the men who put Brian Sewell in your bathtub.'

'You need to take them down, Neil.'

'We will. I'm using every resource at my disposal.' McGovern's phone rang. 'Excuse me, I need to take this.'

McGovern walked out of the room and upstairs to his office where he spoke to the person on the other end. After a few minutes, he hung up and left the house.

Things were getting interesting.

****

Miller left the bank HQ on the A90 and drove back towards Edinburgh, cutting through South Gyle, past the Gyle Centre and heading down towards Saughton, going under the new tram bridge that sat next to the railway bridge. He wondered how long it would take people to shout that it was a complete waste of money again. The whole tram project had gone way over time and budget, making some people very rich. They'd cut the line back to terminate in the city centre instead of going down to the Ocean Terminal Shopping Centre in Leith, despite the fact they'd dug up the roads to lay the tram tracks, and spent millions relocating the utility lines underneath the road.

Up Broomhouse Road where tower blocks had been demolished and left behind a wasteland, another testament to the narrow-mindedness of sixties planning. He wondered if people had become rich from that project back then. He cut along Calder Road, down to Longstone, and then into Redhall Gardens, stopping outside the house he had been looking for.

And did a double-take.

Kim stayed in the car as he got out, he saw the next-door neighbour with his hedge trimmer out, the machine buzzing about on the end of a long orange cord. Miller walked over to the living room window and looked in. There were no curtains covering the glass, and he saw the room was empty. He went to the front door and looked through the letterbox seeing nothing but junk mail strewn about the hallway. The man switched off the trimmer.

'Can I help you, son?'

Miller walked over to him and showed him his warrant card. 'Yes. I'm looking for Rosie Davidson. Can you tell me if the house has been empty for long?'

'Oh, yes, it's been empty for a wee while now. The woman who lived there told me it had been repossessed by the bank. Her husband died a few months back, and she probably didn't have insurance on him. She was nice, her and her wee lassie.'

'Do you know which bank owns it?'

'No, I'm not sure. She said it would eventually go to auction if she didn't pay, so she decided to walk.'

'Do you know where they're going to live?'

'She said she's moving to Spain. Her wee girl already left apparently. She said she was going to work until the school holidays started, then she was going to go.'

'Do you know when the schools finish?'

'Well, I know my wee grandson finished school last Friday, but I'm not sure if that's all the schools in Edinburgh.'

'Okay, thanks.' Miller went back to the car and tried calling Rosie but there was no answer on her mobile phone. He got an automated message saying the number was no longer in use.

Maybe Rosie couldn't manage on her own after Gary died in prison, or maybe everything that had happened to her had made her want to get away from it all. Either way, he wished she had found the time to say one final goodbye to him. Then again, maybe she thought he might try to talk her out of it.

'She's gone. The bank took her house,' Miller said, to Kim.

Miller cranked up the air conditioning in the car and his phone rang before he had a chance to move.

'Neil. How's things?'

'We need to have a little meet, Frankie, my boy.'

'No time like the present. Where are you?'

'Just leaving the safe house.'

'I'm just down the road at Longstone. Where do you want to meet.'

McGovern told him and he hung up. 'Your dad's going to meet us.'

'It must be important,' Kim said, pulling her seatbelt on. 'Where are we going?'

'You'll see in a minute.'

Pulling out from the house, he put the blue flashers on.

'I feel sorry for Rena Stuart,' Kim said, as they shot past the Lothian Buses depot. 'I mean, first of all, her husband cheats on her, and then some vindictive bitch sends her a copy of the DVD, and then her husband dies in a car crash.'

'Abercrombie still maintains that just because Stuart didn't drink whisky, doesn't mean to say he didn't this time, as he was trying to commit suicide.'

'I don't think he committed suicide, Frank. I think he was a pawn in all of this. Adam Stuart and Willie Cruickshank as bank robbers? I don't see it.'

'I would have liked to see how Adam Stuart reacted when we hit him with an arrest.'

'Now we'll never know. It's just convenient how Cruickshank and Stuart are now both dead.'

'Whoever is doing this is trying to throw us off the trail.'

He hit the siren and navigated his way past traffic on Calder Road, and hit the bypass. Five minutes later, he was at Newbridge and made a right into the road where Carl White's dealership was. Neil McGovern was already waiting in a black Range Rover, a driver sitting behind the wheel.

'Hello, sweetheart,' McGovern said to his daughter, as he left the cool comfort of the big SUV. He got into Miller's car.

'Hi, Dad.'

'So what's this all about, Neil,' Miller said.

'I told you I'd make a phone call about Andrew Borthwick's Army career.'

'Yes, you did.'

'A friend of mine called me a short while ago, with everything he knew about the man. He had to go through the MOD of course, but we have files on some of those people too. Anyway, I got a list of men who served with Borthwick, and it was a long list. It also contained the names of men who Borthwick helped.'

'His military patients, you mean?' Kim said.

'I do. Some of it makes very interesting reading, from our perspective.'

'Don't keep us in suspense, Neil,' Miller said. 'Apart from Martin Crawley being one of White's men, how many others?'

Neil laughed. 'Very good. You worked it out.'

'I figured on Crawley when you told us to meet you here. He's the only one who fitted in, age wise.'

'Good thinking. Here, have a look at this list my friend faxed over.' He took a piece of paper from his pocket and handed it over. Miller and Kim both read it.

'So Willie Cruickshank was a patient of the good doc when he was in the Army, but to be honest, I don't see him having the intelligence to carry out a bank robbery. He wouldn't be part of that team. We know he wasn't in the bank, and let me put it to you this way; would you trust somebody like that to have your back?' Miller said.

'Somebody wants it to look like those two clowns are involved, but trust me, Frank, I've worked with Special Forces guys, and two of them are highly trained, and I can assure you, they wouldn't want those two looking after their backs.'

'There are two other names on here that I recognise; Davie Raeburn, who's a friend of Jill White, but we know about him.' He looked at Kim. 'And Chris Mason.'

'How do you know Mason?' McGovern asked.

'He's a driving examiner. We were at Wester Hailes test centre a little while ago, and he quit. His supervisor was giving him a hard time. That man was Adam Stuart.'

'And he left the test centre?'

'Not long after.'

'What does the letter *R* stand for after some names?' Kim asked.

'Restricted file. Does anybody stick out?' McGovern said.

'Yes. One name; Martin Crawley.'

'If he's here, then Frank is going to arrest him. We're just waiting on somebody. They should be here any minute.'

'Why would some of the names be restricted, Dad?'

'They were Special Forces.'

'Chris Mason and Martin Crawley have an R next to their name. So does Ross Brannigan. You remember him, don't you, Frank?'

'It sounds familiar.'

'The male nurse who rode the lift down with us in the hospital when we took Shaun Foxall down to the canteen.'

'Oh yes. Big burly guy. He was Special Forces?'

'He was, and he worked with Borthwick in the Army,' McGovern said. 'As far as I'm aware, his credentials were fudged. He's no more a nurse than I am. More like a security guard with a white coat.'

'So, in theory, those two were more than capable of killing Cindy Shields and making her death look like an accident,' Miller said.

McGovern nodded. 'Oh yes. That's the sort of shit they're trained for.'

Miller looked thoughtful for a moment. 'And let's just say they wanted to get rid of Adam Stuart. They could somehow get his car into the river, more than likely by driving him off the road, and then drowning him, and putting a bottle of whisky in the car to make it look as if he had been drinking.'

'They wouldn't have just put the bottle in the car; the post-mortem would show whether there was whisky in his system or not, so they would make sure he swallowed some of it before killing him.' McGovern looked at his daughter. 'You know what some of them are like. They're very good at killing.'

'I know. Eric said he worked with some real psychos. Highly-trained killers they were, but the government knew what they were doing. They had to train them that way. You don't win wars by sending out Boy Scouts.'

'We know they weren't in the bank HQ to kill Willie Cruickshank though,' Miller said. 'One of the regular staff was there. Raeburn, who I just mentioned.'

McGovern raised his eyebrows. 'His name's on the list, he's a volunteer at the hospital, and who just happens to be a good friend of Jill White.'

The wheels turned in Miller's head for a moment. 'Fuck. I need to make a couple of calls, Neil.' He looked at Kim. 'Now I think we all know who we're looking for.'

Miller pulled out his phone as a black transit van came screaming along the road towards them. Miller was about to get out and confront the driver when McGovern put a hand on his shoulder.

'They're with us, Frank.'

Six men piled out the van. Any one of them more than capable of taking down Martin Crawley should it come to that.

CHAPTER 67

The buzz of adrenaline kicked in as Miller was led into the showroom, McGovern leading the way, Kim behind, and seven men following, including McGovern's driver. None of the men spoke and they stopped just inside the front door.

'Cover all exits. Nobody in or out.' He looked at Miller. 'You ready to go, Frank?'

'Yes. I spoke to Tam Scott. He knows what to do. I couldn't get hold of Jill White though.'

'Try again when we're in there. Right. This is your jurisdiction, so you go first. All you other men, you know what to do if it comes down to it.'

'Yes, sir,' the leader said, a medium-height man who was the smallest of the bunch, but who looked as if he could kill a man while his hands were tied behind his back.

Three men covered the exits, while Miller walked up the stairs to Carl White's office, walking in without knocking.

'I know we have some special offers on, Miller, but slow down. There's plenty to go round,' White said.

'Where's Martin Crawley?' Miller asked, getting down to business.

White didn't look so confident when he saw the group of men standing at his office door.

'I don't know. He doesn't work here anymore.'

'Since when?'

'Since the other day. He got all nasty and quit.'

'Have you seen him since?' McGovern asked.

White stood up. 'I'm sorry, but we haven't been introduced.'

'And we're not going to be. You don't have to know who I am, but let me tell you one thing; you're lucky you're still here. If Martin Crawley got angry with you, then he must have been feeling charitable the day he left, otherwise your next of kin would be arranging a florist for your funeral.'

White went pale. 'Martin? You think he's dangerous?'

McGovern smiled without humour. 'I *know* he's dangerous.'

'Do you know where he is?' Miller asked.

'No,' White said. 'I haven't seen him since. Maybe he's at home.'

'We're checking that right now. We got his address when we interviewed your staff the other day.'

McGovern stepped up to White and there was no arguing with the smaller man's status. 'You need to tell us all you can about Martin Crawley. Sit down.'

White didn't protest, but sat back down behind his desk. Kim sat while the two men stood.

'Martin's worked here for a few years. He's a good worker – or was – and I never had any cause to doubt him. I was pissed off the other day and snapped at him, and that's when he walked out, but apart from that, I've had no problems with the man. What has he done?'

'Where was he around the time your son was kidnapped?' Miller said, ignoring the question.

'He was here.'

'Can anybody confirm he was actually in the showroom?'

'Well, Cindy was the only one who was here at the time. And now she's dead.'

'Did he ever meet other men here, men you didn't know?' Kim asked.

'No, never.'

'Did he ever talk about meeting anybody at the Royal Scottish Hospital?' McGovern asked.

'He didn't say anything to me, and I didn't hear him talk about going to the hospital.' White looked as if he was going to vomit all over his desk. 'You don't think he had anything to do with Terry's disappearance, do you?'

'We're not sure, Carl,' Miller said, 'but if he comes here, you need to call us. Don't aggravate him, don't confront him. Just call us. Your life might depend on it.'

Kim stood, sensing that the conversation was over. They all left White's office and regrouped outside.

Miller's phone rang. 'Hello?' He listened to the caller before hanging up. 'That was Tam Scott. Crawley's house is empty. And I mean empty. It's bare. A neighbour said he hasn't lived there for weeks now.'

'I wonder where the hell he went?' Kim said.

'Let's go and ask Andrew Borthwick. I'm sure he has all the answers. First though, I want to call Jill White.'

McGovern turned to his men. 'Right boys, back in the van. Royal Scottish Hospital. One of your own works there, but don't let him fool you; he'll try and take you out as quick as look at you.'

The leader smiled at the boss. 'Let's hope he tries,' the man said, in a quiet voice.

****

Jill White was in her office going through paperwork when she decided she needed more caffeine. God knows she hadn't slept since Miller told her about her little boy.

Along the corridor, she went into the small room they used as their break room. It was a table surrounded by four chairs, with a fridge in one corner, a microwave on a countertop, and a kettle.

Jill switched it on and waited. Thought about her life and where it was going. *Not far.*

'Look at yourself now, Jill,' she said aloud. 'You're touching forty, you're not married and you have no kids.' Then she broke down, and the tears started coursing down her face like a flood.

'Oh, God, I'll never get my little boy back.' She sobbed harder. After a while, the kettle clicked off. She took a deep breath and wiped away her tears. 'Get a grip of yourself, woman. You're supposed to be the one who helps people, the one who lends a shoulder to cry on. You don't cry on shoulders.'

She poured herself a mug of coffee. 'I can't help it,' she said out loud, as if this would ease the pain. She had told this to a patient a long time ago, believing with all her heart that the therapy would work. Now she was seeing that it didn't. 'I see my little boy every time I close my eyes, I hear his voice as if I heard it only yesterday. I can hear his laugh as he played on the swings when he was little. I can hear his cry when he fell and scraped his knee. I can look into his eyes and see the man he was going to be.'

She stepped back into the corridor when her mobile phone rang. She finagled it out of her pocket and hit the answer button. 'Hello?'

Before she heard the caller's voice, a hooded figure stepped into view along the end of the corridor, outside her office door, holding a large knife that glinted in the sun coming through the corridor windows, making it look even more menacing.

'Jill, it's Frank Miller. If you're at work, get out. Trust me on this but I think Davie Raeburn is coming for you.'

She dropped her cup of coffee and turned to run. 'He's already here.'

CHAPTER 68

'Jill? Jill?' Miller shouted into his phone, as the line went dead. He tried calling the number again but it went to voicemail. He turned to Kim. 'Call in a Code twenty-one. Astley Ainslie Hospital in Morningside. Jill White. Get some of our team there. I'm on my way.' *Code twenty-one: Abduction In Progress.*

'I'll come with you.'

'No, go with your dad. He'll need you there. Get the rest of the team to go there and make sure there's an ARV there. If Borthwick makes a run for it, shoot the bastard.'

He jumped into his car and flew out of the car park, hitting the blues and twos. Screaming out of Loanhead Drive, he hit the roundabout, shooting straight over and on to the A90 back to Edinburgh, knowing full well members of his team were going to get to the Astley first, and still they were all going to be too late.

Davie Raeburn had seemed a pleasant man. Miller had met a lot of low-life over the years, he deemed himself a good judge of character, and Raeburn just did not give off an air of underlying psycho.

That's what they train for, Frank. Raeburn was in the Army. Jill had told him. She hadn't said what branch. Now he knew.

He wondered what Number Raeburn was. Five? He'd thought maybe Willie Cruickshank had been Number Five, but now he knew better. Willie was no more a bank robber than he was. They'd been played. Everybody had, including Jill.

It took him twenty-five minutes to get across to Morningside, skirting through the heavy traffic.

He made his way past the two patrol cars in front of the rehabilitation unit and parked next to Tam Scott's unmarked Vauxhall. He cut the siren and the lights and turned the engine off. Walked into the hospital, past the group of onlookers, both staff and patients, all of them eager to get a glimpse of what was going on inside.

The sun was up in a clear sky, and Miller felt the heat as he stepped out of the pool car. Inside, the heat was still apparent. The health board obviously couldn't run to air conditioning.

Scott was standing outside Jill's office. Miller saw the coffee mug still sitting on the carpet where it had fallen in the corridor.

'She's not here, is she?' Miller said, knowing the answer but wanting Scott to confirm it.

'No, sir,' Scott said, in front of the uniform. He was a sergeant in his fifties, but he always showed respect to his senior officers in front of the ranks. They walked into Jill's office, Miller following suit and pulling on a pair of nitrile gloves like Scott was wearing.

'What the fuck happened?' Scott said, once the door shut.

'We fucked up,' Miller said. He looked around the office but there was no disturbance. Nothing to show that a struggle had gone on, nothing except the empty mug on the carpet outside, its contents bleeding across the short pile.

DS Jimmy Gilmour came in. 'Sir, I've checked with the staff, and nobody saw a thing. No witnesses to what happened. It's as if Jill just vanished.'

'None of the ground staff saw anything?'

'I spoke to their supervisor, but nothing. People come and go here all the time. By its very nature, this is an open hospital, with day patients coming and going all day.'

Miller couldn't believe their timing. The question was, why would Raeburn abduct Jill? Then a cold thought tore through him; Jill had said Raeburn had been there for her when Terry had gone missing. What if Terry had gone missing *because* of Raeburn?

'Tam, I'll leave you in charge here. I'm going over to the Royal. I don't think we're going to find anything here. I think they're long gone. We'll meet back at the station later for a debriefing.'

'Right you are.'

The entrance to the Royal Scottish Hospital was almost exactly opposite Canaan Lane where the Astley Ainslie was situated, so it was less than a five-minute drive for Miller.

He could see right away that McGovern and his crew were already there along with Kim. A patrol car was stopped at the gatehouse, and the uniform directed Miller in. The black Range Rover and Transit van were at the front door, as well as more patrol cars, and another Vauxhall with flashing blue lights behind its grill.

Miller parked behind one of the patrol cars and ran inside.

McGovern was at the reception with Kim. The leader of the six men stood next to McGovern, looking frustrated that he hadn't had the chance to slap somebody.

'Ah, Frank, it seems that our good doctor has done a disappearing act. Along with his buddy, Mr. Brannigan.'

'There's no sign of Jill nor Raeburn.'

'They know we're onto them,' Kim said.

'They must have planned this all along.'

'We're spreading out throughout the entire hospital, which is locked down, but there's no sign of any of them.'

Andy Watt came along the corridor with Hazel Carter. 'Hey, boss. None of those arse buckets are here.'

'We searched all over, sir,' Hazel said, 'but there's been no sign of them.'

'Okay. I think we need to get back to the station.'

'Let me know if you need me for anything else, Frank,' McGovern said.

'Will do. Thanks for your help.'

'No problem.'

'One thing; you don't suppose they know Louise Walker is in your safe house?'

McGovern smiled at the Special Forces man before looking back at Miller. 'If they do, they'd better have a supply of body bags with them, because that's the only way they'll be leaving there.'

****

The team gathered in the investigation suite. Paddy Gibb was at the front of the room, standing by the updated white board, looking as if he could kill somebody with a sharpened cigarette.

'Right, listen up. I got everybody here, because these bastards are playing games with us, and right now, there's no doubt they have the upper hand. I want that changed. And it better happen soon. You all know Doc Levitt, who has been going over this case for us. Doc, you have the floor.'

Miller stood to one side with Kim next to him. He didn't think he'd seen Levitt looking so tired.

'Ladies and gentlemen,' the American said, 'we have a bad situation here, and by that, I don't mean the Scottish National Bank have lost some money. No, I mean a woman is dead, and as of this morning, a woman has been taken, both at the hands of this ruthless gang. However, we have gathered some leads together, which DI Miller will go over with you shortly, but I've been asked to go over the profiles of these perpetrators.'

Levitt paced back and forward for a moment, looking down at his shiny brogues, perhaps thinking he'd missed a bit of polish that morning. Perhaps thinking he'd like to give somebody a kicking with them.

'I don't need to tell you how dangerous these men are. They casually took a life, and from what we can gather from witness statements, it was unplanned. The woman, a female bank worker, panicked and tried to scare the robbers. It looks as if one of them shot her, not meaning to, but shooting her nonetheless.

'Which tells me two things; one, they're used to handling guns, and they're comfortable around them, and two, they will not hesitate to use them if cornered. We have several names, and again, Inspector Miller is going to talk to you, but my assessment of them is, they are ruthless and will not let anybody get in their way. They will shoot again. And now, Detective Miller.'

Levitt stepped aside and Miller walked forward. 'The doc is right. We have some names from a source and these men we're looking for all have military training, some of them with Special Forces. I can't say any more about their military careers, but needless to say, they are all highly trained.'

The faces of his team looked back at him, hanging on his every word. Perhaps it was the heat in the building, or perhaps it was the thought that they were now dealing with highly trained killers, but most of them had broken out in a sweat.

'We believe a man called Davie Raeburn has been in the picture all the time, but we just didn't connect the dots. He abducted Jill White earlier today, for what reason, we don't know yet. Maybe she had suspicions about him herself, or maybe he thought she had found out, but whatever the reason, he took her. And I have to admit, I don't hold out much hope of finding her alive.'

'What about Borthwick?' Andy Watt asked.

'I'm getting to him. He was an officer in the Army, a doctor. He treated several of the soldiers who were injured and had mental health issues, but he was their therapist. He obviously connected with some of them, and even got one a job at the Royal Scottish, even though the man had no qualifications. He's male nurse Ross Brannigan, ex-Special Forces soldier.'

He tapped at the name written on the white board.

'The other names we have are Martin Crawley, who was a car salesman who worked for Carl White. He left his job a few days ago. Then there's Chris Mason, who is a driving examiner who worked with Adam Stuart. Stuart's wife is operations director with the Scottish National Bank.'

Hazel Carter put her hand up. 'So, do you think Mason worked there to get close to Stuart to get information from him?'

'It's a possibility, but that's something we're still working on. However, if that's the case, then it's pretty audacious. I got Tam Scott to make a call; and the training to become a driving examiner is pretty stringent, and the process is a long one. Maybe he did try that, or maybe he got the idea when he started working at the test centre. It seems that Andrew Borthwick let the men gather at the hospital, where they could meet in secret, without getting disturbed. Borthwick is the ringleader and he pulls the strings.'

Miller took a deep breath and let it out slowly before continuing. 'We know from the other staff members in the bank that the robbers identified each other by using numbers instead of their names.'

'Fat lot of fucking good that did them,' Watt said, and they all laughed for a moment, until Miller held his hand up.

'Andy has a point. However, they were numbers one through four; there was a number six who I will tell you about in a second. Now we believe Raeburn is Number Five.'

'Who's Number Six?' Scott asked.

'That was my brother-in-law, DI Gary Davidson. We all know he took the ransom money when Terry White was kidnapped three years ago, killing my wife in the process, but now we have reason to believe that not only did he steal the money, but he was part of the kidnapping team.'

There were murmurs around the room for a moment.

'How the fuck did Davidson get involved with these scumbags?' Andy Watt again.

'Gary was in the Army. He served with those men in Iraq. When they went their separate ways, Gary joined the force, and of course, he was snapped up.'

'Especially since his old man was Detective Superintendent Harry Davidson, our boss,' Watt said. 'I bet he was corrupt as well.'

'Andy, please remember he was also my wife's father, and by association, my father-in-law. We have no reason to believe Harry had anything to do with anything Gary was involved in, and certainly not Terry White's kidnapping.'

Watt looked sceptical but chose to shut his mouth at that point.

'We know Davie Raeburn worked for the bank as a mailman. We also know he was working late last night, and it seems Willie Cruickshank, the security guard at the bank, was somehow involved. There was a notebook found in his house with Adam Stuart's name in it, suggesting there might be more members of the team. There was also some money from a previous robbery in a box in his flat. I believe it was three thousand pounds.'

Hazel again. 'So Raeburn and Cruickshank are at the security control room, and then Cruickshank dies of a heart attack? Just like that?'

'He was a big man, Hazel. It happens. Maybe when the robbery was going down, he was supposed to switch the cameras off, and he ended up keeling over and knocking coffee into the console which fried it anyway.'

'Why wasn't Raeburn there when you guys got the call?' Jimmy Gilmour asked.

'We know he was there, because he told us he was. However, his reason for being there late was to sign for a parcel. Which he did. But we checked the parcel over and there was no sender name. It was a brown box with nothing in it.'

'So he made it up himself and just kept it there?'

'No. Get this: when the console fried, it also wiped the recordings for the bank that was being robbed. That's why we're on the fence about Cruickshank being involved, but the cameras that record the back gate opening and closing were on a different server, and we can clearly see Raeburn going to collect the parcel and sign for it.'

'Did you get a number plate?' Hazel asked.

'That's the thing; the courier walked in the gate with it.' He looked around the room. 'Which means we have five men accounted for, and another dead one, Gary Davidson, which means there were six, and then we have Cruickshank and Adam Stuart, which brings the number to eight that we know about.

'So that means we have another member of their team out there who we have no idea about. All we know from the CCTV footage is he is shorter than Raeburn. He was wearing a hoodie and kept his face down at all times. There was no ID at all.'

'And you're sure Stuart's wife is not involved?' Hazel said.

'We're not sure of anything yet. She has an alibi for last night. Her sister was round her house all evening, and the brother-in-law came round to pick up his wife because they had a few glasses of wine. And they were in the house when the robbery was going down.'

'Did Adam Stuart have an alibi last night?'

'He was in a hotel screwing a prozzy. The DVD was analysed and there's no time stamp on it, but after the action was filmed, it zoomed into a copy of last night's Evening Post.'

'If the others were out last night and taking part in the robbery, whether it was in the bank or in the security room, why wasn't Stuart there in some capacity?'

'I think he already did his job by getting them information from his wife.'

'Do you think he was killed after outliving his usefulness?' Hazel asked.

'That's something we're looking into.'

Harvey Levitt stepped forward. 'That would certainly fit in with the profile. They would use those men for their own ends, and then discard them when they didn't need them anymore. It's not beyond the realms of possibility for both Stuart and Cruickshank to be murdered. The guard had a heart attack, but certain things can be administered to mimic a heart attack, such as Potassium Chloride. And Rena Stuart did say her husband didn't drink whisky and Adam's car was damaged at the back.'

'It's all speculation just now, but what isn't, is Jill White has been taken, and I personally think she might be used as collateral, or she's going to be killed because she knows too much about Raeburn.'

Miller looked around the room. 'Any more questions?'

Hazel Carter looked at him. 'Do we have any idea at all where they could be?'

'No idea right now, but we think they've regrouped, getting ready for the next job.'

'Any idea when that'll be?' Gilmour asked.

'There was a note in Willie Cruickshank's notebook about a big job coming up on Sunday.'

'Sunday?' Watt said. 'Those lazy bank working sods won't get out of their beds to work on a Sunday.'

'That's why we think they'll hit an empty bank. One that has a lot of security boxes. We're getting a list made up now.' He looked around again. 'Anybody else?' Nobody said anything.

'One last thing before we go, those of you who are firearms trained, I want you with me. We're going to the firearms centre at the Pentlands armoury where you'll be issued a Glock. I still have mine from the operation the other day, which is locked away downstairs, but I'll be signing it out again. I want everybody to go on the gun range. When we go looking for these guys, we'll be taking the gun fight to them. And those of you who are not firearms certified, you will be going in groups and each group will be accompanied by an ARV. All leave for those guys has been cancelled until further notice.'

The group went back to their desks, some of them putting their jackets on, getting ready to drive to the firearms centre.

'Please tell me I can carry my own gun again.' Kim said.

'Of course you can, but I just pray we don't need to use lethal force.'

'Me too,' she said, but she was smiling as she walked away.

CHAPTER 69

There were six of Miller's team who were firearms trained, and a call to control at Bilston brought in the uniforms who were trained and currently not on duty.

Miller had one of the team drive them up to the firing range at Dreghorn Link. The road was public until a certain point, then gated for those who didn't belong there.

The range was relatively new, having been built with the new unified force in mind. This was where officers from all over Scotland came to be certified. There were two other gun ranges, one up north just outside Aberdeen, and another in the west, outside Glasgow, but this was the main centre. Since the new force came into being, all ARV units came here for training and certification.

Officers didn't carry guns in Scotland, but the big wigs knew there was a need to fight fire with fire.

As the van pulled up, the Pentland Hills sat before them like a cowering green beast, ready to pounce. They all heard the crack of gunfire as if some of the men were already trying to shoot the beast.

A large man, in his early fifties, approached the van when they started piling out. He had short hair and was heavily built, but Miller knew the man could run if it came to it, and usually it was after some miscreant. He also knew the man could shoot, having spent many years in the Army before joining the force.

'Frank, ye wee bastard,' he said, grinning like a schoolboy. 'How you doing?' He held out his hand and Miller shook it.

'Lloyd, if I didn't have the team here, I'd be teaching you a lesson or two.'

Lloyd Masters laughed out loud. 'Always the comedian, eh?' he clapped Miller on the shoulder. 'And who have we got here today?'

'This is Dr. Kim Smith. She's an investigator with the PF's office.'

'Ah, yes, Miss Smith.' He shook her hand. 'I know your dad. I worked with him a few times in London. A long time ago. I was in the Met for many years, before transferring here.'

'Good to meet you, sir.'

Masters guffawed. 'Listen to her. Sir. I might be Superintendent, but we don't stand on ceremony here. It's Lloyd. Come away in you lot, and we'll get a drink. A cold one, mind, and strictly soft.'

'Sounds good, Lloyd,' Kim said, warming to the man already.

The sun was beating down as it tried to burn the greenery on the faraway hills. Miller was starting to sweat, and yet inside, he felt a little chill. He reminded himself why they were here; killers were on the loose, and any one of his team could be in their firing line.

'Give me a rundown, if you will, Frank,' Lloyd said, leading the team through to a large room where cold drinks were waiting. They all grabbed a bottle of water, and Miller took a long pull.

'We have a team in Edinburgh who have demonstrated to us they're not above killing somebody if they get in their way.'

'Bastards. They need a bloody good hiding if you ask me. Is that the bank robbery crowd?'

'Yes. We're keeping it out of the press for the moment, but it's going to leak.'

'It always does, son.' Lloyd took a pull of his own water.

Miller turned to the rest of his team. 'If you guys want to go through to the range, we'll be through shortly.' He watched them troop through another door, which would lead them through to the armoury.

'How's Jack doing these days? The old bugger doesn't come up and see me anymore.'

'You'll probably see even less of him now that he has a lady friend.'

'What? When did this happen? I'm really out of the loop.'

Kim smiled. 'What Frank means is Jack has a female friend who's a writer. They're neighbours.'

'Neighbours, eh? If I know Jack, he won't be just neighbours for long.'

'I don't want to hear what my father gets up to, Lloyd.'

Masters laughed again. 'I could tell you a few tales, but I won't.' He winked at Kim. 'So what does this writer write?'

'Detective novels. DI Jimmy Callahan, the Edinburgh cop.'

'Away with yourself. I've read her books. She's a great writer. And Jack's her...friend?'

'Again, Lloyd, yes, they really are just friends.'

'Of course they are.' He drank more water. 'I hear you two are an item as well.'

'My dad's an old gossip,' Kim said, smiling.

'He's just being a dad. You'll always be his wee lassie.'

'I know, although I keep telling him I'm not wee anymore.'

'Kim and I have been seeing each other for a few months,' Miller said.

'Good for you, son. Carol was a sweetheart, don't let's forget that, but life moves on, eh?'

'It does that.'

'She was a bloody good shot, let me tell you. She took to the range like a duck to water. Glock seventeen, Heckler and Koch, you name it, she could give it a bloody good belting.'

'Kim shoots as well. Sig Sauer P229.'

'Nice. Much better than the old Browning. They were good, but these new guns are better.'

'I was recently re-certified, though I don't carry in my new job like I did in my old one.'

'I bet you miss it, am I right?' Masters grinned again. He could talk guns all day long.

'Oh yes. Let's just say, I had to use it on more than one occasion.'

'Ah, yes, the great British public don't know the half of it.' He looked at Miller. 'If we didn't have so many stuffed shirts down in Westminster, maybe they would arm all cops. It's the old story, *If you arm the police, then the crooks will arm themselves too.* Load of bollocks. As you saw for yourself, the fuckers are already armed.' To Kim: 'Excuse the French.'

Kim smiled, warming quickly to the other man. 'Frank uses worse.'

'No I don't. Lloyd knows me better than that.'

'Yes I do, and don't forget it. I have enough on you to blackmail you for years to come, so don't forget it, sonny.' He laughed. 'Come on, there's ammunition waiting for us to give it a kicking. So let's not let it wait any longer.'

****

They sat down to dinner later than usual. Jack had invited Samantha round.

'I actually managed to get the bottle of wine along the hallway without Jack smashing it this time,' Samantha said, smiling at Miller's father.

'I'm never going to live that one down, am I?'

'No, sir, not for a long time.'

'Jack said he was going to cook,' Miller said, putting the Chinese dishes on the table, 'but poisoning is still a crime in Scotland.'

'Listen to my son, ever the wit. Or half, I should say.'

They tucked into the food, Jack poured the wine, and Miller chased it with a beer.

'You don't think they'll strike again tonight?' Jack asked.

'No, I very much doubt it. After last night's debacle, I think they'll be laying low.'

'And now they've all gone AWOL. Except the two who are dead.'

'There's one we don't know about.'

Samantha was hooked on Miller's every word. 'How can you tell?' she asked.

'Davie Raeburn had to have a reason to stay behind with Willie Cruickshank, so they came up with an idea to have an important package delivered, and it was in the evening, so he was hovering about with his accomplice, Cruickshank. On one of the servers, we were able to pull up video feed of the courier, and you normally expect a courier to come in a van. But there was no van, but to keep up with the story and so as not to raise a red flag, a courier did appear, but this one was on foot. It was light outside, yet he was wearing a hoodie so he couldn't be identified. I'm ninety percent sure he's one of them, but as of right now, he's the only one we can't identify.'

'And you said you found a notebook at Cruickshank's house mentioning another robbery this Sunday.' Samantha said.

Kim washed down a mouthful of her food with a Pepsi, 'That's why they're laying low tonight. First of all, the stress factor for them must be through the roof. I did a course when I was with the government, and it involved speaking to ex-cons who were willing to talk. One robber told me the stress is sky high. He would go into a jewellers with a sawn-off and in that moment in time, he was running on pure adrenaline. He said if anybody had come near him, he would have blown their head off, he was that wired. So I can imagine what those robbers were feeling last night. That poor woman didn't know any better, but I'm willing to bet killing her wasn't an act of savagery, but a combination of taut nerves and adrenaline.'

'Well, I wish they still had hanging,' Jack said.

'It wouldn't bring that woman back, Dad,' Miller said.

'It would stop them from shooting anybody else ever again.'

They ate in silence for a moment. The sun had gone overhead and left the front of the house in shadow, cooling it off. They had opened the windows and the noise from the traffic below was getting less as time wore on. Miller wondered where the men had holed up. They would release details to the press next week if they didn't get a result on Sunday, but it was a struggle trying to get the right balance; release details now, and maybe somebody would make a phone call about a group of men who had moved into a house, but the other side of the coin was tipping them off and having them go even deeper underground, which might cause them to get even more reckless and kill somebody else.

He was about to speak when his phone rang. He excused himself and answered it. 'Hello?'

'Miller, this is Kate Murphy. The pathologist.'

'I know who you are, Kate.'

'It's Dr. Murphy.'

'Dr. Murphy.' He covered the phone with his other hand and looked at Kim. 'It's your friend from the mortuary. 'Yes, I'm listening.'

'I did the PM on William Cruickshank, the heart attack victim. It was clearly a massive and fatal heart attack. He had a major blockage in the carotid artery in his neck. He was in such bad shape, health wise. Maybe not in the near future, but certainly sometime in the future, he would have had a massive stroke. A piece of the plaque would have broken off and that would have affected one side, if it wasn't fatal.'

'Okay, thanks for telling me.' Miller had the same feeling he'd had when standing in front of his headmistress years ago.

'I also have the report from my colleagues in Dunfermline who did the PM on Adam Stuart. Apparently, it was an open and shut case; he drowned.'

'Was there any sign of foul play?'

'None. He had alcohol in his system, twice the legal limit, which was enough to make his driving impaired.'

'So what was the ruling?'

'Accidental death by drowning.'

'Thank you. I just have one question before I go; how did you get my home phone number?'

The line was already dead.

Miller hung the phone up and sat back down at the table. 'I suppose you heard that?'

'We did,' Jack said.

Kim finished her mouthful of food. 'So Raeburn and Cruickshank were at the security room, making sure nobody saw any of the alarms going off and keeping an eye on the monitors. Raeburn leaves when he sees the robbery has taken place, and takes the package that gives him the reason for being there. Cruickshank is still there, and we suppose he knocked the cup of coffee over the console, and whether anybody believed it or not, it's his story, but soon after Raeburn leaves, Cruickshank has a heart attack and dies.'

'That's about it,' Miller said.

Samantha perked up. 'What about this other guy, Stuart, who drowned?'

Miller looked at Kim to explain. 'We think he became involved because he was having marital difficulties with his wife. They were on the road to a divorce, and whether this was a ruse or not, he and Chris Mason would argue in front of the other staff. Maybe so it wouldn't look like they were partners in crime. Whatever happened, we know Adam Stuart was a big drinker, and his wife knew he would go drinking at lunchtime, so maybe he was panicking after somebody was killed and he was drinking and driving when he lost control and left the road.'

Samantha looked thoughtful for a moment. 'What was he doing driving up through Fife?'

Miller didn't have the answer.

CHAPTER 70

'Everything is going to be alright,' Davie Raeburn said, as he walked into the room, carrying a breakfast tray, with a cup of coffee, toast and a plate of scrambled eggs. 'I remember you saying you liked your eggs scrambled in the morning.'

'Fuck you.' Jill White was sitting up in bed, still fully clothed. 'Who was that prick who came in and untied me? My fucking wrists hurt and he wasn't very gentle.'

'My friend can be a bit rough, and trust me, you don't want him coming back in here and slapping you about, so be a good girl and tuck into your breakfast.'

'Sure. Then maybe you can take me shopping afterwards. I hear Mappin and Webb are having a sale and I really need a new Rolex. You should be able to afford to buy me one after robbing...how many banks is it now?'

'Jill, Jill, please. Your words are having a negative effect on our relationship.'

She swung her legs over the bed.

'Remember what I said about my friend. I might not lift a hand to a woman, but he won't think twice.'

'That's sort of hard to believe when you abducted me at knifepoint.' She walked over to the tray, took hold of it and sat with it on her lap. She wasn't hungry, but remembered what Frank Miller had told her three years ago; a lot of kidnap victims lose their fight because they not only lose hope, but they succumb to fatigue and just when they need strength to fight somebody, their body lets them down, because *they* let their body down.

So she put milk in the coffee and tucked into the eggs. The cutlery was cheap, flimsy plastic. 'Is this how my son was treated when you kidnapped him?'

Raeburn's confidence slipped for a second, but then the smile was back in place. 'Just eat, Jill. We mean you no harm. All we want to do is keep you out of the way until after Sunday, then you can go home.' He turned and walked back out of the room, closing the door behind him and locking it.

Downstairs, there was chatter coming from the kitchen as the others ate their breakfast.

'Just like old times, eh?' he said, walking into the room.

'How's the bint?' Ross Brannigan said.'

'That *bint*, as you so eloquently put it, is not exactly giving a rendition of *Oh What a Beautiful Morning.* She is, however, pissed off and hungry.'

'Did you slip her one, then?' Brannigan laughed as Raeburn walked behind him, and only stopped when Raeburn grabbed him and put the kitchen knife to his throat, dull side against the skin.

'You need to concentrate on your breakfast without trying to be a comedian.'

Brannigan didn't move.

'Ross, one day your mouth is going to get you into trouble, and that day will be today if I hear you say anything like that to me again. Got it?'

'Got it.'

Raeburn took the knife away and put it back on the counter. Nobody else said a word.

Chris Mason, Martin Crawley and Andrew Borthwick carried on eating their breakfast as if nothing happened.

'Gentlemen, we all know what's going down on Sunday, so I want things to go smoothly today. Let's be in no doubt that the ARV patrols in Edinburgh will be on heightened alert. If confronted, they will open fire, so if you're going to start shooting, make sure you hit them. We're already going down for a long time should we get caught, so taking a few coppers with us won't make a difference. Anybody got any questions?'

'Should we shoot anybody today if they get in our way?' Crawley asked.

'Martin, I know you are a highly trained soldier, but it scares me that a wee lassie watched you and Chris the other night and almost managed to get away with some photos. So, yes, if somebody gets in your way, let the bastard have it.'

Crawley smiled, relishing the idea. Selling cars was fun for a while, but it didn't beat going on covert operations.

'What about you, Dr. Borthwick? We fit and ready for today?'

'I feel fucking sick. I'm not used to shooting people like you crazy bastards.'

Chris Mason laughed out loud. 'We take that as a compliment.'

'You can take it any way you fucking like. After this shit on Sunday, I'm off and I never want to see you psycho bastards again.' Borthwick got up from the table and walked outside, going over to the converted barn where the cars were.

'You think he'll be a liability?' Crawley asked.

'He already is, Marty. We can do this job without anybody getting hurt, because we're controlled under pressure. Borthwick, well, he's the noose round our neck.'

'Do you want me to take care of him?' Brannigan said.

'No, we're going to need him on Sunday. I'm not a fan of taking out a team member. However, we'll review the situation and if we think he'll jeopardise the whole operation, we'll let him go.'

Nobody in the room was in any doubt that *letting him go* was more than giving him early retirement.

****

Rena Stuart was sick and tired of the *Poor cow just lost her husband* looks she was getting. Some of them were probably thinking she was better off without Adam after what he put her through, and she thought they were probably right. It didn't make it any easier though.

Adam had been great in the beginning, and it had been a fresh start for both of them. They'd been married before, and both of their marriages had been horrific, so when she met the fun-loving Adam who treated her like a Princess, she was swept off her feet. The first few years had been great; Adam never looked at another woman, which she should have seen as a smoke screen. Her first husband had openly checked out other women, even making comments like, *Oh, I'd like to give her one,* but she hadn't for one second thought he'd ever do it. So she didn't worry and as far as she knew, her first husband hadn't cheated.

Adam, on the other hand, had never once made a comment about another woman, and now she knew this was because he didn't want to raise her suspicions. She didn't know how many women he'd cheated on her with, but it was a few. All the nights he said he was meeting a friend of his from work.

She stared at the screen on her computer, not doing work but looking at funeral directors. God knows when his body was going to be released, but when the PF did release it, she wanted to be prepared.

She browsed through their services online, looking at different coffins, made from different types of wood, although she thought her dead husband didn't deserve anything more substantial than plywood, and if it had been offered, that's what she would have chosen.

She and Adam had discussed death before, not wanting to court it by talking about it more than once but it was in keeping with the other's wishes. He wanted to be cremated, perhaps thinking he was going to be surrounded by flames for all eternity, but whatever the reason, he was going into the big fire.

She looked up, startled, when her assistant knocked on her door for the umpteenth time that morning.

'Sorry to bother you, Mrs. Stuart, but the policeman who came to see you yesterday is here to see you again.'

'Thank you. Could you show him in, please?'

Miller came into her office with Kim, and Rena minimised her screen, looking as if she'd just been caught looking at porn.

'Detective Miller, Dr. Smith, please come in.'

'Thank you. We won't keep you long, but we have a couple of questions, and I wanted to ask them in person, rather than call.'

Please tell me that it's still Adam lying in the mortuary. 'Not a problem. Did your forensics team find anything? They went through my entire house. I had to stay at a friend's house last night, because your people wouldn't let me back until they'd finished.'

'If we may?' He indicated the two chairs, and after Rena nodded, they sat down. 'The preliminary report I received this morning indicates they found nothing incriminating against your husband. I just want to ask if you have any idea why your husband might be driving over to Fife? Was that something he did often?'

'I'm not sure if he drove over there much or not. You see, he may have a woman over there. After what you witnessed yesterday, you can see nothing's beyond the realm of possibility.'

Kim leaned forward. 'You would have no idea if he had been seeing somebody? We're just curious why he was over there. Do you have any property in Fife?'

Rena stared at her for a moment. 'I'm not sure if he had a girlfriend over there, but what do I know? I thought many things about Adam, but it turns out I didn't know him at all. And no, we didn't have property over there. Adam, had, but he sold it when he divorced.'

'He was married before?' Miller asked.

'Yes. He lived in Fife.' Then a light went on behind Rena's eyes. 'You don't think..?'

'That he was seeing his ex-wife? I don't know. Do you know if she still lives there?'

'I don't know.' She looked between her two visitors. 'I didn't think he would ever want to see that bitch again. She was off her head. One minute she would be okay, then bang! Off she went. Adam always said it was because she was a Gemini.'

Miller felt the hairs on the back of his neck rise. Looked at Kim before looking back at Rena. 'Where did she live?'

'In Kelty.'

Rena told them the woman's name.

Miller was already on the phone by the time they were riding the lift downstairs.

CHAPTER 71

Where was her best underwear? Had she brought it out of the washing machine? The woman looked down at the near-empty suitcase and thought, *It's never all going to fit in there.* What was the hurry anyway? Christ, one phone call and she was jumping through hoops. Well, fuck 'im if she was late. She didn't answer to him anyway.

She lit up a cigarette and took a swig of the Bacardi and Coke, even though it wasn't even lunchtime. She had felt a twinge of sadness at reading about the death of Adam Stuart. Times had been good with him, but they both had the same personality, which is what broke them. She liked the company of men, although she didn't want to shag every one of them, but some men had the knack of making her laugh, and sometimes that was all she needed.

Other times, she needed the physical side of things. Adam had never understood that. He would go off his head when she came in late, and sometimes she would smell of a man's aftershave, but Adam couldn't tell the difference between Old Spice and Carly Spesh.

After a few years, she realised he was doing the very thing he thought *she* was doing to *him.* If she'd known he was going to do that behind her back, she would have dropped her drawers for every sailor she'd come across.

The last time she hit him was the last time they'd slept together. Yes, she was the first to admit she had a temper. Something just snapped the wires in her brain, and before she knew it, words were leaving her mouth like a runaway train. *You can't un-ring a bell* her long-dead father had told her, and it was true. And boy, did she ring that fucking bell. She'd told Adam he could get out of her life for good. He could go and live with whatever wee hoor he was banging now. She was probably some wee slut he'd picked up when he was cruising in front of Burntisland Links when the shows were on.

How she'd been wrong on that. Not only did Adam meet a sophisticated piece, he told her she was leaving her husband for him, and they were planning on leaving together.

She walked over to her wardrobe, grabbed a handful of clothes and threw them in the suitcase. She was never any good at packing, but he'd said it was only for a couple of weeks, and surely there would be a washing machine where they were going. She just wished she knew if they were going somewhere hot or cold, but as it was June, she was leaning more towards summer clothes.

Adam always wanted her to wear sexy clothes, even though she didn't feel comfortable in them. Still, she only had them on for five minutes, just long enough for him to rip them off her.

They'd had some good times together, and when it was good, it was really good, but the bad times outweighed the good times. Especially after she lost the baby. She hadn't told Adam, and he never found out, but she went off in a bad mood a lot, and although she wanted to yell at him, to throw it in his face, she never did. She didn't hate him after all.

She zipped up the case, and grabbed hold of it, slipping it off the bed. Looked at her watch. The taxi was late. Bastards. They were always late. She would give them another five minutes, then she'd give somebody a bloody good bollocking on the phone.

Then she heard a noise at the door. As if somebody was there but didn't want to ring the bell. Well, the bastard wasn't getting a tip...

Crash, bang, the sound of running feet. Men in black. 'Show me your fucking hands!' the first one with the big gun was shouting. Then more of them. Shouting, pointing their guns. Then one of them grabbed her and threw her to the ground. Then she was handcuffed by a copper who had been here the other night with Carl White.

'Susan Tay, I'm arresting you on suspicion of aiding and abetting the act of armed robbery. Anything you say, can and will be used against you...' Frank Miller was talking, but she wasn't listening anymore.

Her brother was going to get a fucking kicking when she got hold of him.

****

Normally, Glenrothes dealt with any serious crime matter, but they were one big unified police force that sort of deal could be negotiated. The local police commander in charge of Fife Division had been informed and was agreeable to allow Susan Tay to be taken to Edinburgh for questioning, which Miller thought was a mere formality at this point.

They had come across in two black vans, and two Special Operations Range Rovers, and liaised with the Fife Police, but ultimately, this was an Edinburgh operation.

A uniformed superintendent was on scene, more for show than anything else. 'We're looking for a woman who's been abducted,' Miller explained to the super. 'I need your forensics crew to go through this place with a fine tooth comb. You can liaise with Edinburgh on this, but we need you moving on it now.'

'Leave it with me,' the burly man said, eager to get in on the action.

Susan Tay had been unceremoniously dumped on the floor of the van and driven through to the High Street where she was taken down to the high security suite, one level below the holding cells. This area had its own holding cells, and interview rooms with no windows.

'What am I supposed to have done?' Susan said, sitting across from Miller and Kim. Paddy Gibb stood behind them, chewing on a fingernail, no doubt dreaming of the little fellas in their packet.

'We know you were married to Adam Stuart,' Miller said, sitting drinking a cup of coffee.

'You know that twat who burst my front door will be paying for the damage.'

'You need to co-operate,' Gibb said.

'What's this? Good cop, twat cop?' She curled her lip at Gibb. 'I want a lawyer.'

'You're not getting a fucking lawyer. We're holding you here under terrorism charges.'

'What? Do I look like a terrorist?'

'I don't know; what does a terrorist look like?'

'This is a wind-up.'

'This is deadly serious,' Miller said. 'You need to start listening to us. We can have you taken away and interrogated by specialists, but we don't think you'd like that.'

Susan sniffed and sat back in her seat. 'Yes, I was all but married to Adam Stuart.'

'Why is your name now? Tay?' Kim asked.

'Adam and I weren't legally married. I was his common-law wife. I had been married before, and when we divorced, it was easier to keep my married name rather than go around changing everything.' Her cockiness had left her now, and she knew she was in some sort of trouble. 'Look, whatever Adam was into, I had nothing to do with it. He was married to that snooty cow, and I hadn't seen him for a long time.'

Miller studied her face, and he'd studied a lot of faces sitting opposite him over the years, and had a sinking feeling that this woman was telling the truth.

'We have reason to believe Adam was coming over to see you yesterday when he lost control of his car and drowned. He'd been drinking, which must have impaired his driving skills.'

'I don't know why he'd be coming over to see me. I haven't seen him in ages. In fact, the last time I met him, was in Asda in Dunfermline, but that was over a year ago.'

'Why would he be in Dunfermline?' Kim asked.

'He was a driving examiner.'

'Yes, we know that.'

'Well, all the area managers from around here met in the driving test centre in Kirkcaldy. He came over to Fife all the time.'

Miller looked at Kim. *Have that checked out.* She got up from her seat and left the room. Gibb sat down in her vacated chair.

'How did you know Carl White?' he asked.

'I met him when I was in Edinburgh.'

'You bump into him or something? Meet him in a bar?'

'No, I was introduced to him by my brother.'

'Your brother knows Carl White?'

'Yes, they know each other very well.'

'In what capacity?' Miller said.

'Look. Detective Miller, I've had a few drinks already today, and I need to pee.'

Christ. Miller knew if he refused a human rights lawyer would have his pension. 'Okay, we'll get a female officer to escort you.' He turned to the uniform who was standing just inside the door and asked him to get one of his female counterparts. Two minutes later, a female took Susan Tay to the bathroom.

Kim came back in. 'I made a call and there was a meeting with the area managers yesterday, but it was in Glenrothes, not Kirkcaldy, although they do have them there too.'

Susan was brought back in. She sat back down, still looking unhappy.

'Where were we?' Miller said.

'You asked me how my brother knows Carl White.'

'Oh yes,. So, how *does* he know your brother?'

'Through the Royal Edinburgh Hospital. My brother's a volunteer there. Carl's wife worked there at times. I was introduced to Carl. We started seeing each other.'

For the second time that day, the hairs on the back of Miller's neck were standing. He thought he knew the answer to the next question, but it turned out he was so wrong.

'Is your brother Andrew Borthwick?'

Susan laughed. 'That balloon? You've got to be kidding me.'

'Then who are we talking about, Susan?'

She looked at Miller, feeling her confidence growing back. 'Why Davie, of course. My brother is Davie Raeburn.'

CHAPTER 72

Miller was pacing his office like a caged tiger. 'This is all going to shit. I think we've been underestimating those bastards. They're not just a bunch of dumb hicks who get lucky with a shotgun. They're professional soldiers who have decided to use their skills for robbing banks. But they're also thinkers, planners. Very skilled men.'

Paddy Gibb was openly smoking now, taking deep draws on the little fire stick, and blowing the smoke in a *fuck it, I don't care* fashion. 'Shower of bastards. What the fuck are we supposed to do with this?' He tapped the sheets of paper sat on Miller's desk.

Rena Stuart had faxed over copies of the locations of banks that had security deposit boxes, which turned out to be all of them.

'This is a nightmare,' Kim said. 'However, this is what I'm thinking.'

Both men looked at her.

'Right now, we know there are eight of them. Or that's what we're supposed to believe. But hear me out on this; Adam Stuart was one of them because his wife is high up in the bank, and they knew this. He worked with Mason, so we are meant to believe he's one of the team. Maybe not one of the front men who actually rob the banks, but one of the support staff. Yet, from what we've seen, he's done nothing more than fool around on his wife. And let's take Willie Cruickshank, the security guard.

'Davie Raeburn was in the Army with him, and made sure Willie got help after he was discharged from the Army. Just because he died of a heart attack, doesn't mean to say he wasn't given something to induce it, like Harvey Levitt said. I've seen it done before. It would have been easy for Raeburn to slip him something and then plant some incriminating stuff in Cruickshank's flat.'

'That's one theory,' Gibb conceded. 'If that was the case, then we're down to looking for five again.'

'Six,' Miller corrected him. 'The courier who we don't know about.'

'And you're sure it wasn't Susan Tay helping out her brother by pretending to be a courier?'

'We're sure. I had that superintendent from Fife check out the pub she said she was in at Kelty, and the manager said she was blootered last night and had to be poured into a taxi. We're checking out her other alibis, including the fact that she booked a holiday to Spain a few weeks ago, thanks to her brother giving her money.'

Kim smiled without humour. 'I don't think a professional team like that would rely on Adam Stuart, Cruickshank or Raeburn's sister. They're not in the same league, and would you risk something going awry because some doughnut couldn't think straight?'

'It still makes me suspicious about Carl White, especially since he was involved with Susan,' Gibb said.

'He was dragged into their little game three years ago. Raeburn knew Jill White had a little boy. They knew Terry shared the same grandmother as Shaun Foxall, and therefore, they knew Margaret White was loaded. So, if they took Terry, the grandmother would have the money to pay for his ransom. Susan Tay was being used, even back then. Raeburn introduced his sister to White so he, Raeburn, could glean information from her.'

'So, if Cruickshank, Stuart and Susan Tay are all meant to throw us off the scent, then who the hell is the courier we saw on the CCTV footage?' Gibb said.

'Could it be somebody Gary Davidson knew?' Kim said.

'And why did they kill Brian Sewell and bury his body in the cemetery?' Miller said.

The older detective flicked his used cigarette out the window. 'So many questions. Was Sewell part of their team? We have to assume he was now, since he was buried near the house where he was caretaker. Christ, the list gets longer and longer. Even if we still discount Stuart and Cruickshank as pawns, it still leaves the four robbers, Raeburn and the courier, and the two dead men, Sewell and Gary Davidson. Eight of them. That doesn't seem credible.'

'Look at this way, Paddy; they were all in an Army unit, used to dealing with small groups of people, working hand-in-hand. That's how they roll. Each of them has a part to play, and each of them gets a cut. If they do it often enough, then they can all make money.'

Gibb picked up his coffee mug, saw it was empty, made a face and put it back on Miller's desk. 'So they're playing their little game, robbing banks and splitting up the money.' He looked from Kim to Miller. 'Why have they all gone underground now? Why not keep doing what they were doing?'

'Maybe the odds were stacking against them, and they'd only planned to do it for so long before going out with a bang,' Kim said.

Miller was sweating. The sun was coming in through the window, relentless in its pursuit of trying to kill them with heatstroke. 'There's something not right. Something they've thought of that we haven't. You know like sometimes if you're doing a crossword puzzle and you know the answer and it just won't come to you?'

'If we don't get the answer soon, they'll have fucked off, and in their wake, they'll leave Jill White's corpse.' Gibb strode to the office door. 'I'm going to get a bottle of water before I pass out.'

When it was just Miller and Kim left, Frank doodled on a piece of paper next to his computer. 'What we have to figure out is, have they gone to ground because of the shooting last night, or was this part of their plan?'

Kim looked tired and rubbed her hands over her face. 'Knowing how professional they are, I want to say this was part of their plan. The shooting was a mistake.'

'A coincidence?'

'I know, I know, but sometimes life throws a coincidence at you. I mean, there's a woman dead, sure, but they won't let that get in their way.'

'You're right. Also, if you're right about Cruickshank being a pawn, why would they leave a note basically telling us they would strike on Sunday? Why wouldn't they let us keep on guessing?'

'I don't know the answer to that. Unless that too was a mistake, and the note wasn't supposed to be left there.'

'These men call each other by numbers, and they've left no DNA at any scene. I don't think they would leave a note by mistake. No, it was left there for a reason.'

Miller picked up his phone and put it on speaker. 'Mrs. Stuart? DI Miller. I have you on speaker with Kim Smith.'

'What can I do for you, Detective?'

'I have a question for you regarding the sheets you faxed over; are any of the banks open on a Sunday?'

'No, none of the banks are.' Silence for a moment. Then Rena Stuart hit the motherlode. 'I do know one place that's open on a Sunday.'

CHAPTER 73

Sunday

It was a tactic known as shock and awe. They'd used it many times before; hit a person or a group of people with overwhelming violence so they would be so shocked they couldn't react.

One of them walked up to the glass doors and showed the warrant card. The security guard came over and looked at what was a pretty good fake.

'What's the problem officer?' the guard asked, through the intercom.

'Don't be alarmed, but we think this building is going to be compromised. I have a team on its way but I need to get in now.'

The guard waddled over with a bunch of keys in his hand and unlocked the glass door. 'Oh my God. Is it the same crew who hit the bank the other night?'

'We think so.'

The guard locked the door behind him and they walked back to the reception desk.

'I need access to a computer. I have to organise a firearms team to come here.'

'Sure. There's a computer you can use in an office back here.' The guard swiped his card through a card reader, and in that instant, Ross Brannigan knew it was going to go smoothly. He pulled out his gun and rammed it into the man's face. This was the shock and awe part, when they didn't see it coming. 'You give me any trouble and you'll end up like that old cow who was shot last Thursday. You got it?'

Brannigan was shouting at the top of his voice. Part of the shock. The awe part was when he pistol-whipped the guard, who fell over. Brannigan pointed the gun at him. 'Up on your feet or I'll shoot you where you lay.'

The older man got to his feet, his face bleeding.

'Good. Now you might not die today.' He looked at his watch. Timing was everything on this. 'Walk me through to the loading bay.'

The two men hurried, Brannigan frog marching the older man. They went through several doors, the guard swiping his card each time, then down two levels where they entered through a high-security area, with signs on the wall that read, Authorised Personnel Only!

'Get that door open,' Brannigan ordered.

'We're not supposed to.'

'You want to die or go home to see your grandkids? Your choice. I can kill you and take your swipe card off you.'

'This one needs a code as well.'

'I'll fucking kneecap you, then.' He pointed the gun at the man's leg, but before he could pull the trigger, the guard had entered the code and swiped his card. The door clicked and Brannigan pushed the man through. 'Good man.'

They walked along another corridor, this one vastly different. More industrial, with no carpeting on the rubber floor, pallets of plastic bags with denominations printed on them lining one wall. A glass-fronted area looked onto the corridor, and Brannigan looked through to where the counting machines were.

He looked at his watch. It had taken him exactly seven minutes to get from the front door down to the coin-sorting warehouse.

'What's your name?' Brannigan asked the guard.

'Fred Summers.'

'Well, Fred Summers, here's what's going to happen; you're going to unlock one of the doors in the loading bay, and my friends are going to drive their van through. Got that?'

Fred nodded. 'Yes, sir.'

'Go to it. They're waiting outside. If you try to run, one of them will kill you. If you let them in, I will let you sit somewhere quiet until we're done. Then you can go and have a pint with your friends and brag about how you managed to stand up to the gunman, and how you would have battered him if he hadn't been armed. Now go do as I say. Open the end bay door on the left.'

The four inner bay doors lining the wall wouldn't open when a truck was reversing in, only when the truck was in and the outer door was secure. One end housed a heavily fortified door, which would have looked like a normal house door if it hadn't been for the armour plating on it. Above the doors was a monitor. They could see the dark van sitting outside one of the bay doors.

Fred punched in a code and swiped his card. The heavy door hissed open as if he was going into an airlock. He entered the control room in the small anti-chamber, the door closing behind him. For fire safety, when the door into the bank proper locked, the other door to the loading bay would open.

Fred opened the outer door, and the promised van reversed in and stopped. The outer door closed and the remaining three men jumped out of the van. The three of them and the guard came back through the heavy door, so now there were five men in the corridor, including Brannigan. There were no masks this time, no number calling.

Martin Crawley and Chris Mason looked in their element. They were carrying shotguns, happy at the prospect of using them. Only Andrew Borthwick was looking nervous, but as they were all dressed in black, they still looked menacing.

'Right, all we need to do is sit tight and wait,' Brannigan said.

'How long will they be?' Borthwick asked.

'Raeburn and The Boss will be along in ten minutes,' Crawley said.

Brannigan sneered. '*The Boss.*'

'Don't let Raeburn hear you say that,' Mason said.

'I think we'll have to have a little conference about who's really the boss when we're done.'

Crawley was looking around, smiling. 'Six million. Who would have thought it? Can you imagine how much the depository holds?'

Brannigan smiled as well. 'That's right, lads, six big ones. They bring the notes in, swap them for the coins and take away the counted coins to leave at the depository. Only now they won't be taking away anything, and we'll take their truck with six million in it. How simple is that?'

Mason looked at the boxes just inside the warehouse doors. 'Is that where they keep the coins?' he asked the guard.

'Yeah. They're counted in machines and packed then put into those boxes. Then the depository handles them from there, and they are split up and sold to stores and big businesses.'

'Enough of the history lesson, old man,' Borthwick said. 'I couldn't give a fuck where the coins go, I just want to get the notes out of that truck.'

'Where's Raeburn?' Mason asked.

'Give him time. He and The Boss were disabling the system at the HQ. They'll be here.'

At that moment, they all turned to look at the monitor and saw the money truck reversing in.

****

Raeburn wasn't at the HQ disabling any system. At the same moment the truck was reversing into the loading bay, he was walking slowly along an underground tunnel, taking his time, making sure he didn't make a noise. The Boss walked behind him, not saying a word. They were both pumped up, and knew this had been in the planning for a while, and it was all going to come together. Maybe not as long in the planning as the bank truck heist, but this was even more genius. And more satisfying.

He had a small LED flashlight on his head, which lit up the old stone walls and was holding a sawn-off in the other. The underground passageway smelled old and musty, which was to be expected since it hadn't had any fresh air in a very long time.

He'd studied the map over and over so that he knew it off by heart, and was picturing it in his mind as they walked. The entrance to this place was behind an old, boarded-up service entrance belonging to an old, empty building that backed onto this place. They had been connected once, a very long time ago, and when they went their separate ways, the service entrance had been boarded up. If you didn't know it was there, as Raeburn did, then you would think it was an old, walk-in storeroom. It had been empty ever since the crash back in oh-eight, when stores went under and property tanked. It had been up for sale for the longest time, and would probably be demolished and built on again, but in the meantime, it lay empty and abandoned.

Which was fortunate for them.

Nobody ever ventured along the small lane leading to the service entrance, so nobody noticed them pulling the boards back. And now they were walking along the dark, smelly passageway, which was big enough for them to stand up in.

Raeburn had spent time building two carts with large wheels, which he had hidden behind the boarded-up entrance, and which they now pulled behind them.

They turned left, and walked further along. It was getting closer. The connecting wall had been broken a long time ago, and Raeburn had been down here removing more of the bricks, making the hole bigger to make their job easier.

They turned right, then left again and then the air started to smell a bit fresher. A couple more turns and then they were in the last of the passageways before making one final turn.

Raeburn stopped and put out his light, but keeping the headband on. Before them on their left hand side were the vaults. Loaded with money. He'd seen it before and knew there was at least three million down here. They wouldn't be able to carry it all, but if they got a million and added it to their share of the other heists, it would keep them ticking over for a long time to come.

They walked forward. Low-wattage bulbs hung from the ceiling, casting shadows around as if they were in a horror movie. Raeburn walked towards one of the doors, which was ajar, as were some of the others. They probably kept them open all the time. After all, who came down here, except some of the men to make a deposit.

He kept his shotgun in front of him and was about to lower it when a man stepped out from the vault. He didn't see Raeburn, or didn't react if he did. Either way, Raeburn stepped silently up behind him and shoved the gun hard into his back.

'Nice and easy, Twinkle Toes, and we won't have to bury you somewhere.'

CHAPTER 74

The armoured truck backed into the bay and the doors to the outside world closed.

'Gentlemen, I give you six million pounds,' Brannigan said.

The reverse horn on the truck died, its back doors almost touching the bay doors it had backed up to. The security guard was in the control booth again, and he stayed there to control the bay doors leading from the truck to the corridor.

They slid up quietly, and the back doors to the truck started to open then stopped. Then the truck exploded.

Flash bangs erupted from the back of the truck, tear gas canisters flying out. Brannigan, thrown backwards by the blast, managed to remain on his feet. Martin Crawley fell over a pallet of boxes. Chris Mason put his face forward, wanting to shoot but not seeing anything to shoot at.

Andrew Borthwick stood where he was, choking and coughing.

The explosion took almost two seconds, and as the wave of tear gas erupted, the Tactical Unit remained in the truck behind their armoured shields.

'Police! Drop your weapons!'

Before Brannigan had a chance to fire, the cardboard boxes erupted. Black masks appeared, then Heckler and Koch MP5's. His instinct to fight kicked in. He swung his shotgun at the first officer leaping from the cardboard box, about to pull the trigger.

Miller was in one of the boxes along the back wall, strategically placed so when each of them burst out, they wouldn't be in each other's line of fire. More importantly, they wouldn't be in the way should the tactical team have to start shooting. There was only one way the robbers could run, and that was the way Brannigan had come in, but there was another tactical team waiting there.

Miller heard the truck reversing, Andy Watt doing a good job playing security guard, *Fred Summers.* Watt had first suggested they use the name *John,* as in *Wayne*, but Miller decided to go for *Fred* as in *Flintstone. Summers* Watt had plucked out of the air, but Miller thought it may have something to do with the Ann Summers store in Princes Street.

He was quiet, his tear gas mask in place, making him sweat. They had come round yesterday and made the boxes comfortable with another, smaller box inside to sit on. Each one large enough to hold a man brandishing a submachine gun.

He slowed his breathing and listened to the back loading bay door open. Counted down. Five, four, three, two, one...bang!

He heard the tactical team's warning, 'Armed Police! Drop your weapons!' his cue to get the top of the box open.

Ross Brannigan, the first to recover, swung his shotgun round, and Miller took the shot at the same time fire spat from the back of the truck. Brannigan was down. And he stayed down.

Chris Mason was bent over but stood up straight. The tactical team shot him and he too went down.

Martin Crawley started screaming and in that instant, Miller knew the former car salesman was going to die, and the blast of gunfire from the truck confirmed his thoughts.

He saw an armed man run past him, towards the other end of the corridor.

Andrew Borthwick.

Miller was out of the box and running after him as other members of his team leapt out of their boxes.

In the noise and confusion, Miller was the only one running. He caught sight of Borthwick turning at the end of the corridor and disappearing. He pulled off his gas mask, threw it down, keeping hold of his gun.

He stopped before he reached the corner, then swept round, holding his gun out.

Nobody there! There was a door swinging at the end of the corridor. Miller ran, once again, cautiously entering the room.

It was a staff canteen, the tables empty, the stainless steel serving trays empty and cold, until tomorrow when they would be filled with hot food to be served to hungry workers.

Now though, the large room was deathly quiet. Miller ducked behind the serving counter.

'Andrew, it's not too late to come out with your hands up.'

'I'm not going anywhere, Miller.'

'Talk to me. I'm listening, Andrew.'

A laugh sounded from the far side of the room. 'You don't understand, Miller; I'm not like them. I shot that woman on Thursday by accident. Nobody else panicked, only me. If they had hanging, I'd be swinging in the wind. I can't go to prison.'

'We can talk about this. I can help you. I want to know where Raeburn is.' Silence. 'Andrew? Andrew?'

Miller felt the adrenaline blast through him. Borthwick was probably trying to get around him, to get back out the door, and just admitted he was a killer.

He was wrong. As he moved position, he saw Borthwick standing on a table. Holding the gun by his side.

Miller stood up, holding the Koch. 'Put the gun down, Andrew. Please. I'm asking you man to man, put the gun down.'

Borthwick smiled, a sad smile, and Miller had a sudden urge to be sick. He felt the acid pump into his stomach as he knew what Borthwick was doing.

'Andrew, please don't do this.'

'I have to, Frank. I told you, I can't go to prison. Raeburn and The Boss are ruthless. They'll kill me. You're going to have to take care of this.'

Borthwick raised his shotgun. Before Miller could pull his own trigger, a sharp crack from the doorway rang out. Lloyd Masters watched as Borthwick flew backwards off the table to crash onto the floor.

He walked over to Miller. 'I know you could have taken the shot, son, but this way, you didn't have to.'

In truth, Masters saw Miller hesitate just a fraction too long for his liking, and thought Borthwick might actually have killed Miller, but that's not what he would say on his report. He would say Miller tried to negotiate and he, Masters, already had Borthwick in his sights.

'You know something? There was a small part of me that actually thought they might give up without a fight.'

'They're trained soldiers. There was no way they were going to give up. Your men did well. Those tactical boys and I have been training for months for such an occasion. So for them, it was just another day at the office.'

'The robbers are all dead?'

'Yes they are.'

'Now we just have to find Davie Raeburn. And I think I know where he'll be.'

CHAPTER 75

Miller felt the ache in his bones as he sat down on the armchair and drank the coffee. It had been a long time since he had sat in this chair, and it felt good to be back. He recognised the smell as he walked through the door. Not a nasty smell, more of a *signature* smell. Like smelling a perfume and associating it with somebody. This house had its own unique smell, and it brought the memories flooding back to Miller.

He heard the car coming up the driveway. Or the van, to be correct.

He remained seated, sipping the coffee. He wished he had his gun right then, but after the robbers were shot dead, all weapons had to be surrendered so they could figure out which guns fired the fatal shots. Net curtains on the windows let him see out, but the occupants of the van couldn't see in. He saw the van stop and the two people get out. Raeburn and The Boss.

The front door opened and the first person through stopped suddenly.

'Hello, Rosie. I hope you don't mind, but I helped myself to a coffee. I know Harry always liked a good cup of coffee and I was glad to see there was still some in the kitchen.'

Davie Raeburn came in behind her. Looked over to the stairs at Miller's side.

'Jill's gone. I told her to take my car. She's somewhere safe,' Miller said, putting his cup down.

'How did you know we'd be here?' Rosie asked.

'At Harry's house? Where else would you be? Harry died and left his house to Gary. Carol was already dead, so it all went to him and you.' He looked at her. 'I went round to your house in Longstone on Friday and your neighbour said your house was in foreclosure. That you were going to live in Spain and your daughter was already over there.'

'So, what are you doing here, Frank?'

'Well, considering we're looking for Mr. Raeburn there in connection with several bank robberies, I think you know what I'm doing here.'

'Oh, Frank, you're so adorable. And to think we would have been away tomorrow morning. Oh, wait a minute, we still will be.' There was a hard edge to Rosie's voice now, and Miller saw her for who she really was; a ruthless, calculating bitch. No wonder she was the boss of their little gang.

'That's a matter of opinion.' Miller stood up and Raeburn looked round at the van through the open doorway. 'Thinking of getting your gun, Davie? Go ahead. Put one hand on it. You won't see it coming, I can promise you. Every one of those tactical firearms men are highly trained snipers. Your buddies thought they were better than my guys, but you can go and ask them down at the mortuary if you like. Brannigan was the first one to go down, in case you're interested.'

Miller picked up his cup and drank more coffee. 'I wish Harry was here to see his daughter-in-law, to see what she turned into. Oh, you were the courier the other night, weren't you? The one who delivered the package to Davie here at the bank, to make it look like he needed to be there.'

Rosie shrugged her shoulders like a child.

'I'll take that as a yes, then.' More coffee.

'Why did you think I was involved in all of this?' Rosie said. They hadn't moved since they came in.

'It was Gary really. He killed my wife, his own sister. He told me that, told me he had big gambling debts, and needed the money. So he took the money from Carol. But you knew all that. What I didn't realise was he was part of the kidnap ring. He was there, he knew every move that was being made, and fed that information back to you lot. I thought you had to have known what he was doing. It was fifty-fifty though; you did, or you didn't. I'd asked myself that many times, but then there was that debacle the other day in Princes Street gardens with Shaun Foxall. Now, that was very clever. You are sent emails from Foxall, and get him out of the picture. What were you hoping for? Us to shoot him?'

Rosie smiled, turned to Raeburn then looked back at Miller. 'That was plan A, but we thought it was more likely going to be plan B; kill him in the hospital.'

'Because he had seen you guys in the hospital, and more to the point, he had overheard you. Is that right, Davie?'

Raeburn was also smiling. 'That's right. He saw Borthwick talking to Gary on occasion but that wasn't something we worried about. Rosie was a volunteer at the hospital, Gary was her husband so naturally he would come to pick her up. Nothing to worry about.'

'Except he overheard Gary talking about things, and he knew Gary was a bad man,' Miller said. 'He overheard Gary saying he had killed Carol. And then he saw the lot of you together in the hospital and he had to go. So you concocted a plan to have him flash a gun at the police and bingo, he'd either be dead or be right back in the hospital for a week, giving you a chance to kill him, but it didn't work out that way.'

Rosie looked bemused. 'If you hadn't taken him from the hospital, we would have killed him.' She looked Miller in the eyes. 'You still haven't told me how you knew for sure I was involved.'

'Simple deduction. You got used to living it large. Not on Gary's salary, of course, but with the proceeds of the robberies, and the gambling. You had to know the money went to pay off your house, yet it's been taken by the bank. Gary's debts again. Once a gambler, always a gambler. He owed big money to somebody so once again you re-mortgaged your house. And you're the connection between everybody. Shaun Foxall, the Royal Scottish.'

'You're right of course. Gary sometimes brought home loads of money, and we'd have a good time with it, but then he'd go and lose it all again. We were about to lose the house, and then he got money again. Talk about being on a bloody roller coaster.

'Then Andrew Borthwick and Jill White treated some of his ex-Army buddies, and they got together at the hospital one day and that was it. Why don't you tell him, Davie?'

'We were just talking about how Gary was a copper, and how coppers weren't as well trained as Army, and how we could do anything we wanted and get away with it. And Gary laughed. It was a dare really.'

'So you thought you'd rob a bank?' Miller said.

'No, that came later. It was the kidnapping thing first. We knew Jill had a little boy, Terry. We also knew her estranged husband had a rich mother. So I introduced my sister to him one night, and they became friends. She didn't know what I was doing. One thing about Susan is she loves the sound of her own voice. It was Carl this, Carl that, Carl has a little boy who goes to a posh school.'

'You used your own sister to orchestrate a kidnapping?'

Raeburn laughed. 'Yes. It was too easy. She was with him the day we snatched Terry. She isn't involved in any of this though. We just used her.'

'And then you killed Terry.'

Raeburn's smile dropped. 'Not on purpose. He was being held in the caretaker's house by that half-wit Brian Sewell. I told the others he shouldn't be trusted with such a thing, but they liked him. He was around the hospital, and became part of our group. So one day, we get a call from Brian, all panicked. He said the boy had tried to get out of the basement and they'd struggled, and Brian had pushed him down the stairs, and Terry broke his neck. I said I'd go over there and I'd sort it, but then Brian calls again, and said he'd set fire to the house. By the time I got there, it was well up and the fire brigade were there, but there was no sign of Brian. Later on, I found out Mason and Crawley had gone round and killed Brian before the fire brigade got there, and then they later buried him.'

Miller took a step towards Rosie. 'Nice story, but not quite true, is it, Davie? Is that the story he told you? That Brian had killed the boy?'

'Yes it is. Why? What are you saying?'

'I'm saying that's not quite how it happened. The post-mortem was done this week on Terry's cadaver, and it was found that he had a broken neck, but it was broken in a certain way, as in the way Special Forces soldiers are trained. A neck is a very hard thing to break, contrary to what people might think, so there is a certain way that can break the neck more easily. Terry died this way, and so did Brian Sewell.'

Rosie turned to Raeburn. 'You killed a little boy?'

'He recognised me. I wore a mask to go and feed him, but then he said my name out loud one time. I couldn't let him live after that. My God, we would have all gone to prison. We just wanted the money and we would have dropped him off somewhere, if it wasn't for that outburst.'

Rosie looked shocked.

'And then he torched the house after killing Brian, to make it look as if Brian had killed Terry and taken off. Nobody could find him, because Davie and his friends buried him in the private garden belonging to the caretaker's house. But there was one little flaw in the plan, wasn't there? One of the walls collapsed onto the basement floor where you had buried the little boy. Now nobody would find him, but at least people wouldn't know he was there.

'And then Rosie comes across a notice in her work at the council. They were going to tear the house down. Chances are, they would find Terry and we would start asking questions again, so best to try and get Shaun Foxall out of the picture. You were cutting it fine though, getting us there on the same day the demolition team found Terry.'

'It wasn't planned that way,' Raeburn said. 'They weren't supposed to come for another week, but there was a mix-up with the paperwork, and some desk jockey told them to go ahead. Otherwise, Shaun would have been in the hospital and committed suicide, with our help.'

Rosie took a step away from Raeburn. 'You killed a little boy.' she said again.

'It's what we're trained to do. You don't know the half of what Special Forces are asked to do. It's part of war, whether it's fighting terrorism or another country.'

'That wasn't a war you were fighting, and that little boy wasn't the enemy!' she screamed at him.

'Don't tell me you wouldn't have shot Molloy's man in that vault if he'd had a go with you. You would have pulled the trigger the same as I would have.'

'I think it's all over now,' Miller said. 'None of you got any money, so I hope you think it was worth it.'

'Who said we didn't get any money?' Rosie turned and said to Miller, spittle flying out of her mouth. 'We figured there was a good chance you'd figure out where the team were going to hit next, but we had already figured on doing our own little robbery. Robert Molloy is a gangster, pure and simple, making people scared of him, including my husband. That's where Gary gambled, at Molloy's secret gambling den. That man makes an absolute fortune from that gambling, and Gary was down in those tunnels under the club, where Molloy has his vaults, the ones that were there when the place was a bank long ago. Me and Davie found out it was connected to an abandoned building so we went in and took his money. Or should I say, I took back *my* money, the money Gary had lost to him.'

'I'm sure Robert Molloy will be pleased when he finds out,' Miller said. 'But you thought you had a soldier to look after you now. At least until Molloy gets back from his annual holiday in Spain. By which time, *you* would be in Spain.'

Rosie turned back to look at Raeburn. 'You killed a little boy and I was going to have you live with me and my little girl. How could you?'

'As I said, needs must. It's what I do. I killed Willie Cruickshank on Thursday night. He wasn't in our team, but we made it look as if he was. It's all smoke and mirrors. I gave him laxative, which made him run back and forward to the toilet, and when he was dehydrating, I persuaded him to take a drink of water. Laced with Potassium Chloride of course. Then he dropped down dead from a heart attack and I poured coffee into the console and fried it.'

'Jesus, you're ruthless.'

'Of course I am,' Raeburn said, as if she'd just paid him a compliment.

'What about Adam Stuart, the driving examiner?'

'Again, smokescreen. Two of the others killed him. It was just enough to try and throw a spanner in the works.'

'Who was the woman he was with in the hotel room?'

'Just a decoy we've used in the past. She works with a guy who hides in the wardrobe and films them getting it on.'

'And you just killed him when you were done with him.'

'We did, although that was Mason and Crawley who did that. Ran him off the road, put a bottle of whisky down his throat and held him under the water until he drowned.'

'You're a sick bastard,' Rosie said. 'You told me he'd be left alone. That he was just being used.'

'Oh get over yourself. You knew all along what we were doing.'

'I didn't know you'd killed that little boy.'

'Look, there's the best part of three million in that van, and you're either coming with me or you're not.'

'The snipers will take you out before you get behind the wheel,' she said.

'There's no snipers there. They would have been in here by now.' He looked at Miller. 'You forget that I know how this works.'

Miller looked at him and for the first time, thought he might have lost the upper hand.

'Come with me, Rosie. We can still make this work. I'll even let the copper live.'

'I'm not going anywhere with you. You killed a little boy. How do I know you won't kill my little girl? Or me for that matter?'

'You don't.' He stepped closer to her as if he was going to kiss her, then he reached up and grabbed her head, twisting and pulling her neck in the way he'd been trained. The snap was horrific in the large room, and the life went out of Rosie's eyes as Raeburn grabbed her and threw her at Miller in one quick movement.

He ran out the door as Miller caught the lifeless corpse of his brother-in-law's wife and fell backwards onto the wooden floor.

He saw Raeburn reach into the van and then he heard the roar of a vehicle coming up the long driveway. After he'd found Jill White, he'd called Kim and told her to alert Lloyd Masters. He crawled out of the line of sight in case Raeburn turned and shot at him.

The car stopped, and Miller heard raised voices. 'Police! Drop your weapon!'

Raeburn let off a shot at whoever was shouting, and didn't hear the return of gunfire. Christ, it wasn't Lloyd Masters and his crew. They were on their way, but hadn't got here yet.

Somebody had though.

He stood to one side of the main door and saw Raeburn run across the wide yard and duck inside the barn where Harry had kept his car and an old tractor with grass-cutting accessories attached to it. *I wish I hadn't thought buying an old farm was a romantic idea for retirement* he'd said to Carol one time.

A car screamed up and stopped behind the van. Tam Scott got out from behind the driver's seat, and Kim jumped out of the back.

'This is his van,' Miller said, running to the side of it. 'There's another haul in there. They ripped off Molloy's place. He'll want to take it with him. Right now, he's in the barn and there's only one way in and out.'

'I have my gun,' Kim said.

'There's no way I'm letting you go anywhere near him,' Miller said.

'I'm a better shot than you.'

'We'll wait for Masters and his team to get here.'

'They're ten minutes behind. Raeburn will be away by then.' She sprinted over to the barn, ducking round the side of it.

'Oh, fuck me,' Miller said, as he saw Tam Scott sprint after her, his own weapon drawn. Miller ran as fast as he could.

They were standing at the side of the barn when they could hear the sirens approaching in the distance.

Then Raeburn was shouting at them. 'Frank? I can hear the sirens. I know it's no good now. I want to give up. Don't shoot. I'm going to throw the shotgun out.'

They looked at each other for a moment, before Scott spoke.

'You two stay here. I'll get the gun.' He cautiously looked round the corner. 'Okay, Raeburn, throw the gun out.'

Scott watched as the gun was thrown through the gap in the door. He kept his gun up as he approached, and saw Raeburn standing in the shadows with his arms raised. 'Keep your hands where I can see them,' Scott said, tucking his gun away.

Then a thought struck Miller like a lightning bolt. Words Raeburn said when he was arguing with Rosie.

'Don't tell me you wouldn't have shot Molloy's man in that vault if he'd had a go with you. You would have pulled the trigger just like I would have.'

They had both been armed.

Raeburn had another shotgun.

CHAPTER 76

'Tam! He's got another gun!' Miller shouted, as he ran out from the side of the barn, but it was too late.

Scott bent down to pick up the shotgun lying in the dirt just outside the barn, and Raeburn stepped forward, smiling. Miller saw the look on Scott's face as he heard Miller's words and saw Raeburn with the gun at the same time.

Miller felt Kim beside him but neither of them could do anything to help Scott. It was like watching a small child standing on a railway track and not being able to reach out to grab him as the train was bearing down.

The flames from the shotgun seemed more intense as they exited the barn, the buckshot flying from the barrel and starting to spread from no more than six feet away.

The destruction was complete and fatal. The buckshot ripped into Tam Scott, blasting through his clothing, and although they were spreading, the deadliest ones shredded his heart, killing him instantly.

Kim didn't utter a warning, although she would swear blind later on that she did, but she saw the barest window of opportunity. What felt like minutes was probably only a couple of seconds, if that. Raeburn had stepped out from the barn before Scott was even dead, bringing the gun round to blast Miller. Kim saw Raeburn's face just to the left of Miller's shoulder. The gun hadn't completed its arc yet and Kim would tell Miller she took the shot on nothing more than instinct. There was no time to think, aim and fire. It was just, fire.

It wasn't accurate, but it was certainly deadly. The bullet would have ideally hit Raeburn in the forehead, but instead, it hit his right eye and went tumbling through his brain, switching his lights out for good. He fell down on the ground not three feet from Tam Scott. Had he been alive, Miller felt sure Raeburn would have been impressed by Kim's shot.

As it was, Miller ducked as Kim's shot went past his head, and he fell on his knees beside Scott.

'Tam! Tam, for fuck's sake.' He knew he couldn't do anything for his friend, but he picked him up and held him.

He didn't hear Lloyd Masters coming up with the firearms team. Didn't hear the sirens, didn't hear the screams as orders were given. Didn't hear the paramedics tell him to let Scott go.

All he heard were Davie Raeburn's words to Rosie, over and over again.

You would have pulled the trigger just like I would have.

Too little, too late.

CHAPTER 77

Two weeks later

There had been a little drizzle first thing in the morning, which made the grass look shiny. Miller parked the car and walked across the grass, past the other headstones until he reached Carol's grave, holding the little bunch of flowers carefully.

He looked at her name. And the name carved below it.

Harry Miller.

'I know you said you wanted to name a boy after your dad, or if it was a girl, after my mum. I thought it was time to let the world know we would have had a little boy.' Miller felt his voice break as he laid the flowers down, leaning them against the black headstone.

'The mason did a good job adding Harry's name.' He stood up straight and looked around at the other gravestones. The sun was out now, and the heat was beginning to kick in. He felt his shirt starting to stick to him.

'It was Tam's funeral on Friday. They wouldn't release his body until the preliminary hearing was over. They grilled Kim and me, and of course, there was a trial by newspaper. At the end of it all, we were absolved of any blame, but it will still go before the PF at a further enquiry later on. I can't believe Tam's gone. At least Davie Raeburn got what was coming to him, but that's another thing; not one of those men are alive. They'll question that next. Lloyd Masters gave a testimony saying there was no other way. Those men weren't going to be taken alive. That's how they were trained, and that's how they lived.'

A breeze whipped through the trees in the distance, as if she was answering him.

'It was Terry White's funeral yesterday. They didn't want it on the same day as Tam's. Jill wanted me to be at her side when they laid Terry to rest. He's not here though. He's up at Mortonhall, where Tam was cremated. Carl White was a mess. His mother, Margaret, felt she couldn't attend. Too much for her, she said. Shaun wasn't there either. He's back home with her, and Carl is helping him. He's back staying with his mother for now.

'You don't know Louise, but she's nice. The insurance is paying to fix her house and she's going to sell it. She said if I ever need a car, then to go see her. Jack's Audi is just fine for now. He always lectures me when I want to borrow it, and I think sometimes he forgets McGovern got it for me. Oh, and he's actually dating a writer now. He said it was only friendship at first, but last week, he asked her out on a proper date. She said she wasn't sure at first, as her divorce papers weren't signed, but then, out of the blue, her estranged husband sent her the papers, signed. So they're both happy.'

Miller looked at his dead wife's name on her headstone and felt nervous. He'd actually talked to Harvey Levitt before coming here, and the psychiatrist had told him there was nothing to worry about.

'I know you would have liked Kim, and might even have been her friend in another world, but I wanted to tell you she finally moved in with me. Her and her little girl, Emma. Her dad brought her home after she was visiting him in London, and we had a talk. I told him I'll look after his daughter as if she were my own.

'It makes me sad that we didn't go through life together, but neither one of us chose this. I just hope you're happy that we finally got the men who were responsible for Terry's death. I wish you were here with me now, but it wasn't meant to be. I hope you understand that.'

The wind whispered again. Miller said goodbye to Carol. And to little Harry.

CHAPTER 78

'I don't know where all this stuff came from,' Kim said, putting the last of the boxes down.

'A lot of it's my toys,' Emma said. 'I don't want to get rid of them, Mummy.'

Miller laughed. 'You don't have to get rid of them, sweetheart. Not until you outgrow them.'

The little girl laughed then skipped out of the room.

'You sure Jack doesn't mind us moving in?' Kim said.

'Don't be silly,' Miller said, lifting another box and taking it through to the bedroom. Kim had neatly marked each one. 'He loves company, and he loves you two. Besides, I don't think it will be long before he and his writer friend will be calling *her* flat home.'

'You think he would move in with her?'

Miller put the box on the bed. 'I think he would to be honest. He's had a few female friends since my mum died, but nothing serious. That's why he's still here with me.'

'I love him being here. I wouldn't have moved in otherwise.'

'It's working out perfectly for us. Emma will be going to her new school and we're just down the road from work.'

Kim walked over to a drawer and opened it. 'I won't make a habit of going through your drawers except to put clothes away, but I did see you take this down from the cabinet in the living room.' She held up Carol's photo. One where she was at Burntisland. They'd driven over one summer evening when the fair was on at the Links, and they'd gone on some of the rides, and she wanted a Mr. Whippy ice cream. He'd caught her with the camera as the wind tousled her hair and she was smiling, holding her ice cream like a kid.

'Put it back, Frank. She was part of your life, a very important part. I want Emma to know it's alright if her mum or dad were married before, that not every child has parents who stay married forever.'

'If you're sure.'

'I am.' She passed the photo over and then the doorbell rang. 'That'll be my mum and dad. They said they'd pop round this afternoon.'

Miller put the photo on the dresser then opened the door with a smile. 'Mum and Dad,' he said to McGovern and Norma Banks, his future in-laws. "You don't mind if I call you that, do you?'

'Oh, Frank Miller, don't tempt me,' Norma said. 'Jack said you need to be put across somebody's knee.'

Miller laughed. It was good to see Norma in casual clothes for a change. Same with McGovern.

'Neil will do fine, me old son,' McGovern said, with a smile, and was about to hand over the bottle of wine when he stepped back and looked round the corner of the hallway. 'Come on, he doesn't bite.'

A woman stepped into view. 'I brought some wine, too,' Kate Murphy said. 'I hope you don't mind.'

Miller faltered for a second. 'No, of course not. The more the merrier.'

****

Emma was along the corridor at Samantha's house, and she had persuaded Jack to play tea parties with her and her dolls.

Now, the five adults in Miller's flat were sitting back with a glass of wine.

'We wanted to raise a toast to you two, and wish you all the best of luck.'

'Thanks, Neil,' Miller said, and they clinked glasses.

'And now to the elephant in the room,' Norma said. 'Kate Murphy, our new and esteemed pathologist.'

'Here's to Kate,' Miller said.

'That's not what we're here for, Frank,' Norma said. 'Tell him, Neil.'

'When Norma told me what a hard time Kate was having integrating, I thought it was time we shared something with you two. Only you two mind, and for obvious reasons.'

'I don't think I can do this, Neil,' Kate said, putting her glass on Miller's table.

'You can. And you'll see these two people will be friends of yours, if you'll let them.' He looked at her, waiting for her permission to go on. She nodded and picked her glass back up.

'Kate's in witness protection. She wasn't always Kate Murphy. She used to be Arlene Donaldson. She was a pathologist in London, so she's fully qualified, but back then, she witnessed a murder, by some psycho called Jared Flucker. Yeah, I know, take the 'L' out of his name, and you can guess what the bullies called him at school. He was a real mean bastard, but let's not get into his past. He escaped from police custody after he killed a copper, and went looking for Arlene. He broke into her house but didn't find her, but he was disturbed by Arlene's mother, who had dementia. He strangled her mother but somebody saw him breaking in and the police quickly re-arrested him, but not before Arlene's mother died.'

Norma put her hand over Kate's—Arlene's—hand and gave it a gentle squeeze. Then Kate looked at Miller.

'I don't know who to trust anymore. After Flucker was arrested again, he promised he would find a way to get out and find me. This was after they locked him away in a psychiatric hospital.' She looked at Kim. 'I'm sorry I was rude to you in the cemetery the other day. I don't make friends easily. The therapist said if anybody gets close, I shove them away, because that way, nobody close to me will die.'

'The only two people who know she's here as Kate Murphy are me and Neil,' Norma said. 'And other members of Neil's department, of course, but nobody else outside. She needs friends.' She looked at Kate, who looked horrified for a moment. 'You do, Kate. Arlene's a different life. You're Kate now, and everybody needs a friend.'

Kate started crying uncontrollably, and Kim indicated for her father to swap seats with her. She sat down and put an arm around Kate's shoulders. 'Don't worry, Kate, I think you and I are going to be best friends.'

Miller looked up at Carol's photo on the dresser. He knew she would have been Kate's friend, too.

CHAPTER 79

The hangar holding the private jet was much cooler than the sticky heat outside. Not as cool as the Lincoln Town Car had been, but cool nonetheless.

Both men stood outside the Lear jet, at the bottom of the steps leading into the aircraft.

'You sure Frank Miller thinks you were in Spain?'

'Yes. A friend of mine called me a few weeks back.'

'After the robbery?' the younger man said.

Robert Molloy shook his head and spat on the concrete floor in disgust. 'I wish Gary Davidson were still alive so I could have him topped all over again.' He looked out the hangar doors at the blue New York sky. It had been great being here on holiday, and doing personal business, but it was time to go back home to sunny Scotland.

They boarded the plane and were welcomed by a young woman who gave them a smile and settled them in.

'I like using this service,' Molloy said to his companion. 'You can't beat a private stewardess.'

'They're called flight attendants nowadays.'

'Bollocks. Who came up with that PC crap?' He looked out the window as the jet taxied out of the hangar. They were at Stewart International Airport in the Hudson Valley, in Upstate New York. Quieter, Molloy said. 'Not as many dogs going around sniffing your luggage.' Not that they had anything to hide, but he was never happy at an airport where they thought it was okay to have a Beagle poke around your Gucci.

Fifteen minutes later, they were airborne and Molloy watched as the pilot took them over the Hudson River below.

'You know, I've been giving some thought to buying a property here. It's dirt cheap since the crash, and I'm getting to like it here.'

'You *should* buy a place. That way, when you piss me off, you can be three and a half thousand miles away.'

'Sod off.'

After they levelled off, the young girl came round with a pot of coffee. When she was gone, the younger man looked at Molloy.

'What do you think Frank Miller will say when he sees me?'
Molloy thought for a moment. 'I think he'll say, *I thought you were dead?'*

Afterword

All the characters in Silent Marker are fictitious and not based on anybody I know, either living or dead.

A long time ago, I had a stint as a Driving Examiner, taking people on their driving tests. None of the driving examiners in this book are based on anybody I worked with, and as far as I know, none of them went out drinking at lunchtime.

Thanks to the many people who bought my first book, Crash Point. And who left a review. If I could just ask if you could leave a review for this book too, it would be greatly appreciated.

I would like to thank my daughters, Stephanie and Samantha, for their faith in my work, to Nancy for always believing this would work. To my friend and fellow writer John Walker for supporting my writing through the years and to all my friends on Facebook, both old and new.

A special thanks to my wife Debbie, who is my right hand and who is the calm sea when all I see in front of me is a storm.

And last but not least, a big thanks to you, the readers, for making this possible.

'Til next time!

John Carson
New York
October 2017

CPSIA information can be obtained
at www.ICGtesting.com
Printed in the USA
FSHW010957191218
54526FS

9 781977 978998